Love Is for the Birds

Copyright © 2025
Love Is for the Birds by Deborah M. Hathaway

All rights reserved.
Except as permitted under the U.S. Copyright Act of 1976, no part of this book
may be reproduced, transmitted, or distributed by any part or by any means
without written consent of the author.

Printed in the United States of America

Published by Draft Horse Publishing
© Copyright 2025 by Deborah M. Hathaway
© 2025 Cover Art by Ashtyn Newbold

First Printed Edition, June 2025

This book is a work of fiction. All character names and personalities are entirely
fictional, created solely in the imagination of the author. Any resemblance to
any person living or dead is coincidental.

ISBN: 978-1-956091-19-9

Deborah M. Hathaway

Books by Deborah M. Hathaway

A Cornish Romance Series
On the Shores of Tregalwen, a Prequel Novella
Behind the Light of Golowduyn, Book One
For the Lady of Lowena, Book Two
Near the Ruins of Penharrow, Book Three
In the Waves of Tristwick, Book Four
From the Fields of Porthlenn, Book Five

Belles of Christmas Multi-Author Series
Nine Ladies Dancing, Book Four
On the Second Day of Christmas, Book Four

Seasons of Change Multi-Author Series
The Cottage by Coniston, Book Five

Sons of Somerset Multi-Author Series
Carving for Miss Coventry, Book One

Christmas Escape Multi-Author Series (RomCom)
Christmas Baggage

Castles & Courtship Multi-Author Series
To Know Miss May, Book Two

Men of the Isles Series (RomCom)
Winning Winnie's Hand, Book One
Driving Maisie Crazy, Book Two
Ruling out Robyn, Book Three

Bachelors of Blackstone's Multi-Author Series

Love Is for the Birds, Book Five

For Mom—

*From the beginning, you have watched over
your little flock of nine.*

We truly owe you everything.

CHAPTER 1

London, April 9, 1817

The cold eyes of a silent crocodile stalked Henry Branok as he strode down the gallery. A bear was next, staring motionless at him before Henry passed by an orangutan, followed by a mountain goat, then a shrew, then an emperor penguin. More than five hundred animals, more than a thousand eyes, all of them surveying his every move.

His footing was swift, though not because of their watchful eyes. The animals would not attack—they wouldn't even move a limb. Henry's safety was secure due to the sole fact that each and every one of these animals now watching him was long dead.

That was why he flew down the gallery as swiftly as a swooping sandpiper. Taxidermy, while an accepted and admired practice to most in Society, was Henry's version of a living nightmare.

Or *dead* nightmare, he supposed.

Hundreds of heads were propped up on shelf after shelf, and gulls with their wings outspread hung from the ceiling above.

Muted lighting cast frightening shadows across their faces to distort the animals further.

Lord Blackstone—the viscount who owned the monstrous creations—was quite proud of his collection, hence why every inch of the long corridor leading to the man's study was filled with animals from around the world.

"Each of these animals died a natural death," the viscount often said. *"We honor them without placing them behind glass cages. Free in life and in death."*

The man was likeable enough, but he was clearly living in a world of his own making.

Henry could never understand the appeal of staring at animals once living. He was fortunate enough to have seen many of the wildlife in their natural homes, and nothing —*nothing*—could compare to that. Especially when it came to birds.

Birds that blinked, breathed, and possessed a heartbeat.

Henry lived for observing them, writing about them, and sketching them. Unfortunately, it was Lord Blackstone who made such things possible for Henry—which was the only reason he now walked through this corridor of corrupted creatures.

He gripped his leather satchel tightly in his right hand, walking past the last of the long-gone animals before finally reaching the end of the corridor and tapping lightly on the thick, wooden door.

He ignored the feel of the eyes searing through his back as Lord Blackstone finally responded.

"Yes, yes, do come in," came his muted voice from within the study.

Opening the door and stepping foot into the room, Henry was instantly set upon by the overwhelming scent of tobacco and leather, and he stifled a cough.

More animals adorned the study in various locations—

muntjacs behind the desk and a hare close to them—while books lined the shelves from top to bottom. A single, closed window to the right of the desk produced enough light to showcase the smoke swirling in the air.

"Ah, Branok," Lord Blackstone greeted, lowering his pipe and beckoning Henry forward with two fingers close together. "Come in, my friend. Come in."

His gray and white hair curled up at the tips, making room for a broad receding hairline that brought to mind the tufts of feathers the guan boasted on its head. Henry had only just seen the bird that had resembled a skinny, black hen two months past in the West Indies.

He'd hold his tongue about that, though. Henry had learned his lesson that men did not take kindly to being compared to birds. The last time he'd done so, he'd been blackballed from every club in London, never again to be allowed in Boodle's, White's, or Brooks's.

This had worked in Henry's favor, however, as Lord Blackstone had subsequently sought him out and invited him to join the viscount's own club meant solely for misfits and other blackballed gentlemen.

"How was your journey back?" Lord Blackstone asked.

"Uneventful, my lord."

"Fine, fine."

"I trust you are well," Henry said next, his boots thumping against the floor as he approached the man seated behind his large wooden desk.

Books, papers, and various golden instruments for measurements and writing were splayed out across the surface. But what stole more attention than anything else was the portrait behind the desk—the painting depicting a badger, bearded and sporting a mourning coat.

The viscount certainly had...*unusual* taste in décor.

"Yes, yes, very well, indeed." Lord Blackstone waved him

closer. "Are you come to deliver something of mutual interest to us?"

Henry ignored the purple water-hen accosting him with its beady eyes and cleared his throat. Would Lord Blackstone notice if he just reached over and propped the window open, letting in just a touch of the cool, spring air?

He'd been back for nearly two weeks now, and still, he relished England's colder weather as opposed to the sweltering heat he'd been constantly confronted with in the West Indies.

"I am, my lord," he said, opening his satchel.

He pulled out a thick stack of unbound, printed pages and extended them. "The proof, to be printed and bound upon delivery of your signature. On time, as promised."

Lord Blackstone gave a slight exclamation of delight as he accepted the pages, making space for them on his desk.

"I have eagerly awaited this moment, Branok," Lord Blackstone said, swiftly thumbing through the large stack of papers Henry had spent weeks writing.

"As have I, sir."

Even more than you, he added for only himself.

Henry had spent October through February in the West Indies, exploring every inch of the land and sky, recording every detail about every bird he witnessed to be ready for this moment.

After suffering nearly seven weeks at sea returning to England to deliver these pages to Lord Blackstone, Henry was more than ready to have his work seen by others.

"When will the book be printed?" Lord Blackstone asked.

"A week from approval, as discussed."

Lord Blackstone nodded, pleased.

Years ago, he'd arranged for the publisher and printer to deliver the books in a swift manner in exchange for a sizeable donation from the viscount. The volumes of work were hardly

LOVE IS FOR THE BIRDS

bestsellers—people preferred fiction to research—so the companies would never consider publishing them otherwise.

The viscount adored seeing his name in printed form, whether he did any writing or not, so he would stop at nothing to keep the books going.

"Quite a thick collection," Lord Blackstone observed. "Larger than Gibraltar's."

That wasn't difficult.

Henry's excursion to Gibraltar in 1814 had ended in two hundred and fifty-seven species of birds observed with at least forty of them he'd never seen before.

"Much larger, my lord. It includes observations for nearly five hundred species—including two hundred birds I hadn't recorded until now."

"Spectacular," Lord Blackstone mused, nearing the end of the papers. "Though I can see from these birds that South Africa has still provided you with the most diverse list."

Henry had been sent out on eight excursions now in the last five years, and each location varied more than the last.

Perhaps if the viscount and other wealthy members of the *ton* would cease killing, disfiguring, and stuffing birds for their own vanity, there would be more birds to find and observe.

He drew a deep breath, soothing his own ruffled feathers. "Not quite as large or diverse, but still a success."

"Oh, quite, quite," Lord Blackstone said distractedly. "I meant no offense, of course. Nearly five hundred is still quite a feat. Ah, here we are."

He reached the final page—the title page Henry had purposely slipped to the back of the stack.

His eyes dropped to the bottom of the paper, and a small smile thinned his lips. Lord Blackstone had obviously found what he'd been searching for.

Deborah M. Hathaway

A Compilation of Birds Observed
Vol. VIII

Containing the Description of Birds
as Found in the West Indies
by H. Branok

Excursion appointed and fully funded by
Egbert Percival Ptolemy, Viscount Blackstone
Naturalist

Lord Blackstone had never read one of Henry's books. He only ever saw his name on the title page before signing off on the proofs, so Henry liked to make him work for it. The man was obviously more inclined to appreciate the acclaim he received for funding expeditions—as the king did—than he was to appreciate breathing birds.

Henry didn't really mind. After all, his traveling, researching, observing, and writing was for individuals who *loved* birds. *Living* birds.

But Henry would accept whatever mere glance at his words Lord Blackstone could muster, so long as the viscount continued to send Henry all over the world, using contacts and connections to observe more birds and to print books faster than Henry ever could himself.

All he had to do was get past his own loathing for the man's dead animal obsession, and he would last another decade or so doing this very thing. At any rate, Henry was advancing the understanding of living animals with each book he finished. That was worth any sacrifice needed, as far as he was concerned.

"Very fine work," Lord Blackstone said, admiring his own name written in big, bold letters—one of his requirements.

"If you remain in my special club, devote the entirety of your

attention to these excursions, and attribute your findings to me, I shall send you all over the world," he'd said five years before.

They'd both made good on their promises.

"All is accurate and in order?" Lord Blackstone asked next, slipping the title page to the front of the papers. "A full account of your findings?"

"Yes," Henry replied. He cleared his throat, glancing again at the window.

"Excellent," Lord Blackstone said. "Everything appears in order on my end."

He dipped his pen in his ink well, slid the tip on the edge of the glass container, then signed the front page to send the proof back to the printers.

Henry felt a weight lifted from his shoulders.

Book eight, complete.

He accepted the pages and slid them back into his satchel. "Thank you, my lord."

"Thank *you*, Branok," Lord Blackstone said, lacing his fingers on his desk and leaning back. "So what is next for you? Rest, I trust?"

"Not quite. I have been requested by an acquaintance, Mr. Chumley, to join an excursion across England over the coming months. We leave this morning."

"Indeed? The very wilds of England. How ever shall you manage such excitement?"

Henry laughed, thinking Lord Blackstone had made a joke, but he realized all too late the viscount did not possess the wit. Instead, his wide, round eyes were as blank as the rabbit perched behind him.

Henry cleared his throat. "Oh, well, I…That is to say, I shall take it day by day, I suppose."

That wasn't too far from the truth. He'd spent the last five years exploring Greenland, Europe, South Africa, the Americas, the East Indies, and now the West Indies. He'd experienced nearly every sort of weather, observed countless animals and peculiar birds, and witnessed vast cultures.

And now...now, for the first time he would be crossing England with a group of inexperienced individuals who merely dabbled in observation.

He would either be terribly bored or entirely unfit to lead such rabble. Only time would tell.

"I must take my leave now," Henry continued. "I fear I am already late."

"Oh, but of course. Allow me to see you out."

"No, please—"

"I insist."

Henry hid a grimace, knowing what was coming next.

"While we're walking, I may as well point out my latest additions," Lord Blackstone predictably said. "Although, you might have already noticed them on your way in."

"I did notice quite a few specimens, my lord," he responded mutedly.

As they walked through the doorway and entered the gallery, Lord Blackstone placed an arm around Henry's shoulders—or attempted to, at least, as Henry was more than a head taller than him.

"Now," the viscount continued, "I know you are partial to *living* animals, but I shall convert you to my collection yet. Have you seen my weasel? Oh, she is a remarkable creature. Now, where is she?"

He led the way forward, talking to himself as he moved through the different animals, and Henry followed him with barely restrained repulsion.

Soon, however, footsteps sounded down the corridor, and Mr. Sebastian Drake appeared at the other end.

Praise heaven. Henry was saved.

"Drake!" Lord Blackstone cried out, releasing Henry as he faced the other gentleman. "You have arrived in the perfect moment. I was just about to show Branok my lovely weasel. Have *you* seen her?"

"I have indeed been granted that very distinct pleasure, my lord," Mr. Drake responded.

Henry snatched up his chance to leave before it could be taken from him.

"I must see these arrive at the printers," Henry said, lifting the satchel and backing away with a bow. "Good day."

"Oh, but of course. Good day, Branok. Now, Drake. Come. I have found her. Oh, no. That is not a weasel. That is a marten. I know she must be nearby."

He continued mumbling to himself as he searched through his countless animals, and Henry reached Mr. Drake.

"Branok," Mr. Drake greeted. "How were the West Indies?"

"Stifling." He lowered his voice so the still-muttering Lord Blackstone could not hear. "But preferable to this gallery."

Mr. Drake chuckled. "How long have you been trapped here with him?" he asked from the side of his mouth.

"Thankfully only a moment before you arrived. But I'm afraid you shall have to suffer with tales of his weasel now."

"I'll manage," Mr. Drake responded, though he looked at the viscount with impatience before glancing back at Henry. "Care for a game of billiards later?"

Henry clicked his tongue in disappointment. "I do wish I could, but I am slated for another expedition."

"Gads, man," Mr. Drake said, "do you never rest?"

"Not if I can help it."

"I know she's around here somewhere," Lord Blackstone said from behind Henry.

The man's eyes focused on the ceiling where the birds hung. Why he'd find a weasel flying with the stagnant fowl was beyond Henry.

He faced Mr. Drake again. "I shall return next month for a week or two, though. We can meet then?"

"Yes, fine. I'll be here for the entirety of the Season."

Henry nodded. He didn't know much about Mr. Drake, but he assumed he was in London for the same reason as the rest of the single gentlemen—they were all in search of a wife.

Henry, however, was the furthest from even *wishing* to find a wife. He'd almost been coerced into marrying a woman before, but when he'd returned from Greenland, she'd already married another.

It was just as well. Henry hadn't really liked her anyway. Besides, he did not want a wife to leave at home—a wife who pined for him or whom he pined for while he was away. It wouldn't be fair for either of them.

At any rate, Lord Blackstone had made it clear that, should Henry ever marry, the excursions, the personal guides, and the connections with the printers would be eliminated.

"I shall keep you and your attentions for as long as possible, Branok," Lord Blackstone had said. *"And if you marry, I shall be the first in line to congratulate you. However, I cannot fund excursions for a distracted gentleman, and there is no one more distracted than a married man. Take it from me."*

Henry had taken his advisement under careful consideration. He'd attempted to carry out his own excursion six years ago to India, but the costs to travel had been extortionate, and obtaining the proper permissions as well as finding the right guides, accommodations, and crew members, had been impossible.

Not only did the viscount have extensive wealth, but he also had an astonishing amount of connections. From the start, he had been able to consistently provide Henry with knowledge-able locals as guides, a safe and swift passage to each country, permits to travel, and a dependable way to publish his volumes of work.

In short, Henry had seen more birds with Lord Blackstone's aid than he ever could have on his own. As such, he had decided that he would remain single until he was finished traveling—which would be on his deathbed. So if he found a woman interested in an old, decrepit gentleman with less hair than the lifeless naked mole rat standing at his right, then certainly, he would marry.

Until then, he was quite content to be a bachelor. He had a comfortable living, a fine steward caring for his large estate in Kent, maintained good health, and his parents, God rest their souls, were surely looking down on him in delight for their son was truly living the best life he could.

He was happy, so why would he change a thing?

"Ah ha! I have found her! Come, Drake, come!" Lord Blackstone waved his hands toward him, his eyes fixed on the animal as if he feared the dead creature might scamper away and be lost to him again.

"I am beckoned," Mr. Drake said, then with a nod in departure to Henry, he walked toward the viscount.

Henry, on the other hand, left directly. He would not have to return to the gallery—or the club itself, for that matter—for over a month, and he wasn't upset about it in the slightest.

Until he returned, he was determined to enjoy himself around his own country. Even if he *was* destined to be bored or was truly unqualified to teach about the birds in England, this would be more of a rest than tramping across jungles in sweltering heat or being tossed about for weeks at a time across the Atlantic.

He'd even heard that women had been invited on this excursion. He'd never seen a woman take up bird observing before. That alone would be entertaining.

At least more entertaining than a club full of dead animals.

CHAPTER 2

Standing in the Chumleys' grand parlor, Lark Fernside bounced up and down on the balls of her feet, shifting her leather-bound journal from her left hand to her right, then back again.

"Nervous, my dear?" Aunt Harriet whispered to her right, an amused smile playing on her lips.

Lark stopped her bouncing at once and looked over at her aunt with a sheepish grin. "More anxious than nervous."

Aunt Harriet faced forward with another smile. "We will be on our way soon, I'm certain of it."

As she and Aunt fell silent again, Lark took up the less conspicuous activity of wiggling her toes in her half-boots. She knew she ought to be still, but she couldn't manage her excitement.

She'd awaited this moment for so long—more than seven months—but now that the time to depart had nearly arrived, she found herself swiftly losing patience.

The two of them—along with Uncle Francis who stood on Aunt's other side—had arrived at the Chumleys' only moments before, having been ushered into the parlor where the rest of the attendees stood to await the beginning of the bird observing excursion.

The parlor was adorned in a soft blue floral wallpaper reminiscent of the sea, though the windows at the far side of the room revealed the bustling London streets below. At least a half a dozen paintings of English landscapes were scattered about the walls, and a large crystal chandelier hung down from the ceiling ornamented with gilded paint.

The room was magnificent, but what drew Lark's attention more than anything were the other attendees scattered about the space. All eleven of them stood by in near silence, their bags and trunks already loaded onto the private carriages by the help. Lark's own lady's maid, Penelope, would be riding with the rest of the servants in their own carriages. For now, however, they awaited out of doors for the guests, who in turn awaited further instruction from the Chumleys, their hosts. The handsome couple—who appeared to be in their forties—stood at the front of the room, speaking with their butler in whispered tones.

Lark shifted her leather journal to her other hand again as she stared at the Chumleys, willing them to begin, but they continued their whispers. They were still smoothing out the last-minute details for the two-month-long excursion, no doubt.

"So which one is Mr. Branok?" Aunt whispered, leaning close to Lark again.

At the mention of the name, excitement and nerves simmered together at the base of Lark's stomach, making it difficult to breathe.

Mr. Henry Branok.

She couldn't believe she was finally going to meet the man whose work she'd admired for five years now. Lark had read each book by the esteemed naturalist so often—had effectively memorized most of them—that his works had become a permanent fixture in any conversation she held with her aunt and uncle.

In truth, Mr. Branok was the reason Lark had wanted to join the excursion in the first place, but she had yet to meet or even see a likeness of the gentleman.

As such, the moment she'd entered the room, she'd inconspicuously examined each individual to decipher which one he could be.

The Chumleys were not candidates. And the dark-haired man nearby who stood next to his wife—the two of them like preening peacocks with an apparent knowledge of just how very handsome they were—was too young to be Mr. Branok.

The red-headed gentlemen at the far side of the room were no doubt brothers, but Lark had never heard word of Mr. Branok's family, so she doubted that one of those men would be him either.

Between the remaining individuals—a younger gentleman with a small patch of hair above his lip and a middle-aged gentleman with a head free of any hair at all—Lark had deduced Mr. Branok to be the latter.

He appeared the eldest and wisest of them all, as if he had sailed around the world a time or two, which was essentially what Mr. Branok had done.

Settling once more on her decision, Lark leaned toward Aunt Harriet. "I admit, I do not know for certain. But I do believe it is the gentleman closest to us."

She motioned toward him, his head as bald as the King of the Vultures she'd seen in Mr. Branok's book, *A Compilation of Birds Observed, Vol. IV, Containing the Description of Birds as Found in the Americas.*

Light shone off his empty scalp as bright as the sconces on the walls, and he held himself in a commanding sort of way. No nonsense, quite like Uncle. Quite like someone who knew how to find a bird or two.

Aunt Harriet nodded. "We shall have your uncle make his acquaintance directly, so that he might introduce the two of you."

Lark smiled her gratitude. How blessed she was to have Aunt and Uncle as her chaperones on this new adventure. She would not be on the excursion at all, were it not for them.

Months before, in September of last year, she'd seen advertisements for the excursion around England. She'd spotted many similar announcements before, but all of them had the same stipulation:

"For gentlemen only."

Or, on the rare occasion,

"For gentlemen and their wives, if applicable."

Lark understood the reticence. Single females were often seen as unnecessary distractions for gentlemen who wished to remain focused on nature. More than that, they were considered to be most burdensome, unable to withstand rigorous traveling circumstances and incapable of braving the elements to remain out of doors long enough to spot birds at all.

Lark did not agree in the slightest with either accusation, but she'd resigned herself to their prejudice. That is, until she'd heard news that Mr. Branok would be joining this particular venture. Not only would he be sharing with them the marvelous creations he'd witnessed over the years, but he would also be instructing them on how to best observe birds.

Naturally, Lark could not pass such an opportunity, and though Mr. Chumley resisted, he finally allowed her to join only after she promised that her presence would go by veritably unnoticed—and after she'd agreed to pay for four retainers of six hundred pounds each, instead of the three for which she had planned.

Mr. Chumley had written to her that if he allowed her as a single female to join, he would be potentially missing out on filling a whole other entry for another couple.

Lark was not stupid. She knew full well the man was taking advantage of her determination to join, but she allowed it anyway. She'd also kept the true costs hidden from her aunt and uncle, paying for their entries, as well, despite their protests.

They were perfectly capable of paying the sum themselves, but Lark had insisted. Aunt and Uncle were not great admirers of birds, but they *were* great admirers of Lark and would do anything for her. Paying for them was a simple way to express her gratitude.

At any rate, no matter the cost, Lark was simply happy to be there—and to be allowed the opportunity to prove her worth as a valuable member of the bird observing community, female and single, or not.

And if Mr. Branok just so happened to see how much value she brought to an excursion, she would certainly not be upset about that either.

She stared once more at the back of the man's pale scalp. She'd brought each of her copies of his books with her. Would it be too much for her to request that he sign them? How she wished she could abandon all sense of propriety by marching up to him and expressing how much his work had meant to her over the years.

But she would maintain her dignity, if only to prove to Mr. Chumley that she would keep her word and remain relatively invisible—which was how she preferred to live life anyway.

"They are running behind schedule," Uncle Francis whispered, leaning forward to address both Lark and his wife. "This does not bode well for the rest of the journey."

Lark glanced toward him, noting the worry creasing his brow.

"I'm certain we shall leave soon, my dear," Aunt soothed.

He nodded, though he glanced at his pocket watch again.

"Would you care for me to tell them to make haste?" Lark teased.

Uncle Francis cracked a smile. "Thank you, but I don't believe that will be necessary this morning, niece. Anyway, did you not promise to hold your tongue on the journey? As impossible a notion as that is." He winked, and Lark smiled in return.

He was not wrong. Lark was not an unkind person by any means, but when her peace was threatened, she was not afraid to speak her mind.

She'd told Aunt and Uncle of her promise to remain unseen, and though they hadn't liked the idea at all—loving her and accepting her the way she was—they'd agreed to support her, just as they always did, for they loved her as the child they never had.

Ever since Father had died eighteen years ago, and Mother had spent each subsequent Season in London, Uncle and Aunt had remained behind to be her protectors, her chaperones, and her advisors. Lark hadn't minded Mother leaving. She got along better with her aunt and uncle anyway.

But even though she appreciated them and their presence in her life to no end, she could not help but long for an existence where she could move beyond her twenty-six years and lead a life without chaperones.

She wanted to go where she wished, when she wished. She dreamt of traveling across England and Europe. Of exploring birds in the East Indies. Discovering more in India, perhaps even in the Americas, like Mr. Branok.

She glanced again at the hairless man in front of her. What a life he must have led. What adventures he must have been on, and what birds he must have seen. She *would* have that life one day. It was only a matter of time.

Lark looked over her shoulder at the light pouring in from the windows and was half-tempted to move closer to the glass to spot a few birds as she waited.

However, when she heard footsteps shuffling about the room, Lark faced forward as the Chumleys' butler departed and the host and hostess finally turned toward their guests.

"My friends, welcome," Mr. Chumley began. His thick curls were brushed forward to frame his features like a lion's mane. "I do apologize for the delay. We have had a few problems arise, but I assure you, all is well now, and I am so pleased to have you here." He held his hands together in front of him, his white collar high and skimming his jaw as he spoke. "Now, would you all gather closer? Take a seat if you wish. If we are to be friends on this trip, we may as well begin now."

The group drew closer together. The peacock couple sat down on the settee, and Aunt Harriet took a single chair on the outskirts of the room while everyone else remained standing.

"Do you wish to sit, Lark?" Aunt Harriet whispered, motioning to a nearby chair, but Lark shook her head.

"I prefer to stand, thank you," she responded.

She needed to work out her excess energy still, and sitting would hardly do her any favors.

The men drew closer, too, and Mr. Branok—or who she was fairly certain was Mr. Branok—stood near the center of the room. That is, until he moved directly into Lark's line of sight.

He angled his large body so Aunt and Uncle could see the Chumleys in front of them, but Lark's view of the host was entirely prohibited. She looked left and right to see if anyone noticed, but Mr. Branok was far enough ahead of her to make it appear that she *could* see around him. As such, all eyes, including Aunt's and Uncle's, were on the Chumleys.

Lark pulled in her lips, shifting to the side, but it was to no avail. She could barely see the couple above the tall, balding man's head.

It was no great feat for Lark to not be seen behind him. She had a slight frame and hardly commanded attention. But she struggled not to take offense at his ignorance of her. If he wasn't noticing her now, who was to say she'd be noticed at all during the trip, when that was what she wanted most—to be seen by a famed naturalist and be recognized for her own talents and abilities as a bird observer?

"That's better now, isn't it?" Mr. Chumley said, his voice moving around Mr. Branok toward Lark.

She frowned. Surely Mr. Chumley had noticed her behind the man. But then, is that not what she'd promised to be on the excursion—invisible to others?

She shook off the feeling of embarrassment that accompanied being ignored, refusing to become bitter. This adventure would still be amazing, with or without being seen.

She shifted a step away from Aunt, moving until she could see at least half of one of Mr. Chumley's eyes.

"I hope you've all felt a little comfort in our home this morning," he continued, "enough to sustain you on our long journey ahead." He paused, as if for dramatic effect. "Speaking of long journeys, I would like to formally welcome you all to our first bird observing excursion across England."

The group clapped, and Lark tucked her book between her arm and side to join in. Her gloved hands produced a muted thwapping sound. She longed to whoop and whistle, so ready she was for this journey to begin, but she forced herself to remain reserved, just as she'd promised.

"Now," Mr. Chumley said, motioning to his wife beside him, "I must begin by drawing your attention to my lovely wife, Mrs. Emmeline Chumley, who has taken upon herself the title of hostess. She has been the one to see through the grueling details of planning, including the hiring of private carriages, finding the best travel routes and inns, ensuring we have wonderful homes to stay within in three different counties, and countless other decisions. Let us all show our appreciation for Mrs. Chumley, if you please."

The group clapped again, and Mrs. Chumley ducked her head in modesty. "I was happy to do so," she said softly, a kind smile on her lips.

"She has been wonderful," Mr. Chumley carried on, then he spoke to the group as if his wife couldn't hear. "Do not tell her I said this, but that is the reason I invited her—so I would not have to do any of that terribly draining work. She is much better at it than I am."

Laughter sprinkled around the group. Mrs. Chumley and the peacock woman smiled amusedly, as well.

Lark, however, being hidden behind Mr. Branok, fortunately did not have to pretend to be amused at the comment.

She longed to call out, *Is this the only benefit of having a wife?* But she held her tongue.

This was one reason Lark would never marry. If she wanted to observe birds for the rest of her life, she would have to find a gentleman who *allowed* her to join *him* on his excursions, never the other way around. Otherwise, she would be expected to remain at home—like the wives of these other men, no doubt.

Even Aunt would have been left alone had she not chosen to come as another chaperone for Lark.

"I am thrilled to begin this journey with you all," Mr. Chumley continued.

He launched into a description of how this had been a dream of his for years, but Lark's attention was stolen by a movement at the door.

She thought perhaps the butler had returned to deliver some other unfortunate news that would cause another delay, so she glanced away from the entry way, only to return her gaze a moment later when someone else entered instead.

Hesitating in the doorway, hidden to all others in the room aside from Lark, the man and his entire stature commanded attention—broad shoulders, tall figure, tanned skin, dark blond hair. Then there was the matter of his features, his cut jawline, masculine lips curved in a slight smile, and his eyes—deep blue and striking like the sea.

He stood there for a moment, hesitant as he leaned around the doorframe. He paused, smiled, then entered the rest of the way with silent footsteps.

Lark tore her gaze away, looking to see if Mr. Chumley had motioned the man forward, but she remembered too late that she couldn't *see* Mr. Chumley.

But she *could* see this new gentleman.

She looked at him again as he walked toward the back of the group where she stood. His attention was on Mr. Chumley, then his eyes found hers, and Lark's stomach pulled down in pleasant surprise.

CHAPTER 3

Lark looked away in a rush, praying the man hadn't thought she'd been staring, even if that was exactly what she'd been doing. Yes, he was handsome, but she was more concerned about his tardiness. Was this why matters had been delayed? Had the butler been informing the Chumleys of their final latecomer who would push them all back a quarter of an hour?

The man stopped a foot or two away, his gaze on her. She fought a good fight for ten seconds or so, then relented and met his stare.

He smiled, the wrinkles at the edges of his eyes appearing first.

She returned his smile with one of her own, then faced forward again, staring at the back of Mr. Branok's bald head. She couldn't lean to the side any longer to see more of Mr. Chumley. She would not wish for this man—this very attractive man—to think she was leaning closer to him.

"Typically," Mr. Chumley was saying, "I venture forth on these excursions alone, spending weeks at a time away from my wife. She has never wished to join me on such dull outings, you see."

More chuckles from the men sounded, but the gentleman beside her merely smiled.

Mr. Chumley continued. "This time, however, she is simply thrilled to join me, purely based on the fact that she shall have female companions to keep her company over the next two months. You women are a godsend to her, I assure you."

Lark caught Mrs. Chumley nodding her head enthusiastically beside her husband, and most of the women laughed.

But once more, Lark didn't join in. How could she? She hadn't come on this excursion to play companion to some poor woman whose husband did not care to be around her. Lark was there to observe the birds herself. Was there no other woman attending with the same wish?

Aunt certainly wasn't. She'd merely come to keep Lark and Uncle Francis company. The peacock woman was here for her husband, too, no doubt.

Did this mean Lark would be expected to keep company with the women instead of with the birds?

She internally shook her head. She had paid double her own fee—and both Aunt and Uncle's charges—to join this tour. And while the price was nothing to her fortune of forty thousand pounds and being the sole heiress of a large estate in Suffolk, Brackenmore Hall, she would not waste another pence on spending a day indoors when she could be venturing forth and adding to her list of birds. Uncle would see reason, surely, and help her to be out with the others, would he not?

The tall gentleman beside her shifted his footing, and she caught the earthy scent of his cologne. It was quite a pleasant smell. One with which she wasn't entirely familiar.

"Excuse me."

Lark nearly jumped as the same man whispered to her, leaning slightly down so he was hidden by Mr. Branok, too.

This gentleman certainly wasn't worried about propriety, was he? Speaking in the middle of the host's instructions with a woman to whom he had not been introduced.

"Yes?" she asked in a returned whisper, stealing a glance at her aunt and uncle.

Both seemed entirely unaware of the man's words.

"For how long has Mr. Chumley been speaking?" the gentleman asked.

Lark was having a difficult time focusing on his question, what with those sea blue eyes staring down at her.

"Only for a moment or two," she finally responded.

He nodded. "Have I missed anything important?"

Other than Lark being classified in the same group as the other women *not* there for the birds? No, he had not. But then, that didn't concern him anyway. He'd probably left his wife at home, as well.

"No, you haven't," she responded.

"Excellent. Thank you," he whispered again.

His eyes remained on hers after she nodded, and she could see the clear curiosity in his gaze, but she stared straight ahead at Mr. Branok's bald head, pretending to see Mr. Chumley.

"Now, according to the itinerary," Mr. Chumley said, "we shall begin our adventure in Yorkshire, where we shall stay for a fortnight, exploring a few seaside towns, as well as the North York Moors. There, as I'm certain you are all aware, the common redstart has been known to inhabit this time of year."

Lark bit her lower lip to keep from grinning too broadly. She'd been desperate to catch a sight of the bird ever since she'd read about it in Thomas Bewick's book, *History of British Birds, Vol. I.*

She was hopeless when it came to colorful birds. Then again, she was hopeless when it came to *all* birds. She couldn't wait to see the puffins at Bempton Cliffs, choughs in Cornwall, even mallards in the Lake District. Each bird was so marvelous, so different and unique, that she could not help but love them all.

Her journal was filled with well over one hundred species she'd found in her little corner of east England. But after this trip, her list would be as comprehensive as Mr. Branok's.

Or so at least she could dream.

She looked at the man's shining head, and she caught him stifling a yawn into his fisted hand.

Lark pulled back, forcing her frown to remain at bay. He was yawning? Did that mean he was bored? Or was he merely exhausted from traveling back from the West Indies?

She prayed it was the latter. She couldn't abide the great disappointment she'd experience if this man did not love birds as deeply as his books would suggest.

Her thought didn't last for long as the gentleman beside her leaned down once more to whisper. "Can you see well enough from there?"

Her cheeks warmed. He'd noticed, then. How had he seen her struggles when not even Aunt and Uncle had? She supposed she shouldn't be too shocked, as they had yet to acknowledge the whispering man at the side of her either.

"I can, thank you," she whispered back.

The man didn't pull away. "Are you certain? You're welcome to move closer over here. I'm happy to give up my spot for you."

She glanced up at him, saw his friendly smile, but shook her head all the same. "No, but thank you."

She faced forward more directly, hoping to dissuade him from speaking to her further. He was kind enough, but she wasn't entirely aware of *why* he was being so kind. In her experience, if gentlemen behaved in such a way, it was to get to know her—or rather, her fortune—better.

He peered down at her again with that curious gaze, then looked at Mr. Chumley—whom *he* could actually see.

"Our journey to Yorkshire will be arduous," Mr. Chumley

said. "Three days of travel. This will be particularly difficult for the women, but I assure you, Mrs. Chumley has taken special care to ensure we have the best inns in which to recuperate."

Lark fought the urge to roll her eyes. For heaven's sake. Why did gentlemen feel the need to point out how difficult traveling was for the women? And why did some women feel the need to essentially swoon at the mere mention of a carriage ride? Coaches were not so very bad.

Of course, Aunt and Uncle would beg to differ. The poor dears both suffered with terrible sickness each time they *sat* in a carriage. She did not relish the upcoming journey for their sake.

Still, Uncle suffered just as greatly as Aunt, so why were only women singled out?

"Have you ever attended an excursion like this before?"

Lark started.

The gentleman beside her...He was speaking with her *again*. Did he not care about what was being said? She was trying to listen. Not that she needed to. She'd already memorized the itinerary months ago. Still, it was terribly rude to speak over their host in such a manner.

"No, I have not," she stated. She gave a single nod, then faced forward again, leaning slightly away from him, even though that proved to hide her from Mr. Chumley even further.

"Not even around England?" he whispered next.

He was either oblivious or far too determined.

"No," she replied simply.

"I have been fortunate enough to have attended a few myself," he whispered with a smile.

Just then, Mr. Branok's bald head swiveled round until he made direct eye contact with Lark. He sent her a clear look of intolerance, then shifted to face Mr. Chumley again—all the while still blocking Lark's view.

Lark couldn't believe it. This was not the way she'd hoped her first interaction with the naturalist would be. How utterly humiliating! What was even worse was that she was not to be blamed in the slightest. It was the gentleman next to her. He simply could not keep his mouth closed, so what was she to do? She glanced round for aid, but Aunt and Uncle were still both focused intently on Mr. Chumley.

"We have a lovely estate set up for us," he was saying. "The very best. Quite large…"

"Are you joined by your parents?" the gentleman whispered to Lark next. "Or your husband perhaps?"

Lark closed her eyes with barely restrained patience.

Just as she'd suspected. *This* was why the man was paying such close attention to her. He must be aware of her wealth, what with her being able to afford an excursion like this, and was now in search of adding to his.

This was exactly as it had been her entire life—exactly as it had been when she'd had her heart broken at the tender age of eighteen and exactly as it had been only a week before when one Sebastian Drake, a fortune hunter and supposed gentleman, had proposed to her after a mere week of knowing her, simply to benefit from her prosperity.

This was why she despised being wealthy—and why she would never marry. Certainly, wealth had its perks, and she knew how fortunate she was because of it. But she would rather be ignored during this entire excursion than to be paid attention to merely because of the fortune to her name.

Well, this gentleman had no idea whom he'd chosen to target. But he would soon enough.

As quietly and succinctly as possible, she discreetly shifted toward him and replied, "No. I am not joined by my parents but my aunt and uncle. As for the other matter, I do not have a husband. However, I will save you and I both the time and embarrassment by informing you that I intend to *never* have a husband. Now, if you will excuse me, I must end this conversation before we disturb Mr. Branok further."

The gentleman pulled back. "Mr. Branok?" he whispered with a look of confusion that swiftly shifted to amusement.

"Yes," she said, ignoring whatever it was he found humorous and tossing her head in the bald man's direction. How could this man not know who was in his presence? Surely he'd seen the advertisement.

"Are you not aware that he is the esteemed and talented naturalist?" she continued. "I should hate to upset him more due to the incessant whispering of a gentleman who clearly does not take bird observing very seriously."

"Madam," the gentleman began, shaking his head, "you are mistaken…"

But she stopped him at once. Pulling a finger to her lips, she signaled to him as one would a disobedient child, then she faced forward with a frown, attempting to ignore the bemused look across his features.

What sort of gentleman found it humorous to be chastised? Clearly one with whom she did not wish to be acquainted.

"Let us now move on to introductions," Mr. Chumley said, finishing his explanation of the schedule. "Then we may all proceed to the carriages."

The group nodded in response, and Lark forced her eyes to remain off of the man still smiling beside her.

"You all know me, Mr. Daniel Chumley, and my lovely wife," Mr. Chumley began, then he shifted to the peacock couple, who nodded at his words. "Mr. Charles and Mrs. Marie Shepherd."

Mrs. Shepherd raised her arched eyebrows in greeting, and Mr. Shepherd bowed ceremoniously.

Next, the red-headed gentlemen nodded as Mr. Chumley introduced them. "Mr. Michael Kay and Mr. Joseph Kay are, indeed, brothers, as I'm certain we all already established. And then we have Mr. Stephen Gibbon." The man with the small mustache tipped his head in greeting. "At the back of the room are Mr. Francis and Mrs. Harriet Haskett with their niece, Miss Lark Fernside."

A few eyes turned to look at Lark, no doubt at the introduction of her being single. Even Mr. Branok shifted his rotund body from in front of her, his eyes focusing condemningly at her.

Blast and wretch. Of all the people to have annoyed, why did it have to be him?

She smiled nonetheless, praying for another chance to make a good impression.

Then Mr. Chumley continued. "Next, we have Mr. John Dunn, who has traveled from Somerset. Welcome, sir."

Lark looked to the man beside her, expecting him to bow in response to Mr. Chumley's introduction, but when Mr. Branok bowed instead, she stiffened.

Mr. Dunn? The bald gentleman was Mr. Dunn? But then, if he was not Mr. Branok, who...

Slowly, her eyes shifted to the gentleman standing beside her. He was already watching her with a happy, knowing smile.

CHAPTER 4

Lark could hardly breathe, her head spinning.

"Finally," Mr. Chumley said, his voice distant in her embarrassed haze, "a man who needs no introduction, our wonderful guest of honor, Mr. Henry Branok."

The group clapped, but Lark was so stunned, she could not move. The gentleman—the real Henry Branok—grinned as he bowed in response, his eyes sparkling with delight.

"Come, join me at the front of the room, sir," Mr. Chumley invited.

Mr. Branok nodded, moving a step forward before seeming to think better of it and glancing back down at Lark. He took a subtle step toward her, clearly ignoring all propriety and caring not an ounce of what others might say as he shifted closer.

With barely moving lips, he whispered, "I did try to tell you who I was. But you *were* right about one thing...I certainly do not take bird observing very seriously."

With a twinkle in his eye, he moved to the front of the still-applauding group, running a hand through his thick, dark blond strands.

Lark was left behind to suffer with burning cheeks and

limping pride as she contemplated how she would ever be able to show her face around Mr. Branok again.

What a nightmare.

Aunt Harriet gently tapped against Lark's arm, and Lark bent down to level her ear with her seated aunt.

"*He* is Mr. Branok?" Aunt whispered, her dark eyes focused on him as he reached Mr. Chumley.

The gentlemen clasped hands with friendly smiles.

"Apparently," Lark responded.

"But he is so very young to have accomplished so much, is he not?"

"He is," Lark said.

Which was precisely why she had guessed Mr. Dunn to be Mr. Branok instead. Writing novels, receiving awards, exploring the world—achieving so much at what could only be eight and twenty? He was so very capable.

And Lark had shushed him like a schoolboy. She had accused him of *not being serious in his bird observations.*

An ache in her brow pulsed.

"What did he say to you before he left just now?" Aunt asked next.

Lark hesitated, swallowing hard. "Oh…He simply apologized for the disruption his late arrival caused."

Aunt nodded, leaning back as she seemed to accept Lark's falsehood.

Lark straightened, guilt poking at her conscience.

She wanted to tell the truth, but she would not reveal a word about what she'd said to him. She was far too humiliated to admit her actions aloud. Especially when she'd so wrongfully assumed that he'd been seeking her marital status due to being interested in her fortune. He was obviously simply curious that she was a single female on an excursion, that was all.

She gritted her teeth. This was all Mr. Drake's doing. Lark had been on edge ever since his swift and loveless proposal. Had it not been for Mr. Drake dredging up her past—reminding her of the last time she'd been proposed to—she never would have assumed something so unjust of Mr. Branok.

"Now, ladies and gentlemen," Mr. Chumley said, motioning to Mr. Branok, "I must share with you how often I have attempted to coerce Mr. Branok to join me on an expedition around England. He leaves our fair country so often, it has taken me years to find a time for him to finally be here. Is it not wonderful to have him join us? We shall surely be educationally fed by him over the next two months."

The group clapped, and Lark did her best to join in, though her limbs had grown weak due to the distinct depletion of energy she was still overcoming from her mistake.

Mr. Branok—the real Mr. Branok—clasped his hands behind his back and smiled around the room. "Thank you all so much for your warm welcome," he said, his voice deep and rich as opposed to when he'd whispered. "While I cannot claim to be a master in the art of observation, I have experienced a great deal over the years in relation to viewing birds that I will be happy to share with you. I do hope, however, that we may learn from one another as we delight in observing God's beautiful creatures together."

The group clapped again, and this time, his eyes landed on Lark's. She could have sworn she'd seen them sparkling once more, but she looked away, unwilling to acknowledge the interaction that had already taken place between them.

How was she to behave around him? If he was old and married like Mr. Dunn, she could have easily told him how she admired his writing and wished for his signature to be on each of his volumes of work she'd brought with her.

But now that she was so painfully aware of how he was young and handsome—and single? He had not brought a wife with him. Either way, saying such things would hardly be proper. Suppose he thought her too forward? That she was attempting to express a certain fondness for him? Although, she had no notion how he could think such things, especially after she'd explained her desire to remain unmarried.

She chewed on her lower lip, the pinching above her brow growing steadily stronger.

"We certainly cannot wait to learn from you, sir," Mr. Chumley said, clasping Mr. Branok's shoulder and delivering a firm nod of his head, then he faced the others. "So let us begin this journey, shall we? Three carriages await our departure just outside. We thought it best to assign individuals to specific carriages for the duration of our journey to avoid any confusion and prevent anyone from being left behind. So, the first carriage shall house me and my wife and the Shepherds. The second carriage shall hold the Kay Brothers, Mr. Dunn, and Mr. Gibbon. And the third will be for Mr. and Mrs. Haskett, their niece, and Mr. Branok himself."

Lark blanched. They would be riding in the same carriage? That would be days of travel to reach Yorkshire alone, not to mention the next two months they would be stationed together.

Well, if she hadn't been worried enough about the coming interactions with the gentleman, she certainly was now. Would he tell Aunt and Uncle about her shushing him? Would her aunt and uncle blather to Mr. Branok about how greatly she'd long admired his work? That would be one surefire way to seal the fate of her never speaking with him again.

Mr. Chumley finished, then led the way forward, his wife on his arm and Mr. Branok close behind. The group swiftly followed, clearly anxious to seize their chance to speak with Mr. Branok before the long journey ahead.

Lark would have done the same. But now...

Aunt stood from her seat, and the three of them brought up the rear.

"This is a most happy circumstance, is it not?" Aunt whispered, her eyes shining as she looked at Lark. "Sharing a carriage with Mr. Branok? How fortunate!"

Aunt Harriet did not know Mr. Branok from Adam, but her excitement was for Lark more than anything. And yet, Lark could not even manage a smile.

"Are you not pleased with him riding with us?" Uncle asked, his brow furrowed as he must have noticed Lark's lack of enthusiasm.

"Oh, I am quite pleased," Lark said, looking at the group ahead to ensure they would not overhear her. "Merely nervous, that is all."

Aunt smiled at her with understanding. "Your uncle and I will help with your nerves, my dear. Worry not."

But that was precisely why Lark *was* nervous. "Perhaps..." she began, "perhaps we ought not share just how often I have read his books."

Aunt paused. "Whyever not?"

"It is only that," Lark continued, still ensuring no one was near enough to overhear, "I should hate to draw too much attention to myself and cause him discomfort." Or rather, cause *herself* discomfort. "After all, I did promise to remain inconspicuous on the trip. I simply would not wish for him to think that I am anything but an admirer of his works—and his works *alone*."

She emphasized the last word, giving them both a telling look.

Aunt and Uncle exchanged a look of their own, then nodded in unison.

"Of course," Aunt Harriet said, "we understand perfectly, my dear. We shall ensure platonic friendship at all times."

Lark knew a small degree of relief, and she nodded her gratitude as they left the parlor with the others.

She was comforted to know she could rely on her aunt and uncle, just like always. She cringed to consider what might have occurred had Mother joined her on the expedition instead.

"He is single, handsome, has a fortune, is your favorite writer, and loves birds as you do?" she would say. *"What in the world are you waiting for, my darling Lark?"*

The truth of the matter was, Lark was waiting for freedom. The freedom to explore the world and observe birds at her own bidding. The freedom to leave her home without a chaperone. The freedom to simply do as she pleased.

Having a husband would not provide her with any of that, aside from allowing herself to leave her home without a chaperone. But even that was not guaranteed, depending on the husband one possessed.

She'd learned after her experience as an impressionable eighteen-year-old, that in order to be happy, she would have to extricate herself from nearly all social gatherings. So, that was precisely what she did, remaining with Aunt and Uncle in Suffolk while making it clear that she would stay indelibly unmarried.

For the last six years, however, Mother had not once stopped attempting to pull Lark to London—and toward every available gentleman in remotely good standing in Society. Lark, however, had stood her ground...until this year.

"If you wish to have my blessing for you to attend this excursion," Mother had said, *"I would ask that you first agree to attempt to find a spouse for one final Season."*

Reluctantly, Lark had agreed. She loved and respected Mother, despite the two of them having less in common than a siskin and a smew. Where Lark loved peace and quiet in nature, Mother loved the hustle and bustle of the city. And where Lark loved being seen for who she was inside, Mother loved the attention she received from her wealth and status.

Their relationship had always been strengthened rather than hindered after time apart, so Lark had done her best to please her mother, consenting to attend all the balls and parties Mother pressed her to, before, during, and after the excursion.

Lark had already fulfilled a fraction of the bargain, attending a number of social outings before today, but after Mr. Drake's treatment of her—which Aunt and Uncle knew of, but Mother did not—Lark had changed the agreement on her end.

She would still do as Mother begged, but Lark would no longer attempt to catch a husband by playing the ever-demure, ever-unopinionated, ever-the-non-bird-loving individual she was forced to be in Society to be accepted.

Instead, she would be unabashedly herself.

Except while on this tour...all thanks to Mr. Chumley.

She puffed out a breath of air as they moved through his fine townhouse. The next two months would be a test on her will, and that was putting it lightly. She hadn't even made it through Mr. Chumley's introductions without scolding his guest of honor.

But that was in the past. She would move forward, apologize to Mr. Branok for her discourteous words, *reservedly* express her enjoyment of his books, and then spend the rest of the expedition observing birds in silence and not dwelling a single moment more on Mr. Branok and his sparkling blue eyes.

And yet, just as she was beginning to be certain she could fulfill these goals, she caught Mr. Branok looking over his shoulder at her, and she realized with a skipping heart that those goals had been lofty at best.

CHAPTER 5

Henry had a mind to ask the Chumleys to excuse him so that he might walk beside Miss Fernside and tease her again. He wanted to bring out that lovely blush he'd witnessed earlier across her high cheekbones. But when he looked back at her over his shoulder through the Chumleys' corridors, spotting her cheeks pinking instantly, he faced forward again with a satisfied smile.

He supposed a look was all it took, then.

It was just as well. Thanks to the Chumleys' carriage arrangements, he would have all the time he needed to get to know the woman better.

He followed the Chumleys as they led the party through the entryway and out the front doors held open by a footman standing at attention.

Henry drew in a deep breath of the cool weather. The air was smokier here compared to the West Indies—at least where he'd done most of his observations—but it was far crisper than Lord Blackstone's office. And while he wasn't used to living again in the smoke and bustle of London, far preferring the countryside, he had to admit the city had a charm of its own.

The streets were already filled with carriages rumbling and rattling their ways across the cobblestones, and the pavement was constantly marked with passersby—couples meandering from their fine townhouses, mothers and daughters skittering toward newly opened shops, and friends whispering to one another of whatever the latest gossip was amidst the *ton*.

The energy here was contagious, but he could not deny how he longed for the peace he'd grown used to in nature—the peace he craved more than anything now. As such, his attention was soon arrested by the sight of the six large coaches lined up before and beyond the Chumleys' home.

Each privately hired equipage was of the finest caliber with black leather tops and polished wooden bases, pulled by matching pairs of dashing, black horses. The trunks and bags of each attendee were already secured behind each coach, and the help stood by in their finest livery, ready to accompany the party within the final three carriages all the way to Yorkshire.

The sight was grand, indeed, and more than a few spectators paused to glance curiously at the twelve individuals gathered on the pavement with smiles and excited chatter.

Henry, too, felt that initial hum of excitement that always appeared at the beginning of an excursion. In truth, he hadn't expected the feeling for this trip, so he was more than pleasantly surprised as his level of enthusiasm matched the others. He was grateful he'd powered through his initial inhibitions and kept his commitment. This already had the promise of being quite the memorable experience.

"Mr. Branok," Mr. Chumley said, pulling Henry from his thoughts, "would you mind waiting a moment? I'd like a quick word if we can manage it."

"Of course," Henry immediately agreed, standing near the edge of the pavement and away from the carriages to allow others to pass him by.

Mr. Chumley nodded his gratitude, then redirected his

attention to the rest of his party, maneuvering through the busy crowds as he moved from person to person to show them which carriage was theirs and which ones belonged to the servants.

Henry watched him for a moment before catching sight of Miss Fernside. She walked behind Mr. and Mrs. Haskett, heading in the direction of the third coach—theirs and Henry's —before she paused and looked at the grand plane trees across the street.

Her aunt and uncle carried on, but Miss Fernside remained still, opening a leatherbound book and scribbling away at the paper with a small pencil.

Henry glanced up to see what had caught her eye, discovering a house sparrow chirping away within the trees, its brown and grey feathers barely visible through the thick green foliage.

Miss Fernside appeared very excited about the sighting, continuing with what he could only assume was a sketch as she remained entirely unaware of her aunt and uncle moving toward their carriage.

Henry could not stop his smile. The bird was nothing special —more common than anything. Yet, still, she found it necessary to make note of it. It was all rather endearing. Just as it was when she'd mistaken him for the bald gentleman in front of them.

He grinned at the thought of her words.

"I will save you and I both the time and embarrassment by informing you that I intend to never have a husband."

And then, *"I should hate to upset him more due to the incessant whispering of a gentleman who clearly does not take bird observing very seriously."*

Never had he known a woman to speak so plainly. It was refreshing. And the fact that she was an unmarried, female—and clearly enthusiastic—bird observer? She certainly was unique, not to mention stunning in her physical features, as well.

He couldn't help but wonder more about her—why her aunt

and uncle accompanied her instead of her parents, why she'd *chosen* to remain unmarried, and how much she truly knew about bird observation.

Perhaps he would do a bit of digging on their journey over the next three days. Although, with how readily she'd distributed the information he already did know, perhaps digging wouldn't even be necessary.

"I do apologize for keeping you waiting, Mr. Branok," Mr. Chumley said, coming up to stand directly in Henry's line of sight.

"I was happy to wait," Henry responded.

He shifted an inch to the right to better see Miss Fernside, who had wandered closer to the carriages, half-hidden behind the open door of the first coach. Mr. Chumley had walked right by without noticing her. And what of the Hasketts? Were they aware of their niece's absence, or were they used to her doing such things?

Mr. Chumley spoke again. "I wanted you to wait so that I might ask your feelings on the carriage arrangements."

"Oh, of course I am happy to travel in whatever carriage you allot me."

Blast. Was the man attempting to alter the arrangements? Henry had been looking forward to being with Miss Fernside.

He glanced at the woman, her eyes shifting from the bird to the book, then back again. Could she hear their conversation? Or was she too transfixed with the house sparrow?

"Are you certain?" Mr. Chumley pressed. "I would not wish for you to feel as if you were an afterthought in the last carriage. I assure you, a great deal of care was given to the arrangements, but, to put it frankly, Miss Fernside's presence has complicated matters to the highest degree."

At the mention of her name, Miss Fernside snapped her hazel eyes to Mr. Chumley's, peering at him coolly from around the carriage door. When she noticed Henry observing her in return, however, she blushed and swiftly restored her attention to her book.

He anticipated her departure, but she remained planted to her spot. Did she wish to remain there in case she needed to jump to her own defense? Or was she really that determined to finish her recording of the house sparrow?

"You see," Mr. Chumley continued in a level tone, so clearly taken with his own concerns that he did not seem to notice Henry's roving eyes, "I could not separate the Kay brothers, and Mr. Dunn and Mr. Gibbon have struck up a recent friendship, so they requested to sit with one another. My wife"—he broke off with a sigh—"she has need of riding with her dear friend Mrs. Shepherd, who must be with Mr. Shepherd. And with Miss Fernside needing to be with her chaperones, that left only a single spot more…"

He trailed off, clearly troubled with the whole affair as he wiped small beads of sweat from beneath the curls pressed against his brow. "I tell you, the next excursion I conduct shall only include gentlemen. Women have no place on these sorts of things. They only complicate matters in the most infuriating manner—my wife more so than anyone."

With another flick of his gaze, Henry found Miss Fernside's frown growing, this time her lips parting in indignation as she glowered at Mr. Chumley. With another look at Henry, she stared again at her book.

Henry could only imagine the great deal of restraint she had to be practicing to not blast Mr. Chumley right then and there. Honestly, Henry supposed he ought to say something himself in response to the man's obvious frustrations, but with the look of ire across Miss Fernside's features—her petite nose wrinkling in disgust and almond-shaped eyes narrowed—he quite forgot to respond at all.

"I swear, Mr. Branok," Mr. Chumley continued, straightening his waistcoat, "you are the wisest man I know simply due to your decision to remain single."

How Henry longed to look at Miss Fernside *now*. But he kept his eyes on Mr. Chumley, not wishing for the gentleman to discover the eavesdropper. Not only would Mr. Chumley question Henry for not warning him of her presence—but Henry wasn't entirely sure he had an answer to satisfy him.

He supposed he kept her presence to himself because he was merely curious to see what the woman might do next.

"At any rate," Mr. Chumley finally finished, "please tell me if any issue arises with your riding with the Hasketts and Miss Fernside. I have been assured that she shall be veritably imperceptible, but…" He glanced from left to right—omitting looking backward toward Miss Fernside. "I do fear, as she is unmarried, that she may begin to conduct herself as other young ladies do around amiable gentlemen such as yourself. Silly and flirtatious, you know. If this occurs, do alert me, and I shall deal with the matter straightaway."

Henry had thought the entire situation mildly humorous before. Now? He had to stop himself from laughing at Miss Fernside's mouth fully dropping open in utter astonishment.

"I'm certain she will be no trouble at all, Mr. Chumley," he reassured him, if only to prove to Miss Fernside that he was capable of behaving gentlemanly. "And as for her pursuing me, do not concern yourself. I have it on good authority that Miss Fernside has absolutely no interest in marriage."

Mr. Chumley narrowed his eyes. "Are you acquainted with her?"

"No, it is merely…an inkling. My reliable source is merely my intuition," he joked.

He looked back at Miss Fernside, and just as he'd hoped, a blush spread about her pale cheeks as red as a male bullfinch.

She clamped her mouth shut, blinked mutely once, then closed her book and finally moved down the pavement.

Now was Henry's chance. He placed a hand on the gentleman's shoulder. "Worry not, Mr. Chumley. I am quite content riding in whatever carriage I can. I am merely happy to be here." Mr. Chumley delivered a relieved smile before Henry continued. "Now, you had better get into your carriage before Mrs. Chumley becomes impatient with you."

He tossed his head, and Chumley sighed. "Quite right, quite right," he mumbled to himself, then he entered his coach at the front of the line.

Henry didn't miss a moment. With swift footing, he caught up with Miss Fernside, thanks to a slow-moving group who had spread themselves across the entire pavement, preventing any passing of them.

He fell in step beside Miss Fernside, but she kept her gaze focused ahead, as if she'd expected him to join her.

"Good morning," he began. "Miss Fernside, is it?"

"It is." She pressed her lips together before continuing, holding her book at her middle with both hands. "And you are the *real* Mr. Branok."

He smiled. "I am. I must apologize for not making myself known to you sooner. And for speaking with you when we had not yet been introduced. I fear spending five years on and off away from the finer side of Society has taken its toll on me, and I took leave of my senses as I was, I admit, quite filled with excitement."

This time, she managed a sidelong glance at him. "Because of the expedition?"

"In part. But mostly due to the fact that I have just turned in my latest book to the printers."

Enthusiasm lit in her eyes. "Truly?" she asked before checking her interest and feigning a look of placidity. "I believe I recall Mr. Chumley mentioning you had drafted a book or two. What volume is this, then?"

He hid a smile. Had she read his work? She *had* called him—what were the words again, esteemed and talented?

"The eighth," he replied.

"Oh, that is very…fine."

He held his hands behind his back as they continued to move at a snail's pace behind the group still meandering. They'd only just reached the beginning of the second carriage. At this rate, they wouldn't reach Yorkshire for four days instead of three.

Not that he minded. All it meant was more time with Miss Fernside on her own. "Have you perchance read one?"

"Oh, I-I am uncertain. I read so many books about birds, it is difficult to tell one from another."

Henry did not believe her for a moment. Still, he would allow her to keep her secret.

For now.

They finally reached the horses of the third carriage, but instead of continuing forward, Miss Fernside, to his surprise, stopped at the center of the pavement and faced him directly.

"Mr. Branok," she began, staring at the ground between them, "before we go any farther, I must apologize for my behavior within the Chumleys' parlor. Specifically for hushing you. I can assure you, it will not happen again, and I beg your forgiveness for offending you."

Henry could only smile. "Allow me to set your mind at ease. You did not offend me in the slightest. It certainly was not the first time I have been hushed, and I daresay, it will not be the last."

She eyed him for a moment, opening and closing her mouth twice without a word. Why did she stop herself from speaking now, when before, she'd voiced her opinion without hesitation?

"Was there something else you wished to say?" he pressed.

Her lips tightened, then she took a step toward him, clutching her book to her chest as if it were a breastplate that would guard her from any wayward attack. This time, her eyes were on him squarely. "Yes. I would like to clarify, in reference to Mr. Chumley's words..." She paused, her small nostrils flaring before she drew an apparent, calming breath. "I will be neither flirtatious nor silly, but as dignified as the gentlemen attendees, if not more so. It is true that I have promised, as Mr. Chumley said, to remain invisible during this expedition, and invisible I shall be. So our time in the parlor will be the last disturbance I cause."

She ended with a prompt nod, and once more, Henry had to hide his smile. This woman was utterly amusing, especially her concern over matters of which he hadn't thought twice.

He did have more questions about why on earth she was required to remain invisible on the trip—and if Mr. Chumley was the one to come up with such an absurdly antiquated idea—but he set the notion of asking her aside. There would be time for that over the coming months. Right now, he could not, in good conscience, allow her worries to last a single moment longer.

"Thank you for your explanation," he said. "While I cannot understand why you must remain invisible, or Mr. Chumley's reticence in involving women on this excursion, I will apologize on his behalf and heartily welcome you—an unmarried female —on this expedition."

Surprise spread across her features, which made Henry's words more than worth it.

"Thank you, sir," she sputtered.

"Of course."

He had spoken the truth in every regard and would have said the same to Mr. Chumley, had he thought it would have made any difference at all.

Henry had known the gentleman for a few years now, but their relationship was merely a respectful friendship—no camaraderie or closeness involved—and there was a reason behind that. Mr. Chumley was clearly of the old guard, leaving others out of his personal bird-observing community if the man—or more specifically *woman*—did not fit into Mr. Chumley's mold of expectations.

That was precisely why Henry despised the gentlemen's clubs around London. Each of them was filled with pretentious, judgmental gentlemen who spread their fastidious requirements and prevented toleration and acceptance.

Except Blackstone's, of course.

However, while Henry could not agree with Mr. Chumley's rulings, he would allow him his opinion, in the hope that Mr. Chumley would allow Henry to keep his own.

Seeing Miss Fernside's appreciation made him realize all the more that his belief in welcoming all to the bird-observing community was one he would never change his mind on.

But that did not mean a little teasing could not occur.

"However," he began again, and her features fell, "there is one more matter I wish to address."

"And what is that?" she asked.

He delivered a small smile. "When you said you would not create another disturbance…I certainly hope that is untrue. For what is life without a little disturbance now and again?"

He thought he saw a flicker of a smile shining in her eyes, but as Mrs. Haskett's head popped forth from within the carriage, calling after her niece, their solitude ended.

"Lark! Heavens above, there you are," Mrs. Haskett said, stretching out her hand toward Miss Fernside, though she hardly looked concerned. "I do not know how we became separated."

Miss Fernside approached the carriage, making ready to give her excuses, but Henry walked forward and spoke first.

"Forgive me, Mrs. Haskett, but your niece and I were held up by Mr. Chumley," Henry said, ensuring he spoke the truth, if not all of it. "He wished to speak on a few matters."

"Oh, that is more than fine, sir, of course," Mrs. Haskett said with a warm smile. Her soft, graying temples and wrinkled features tempered her words further. "I believe we are to share the same carriage, Mr. Branok. Do join us."

"With pleasure," he responded.

She pulled inside, and Miss Fernside looked up at Henry with gratitude. He gave a subtle nod before offering her help to enter the carriage.

She stared at his hand for a moment, then accepted it graciously. Her gloved fingers, so slender and petite, curved around his, fitting so effortlessly in his hand that his heart responded with a soft pattering.

He quickly put it back in its place. There would be no time for such nonsense, no matter how enticing the feeling.

When it was his turn to enter the carriage, he removed his hat and ducked inside, realizing a half a second later that each spot was taken, apart from the backward-facing seat beside Miss Fernside. She glanced at him, then quickly averted her gaze, as if she'd only now just realized the same as he did.

He had sat next to handsome women before this—though admittedly not as beautiful as Miss Fernside. There was nothing to be done but enjoy himself.

He settled upon his cushioned seat, then faced Mr. and Mrs. Haskett with a smile. "I do trust you will forgive my intrusion on what might have been a family affair."

"Not at all," Mr. Haskett responded. He boasted a high brow and tight lips with an overall no-nonsense air about him. Still, his smile was welcoming enough. "We hope you do not mind sitting with your back to the horses, sir. I fear my wife and I become quite plagued with illness when we ride in any carriage, but facing forward seems to help to a degree."

"I am sorry to hear about your illness," Henry responded. Now the seating arrangement made perfect sense. "But worry not. I suffer with no such malady."

He settled deeper into his seat, aware of Miss Fernside

slightly shifting farther away from him, as if she feared them touching.

He turned his eyes toward her, though was careful to keep his legs pointed away. "I assume you do not suffer from the same illness as your aunt and uncle, Miss Fernside?"

She held her book on her lap, her gloved hands gracefully folded atop the dark leather cover. "No, fortunately, I do not," she replied.

"I suppose it is a very good thing you do not have such an illness, Mr. Branok," Mrs. Haskett began. "Or you would be very miserable, indeed, on so many of your excursions."

"Oh, yes," Henry said. "However, I will admit to becoming quite unwell a time or two during particularly stormy days. There is nothing quite like traveling across an angry sea."

"Do tell," Mr. Haskett said. "We have all been waiting to hear more of your trip to...where was it again?"

"The West Indies, sir."

"Ah, yes. We would love to hear all about your travels."

Would they—including Miss Fernside?

Before he could say a word in response, a footman secured the door closed, and a moment later, the carriage jerked forward, causing the four of them to sway back and forth in their seats as the clip-clop of horse hooves and the rumbling of carriage wheels filled the air.

"And so we begin," Mrs. Haskett said, looking at her niece with bright eyes.

Henry glanced at Miss Fernside just in time to see her grinning in return, and he was struck with the ethereal beauty of her natural smile that changed her features from fine and regal to soft, approachable, and dazzling.

And he had the woman and her family all to himself. His parents were certainly looking out for him from up above.

CHAPTER 6

Lark could not contain her excitement as the carriage carted them away from the busy streets of London and out into the fresh air and open roads of the countryside. What a dream she was living, setting off on her first excursion while being seated right next to arguably the greatest bird observer of her time.

She was glad to have cleared the air between them, if only so she could now sit back and enjoy listening to his tales of his exhibitions all over the world. The East and West Indies, South Africa, Norway, Greenland—she listened to him speak about them all as Uncle continually and skillfully maneuvered the conversation away from Lark's very near obsession with Mr. Branok and his written knowledge about birds.

"Now, have you been to India yet?" Uncle asked at one point.

"I have not had the great pleasure to, no," Mr. Branok responded. "Though I must admit it has been a dream of mine for many years."

Uncle continued, doing so well with his engagement that by the third hour, Lark was certain Mr. Branok was going to lose his voice. Lark could not complain, however, for she lapped up the gentleman's words as if she were a parched dog at a fresh stream.

By the time they stopped for luncheon at the inn in Luton in Bedfordshire, she was certain Mr. Branok was in sore need of rest, despite his enthusiasm in graciously responding to Uncle's inquiries.

However, Mr. Branok seemed doomed to speak forever, as the moment he exited the carriage, he was set upon by the Chumleys and the Shepherds asking after him and his journey.

Mr. Chumley paid no heed to Lark, and by extension, her aunt and uncle, in the process. Fortunately, Uncle Francis and Aunt Harriet—who had both spent the carriage ride feigning wellness—were in clear need of respite.

"Mr. Branok's conversation was a lovely distraction, was it not?" Aunt Harriet asked in a weak voice as the three of them sat at their own table near the back of the inn.

Her features were contorted in distress, but the color had returned to her skin somewhat, leaving behind the sickly green she'd tried to hide in the carriage.

"His experiences in the West Indies were remarkable to listen to," Uncle Francis agreed.

He did not appear as colorless as Aunt Harriet did, as his malady revealed itself in the form of headaches instead of nausea. However, he had often winced in the carriage as he experienced an equal level of discomfort—despite managing to push past his pain to speak with Mr. Branok.

Lark suspected their pretended wellbeing would not last for the latter leg of their journey, and sure enough, after returning to the carriages, Uncle and Aunt both fell fast asleep within a matter of minutes.

Aunt Harriet rested her head on Uncle as he leaned against the frame of the carriage, the couple a picture of peace that Lark desperately needed to see. She knew no small amount of guilt for having requested the two of them on this journey, knowing how carriage rides pained them so, and she would do whatever it took for them to feel her gratitude for their sacrifice.

However, soon enough, thoughts of her aunt and uncle faded away as Lark became all too aware of the fact that she and Mr. Branok were now essentially alone.

She chanced a glance at him, but thankfully his focus was centered out of his window. Had he noticed Aunt and Uncle sleeping? Or had he simply chosen to politely ignore them all so that he might rest, as well?

Either way, Lark would not disturb him. Opening her journal, she flipped through the pages, examining the sketch she'd made that morning of the house sparrow. She'd seen the bird a hundred times over across Suffolk and London, but she'd decided long before the excursion that she would compile a list of each bird she would see on this journey and gift the collection of birds to Mr. Chumley. That way, if he so desired, he could use her list to persuade others to join in his next excursion.

Overhearing him speak with Mr. Branok about women not having a place on such journeys merely amplified her desire to create the list, if only to prove Mr. Chumley's pretentious words wrong.

Hateful man. She had so longed to make herself known to him after overhearing his words, but she'd managed to hold her tongue in that one instance at least. She really shouldn't have been listening in the first place, but she had convinced herself that she'd needed to know what he said to Mr. Branok so that she might defend herself after the fact—which, inevitably, she had.

But then, Mr. Branok had made everything well again by welcoming her on the excursion himself. She knew he was not the host, but as he was the guest of honor—and as he knew more about bird observing than Mr. Chumley and undoubtedly the rest of the party combined—Lark would put his words above the others readily.

She watched him from the corner of her eye for a moment, his fingers laced together on his lap, knees apart in a comfortable manner, and broad shoulders resting against the back of his seat. His eyes were still focused outside, and with the angle of his turned head, the ridge in his neck and the sharp corner of his tanned jawline were just visible above his crisp, white collar.

He was astonishingly handsome. She had wondered earlier if he was married until her eavesdropping had succinctly given her that answer. He had chosen to remain single, just like she had. Would that she could ask after *his* reasoning.

He shifted beside her, stretching out his legs for a moment with what little space he'd been allotted across from Uncle Francis, then moved back to his same position from before. Was he restless, perhaps? Wishing he was traveling by ship to some distant country so that he might smell the salty sea air and stretch his legs to his heart's content—rather than moving about England in a stuffy, rumbling box?

At least the day was cool enough so they would not be made to suffer through sweltering heat. Still, she wished she could distract him. Reassure him that this expedition would be one of his finest. After all, how could it not be when one had the chance to explore one's native land?

Or perhaps she ought to tell him the truth about her bringing his collection of his works—and how many times over she'd read them. She'd decided to behave around Mr. Chumley, if only to remain on the tour, but surely Mr. Branok would not mind a bit of praise.

Then again, at the thought of how he might tease her, she hesitated. Her pride was still resistant to admitting how greatly she admired him.

No, not *him*. His *works*.

Before she could follow through with any errant thought,

Mr. Branok startled her by speaking first, shifting his attention to her in a soft whisper. "I know you do not approve of this way of speaking, but I trust you will allow my whispers now to avoid disturbing them?"

She looked at him in surprise, noting the twinkle in his eyes. "I'll allow it," she whispered back, attempting to respond in the same casual manner. "For their sake."

She was talking to Mr. Branok. *The* Mr. Branok. When would she awaken from this dream?

He smiled, clearly pleased with her consent. He motioned to Aunt and Uncle again. "It would appear they are finally receiving much-needed rest."

Lark observed her aunt and uncle slouched together, mouths slightly parted, deep breaths of sleep coming in between the occasional snore.

"To my relief as much as theirs," she returned in a low voice. "I cannot bear to see them struggle so."

Mr. Branok looked at her next. "You carry the weight of their discomfort?"

"How could I not?" she asked, still watching them to ensure they did not awaken from her words—and to avoid looking at Mr. Branok. His eyes were far too focused on her at present, and the mere hat's length between them was certainly not enough. "I was the one who coerced them to join the excursion in the first place."

"Were you?"

The curiosity and amazement in his words were too great to avoid, and she finally met his gaze. He was much closer than she'd expected, their shoulders only a few inches apart. Her heart gave a sharp thump against her chest.

"Does this surprise you?" she replied.

"It does. Although I suppose now, I should expect to never be surprised by you." He paused. "Does this mean they did not wish to attend?"

Lark shook her head. "With their carriage sickness, it is very difficult for them to travel at all. My aunt does not take to birds, and though my uncle favors them more than her, I am the one who has the obsession. I fear I had to have them come with me, as I was not welcome on my own."

"Due to Mr. Chumley and his rules."

"Due to Society and *its* rules," she corrected—though Mr. Chumley was just as much to blame. "Fortunately, I was able to persuade Mr. Chumley to accept my presence."

Mr. Branok was silent for a moment. "By agreeing that you would remain unseen, as you—and Mr. Chumley—mentioned earlier?"

That...and by paying the fee for four entries instead of three. But still, Lark hesitated to say a word. She could not risk warranting Mr. Chumley's dissatisfaction by speaking of such things.

"I was happy to acquiesce," she said. "I am capable of behaving appropriately, when the outcome is favorable." She sent him a small smile, which he returned in full force.

"Well, I am happy you have found your way around his requirements." He leaned closer toward her, that earthy scent of his cologne swirling about the carriage walls. "And I trust you will find in time, that I, like you, care not for most of Society's standards—or Mr. Chumley's. I do not enjoy behaving either."

Her breath caught in her throat at the look of something akin to mischief in his eyes. What he was referring to, she hadn't the slightest notion, but she hardly thought Aunt or Uncle would approve either way.

She pulled in her lips, then drew her attention outside instead of responding. The green hills beyond them rose up and down, thick trees scattered playfully across the slopes. What birds did they mask behind their leaves and branches? She could hardly wait to walk amongst trees such as those and discover birds she'd not yet seen before.

"You must be a formidable bird observer to have fought so hard to come on this excursion," Mr. Branok whispered.

All thought of those distant trees flittered from Lark's mind. *Was* she a formidable bird observer? Or was she simply obsessed with Mr. Branok and would stop at nothing to learn from him?

The former. Most certainly the former.

"For how long have you observed them?" Mr. Branok asked next.

"Since I was a child."

"And you said this was your first excursion?"

She nodded.

"You must be thrilled. Where else in England have you traveled?"

She strengthened her defenses. This topic always managed to pierce her pride. "I have only ever spent time in London and Suffolk, where I call home. With how trying it is for Aunt and Uncle to travel—and with my mother's lack of desire to visit anywhere but Town—it is quite difficult to go any farther than our little county." She paused, not wishing to sound ungrateful. "But I am thankful for what I *have* seen."

And that was the truth. She had observed well over one hundred unique birds in her little pocket of England alone, and that was more than a triumph. But to Mr. Branok or any other specialized observer, the number would no doubt be an embarrassment to admit, so she redirected the attention to him instead.

"How old were you when you began your observations?" she asked.

He leaned back with a sigh. "I always loved being out of doors and observing birds, but I admit, I did not begin seriously until I was eighteen or so."

She pulled back. "Truly? That is even more surprising, what with your list of accomplishments. And you cannot be above the age of…"

"Eight and twenty," he finished.

Just a couple of years older than her six and twenty. And what had she accomplished? Nothing, short of inheriting a small fortune and deciding never to marry.

"I fear I neglect everything else to achieve that list of accomplishments," he said. "But once one has seen more of the world, one cannot stop until one has seen it all."

Lark had no experience with such matters and therefore fell silent, but Mr. Branok continued, his eyes distant.

"There is nothing that quite compares to observing a bird in the wilds of Africa or the Americas," he said. "Should the opportunity ever present itself to you, I would highly recommend traveling beyond England."

Lark pursed her lips with a silent nod. Had she not just explained why that would never happen? Not only was she not of age to make such decisions herself or without the approval of her mother, she also did not have the companionship of one who wished to travel with her. She had resigned herself to being old and grey before she could explore the world, and she was attempting to be patient with that fact.

Yet, when other bird observers discovered her lack of exploration, she felt as if she had to prove that she still held value in the community—that she was still worthy of being a part of gatherings, excursions, conversations, and sightings. More often than not, however, when she met with the local bird observing groups or she managed to find gatherings in London, she was ignored, passed over, and very clearly humored if anyone did chance to look at her or speak with her. The fact that they did *not* accept her—simply because she had not seen as much as they had—always left her feeling jaded and regretfully cynical.

Mr. Branok had been nothing but kind to her and would have no notion that his words had stirred this turmoil within her. As such, she attempted to set her defenses aside, but the pride within her refused to be satiated, and her compulsive need to prove that she was more than happy with her circumstances strengthened—even if, truth be told, she was not pleased with them at all.

"Have you any desire to travel beyond England?" Mr. Branok asked next, apparently unaware of why she remained silent.

"I suppose," she said stiffly. "But I am quite content with what I have already seen in the east of England."

"Truly? I consider it a shame you haven't been able to see more."

Lark's lips parted, but she snapped them closed once again. He was merely expressing an opinion, that was all. At any rate, he spoke the truth. It *was* a shame she hadn't seen more.

"Observing the sketches in books and articles certainly satisfies my desire to see other birds," she lied. Pulling her lips to the side, she continued, wishing to end on the truth instead. "The written word has allowed me to see far more than I ever would have dreamed, and I will be forever grateful for the books I have read that have provided me with literary trips around the world."

Including Mr. Branok's books. But she wasn't about to admit to that now.

"Books *are* worth their weight in gold," he agreed, his eyes on her again. "After all, I have written seven volumes—now eight—in an effort to share my experiences with others so that they might know of the vast number of birds there are of all colors and sizes. Reading about the creatures certainly helps those less fortunate than I. But nothing could ever compare to seeing birds in person. Surely you agree."

Of course she did. She was not a simpleton. But she did not like this superior tone he had assumed. Not one bit.

Eight books...Vast number of birds...Those less fortunate.

She longed to scoff at his putting himself above others—including herself. She doubted he was attempting to sound as pretentious as he did. But his pressuring her to agree with him prickled her pride further. He was accurate in his description of himself before—he had clearly lacked the influence of fine Society for the better part of five years.

Still, she needed to manage decorum. Anything she said to Mr. Branok might get back to Mr. Chumley, despite the former seeming trustworthy enough. Still, better to be safe than sorry.

"I suppose," she replied simply.

His eyes burned a hole in her temple, but she refused to meet his gaze. Instead, she observed Aunt and Uncle for a moment, willing them to awaken so that she might extricate herself from the conversation, but of course, they remained asleep.

Just as she suspected, Mr. Branok spoke again. "You mean to say you believe seeing sketches of birds in a book is the same as seeing birds in reality?"

Lark needed to retreat before she said something she regretted. But once more, she could not bring herself to abandon her pride. "I meant to say that seeing sketches of birds is better than seeing nothing at all."

Mr. Branok was silent for a moment. "But I was specifically asking if you thought seeing birds in books was better than seeing them alive… with your own two eyes."

Just be humble for once in your life, Lark Fernside.

Drawing a deep breath, she swallowed her vanity. "Certainly not."

She'd hoped relinquishing her opinion would have ended the conversation. Unfortunately, Mr. Branok was not quite finished.

"I am happy to hear your stance is the same as mine," he replied. "After all, if one merely looked at birds in books alone, could he or she call himself or herself a true observer of birds? I think not."

Annoyance swarmed in her chest. She ought not speak. She ought to lay the conversation to rest. And yet…she couldn't.

She shifted her person away from Aunt and Uncle, no longer

caring if they awakened or not as she turned to face Mr. Branok squarely. "So you believe that those who look at sketches of birds are not called true observers merely because they observe drawn birds instead of living ones?"

"Well, yes," he said matter-of-factly. "They are not observing birds, then. They are observing drawings. They cannot compare."

Lark could see his reasoning. But the way he said it with such resoluteness, as if he believed himself to be the most accurate gentleman in all the world and no one could ever persuade him otherwise—it irked her beyond reason, and all her sensible warnings flew away from her grasp.

"What would you say in regard to those who are restricted to their homes yet still have a deep and abiding love for the creatures?" she pressed. "Would you dare tell them that they are not true observers?"

He shifted toward her, then, too, that twinkle in his eye missing, replaced with a narrowed gaze. She was only vaguely aware of how close their knees were to touching, but she was so frustrated with the conversation, she couldn't be bothered to pull away.

"But what person could not manage to leave one's home to see the birds in one's own community?" he asked. "Even *you* manage that."

Lark's mouth dropped open. This time, she did not care to close it. "I beg your pardon?"

Mr. Branok didn't look repentant in the least. In fact, he had the audacity to raise a shoulder in a flippant shrug. "You've spoken of your unfortunate circumstances. What excuses do others have if even *you* can manage to leave your home to see what few birds you have?"

Lark could hardly believe his ungentlemanly words—highlighting her unfortunate circumstances and assuming the number of birds she *hadn't* seen.

She supposed this was the *real* Mr. Branok. He was not old and bald and bored of birds, nor was he benevolent and inclusive. Instead, he was just like the rest of them—the type of person to exclude individuals from the community simply because they did not fit into his idea of what they ought to be.

How wrong she had been about him. And how her admiration for him crumbled beneath her like a foundation made of sand.

She was finished with being pulled this way and that due to her interactions with him—embarrassed, flattered, wounded. Let Mr. Branok complain to Mr. Chumley. Lark would no longer hold her tongue.

"I manage to see birds because I am capable of doing so, *sir*," she stated, indignation burning in the center of her chest. "And I assure you, I do very well despite my *unfortunate circumstances* and have seen more than just a *few* birds."

One hundred and fifty-four to be exact. But she wasn't about to share that number with him, as he had to have somewhere near nine hundred on his own lifelong list.

To her surprise—and even further infuriation—the man cracked a smile, that glimmer in his eyes returning full force. "Of course," he said.

Did he tease her? Was he satisfied now that he'd riled her up? What she wouldn't give to throw her journal toward him and prove just how many birds she *had* seen.

"I *have*," she restated in a raised voice, checking her tone with a quick glance at Aunt and Uncle, who remained fast asleep.

She wouldn't wish to wake them—not when she was finally allowing herself to speak freely. Aunt and Uncle would no doubt remind her of her desire to hold her tongue, but she was past the point of caring now.

"I trust you keep a lifelong list of the birds you've seen?" Mr. Branok asked next.

"I do."

LOVE IS FOR THE BIRDS

"Would you care to share a number?"

"No, I would not. Only know that it is more than sufficient."

He smiled again. "Very well. You may keep your secret. At any rate, I do not doubt that you have seen many birds."

He leaned against the back of his seat with arms folded, and his leg moved toward her in the motion, grazing Lark's knee. A shock of energy sailed up her thigh, and she pulled back with a frown, but he did not seem to notice that he'd even touched her.

He smirked as he continued. "But you cannot deny that you would see *more* birds, should you leave your home and your books behind. After all, is that not the reason you are here on the excursion?"

Her gaze faltered for just a moment as she thought of her *real* reason being that of Mr. Branok's presence, but she readily set that notion aside.

He was a reason no longer, of that she was certain.

"I am on this excursion to see more birds, yes," she returned in a soft tone, keeping her knees tucked and safely away from the man's encroaching movements. "But I do not do so to raise myself above others. I simply wish to see more birds because of my love for them. I assure you, however, that I witnessed enough in Suffolk to be more than satisfied with the amount I've seen." She paused, knowing full well she was not being truthful, but she greatly lacked the desire to stop her words. "Oh, but I forget, I am not considered a true observer of birds unless I leave England, explore the world, and write seven— sorry, *eight*—books, as you have done."

"Now, Miss Fernside," he said with a knowing tip of his head in her direction. He had a look about him filled with insufferable patience and even, dare she think it, tempered *amusement*. "You know I did not say that."

She raised her chin. "Perhaps that was not your exact phrasing, but that is what you meant, for that is how all gentlemen think."

61

She must have revealed a little too much bitterness, then, for he paused, seeming to think before he spoke again.

"I must apologize," he said softly, flicking his gaze in the direction of Aunt and Uncle. "I did not mean to cause offense. Allow me to start again. All I wished to say was that if you have the chance to leave abroad—I would suggest that you take it, for there is much to see, and you appear keen to see it."

His apology was so graceful, so generous, Lark was minded to accept it instantly. But then, if she did, what would become of her? Surely this was not the last time they would disagree—surely this was not the last time he would cause her offense, for most gentlemen caused continuous offense. Excepting Uncle, of course.

If she relented now, that would only leave her open to feeling more pain and frustration in the future. Better to keep her defenses at the ready.

But she could feign generosity better than even he could.

"Thank you," she stated. "I apologize for any misunderstanding on my part, as well. However, I will end on this—while there *is* much to see of the world beyond our country, there perhaps is more that you haven't seen *inside* of England than out."

She gave a curt nod, then pulled her body to sit straight as she cast a leveled gaze out of the window, determined to ignore Mr. Branok until Aunt and Uncle arose and she would be forced to behave.

But Mr. Branok spoke again. "I must admit, I cannot agree with you," he said, his voice reaching her ears across the rumbling carriage.

She attempted to keep her focus on the trees atop the distant hills again, but his words were too much to ignore. Why did he insist on sustaining their conversation—or rather, their argument? Did he enjoy it? Or was he simply not finished exasperating her yet?

LOVE IS FOR THE BIRDS

Either way, she found responding impossible to resist. "I expected as much," she said. Her eyes traced the favorable angle of his jawline and the golden tint of his skin that resembled the tops of warm, buttered rolls.

"Why is that?" he asked, one corner of his masculine lips lifting.

The look in his eyes as they searched her features held something akin to admiration in them, and her stomach dipped. Swiftly, she looked away. He did not admire her. And even if he did, she would do well to remind herself what sort of person he was, for a handsome face could not make up for a decided lack of character—no matter how her quickened heart begged to differ.

"Have you explored England?" she asked, knowing very well that he had not.

"I cannot say that I have," he stated confidently.

"Then that is why I expected you to disagree," she said. "How can you know what you are missing when you have not even bothered to explore your own country? There are a number of species here. Over four hundred."

"Yes, I am aware of that." He paused. "And nearly eleven thousand in the world." He dipped his chin and looked at her with those sea-blue pools. "Not much of a comparison, is there?"

Her heartbeat stamped an image in her mind of that look, never to be replaced. Drat. He was far too charming for his own good, even when he was attempting to instruct her.

"Very well," she agreed, "there is no comparison when referencing the number of species. However, the level of difficulty of finding birds in one's own country is far greater than finding them in others."

His smile grew. "And just how have you come to that conclusion, Miss Fernside?"

She turned her eyes to face him evenly, careful to keep her

legs away from him this time. "Because when one exhausts all the common and recurring birds in one's own country, one must work harder to discover the scarcer birds. However, when a gentleman ventures forth to countless countries, he can easily find all their common birds and consider himself quite the skillful observer, when in reality, he has only discovered the easily ascertainable birds, as opposed to the rarer birds in England."

He didn't respond for a moment, his eyes searching hers before a dazzling smile broke out across his lips.

Her own smile faded, then. That was not the response for which she'd hoped. Why was he not put in his place, as she had been before?

"Miss Fernside," he began, his eyes delving into hers as he drew closer to her, "are you suggesting you are a better bird observer than I?"

She knew he was meaning to intimidate her with his closeness, but she refused to allow him to see the fact that it *was* affecting her—her skipping heart making it difficult to draw in steady breaths.

She leaned closer to him until their faces were mere inches apart and she could see the dark blue outline of his sea-colored eyes. "I am not *suggesting*, Mr. Branok."

His eyes flicked between hers, shining with barely restrained mirth, but she did not budge. However, when his gaze dropped to her lips for a single moment, her breathing stopped altogether.

Out of seemingly thin air, a peculiar pull occurred between them—a magnetism she could not deny. She had never felt such an attraction before, as if she could not keep herself from leaning forward. And as his focused gaze moved back to her eyes, locking her in place, she felt as if the two of them were the only people left in existence.

"What say you to proving your claim?" Mr. Branok asked, interrupting her drifting thoughts with a low, rumbling voice.

Lark blinked. What claim had that been? Ah, yes. That she was the better bird observer. Her mind was still in a hazy fog, brought on by his proximity, that look in his eyes, and that smirk...That smirk that spoke of just how greatly he was aware of what his closeness was doing to her.

She pulled away at the thought, snapping out of the stupor she'd allowed herself to fall into. This gentleman was utterly too attractive.

"Unfortunately, there is no way to prove such a thing," she stated, quite pleased with how smooth her tone was, compared to how he'd unsettled her.

"Oh, I can think of a way," he said softly.

She may have pulled back, but he, however, remained leaning toward her.

"What way is that, then?" she asked, getting lost in his eyes.

"By taking part in a competition," he replied, "just the two of us."

CHAPTER 7

"A competition?" Miss Fernside repeated. Her voice was soft, only just above the sound of the carriage wheels rumbling along the bumpy road. "What sort of competition?"

Henry saw a spark of interest light up her eyes. He was enjoying this conversation. It was far more entertaining than watching poor Mrs. Haskett fanning herself and Mr. Haskett wincing in pain for hours on end.

The Hasketts' rest was a godsend for them all, but it wouldn't last forever. Once they awakened, he would be duty-bound to be as appropriate as Society wished him to be. No more whispering with Miss Fernside. Certainly no more touching her leg with his, nor gazing deeply into her eyes. This was precisely why he was taking advantage of these intimate moments with her while he could.

"A simple challenge is all I suggest," he whispered in reply.

She eyed him suspiciously. "You mean, like a wager? Like, gambling?" She shook her head. "My aunt and uncle would not approve. And neither would I."

He leaned back in his seat with folded arms. Her attention

lingered on his shoulders before she blinked and glanced at her aunt and uncle. She did that often—as if to ensure they still slept —but only ever when she'd been staring at Henry for a moment longer than propriety allowed.

He couldn't say that he minded her stares. Nor had he minded their proximity before. He'd been teasing her when he'd glanced down at her lips. Most women squirmed or backed away with a swift blush, but not Miss Fernside. She'd drawn even closer, pride glinting in her eyes like sunshine off a stained-glass window.

"No, not like gambling," he assured her. "There will be nothing at stake…aside from a title, that is."

"A title?"

She shifted in her seat, moving farther away from him. Perhaps he ought to stretch out his leg again.

"Indeed," he said. "The title of Best Bird Observer in All of England."

She raised her brows with an unimpressed air. "How prestigious. A title only the two of us would acknowledge."

"I would find it prestigious enough when I inevitably claim it."

Her eyes narrowed as she took his bait. "What makes you so certain you would defeat me?"

"Due to my own experiences," he responded simply.

"And my lack thereof," she retorted.

Henry didn't respond, nor did he refrain from smiling, which clearly vexed her further. Her brow furrowed, and her lips pulled into a sort of pout.

She was simply adorable, and Henry could not help himself. He loved a decent repartee with a woman. Most ladies took such offense that they retreated instantly. Fortunately, Miss Fernside seemed at the ready to volley back each of his servings with aplomb.

That was a most attractive quality in a woman—being unafraid to stand up for herself.

He was just grateful they'd both made it clear to one another that neither had any plans for matrimony. This made his flirting and their verbal jousting more enjoyable, as he could do so without fear of any repercussions. That was no doubt why she behaved as freely as *she* did—without care of being *society approved*. It was not as if her behavior would scare off any potential suitors if she had no wish for them at all.

She turned away from Henry again, folding her arms and settling in her seat with a little wiggle of her shoulders. "Well," she said airily, "I think it all rather childish. A competition to stroke one's ego, really."

He nodded, attempting to appear thoughtful. "Hmm. You are perhaps correct. It is a little childish. But forgive me if I choose to believe your avoidance is merely due to—to put it delicately —a particular fear of not living up to your earlier boasting."

The fire in her gaze told him at once that he'd won.

"You think I'm frightened that I will not be able to win?" she questioned.

"Perhaps."

"Very well." A calm smile spread across her lips, accentuating her high cheekbones. "I shall make two things very clear for you right now, Mr. Branok. The first is this, I have never been afraid of my abilities not living up to *anyone's* standards. Ever. And the second, I am fully aware that you are simply goading me with your irksome words so that I might accept your challenge. And while I am loath to admit that your tactics have been moderately successful, I find myself unable to say no due to my plain and simple desire to see you sufficiently humbled." She raised her chin. "So...what is this challenge of which you speak?"

Henry grinned. "It is fairly straightforward. We simply make written note of each and every different bird we observe over the course of the tour in Yorkshire, Cumbria, and Cornwall. At the end of the excursion, the person with the most unique number of birds listed shall obtain the coveted title."

She took but a mere second to respond. "Very well, I agree." She pulled open the leatherbound book on her lap and flipped to a blank page. "Now, what of the rules?"

She turned to look at him, her head slightly tipping to the side so her blonde curls rested against her temples. She was a gorgeous creature, her curved eyebrows smooth and expressive above those almond-shaped eyes.

"The rules?" he questioned.

"Yes, *rules*," she repeated, looking at him as if *he* were the unreasonable one. "We must have rules and agree to abide by them if we are to partake in this challenge."

Heavens, she was taking this seriously. He wanted to throw his head back in laughter, but he maintained his composure, if only to not offend her.

He'd seen the insecurity in her eyes already—her lack of experience observing birds making her question herself around the others. That was part of the reason why he'd suggested the challenge. Her winning would give her the encouragement she sorely needed.

"I'm afraid I have not given much thought to any rules," he said.

"Why does that not surprise me?" she muttered under her breath.

She scrawled some writing across the top of one page, then flipped to another and did the same again, clearly intending on creating a copy for each of them.

"Rule number one," she stated without looking up. "We shall begin the competition the moment we step foot on the estate in Yorkshire. Otherwise, you will have already fallen behind due to the number of birds I've recorded from London."

"Very fair, indeed," he stated.

"We shall carry on with the competition from Yorkshire to Cumbria, be on hiatus when we return to London for the fortnight, then resume once we set course for Cornwall, yes?"

"Of course."

Henry shouldn't have been too surprised that she'd recorded birds already. He'd seen her writing down her observations about the house sparrow. How many more she'd seen during their stop, he could only guess.

He, himself, had spotted at least half a dozen already, though he would've found more had Mrs. Chumley not spoken to him throughout the entirety of the luncheon in Luton.

But all was well. Henry would certainly have more of a chance to spot birds once they arrived anyway. He really wasn't concerned in the slightest about finding them. He'd spotted the greatest martin in Gibraltar, the transverse striped dove in the East Indies, and the crested hummingbird in the West Indies. He could easily find what he needed to in England.

Not that he had any intention of winning when Miss Fernside so clearly needed a victory. No, he would turn the challenge in her favor.

She finished writing the rule on one paper, then copied it to the next. "Rule number two," she continued. "We mustn't speak of our number until the end of the challenge."

"Agreed."

She wrote the next rule, this time pausing in between pages with a sigh. "You must excuse my penmanship," she said, her voice still lowered. "I am not used to writing under such dreadful conditions."

The carriage jostled as if on cue, and she sighed again, raising her pencil to wait for the passing bumps before progressing.

He leaned toward her to observe her writing, but a cloud

scented of orange blossoms drifted around him. His leg was a hair away from her, their shoulders a mere inch apart.

She stole a glance at him but instantly whipped her gaze away, a blush splashing across her cheeks. He eyed the gentle slope of her neck as she leaned toward her writing again, her movements graceful, and he observed her as if she was the rarest bird in South Africa, instead of the fine woman she was, jostling in a carriage.

"I think you quite flawless, Miss Fernside," he whispered.

She looked up at him, pulling back in surprise and creating more distance between them.

"Your handwriting, I mean," he clarified, though he was quite certain his half-smile spoke the truth more than his words.

She didn't speak for a moment, then looked away with a shake of her head. "You are nothing as I had imagined you to be, Mr. Branok."

"And how did you imagine me to be? Like Mr. Dunn?" he teased.

Once again, her cheeks pinked. "No. I thought you'd be a gentleman with more propriety than a common magpie."

He softly chuckled. "I did warn you."

"I suppose I shall simply have to muster up enough decency for the both of us, then."

"It would appear so."

She continued writing, and he leaned back in his seat, if only to not be caught too close to her by the Hasketts should another jostle from the carriage awaken them.

Henry was not typically a flirt. Well, not too bad of one, anyway. But he'd become starved of feminine attention over the last six months in the West Indies. And the months before that in Europe. And the past five years traipsing all over the world with only men for friendly companionship. With Miss Fernside, he was obviously making up for lost time.

Or…or perhaps that was merely an excuse, and the truth of the matter was, Miss Fernside was the most beautiful and intriguing woman he'd ever met, and she was, therefore, quite simply, irresistible.

"There," she said, pulling back from her writing as she finished inscribing. "Now the third rule."

She looked at him expectantly.

Right. He was supposed to be devising their plan. "I think we ought to make it a requirement that we must observe the bird in nature in order for it to count toward our list."

"Naturally," she agreed, writing his words down. "That will make the challenge fairer, as well."

"And why is that?" he questioned. "Because you would attempt to add the birds you see in your books?"

He dropped the sentence before her, hoping for a reaction, but all she gave him was a sidelong glance and a subtle shake of her head.

"No," she stated. "Because if we were including bird *songs*, I would have a significant advantage over you, as I can recognize a substantial number of birds by their calls alone."

He eyed her. "Is that true?"

"I do not tell falsehoods." Then she looked up at him. "Usually."

Her gaze lingered, and a spark of humor he didn't know she was capable of glinted in her eyes.

Henry felt like soaring.

"The fourth rule," she continued, "ought to restrict either of us from sharing about this challenge with anyone else." She glanced up at the Hasketts. "After all, I hardly think *they* would approve. Or Mr. Chumley."

"Agreed," he said.

"Are you certain? About Mr. Chumley, I mean."

Clearly, she was asking if Henry could be trusted.

"I am certain," he said in earnest, leaving behind his teasing nature for a moment so she could see the truth in his eyes. "I would not wish to create any grief for you—or to detract from the excursion."

She studied him, then gave a single nod before writing further.

A lightness unfurled within him like a spotted falcon spreading out his wings. Miss Fernside trusted him. Why was the idea so satisfying?

"At any rate," he said under his breath as he leaned toward her again, "it is far more exciting to keep this between the two of us, do you not think?"

She merely continued writing. "If you say so."

He would have laughed again but settled with a simple smile. Her attempt at remaining unaffected by his words—the way she shifted subtly away from him though her eyes continued to skirt toward him—was nothing short of endearing.

"The fifth rule would be to ensure that we write down each unique bird, the location where we observed it, *when* we observed it, and a short description of what we saw," she said. "This way we may prove our sightings if necessary."

"Very good."

She wrote more, pausing as they passed over another jut in the road. "The only other rule I can think of is that both of us have to do our very best."

He paused. That would put a damper on his earlier decision to help her win. "Surely that does not need to be said."

"One would think so," she said, still writing. "But gentlemen—even those who have separated themselves from Society—are notorious for their chivalry. I will have none of that. If I am entering this challenge, you must do your best to beat me."

She was so wonderfully confident. But he had little to no faith that she would beat him at this game. He did not wish to appear prideful in the least, but how could a woman who had not left Suffolk hold her own against Henry, a gentleman who had traveled the world?

"So," she continued, "do you agree?"

"Yes. You needn't worry. I shall do my best to win."

So much for ensuring her victory. Because now that he'd promised, he *would* do his best.

She finished writing the final and sixth rule on both pages, then pulled back. "Anything else you care to include?"

"No, I believe you have been more than thorough."

She did not respond, merely tore the two papers from her notebook and extended them to him. "Sign here," she said, pointing to one of the two lines she drew below the rules.

He did as he was told, placing his signature on both papers using her pencil and fighting off a smile as he extended them back to her. "Here you are."

She took them without a word, examining the signatures before signing her own name beneath his. Finally, she returned his paper, which he accepted with a nod.

"This is all very official," he said, folding the paper and tucking it into his waistcoat pocket.

"Indeed," she said, apparently missing his teasing tone as she folded her own paper and secured it behind the front cover of her book.

"We are settled, then," he said. "May the best bird observer win."

"Thank you. I shall," she stated without a glance in his direction.

Then she pulled open her book, tilting it away so he could not see within, and shifted her body toward the window, clearly signaling the end of their conversation.

Henry was sorely tempted to tease her further, but when he found her watching him from the corner of her eye, as if she wished to speak, as well, he shifted away and focused his gaze on the small, stone farmhouses punctuating the hills far beyond.

Perhaps withholding his conversation would make her long for it even more. That would be needed on their excursion, as he had a feeling he and Miss Fernside would be doing a great deal of conversing over the next two months. Conversing...and more.

He couldn't wait to begin.

CHAPTER 8

Yorkshire, April 11, 1817

The rest of the journey to Yorkshire was relatively uneventful. Aunt Harriet and Uncle Francis still suffered, though they did their best to hide it, Lark did her best to comfort them, and Mr. Branok clearly did his best to distract them with pleasant conversation and wild stories of his adventures.

Once more, Lark relished the chance she had to listen to his tales, though this time, she hid her enjoyment. No need to boost his ego further.

In between the conversations, however, the four of them sat in mutually pained silence until finally, in the afternoon of the final day, they rolled onto the property of a grand estate in Yorkshire.

Aunt and Uncle exchanged looks of relief, and Lark knew no small amount of respite for their sakes, as well. She couldn't ease their carriage sickness, but she was determined that the next two months would be worth it for them all.

"It is quite a picture, is it not?" Uncle asked, drawing Lark's attention to the present as he stared out of the window.

Love Is for the Birds

"As lovely a house as I have ever seen," Mr. Branok agreed.

Lark gazed beyond him to see out of the window, too, but immediately sat back when Mr. Branok found her straining.

"Can you see, Miss Fernside?" he asked.

"Indeed," she lied.

"As well as you could see Mr. Chumley from behind Mr. Dunn?" he softly questioned with a knowing look.

She pulled in her lips—something she had grown accustomed to doing over the years whenever she was forced to hold her tongue. She had a feeling she would be doing much of that over the next two months, especially around Mr. Branok.

"Have a look," he continued, leaning back in his seat. "You shan't regret it."

Lark had a mind to refuse his offer, but her curiosity won out. She looked past his broad shoulders to where the grand, red home stood perfectly positioned between towering beech trees, and excitement swarmed in her belly.

The house was nearly three times smaller than Brackenmore, but it was a fine establishment, nonetheless. The structure stood four stories tall, red brick covering the left and right side of the home, while a marble front marked the center of the building with intricate carvings and a grand central staircase leading down to the gravel drive.

Altogether, the estate shone perfect symmetry and care, which Lark could not help but admire. She'd always been fond of keeping neat and tidy surroundings. This home would do quite nicely as a place of residence for the next two weeks. Quite nicely, indeed.

The carriage turned down the drive, drawing them closer and closer to the house until finally, they rolled to a stop, and Aunt and Uncle both breathed out sighs of relief.

"Now to recover," Uncle said softly to his wife.

"Indeed," Aunt responded, still tinted a shade of green. "I feel as if I could sleep from now until morning."

Lark winced again. She knew they were happy to join her for this excursion, but once more, guilt rooted itself firmly around her heart. All of it fled, however, when she caught Mr. Branok's eyes fixed on her, a look of concern on his brow instead of the usual humor she'd already grown accustomed to over the last few days. Had he noticed Lark's discomfort for the welfare of her aunt and uncle?

Instead of saying anything to her, Mr. Branok turned to Aunt and Uncle as they awaited the footman to open the door. "While I am relieved for both of your sakes," he began, "I must admit, I shall miss having my traveling companions all to myself. You three have been so pleasant to journey with and more than welcoming. I must thank you again for allowing me to intrude upon your family."

"Not at all," Uncle said. "We have been most pleased to have you with us. None more so than my niece, I'm sure. She will no doubt be filled with gratitude to have had you for company, while Mrs. Haskett and I have been indisposed. Are you not grateful, niece?"

Lark nodded. "Yes, Uncle. Very grateful."

The humor returned to Mr. Branok's eyes as they shifted to Lark. "I'm sure you are," he mumbled under his breath.

Before she could respond with a muttered retort of her own, the door opened, and Aunt was encouraged to depart first.

"Do not forget the rules, Miss Fernside," Mr. Branok whispered as Uncle helped Aunt gather her belongings. "We begin the moment our feet touch Yorkshire soil."

"I am well aware, sir," she responded with a quick glance at Uncle Francis to ensure their whisperings remained unnoticed. She kept her lips still as she continued. "Now don't *you* forget to keep this just between the two of us. Should you need to speak with me about the competition, I suggest you do so in privacy."

"Oh, gladly." He gave a quick lift of his brows, but Lark turned away, leaving the carriage directly after Aunt.

This blasted competition. Lark never should have agreed to something so utterly ridiculous. Her pride had just been so provoked, she'd been unable to help herself. And she'd made such a fuss over those rules and obtaining his signature that she could hardly reject the challenge now.

Well, never mind. She was in it until the end, and she would not stop until she beat this overly confident, far too flirtatious, stunningly handsome gentleman.

She joined Aunt Harriet on the gravel, discreetly stretching her limbs to rid her body of the tightness she'd been feeling for hours. Were she a bird like a grebe or a cuckoo, she would ruffle her plumage, then splay out her wings at the side of her to feel that wonderful fresh air between her feathers.

Yet another reason birds were freer than she would ever be.

Uncle exited the carriage next, followed swiftly by Mr. Branok, who was set upon at once by Mr. Chumley. The host ignored Lark as he placed a guiding hand atop Mr. Branok's shoulder and led him forward toward the front steps of the grand entryway.

The many servants had already arrived—having left the inn that morning earlier than the rest of the party—and were now lining the entryway to the house.

Lark spotted Penelope in an instant, giving her a smile and nod. Penelope—who was just a few years younger than Lark—responded with a curtsy in return, her smooth, dark hair pulled back in a neat and tidy bun that always remained in place no matter her movements.

"Come, my friends, come," Mr. Chumley said, motioning to the others with a broad smile and drawing Lark's attention forward again. "We have finally reached our destination. Let us not be shy."

The group gathered closer together. Lark remained beside Aunt, who mumbled to Uncle, "I shall never step foot in a carriage again, husband. That was dreadful."

"Think of Lark, my dear," Uncle Francis responded in a whisper he clearly did not think Lark could hear.

Lark looked away, pretending as if she had not heard them, though her guilt was acute.

"Ladies and gentlemen," Mr. Chumley said, stopping a few steps up to be heard by them all, "welcome to Deryn Park, your home for the next fortnight."

He paused, allowing the group to respond as they modestly clapped, far less enthusiastically than they had at the beginning of the trip. Clearly, the journey had taken its toll on everyone—and not just the women, as Lark was quick to spot. Mr. Dunn had dark rings beneath his eyes and one of the redheaded brothers stifled a yawn.

"Now, I know we are all quite spent," Mr. Chumley continued, "but I assure you, you shall have rest soon. First, we will show each of you to your rooms where you will be greeted by certainly the most comfortable beds of your existence. If you can manage to remove yourselves from your bedchambers, dinner will be served this evening, and I promise you a warm meal, matched only by our pleasant conversation. Furthermore, you shall have plenty of time to rest tomorrow, as I have promised Mrs. Chumley I shall not begin the excursion until ten o'clock in the morning."

Lark stifled her rising disappointment. They were going to sacrifice an entire morning simply to recover from traveling? Stuff and nonsense. At least Aunt would appreciate the chance to recover.

"Now," Mr. Chumley continued, "let us show you to your rooms. Mrs. Chumley?"

He motioned for his wife to join him in leading the party up the stairs, and the others followed close behind. Lark fell in step after Uncle and Aunt, eyeing the sheer height of the home as she craned her neck to see the top pillars. As she did so, she caught sight of a bird flying just above the roofing.

Ah, a dunnock. She recognized his song. He would most certainly be going on her list—and the list she would begin anew for her competition with Mr. Branok. The man had no idea what he was up against. He was—

"Oof," she grunted as she came face-to-face with Uncle's back, having been too distracted with the bird to have noticed him pausing on his way up the stairs.

She teetered backward from her collision, attempting to catch her balance as her hands flew out to the side of her. A flash of fear struck through her person as her brain told her where she was destined to fall.

Instead, strong fingers wrapped around her upper arms from behind, settling her back onto the step and holding her securely in place as she regained her bearings.

"Good heavens," Uncle said, turning round to face her with a startled expression. "My dear Lark, are you well?"

Lark stared dazedly at Uncle with a silent nod, the warm fingers remaining around her arms.

Uncle Francis's eyes skimmed beyond her shoulder. "Thank heavens you were there, Mr. Branok."

Mr. Branok.

She breathed. *His* hands were the ones steadying her. He had been the one to have saved her from surely falling down the steps and perhaps ending the excursion for her before it had even begun.

His hands remained around her arms, warmth swirling from his fingertips and straight to her core. When had he moved behind her?

"It is no trouble, of course, Mr. Haskett," Mr. Branok responded, his deep voice reverberating through her ears.

"It is that dratted carriage weakening our limbs," Aunt commented, having stopped on the step above Uncle, her soft brows drawn together. "Are you well, niece?"

81

"Yes," Lark responded. "Yes, I am quite well. I don't know what came over me."

"Perhaps you ought to hold your uncle's arm," Aunt suggested.

Lark nodded, taking a step forward and removing herself from Mr. Branok's touch. A coldness replaced the warmth of his fingers, wrapping around her arms in unpleasant strands.

"Thank you again, sir," Uncle said over his shoulder toward Mr. Branok.

Lark chewed her lower lip. She ought to thank Mr. Branok, too, but she shuddered to think of the teasing smile that would be on his lips.

Still, she did not wish to appear ungracious. So, as she continued up the steps with Uncle's guiding arm beneath her hand, she looked back at him.

Instead of that teasing glimmer in his eye, he simply smiled at her, then mouthed out while pointing up at the sky, "Bird one —dunnock."

Then he winked and made his way up the steps without another glance in her direction.

Winking at her, teasing her, creating challenges she agreed not to tell her family about...The man was a complete scoundrel.

She couldn't wait to interact with him again.

CHAPTER 9

Yorkshire, April 12, 1817

The following morning, Lark rose before the crack of dawn, hoping to find more birds by beating the sunshine. Penelope was quite used to Lark's early rising, so she had already arrived before Lark could even call for her. The lady's maid helped her dress in a simple green gown, then sent her off with a polite curtsy.

Through the dark blue light of the early morning, Lark crept through the many corridors of the house, tiptoeing past closed doors and nodding silently to the curious help she passed by.

Eventually, she found her way through the house, having only taken two wrong turns before discovering the entryway and leaving Deryn Park behind to explore what its grounds had to offer.

To her delight, she not only discovered robins, blackbirds, blue tits, and chaffinches—all of which she'd seen before—but she was also able to spy birds she'd only ever seen in her books, a green woodpecker, a wood warbler, and a pied flycatcher, to only name a few.

A full year had passed by since she had been able to add a new bird to the collection she'd started as a child, so discovering so many, her joy was paramount.

So delighted she was with her additions to her journal that when the sun took residence above the fields and the birds' dawn chorus slowly wound down, Lark wasn't even upset to leave. She simply could not wait to share her findings with Aunt and Uncle. They would no doubt be taking breakfast in their rooms now.

As if on cue, her stomach rumbled, so she hastened her steps along the dirt pathway toward the house. She did not progress far, however, before finding Mr. Branok walking in her direction with the Shepherds quickly in tow.

At the sight of him, Lark's stomach tumbled over itself. Last night had been utterly disappointing. She'd looked forward to hearing even more from Mr. Branok about his travels, then she'd hoped to engage in conversation with those around her about the birds everyone looked forward to seeing. She'd also longed to make her mark, let everyone know who she was and that she was serious about her observations.

However, with Aunt remaining in her room due to illness, Mrs. Chumley and Mrs. Shepherd speaking about fabrics at one end of the table, and the rest of the gentlemen engaging in conversation about their various hunting trips, Lark had not said a word throughout the entirety of the meal. Even Mr. Branok did not speak with her, though that was not entirely his fault, as he was seated at the complete opposite end of the table.

Still, she was so disappointed in the lack of engagement that she left for bed early, checking on Aunt Harriet before falling asleep herself.

Last night was sure to be the anomaly, though, as was evident by the success Lark had found that morning. Would speaking with Mr. Branok now improve her mood further?

One could only hope.

She kept her eyes on the pathway until the very last moment, then looked up to see Mr. Branok already watching her.

"Miss Fernside," he greeted.

"Mr. Branok, Mr. Shepherd, Mrs. Shepherd," she returned.

Mrs. Shepherd tipped her head to the side with a look of concern. "Miss Fernside, what in heaven's name are you doing out here?"

Lark had not spoken with the Shepherds a great deal, though the handsome couple—who could only be a year or two older than Lark herself—had smiled at her from across the table a handful of times the night before.

She glanced between the three of them. "Merely taking advantage of the lovely weather and observing God's beautiful world around us."

"No, no," Mrs. Shepherd said, shaking her head, "I mean, what are you doing out here without a chaperone?" she looked around, though it was clear Lark was alone.

Lark stopped herself from scoffing. This was one of the reasons she stayed away from Society—married women always decided they knew better than single individuals.

Well, she would make it clear that she needed no owner—nor husband. "I am walking," she stated with a simple smile. "As I assume the three of you are doing."

"Indeed," Mr. Shepherd responded. "Are you enjoying the fresh Yorkshire air?"

He eyed her from head to foot with a curious gaze—though quite harmless. Mr. Branok still watched her, too. Though, he always watched her.

She glanced at him, and her stomach pulled in with a pleasant dip.

"I am enjoying it, thank you," Lark responded.

"But…" Mrs. Shepherd began. "But where are your aunt and uncle, Miss Fernside?"

"I assume they are still asleep."

Lark was accustomed to walking without a chaperone. In fact, her aunt and uncle preferred it, as it saved them from waking up early and following her around in utter silence.

Birds fled with any chatter, see.

At times, she brought along Penelope, but Lark always preferred solitude.

Mr. Chumley would no doubt disapprove of her behavior, but then, what he didn't know would not hurt him. Now to ensure the Shepherds and Mr. Branok didn't spread word about her *shocking* behavior.

"I do hope your aunt feels better," Mr. Branok said.

"I believe she does," Lark responded. "It takes her a day to recover from most trips, so she should be back to herself this morning."

"That is quite unsafe, is it not, Miss Fernside?" Mrs. Shepherd asked, clearly not finished with the conversation from before. Her arched brows pointed with overt concern. "To walk on your own, I mean. Especially as we are new to this area. Suppose you fall and injure yourself and do not know where to look or call for help?"

Lark flicked her gaze toward Mr. Branok, who watched the exchange in silence, a restrained smile on his lips. He *would* be entertained—a gentleman who could travel where he wished, when he wished.

"I assure you, I took great care," Lark replied. "At any rate, I am six and twenty and perfectly capable of walking without injuring myself." Mrs. Shepherd opened her mouth to clearly protest once again, but Lark continued. "I thank you for your concern, Mrs. Shepherd. It is so generous of you. But my aunt and uncle are perfectly aware of my amble this morning and can see me quite clearly from their window, just there." She pointed to one of the top rooms—which one was Aunt's was beyond her —then continued speaking swiftly so Mrs. Shepherd might not attempt to find it. "Have the three of you managed to eat breakfast before your walk?"

"Ah, yes," Mr. Shepherd responded with a pleasant smile. The man was quite handsome, tall and lean, with dark hair and even darker eyes. But there was a kindness to his features that softened his gaze—a look that only increased as he peered lovingly at his wife. "Mrs. Shepherd and I enjoyed that earlier. The Chumleys have certainly spared no expense with the gorgeous spread they've put on. Now we're enjoying our little *tête-à-tête* with Mr. Branok before the rest of the group seizes their opportunity. You're welcome to join us."

"Thank you so much for the kind offer," Lark said with a glance at Mr. Branok. He still watched her with that insufferably charming smile. "But I have yet to eat, and I should like to fill my empty stomach before the food is put away for good."

"Very wise," Mr. Shepherd said.

"Do eat enough to sustain your walk," Mrs. Shepherd said. "We young women ought to replenish our energy often."

"Very true, my dear," Mr. Shepherd agreed with a pat of his hand atop his wife's. "But I am certain she knows this."

Lark smiled at each of them, curtsying before excusing herself and heading once more toward the house.

She did not make much headway before footsteps sounded behind her, and Mr. Branok spoke her name.

"Miss Fernside?"

She started, turning around to face him. "Mr. Branok?"

The Shepherds waited for him down the pathway so only she could hear Mr. Branok's words.

"Did you need something?" she asked.

"I merely wished to speak with you for a moment."

She watched him expectantly. "About what exactly?"

He paused. "Well, to be frank, Miss Fernside. I believe I have become so accustomed to being with you on our travels that I must admit to quite missing your conversation."

Heat rushed to her cheeks. Was he in earnest? She could never tell with him—nor his reasons behind such flirtatious comments. Was it merely to ruffle her feathers?

Well, two could play at his game.

"Really, Mr. Branok," she responded, "we hardly spoke in the carriage after that first day. I'm certain you exaggerate."

"No, no. I am quite in earnest. I found myself wishing to speak with you at dinner last evening. You must imagine my acute disappointment in discovering how far away you sat from me—and further when you did not join us for long in the drawing room afterward. I trust nothing occurred between you and Mr. Dunn that forced you to retire early."

She hesitated. Mr. Dunn had been her greatest disappointment and greatest relief from the entire excursion so far. He'd been insufferably dull the night before with snore-inducing words about his various muskets. It made her regret taking the only seat left next to him instead of leaving right then and there at dinner. And yet, she could not help the relief she knew that he was not Mr. Branok after all.

Still, she did not wish for Mr. Chumley to hear that she disapproved of the other members of their party. "No, I was simply tired, that is all."

He nodded, though his look revealed how greatly he did not believe her. "You're certain it had nothing to do with the conversation around the table, then?"

"Oh, no. I love…talking about…hunting."

His eyes settled deeper into hers. "I shan't tell Mr. Chumley the conversations that take place between us."

She hesitated, if only due to her very soul instantly trusting the man's words, as if her heart had more sway than her logic. There were very few men who had earned her trust in life. Why did her heart believe Mr. Branok could so readily be part of that club?

"You do not trust me," he stated without question, obviously reading her expression.

To her relief, he did not appear offended, merely intrigued.

"On the contrary," she said truthfully. "I do trust you."

"But you require a signature from me for you to do so?"

The glow in his eyes and the lure of his teasing lips coaxed out a smile of her own.

"No," she finally stated. "I merely find it difficult to speak the truth with you because, as you said, you are so far removed from gentlemanly manners."

"Perhaps in Society's view," he stated. "But as a true gentleman, I assure you, you will find no man as genteel as I."

Once again, her heart pulled toward him.

"Very well," she finally relented. "If you wish me to be honest, I will be. While Mr. Dunn is not solely the cause, I did leave last night due to the conversation. I cannot abide discussions of hunting, especially when spoken by gentlemen who claim to be bird enthusiasts."

To her surprise, Mr. Branok nodded soberly. "I must agree with you there, Miss Fernside. I, for one, have a difficult time tolerating hunting, as well. Especially when it comes to birds of any sort—even the ones we eat."

She wondered if that was really true, but as she thought of the evening before, she could not recall Mr. Branok joining in with most of the conversation, either.

How had she not realized until then?

As they recognized their similarity, a connection she had not expected filled the air between them. She needed to do something to break it, or her heart would drift senselessly toward him again.

"And yet," she began, "are we not both hypocritical, as we were eating the very hunted pheasants last evening for dinner?"

He stared down at her, then suddenly chuckled, which elicited a soft laugh of her own.

"Quite right, Miss Fernside," Henry said. "I suppose we all have our levels, though I do admit I've never liked the taste of the bird."

"Neither have I." She rested a hand against her lips to stifle her own smile, finding the Shepherds looking in their direction. "I suppose you ought not keep them any longer."

He nodded, not bothering to look over his shoulder. "Yes." He paused, lowering his voice a degree further. "It is a shame we do not have more time together, though. I was hoping to compare numbers, you see, as I assume you were out here early to add to your list."

She pulled on a look of disappointment. "Why, Mr. Branok, have you forgotten our second rule already? We mustn't speak of our lists until the end of the challenge."

"Ah, of course. I suppose it is just as well, then."

"But I will say," she continued, "that was *precisely* what I was doing this morning."

He grinned. "I thought so."

"Is that not why you are out here?"

"That was the plan, yes. But with the Shepherds' jovial but ever-present conversation…"

"You will find it very difficult, indeed, to find any birds at all," she finished.

"Precisely."

They shared a smile, but he broke their gaze in the next moment. "I will take my leave of you, then. Shall I see you in my class?"

His class. She could hardly wait for it. But she wouldn't ever let him in on that knowledge. "I suppose."

He grinned, seeming to take great pleasure in her teasing. "You had better be on time, or I just might make an example out of you."

"I have been warned," she said, then she curtsied, turned on the heel of her half-boot, and walked away.

She felt his eyes remain on her, but she forced herself to keep her eyes focused ahead as she contemplated what on earth had just happened between her and Mr. Branok—for her admiration was swiftly shifting from his writing...to who he was as a person.

And she wasn't quite sure what to make of that.

CHAPTER 10

Henry didn't feel as anxious teaching his first class as he probably ought to have. Before the excursion, he'd been rather unsettled at the idea of instructing a group of individuals how to seek birds in a location in which he had never really explored himself.

Now, however, standing before the eleven gathering members of the excursion party in Deryn Park's conservatory, he felt quite at ease. The group was split up and seated in three rows of four chairs, with plants, trees, and flowers framing the aisle they stretched down. The room was two stories high with glass ceilings and ivy crawling up the interior archways, creating the feel of being out of doors.

The eyes of each individual peered up at him as they entered the space, and he smiled in a calm matter. He'd expected a small amount of nerves for his first teaching experience, but his confidence was bright.

None of these people were experts, nor had any of them traveled outside of England before. The Kay brothers, Mr. Gibbon, and Mr. Chumley were eager to learn, and the Hasketts, Shepherds, and Mrs. Chumley were simply there for entertainment. Mr. Dunn appeared to be the most knowledgeable out of the group, though even he seemed ready to listen.

And then there was Miss Fernside.

She took a seat in the back row beside her aunt, Miss Fernside's eyes focused on her book without a glance in his direction. Did she not meet his gaze on purpose? Knowing her, she did *everything* on purpose. That simply made him like her all the more.

Still, he had yet to decipher if she was as talented an observer as she let on. Today would be as good a day as any to finally discover the truth.

"Welcome," he said, motioning to the Shepherds who entered the room last. "Please, take a seat for a moment or two. We shall be going out of doors soon, but I thought it might be nice to meet in here first where we may sit on comfortable chairs."

When everyone settled, Henry drew a deep breath and began. "Good morning. I'm so pleased to finally begin with these instructional classes."

Smiles reached him at the front of the room, but Miss Fernside did not look up—no doubt intentionally again.

"To begin," he continued, "I would like to ask Mr. Chumley here to distribute these books to each of you." Mr. Chumley stood, doing as he was requested. "These are blank observation journals so that you might begin to record the bird sightings you have. If you haven't started your own field journals yet, I highly recommend you begin today. This is the single most crucial part of becoming a true observer, as nothing will help you learn better and understand more than when you write your own observations down about the birds you see. I know some of you have been doing this for years already."

Miss Fernside still scribbled away in her own journal before accepting the book with downcast eyes.

"But one can never have too many available journals, in my

opinion. There will be a full class on the best ways to record sightings," he continued, "as well as a number of other skills and best practices used in observing nature and birds specifically, but for this first instruction, I should like us to simply get to know one another a little better."

Finally, Miss Fernside's eyes reached his. If Henry didn't know any better, he could have sworn he'd seen disappointment in their hazel depths, but she pulled her gaze away before he could be certain.

"So," he pressed on, "let us go about the room so we may each share the reason we have for joining this excursion. I know we are all here to see the birds, but what I wish to know is the deeper explanation within you—what was the ultimate factor that finally pushed you to come."

Once again, Miss Fernside's attention snapped up, and a blush crossed her cheeks, though he hadn't the faintest idea as to what she could be embarrassed about.

"Let us go row by row," Henry prompted, motioning for Mr. Chumley to begin.

The group took turns sharing their thoughts with the others, their reasons ranging from wishing for a break from their children to longing to see more of the countryside to simply wishing to grow in a talent they did not possess.

Henry responded to each comment in turn, anxiously awaiting Miss Fernside's response.

However, when she did, the answer was so rehearsed, Henry in no way believed it to be the truth.

"I have come to simply find rare birds I have not yet had the opportunity to find," she said.

Her eyes flitted toward Mr. Chumley—who'd turned around in his seat to look at the others as they'd answered—then she immediately focused on her journal again.

Henry hesitated. Was Mr. Chumley the reason behind her rehearsed answer? Would she share the truth with Henry if they were alone? Because he was beginning to notice that he was the only person she was blunt with, and that knowledge, for one reason or another, wrapped his soul in warmth.

"Thank you all," Henry said after her final response. "It really is such a pleasure to be here with you. All of you. After the countless excursions I've been on with only men, I must admit how refreshing it is to have women here, as well."

Henry had made the comment as much for Miss Fernside's comfort as for Mr. Chumley's consideration. He hoped both of them would glean from his words what they needed to.

"Now," he continued, "if you'll indulge me, I'd like to share a bit more about my history with bird observing."

Henry dove in, sharing about his love for nature and birds that flourished after his parents died five years before. "They were great lovers of nature, instilling in me that same love and desire to see the world. They had dreamt of traveling to India as I do, but before they could, they passed swiftly one after another, which led me to seek out a newer life than the one I'd lived before."

He kept his words brief, having no desire to share how truly lost he had become after his mother's and father's deaths—how he'd tried to numb his pain in just about every way. Drinking, avoiding his friends, ignoring his duties, and at one point, pretending he'd had no parents at all.

But when he saw Miss Fernside's eyes focused on him with something akin to understanding, he found himself wanting to share more with her and her alone—if only to decipher how exactly she *did* understand.

But now was not the time nor the place.

"Fortunately," he continued, "I found comfort and purpose when I was approached to join an excursion and rediscovered my love of birds. From that point forward, I found myself in the wilds of Norway, Greenland, South Africa, Hudson's Bay, Gibraltar, the East Indies, Europe, the West Indies, and finally, here." He paused, smiling at each person in attendance. "My parents had a favorite phrase to say. *Nothing helps a lost soul discover solace more than when spending time with Mother Nature.* My primary goal for this excursion is to help each of you discover the truth of that sentence as I have in the last five years."

The group smiled again, but Miss Fernside had taken to ducking her head once more, and then, to his astonishment, she *yawned.*

Was he so entirely unengaging? The knowledge threatened to disrupt his confidence, but he drew a steady breath continuing. "Now, I should like to first ask you all a question. Who might know just how many species of birds there are in England?"

A few guesses were given, but each time, his response was, "Higher," until he motioned to the back. "I know there is one person who knows the number."

Miss Fernside didn't move a muscle until her aunt bumped her subtly with an elbow. Only then did Miss Fernside look up from her book, blinking mutely at Mrs. Haskett, who motioned toward Henry.

Miss Fernside finally met his gaze. "Yes?"

She hadn't even been listening, then. He probably should have been even more offended, but suddenly, he was overcome with amusement. The woman certainly was unabashedly herself.

He smiled. "I merely asked the group how many known species of birds there are in our fair country."

She glanced first at Mr. Chumley, then replied. "Over four hundred, at least."

"Very good," he praised.

She responded by dropping her gaze once more.

"Can that be true?" Mr. Dunn asked suspiciously, seated in

the front row. "Sounds like an outrageous estimation, if you ask me."

Miss Fernside looked at him from beneath a lowered brow, clearly bristling.

"What source do you claim, Miss Fernside?" Mr. Dunn continued, his bald head glistening in the warmth of the conservatory.

She once more glanced at Mr. Chumley, clearly attempting to decide whether or not this was worth speaking for. But Henry gave her an encouraging nod before she finally replied.

"Thomas Bewick's books from a number of years ago," she began. "He recorded nearly three hundred alone, and that is one man. George Edwards also outlined a number of birds around the world, with more being discovered daily. Why should we not assume there are even more in England? Furthermore, recent articles suggest that perhaps six hundred is closer to a more plausible number."

Mr. Dunn, who'd been watching her over his shoulder, frowned, then faced forward without another word.

Miss Fernside appeared more than satisfied that her words had silenced him, and Henry did his best not to smile triumphantly for her in turn.

"Well," he said, "I might just sit down and have Miss Fernside here share more of her knowledge with us."

The Hasketts and the Shepherds smiled.

Mr. Chumley and Mr. Dunn did not.

What he'd really wished for was a reaction from Miss Fernside herself, but she merely ducked her head again and did not look up the rest of the meeting.

After a short lecture about the different birds they might find in Yorkshire, Henry led the party out of doors, sharing more about his experiences as they traipsed across the sunshine-filled grounds of the estate.

"The most important thing we must remember when

observing birds," he said, "is to be as silent as possible. I've been told by other naturalists that some owls can even hear the heartbeat of a mouse underground."

"Heavens," Mrs. Chumley breathed with a hand to her chest. "Perhaps I ought to stay indoors. I'd hate to have my own heartbeat confused for a rodent's."

Mrs. Shepherd laughed with her as they reached the section of trees farther from the house.

The group split up, wandering through the oaks and ash trees as they took notes in their journals. The light was beautiful, muted due to the thick leaves above, and an ethereal pink and yellow tone filled the air around them. Birds chirped overhead as voices hushed, and more often than not, the members of the party pointed up into the branches as they anxiously shared each new bird they discovered.

Mrs. Shepherd, Mrs. Chumley, and Mrs. Haskett fell behind the group, obviously finding it difficult not to speak, but not Miss Fernside. She left all the others and remained mostly unnoticed as she stared at the ground instead of the trees above.

Henry watched, intrigued. She paused in her progress, then bent down to retrieve a small, blue feather from the ground no one else had seen. Her pink gown and white overdress fluttered in the subtle breeze.

She examined the feather, then wrote in her journal before tucking the plume between the pages and looking to the ground again. She certainly appeared to be more entertained here than she had been during his class. Did she find him as dull as Mr. Dunn? He certainly hoped not. But there really was only one way to discover the truth.

He approached her, setting aside whatever half-hearted warning his bachelor's heart was obligated to give him.

"Was my class insufferably dull, Miss Fernside?"

She whirled around to face him in surprise.

CHAPTER 11

Miss Fernside whirled around to stare at him in surprise, then she glanced at the others who were far enough away to not overhear their conversation.

"Whispering again?" she asked.

"I don't wish to frighten the birds." Nor did he wish to draw anyone else toward them. He enjoyed his conversations with Miss Fernside too greatly to share them with others. "But what of my question?"

"What question?"

"Did you find my instruction dull?"

"Oh." She paused, appearing to think for a moment. "I do not know what could have given you such an assumption."

"Perhaps it was the lack of eye contact I received," he returned, holding his hands behind his back and clasping his own observation journal in his hands. "Or perhaps I might have seen you stifle a yawn or two."

She winced. "I did not sleep well last night. That is all."

He chose to believe her words rather than the alternative

option sifting through his mind. *You are as dull as Mr. Dunn, Henry Branok.*

"But I will say that I enjoyed your instruction very much despite my lack of sleep. It was very fine."

Her words were delivered in such a rehearsed manner, Henry nearly laughed, though he daren't scare the birds away or draw undue attention toward him and Miss Fernside.

Instead, he settled with a smile. "You are too generous with your words. However, might I suggest that they sounded just a touch rehearsed?"

"Forgive me for not being a better actress."

"Ah, so it was rehearsed."

She eyed him for a moment, then turned away from him to walk farther down the pathway through the trees, whispering over her shoulder as she did so. "Yes, it was."

He watched her walk away for a moment, her white overdress fluttering about her ankles. Was she trying to coax him into following behind her like a puppy to his master? More importantly, did he mind an ounce if she was?

Smiling to himself, he followed her straightaway. "You must tell me why you felt the need to deliver a rehearsed answer," he whispered upon catching up with her.

"Because that is what all gentlemen wish to hear. They only desire words that encourage them to preen." She pulled on a look of importance with raised eyebrows. "Oh, yes, your cravat is majestically tied. Well done, sir. Heavens, no. I most certainly would not mind you joining in with my pianoforte performance. Your singing voice is far better than my playing anyway. Oh, you wish for me to stay home all the days of my life while you gallivant across the country? But of course, sir. I—"

She stopped herself at once, her eyes snapping to Henry with a look that exposed just how much she'd accidentally revealed.

He waited, anxious to hear what else she might say, but she

clamped her mouth shut and turned on her heel again, walking deeper into the trees.

Henry once more trailed after her. "Forgive me," he whispered behind her, "but you appear to have a very poor opinion of gentlemen. But I cannot seem to decipher if you are referring to a single gentleman or all of them collectively."

She didn't respond for a moment, simply paused in place to stare at the ground before peering up at the trees, as if her attention belonged with the birds above.

The graceful arch of her neck and the accentuation of the hollow of her throat stole his attention entirely, but he forced himself to focus on her response, instead.

"Only a select few, I suppose," she finally responded.

That didn't give him the peace of mind for which he'd been hoping, for he still did not know if she had a poor opinion of *him*.

"At any rate," she said, looking back down from the trees to stare at him next. "I should not have said a word. You have distracted me with your charming little smile and made me say something I should not have."

Her words pushed aside all thoughts of being boring or being put on her list of despicable gentlemen. "Charming?" he repeated. "You think my smile charming?"

She paused, as if only just realizing what she'd said. "I believe *you* think it is charming. And you use it to your advantage often."

He couldn't help himself, smiling down at her with what he hoped was all the charm in the world.

"You see?" she said with a little shake of her head. "You are smiling now to get away with breaking your own rule of no speaking when we, in fact, ought to be silent in our search for birds." She narrowed her eyes. "And I suspect that you are also whispering with me to distract me from adding to my"—she glanced left and right, then whispered softer—*"list."*

She was an astute little thing. "Perhaps you are correct in your assumptions. Or perhaps I merely wished to ask how you enjoyed my class."

She blew out a soft breath. "Very well, since you continue to ask, I shall be honest with you." She waited for his nod, then continued. "I thought you did a fine job. I truly appreciated the new observation journal, as I am always running out of pages in mine. I shall certainly make good use of yours soon enough. Overall, I thought you engaging, instructive, and entertaining."

He had never been more flattered. And yet, he knew she was still holding back. "However...?" he prompted.

She bit her upper lip then continued. "However, I could have done less with hearing from the rest of the party. After all, I joined this excursion to learn from you—not to learn *about* others."

Henry paused. Had that been another slip of the tongue? "You...joined the excursion to learn from me?"

She started, her mouth opening slightly as a blush emblazoned across her features as bright as a sunbird. "No, I-I told you, I came to see the birds. I was simply under the impression that your class would be more instructive, that is all."

Henry did not believe her for a second. Was that why she'd blushed when he'd asked the group their reasonings for being on the excursion? Could that have truly been hers?

Instead of pressing her for more information, he allowed her to keep her secrets. At least until he managed to coax them out of her.

"At any rate," she said with revived composure, "your instruction was fine. For beginners."

Henry grinned. He was beginning to notice each time she had a critique about him, it was most often after she'd mistakenly revealed something about herself. But that proved to make whatever she had to say that much more amusing.

"And you do not consider yourself a beginner," he guessed.

She took a few steps away from him, her eyes focused upward again. "I suppose some might consider me a beginner."

"And what do you consider yourself?"

She pulled in her lips. "I thought you came to ask me how I felt about your instruction, not to inspect me as you would a new specimen."

"Forgive me," he said at once. "I did not intend to upset you. I am merely curious, that is all. If my lessons are not instructive enough for you, please share with me your level, and I shall do my best to accommodate."

"That is very generous, but I could not ask you to do such a thing."

"Whyever not? I would be—"

She held her forefinger in the air between them, silencing his words with the action. Was this the second time in less than a week that the woman was shushing him?

"You did promise you wouldn't do that again, Miss Fernside," he said with amusement.

But she shook her head again. "Shh. Listen."

He watched her, her eyes sweeping across the trees above. What had she heard?

Footsteps sounded nearby as the others rushed toward Henry.

"What was that bird call?" Mr. Gibbon asked in a vehement whisper, his small mustache sticking on his upper lip.

Henry paused. Bird call? He hadn't heard any bird call. Blast. Miss Fernside had truly caused him to take leave of his senses— and quite literally so.

"I'm uncertain," he responded, straining to hear what the rest of them had.

A moment or two passed, and the women joined them, having seen the commotion from beyond.

"What are we looking at?" Mrs. Chumley asked.

Her husband didn't respond as a song rang out around them, a high-pitched chirping that wasn't unsimilar to a cricket's.

"What is it?" the eldest Kay brother asked.

Guesses were made around, but not even Henry was certain without being able to see the bird.

Although, Miss Fernside...

He looked at her, seeing her lips parted, as if on the verge of speaking. "You know what it is, do you not?" he whispered.

She hesitated, then whispered, "It...it is a common kingfisher."

"What is it, dear girl?" Mr. Haskett asked, coming up to stand before her, having not heard her soft voice. "You must recognize the sound, yes?"

She nodded, responding with more certainty that time. "A kingfisher, Uncle."

But Mr. Dunn shook his head. "No, kingfishers frequently visit the lake on my estate in Bedfordshire, and that is not their song. It is no doubt a wren."

Miss Fernside's brow lowered a degree, but she kept her mouth pressed firmly shut.

Henry believed her over Mr. Dunn without hesitation, but when a fluttering of vibrant blue wings and a long, black beak caught their attention, all eyes fell onto the bird in question, everyone eager to see which observer was correct.

But of course it was a kingfisher.

With its large head, orange-rusted belly, and wings the color of the sea, the bird swooped into a clearing long enough for gasps of approval to sound around them, then he flittered beyond their sight once again.

Pride swelled in Henry's chest for Miss Fernside as all eyes fell on her with marked surprise.

"It *was* a kingfisher," Mr. Shepherd said with an impressed look.

"Marvelous, Miss Fernside," his wife agreed.

"My niece," Mr. Haskett began with a puffed chest, "she does know her bird calls."

Mr. Dunn walked away without a word, and Mr. Chumley looked rather perturbed, as well.

Miss Fernside's expression, however, was unreadable. She smiled at her uncle in gratitude, then looked at Henry.

"It is time for you to acknowledge the truth of the matter," he whispered. "You are no beginner."

The smile she tried to hide on her pink lips grew ever wider before she turned away and followed her uncle deeper into the trees.

Henry couldn't help but stare after her as he considered the very real possibility that he had been fooled.

He hadn't made a deal with a novice at all.

CHAPTER 12

Lark was sorely tempted not to go to dinner that evening after the dull conversations that had occurred the previous night. However, with Aunt Harriet feeling better and promising to attend, Lark finally relented and joined the others for the meal.

Due to the relaxed atmosphere of the excursion—and the unequal ratio of males to females—Lark trailed alone behind Aunt Harriet and Uncle Francis, choosing a humble side seat toward the end of the unassigned table.

As the others took their seats, Aunt with her husband to her left and Lark to her right, Lark cast her eyes to the head of the table to where she assumed Mr. Branok would sit near the Chumleys again.

However, when the empty chair to her left scraped against the wooden floor, she was stunned to discover Mr. Branok at her side, instead.

"Mr. Branok, do join us up here," Mr. Chumley said, only just above the chatter around the table.

But Mr. Branok, whether he'd heard the man or not, took his seat beside Lark with a happy smile.

Lark hesitated to return it. While she obviously would not mind conversing with Mr. Branok throughout the meal, Mr. Chumley would not take kindly to her disruption of his plans. Especially not after she'd already upset Mr. Dunn with her accuracy about the kingfisher.

She stifled a sigh. Stubborn gentlemen and their compulsive need to always be correct in everything. They were exhausting.

Still, she couldn't risk being expelled from the excursion.

"Mr. Chumley has summoned you, sir," Lark spoke softly, subtly motioning to the head of the table.

Mr. Branok didn't look up from his place setting. "Did he? I wasn't aware."

He made no motion to move, nor showed any desire to do so. Lark bit her lower lip to prevent a triumphant grin from splattering across her face.

"Are you joining us at this end of the table, Mr. Branok?" Aunt Harriet asked, peering around Lark with a friendly smile of her own.

"If I may, yes," he responded. Then he lowered his voice. "I must admit, I have been missing my carriage companions greatly."

His eyes lingered on Lark for a moment, but Lark didn't meet his gaze, glancing at Aunt instead, but she appeared none the wiser to his little knowing looks.

That was fine by Lark. The last thing she wanted to do was settle any suspicions from her family members that there might be something going on between her and Mr. Branok, when all that was between them was a rocky rivalry, at best.

The conversations were small and short around the table, transitioning to longer and more inclusive as the meal progressed, but Mr. Branok was central to them all, preventing Lark from speaking with him until the third course was served.

As Mr. Dunn spoke loudly at the opposite end of the table

about a bird sighting he'd had at his precious lake on his estate, Mr. Branok finally addressed her.

"How did your list fare today?" he asked in a lowered tone.

She glanced around, ensuring no one else had heard him. "We mustn't speak of such things."

"Of course. The rules." He took a bite of his boiled potato. His jaw worked slowly as he chewed, the small muscle in his temple pulsing. "I am willing to bend them, should you like to ask after my list."

She had to admit she had been curious about how many he'd accumulated thus far. She was now at thirty-four, which she thought was respectable enough after only a single full day in Yorkshire. But Mr. Branok was a professional. How many would *he* have?

Then again, rules were rules.

"No, thank you," she finally stated.

He responded with a smile. "That's fine, then. I will say, however, I found more than I was expecting to this morning."

"Indeed?" she asked, feigning disinterest. "Even with the Shepherds speaking with you?"

He shrugged. "I suppose I'm simply talented. Oh, no. I forgot. I am not a serious bird observer."

She shook her head. "You will never let me forget that, will you?"

"Not if I can help it, no."

They shared a look as he popped another piece of his potato in his mouth, chewing with deliberate confidence. The wrinkles at the edges of his eyes gave away his teasing, but she looked away before she stared too deeply into those blue depths. She could easily drown in such alluring seas.

"I enjoyed our conversation earlier," he began again after he swallowed. "Before you shushed me, that is."

He eyed her sidelong, and she hid her smile. "I can't imagine how you were enjoying it. I wasn't being particularly delicate."

She never should have shared her opinion about his class—even though he'd asked her to. She hated to think that she'd offended him.

"Fortunately I wasn't seeking delicacy," he returned. "I appreciate your feedback and will take it into account. I only regret that we were interrupted. Perhaps we ought to carry on now?"

Lark wasn't sure that was a good idea. Was it not better to leave things on a positive note? "I am uncertain. We almost missed seeing the kingfisher due to that conversation."

"I can see your point," he said. "I shudder to think how many birds you'd miss in this dining room if we continued now." He stared at her from the corner of his eyes. "Unless you are counting the pheasant?"

He motioned to the pile of meat before them left untouched by them both.

"Perhaps that ought to be rule number seven," she said. "Plated birds do not count toward our accumulative total."

He laughed, then held a tanned fist to his lip, checking himself before he drew attention.

A thrill shot through her to know she'd elicited such a reaction.

Mr. Dunn's words drifted toward them for a moment. "But with such a grand lake, I have the pleasure of seeing so many birds. I shall list them for you all. Wren. Robin. Swallow. Brent goose…"

He continued, but Lark didn't hear as Mr. Branok spoke with her instead. "Might you agree to finish the conversation, though? For me?"

He sent her that ever-so-charming smile, and she sighed. She was fairly certain, if he asked her to, she'd eat that entire plate of pheasant before them, just so she could earn another one of those smiles.

"Very well," she relented.

He smiled, satisfied. "I merely wished to know if there was any other advice you might have to make my instruction better."

She humbly shook her head. "Really, sir, you ought not be taking any advice from me. I am no world traveler, as you well know, nor have I instructed others or…"

His grin stopped her, and she pulled back with a frown. "Why do you smile?"

"Because I cannot make heads nor tails of you, Miss Fernside."

"What do you mean?"

"One minute, you are fully confident in your opinions and with your bird observations, and in the next, you humbly and readily set aside your accomplishments."

She shifted uncomfortably in her seat. He was reading her far too accurately. "I *have* no accomplishments."

"You see? Even now you dismiss yourself." He stared over at her. "Now if only I could decipher which one is the *real* Miss Fernside."

He looked at her expectantly, and to Lark's surprise, she *wanted* to explain herself to Mr. Branok. Perhaps it was because he was the first man who had ever truly wished to know who she really was.

She glanced around the table, ensuring the others still listened to Mr. Dunn's droning voice as she responded. "I suppose," she began, "I am a bit of both. I must prove my worth for others to *see* my worth—for I *do* believe I have worth. But then, I do not wish to be seen as ungrateful or pompous."

Mr. Branok seemed to mull over her words for a moment. "I understand your reasoning. And yet, you needn't stifle your talents and abilities out of fear."

"That is easier for you to say than for me to do. You are loved and embraced by all."

His features sobered. "Not all." He peered off, as if deep in thought. "But I have learned these last few years that we needn't prove who we are. We simply need to *be* who we are."

His eyes met hers, his stare delving into her soul as he continued. "You are a naturally humble person, Miss Fernside. I can see it in your eyes. But I have also been witness enough to know you are gifted. As such, if you ever have anything to share with the group—anything at all—I would welcome and appreciate your words and knowledge. For you have just as much right to be here as the rest of us."

Lark didn't know what to say. His words had tugged her spirits out of the cage they'd been locked within since the start of the excursion. And yet, she hesitated. To be her true self— bird-loving, fortune-hunted, society-despising Lark—was a frightening notion.

"Do you disagree with my words, or simply find fault in them?" Mr. Branok asked as she remained silent. "I can only assume both, due to that frown upon your brow."

She shook her head, smoothing her frown with a small smile. "Neither, I assure you. I am merely contemplating your words. And wondering how you came to be so intelligent."

Just like that, the spark was back in his eyes. "I was not born with it, I assure you. Any intelligence I do have can be safely attributed to my parents. They were the picture of perfect marital bliss. If anything could persuade me to be married myself, my parents' relationship would have done the trick."

Lark looked away, unsure if he was even aware of what he was saying. She'd had the thought before, had wondered why he'd remained unmarried. Had he no desire to drag a wife around with him? No wish to leave a family at home?

Still, this was hardly an appropriate conversation for two single individuals at a dinner table. Then again, creating secret challenges and whispering to each other at every turn weren't appropriate either.

Thank heavens Mr. Dunn's words drowned out any other

sound. Even the clinking silverware struggled to make their mark.

Mr. Branok blinked in the next moment, coming out of his stupor and staring at her before straightening in his seat. "But marriage would never suit my way of life. Nor yours, I assume?"

"No," she answered more forcefully than she'd intended. "No, indeed. I enjoy my freedom too greatly." Then she looked at him. "And you. Is that your reasoning for remaining single, as well?"

"Just so."

They fell silent again. Would he listen to Mr. Dunn now? Had he had enough of her conversation?

"Have you any siblings?" he asked.

Her heart trilled. "No, though I've always wanted sisters."

"Only sisters?"

"Yes. Brothers always seemed like too much trouble to me."

Mr. Yates, the man who'd first broken her heart, had had six brothers, and he was the youngest and least sensible of them all. Hence why he had been in search of a young, malleable heiress to help sustain his gambling habits.

Rotten to the core, he was.

Not like Mr. Branok. *This* man's parents must have been blessed to have him.

She hesitated at the thought of his mother and father. She knew what it was like to lose a parent, but she'd had much longer to sort through her grief. Still, she had to say something.

"I...I was sorry to hear about your parents," she said softly. "I, too, lost a father, though many years have passed since."

His features sobered. "I am sorry to hear that, as well. How old were you?"

"Eight years old," she said. "His horse threw him. He never regained consciousness. Aunt and Uncle came to live with us after he passed, and it helped, to a degree." She paused, staring down at the table as she pictured Father's kind eyes and thick mustache. "Father was the reason I fell so deeply in love with bird observing. He was the one to give me the name *Lark*, for woodlarks were his favorite. Together, we would spend hours out of doors, just he and I together, listening, mimicking, and watching them round our estate."

Mr. Branok looked as if he wished to hear more, but she couldn't. If she dwelled on the loss too greatly—especially with someone who'd experienced something similar—her tears would not be capped.

"I will not claim to know how you feel," she continued, "as grief is so very personal, but sorrow, while never gone completely, does become easier to bear over time."

His eyes softened, and an unspoken bond she'd never experienced before passed between them.

"Thank you, Miss Fernside," he said gently. "Your words have given me much-needed hope."

She nodded, her heart warming at the notion.

"I, too, had a bond with my father," he said. "He was my greatest and most trusted ally, as I did not come by friends easily in my youth."

"A feeling I know all too well," she said. "Finding someone who accepts one's oddities and passions can be difficult."

He looked down at her. "And yet, our friendship, perhaps, is not so elusive?"

A burden lifted slightly off her shoulders. "Perhaps not."

"After all," he continued, "we obviously agreed to both pass on the pheasant this evening." He motioned to their plates—and the decided lack of pheasant upon them.

"Certainly," she agreed. "And I do enjoy speaking with you. When you are not attempting to bend the rules of our challenge at every opportunity."

"Bending the rules is what makes life enjoyable."

"If you say so."

"What do *you* say?"

She eyed him, grateful for the lightened tone in their conversation. "I say you're as cunning as a crow and as pesky as a pigeon."

He beamed. "I'll take that as a compliment, seeing as how you admire birds." He leaned closer. "Perhaps you might even one day *admire* me. As a friend, of course."

"Of course. As a friend."

They shared a smile, but instead of looking away as friends ought to have, something very un-friend-like passed between them. His features softened as they perused her face, and her heart twittered in response at the admiration clearly shining forth from his eyes.

She cleared her throat and looked away. She'd been admired by other men before, but never had she felt a stirring in the base of her stomach as she had when Mr. Branok watched her.

Feeling another pair of eyes on her, Lark glanced at Aunt Harriet, who studied her pensively, and dread pulled Lark's spirits straight back to their cage.

She had been so distracted by her conversation with Mr. Branok, she'd forgotten to ensure their words went unnoticed.

She smiled innocently at her aunt, ensured everyone else still listened to Mr. Dunn, then finished the last of the food on her plate, though her stomach had turned the meal sour.

With the look Aunt Harriet had given her, Lark was certain that soon enough, she would be required to explain that only a friendship existed between herself and Mr. Branok.

But, oh, how she dreaded such a conversation because she was finding it difficult to imagine convincing someone of her words when she wasn't fully convinced of them herself.

CHAPTER 13

Yorkshire, April 14, 1817

After a restful Sunday, Lark woke the following morning earlier than usual to take her morning wander about the gardens, managing to record three more birds for her list—an alert linnet, a puffy bullfinch, and an adorable pied flycatcher—before returning to the house.

After a quick breakfast, she met with Aunt and Uncle and the others as they loaded into the readied carriages and set off toward a nearby farm.

Mr. Chumley had shared with them last night after dinner that the farmer who occupied the land east of Deryn Park had spotted two Redstarts tending to their nest in the stone wall at the edge of his property.

Not one in the group had seen the bird before—not even Mr. Branok—so all were willing to awaken early in the best chance to observe the bird who was aptly nicknamed *firetail*, due to its fiery orange chest and tail feathers.

Lark, Aunt, Uncle, and Mr. Branok enjoyed a pleasant carriage ride in the beginning. Together, they attempted to mimic the call of a blackbird, that ultimately ended in fits of laughter from Lark—who had accomplished the call perfectly—and barely restrained humor from Uncle Francis and Aunt Harriet as Mr. Branok simulated a wounded animal, despite his best attempts otherwise.

Lark was relieved that Aunt hadn't mentioned Mr. Branok's attention the night before, though she did cast curious glances at them throughout the duration of the carriage ride.

Still, the journey progressed enjoyably as Lark and Mr. Branok shared facts about the redstart with Aunt and Uncle, specifically how the more colorful male helped contribute to the nest building before the female would sit on her eggs for nearly a fortnight.

Before long, however, Aunt fell ill due to the winding roads, followed shortly by Uncle, and the two grew silent—which in turn caused Lark and Mr. Branok to follow suit—until they finally reached their destination at half past seven.

Lark had hoped the beginning joy from that morning would return, but unfortunately, her spirits shifted lower and lower with each passing hour. Not only did Mr. Chumley whisk Mr. Branok away from the moment they reached the farm to the moment they left, but not a single sighting of a redstart had occurred, despite them being in a position to see the nest tucked securely within the gap of the stone wall.

What made matters worse was that Aunt had not been able to recuperate from the first carriage ride, so the second was far, far worse. They had to stop twice alongside the road on the return journey for her to settle her stomach either by relieving it or by walking about, and though she expressed her apologies excessively, the others—Mr. Branok more than anyone—helped her be at ease by ensuring her that she was not an imposition to them in the slightest.

Relief filled Lark the greatest, however, when they stopped the carriage in front of the stately house. She delivered a departing curtsy toward Mr. Branok—who bowed politely in response, concern etching his features—then she escorted Aunt to her chamber with Uncle before taking leave herself.

She would have loved to stay to help, but she knew Aunt well enough that the only person Aunt Harriet needed in that moment was her beloved husband to wipe her brow and hold her weakened hand.

Lark stayed in her room for a time, but as guilt continued to eat at her conscience for being the cause of yet another bout of carriage sickness for Aunt Harriet, she left her room to occupy her mind elsewhere.

Unfortunately, nothing worked. She read Mr. Branok's books in the library—all while being dutifully watchful to ensure he did not spot her—then moved to the conservatory to update her lifelong list of birds. Shortly after that, she sought more fowl in the trees out of doors, but nothing seemed to pick her mood up from the miserable and dejected depths it had fallen to while being alone with her thoughts.

When she finally meandered her way toward her bedchamber to make ready for dinner that evening, she was stopped by Uncle and was given news that made matters even worse.

"I must stay with your aunt this evening," he said, speaking in a whisper outside of the bedchamber. "She is so very ill from the turns in the road this afternoon, I daren't leave her. Not while she feels so miserable. You must go to dinner yourself. I've already asked Mrs. Chumley to serve as your chaperone."

Lark frowned. The last thing she wished to do in that moment was sit with the others without aunt and Uncle.

Unless Mr. Branok entertained her.

She gave her head a little shake. There would be no secret conversations with Mrs. Chumley as chaperone. Aunt certainly had a more lenient eye.

"Thank you, Uncle Francis," she replied. "But I will take my meal in my room. I'm feeling a little tired anyway."

Uncle pulled his brows together. "Please, Lark. Your aunt feels terrible about all of this. She feels she has prevented you from enjoying your time here due to her constant illnesses."

Lark pulled back. "Heavens above. That is not how I feel at all. If anything, *I* feel terribly to have pulled you both through such misery."

Uncle took her hand and gave a quick peck to the back of it. "Do not concern yourself over us, my dear. We made our own decision and would do far more to see your joy."

Lark's heart warmed. How was she so blessed to have received such a loving aunt and uncle?

"Which is why you must go to dinner this evening," Uncle finished.

Once again, her heart fell.

"It will bring us much joy knowing you are mingling with like-minded bird observers instead of holed up in your room all alone. Please, Lark."

She hesitated, but the look of pleading finally caused her to relent with a silent nod.

Uncle smiled with relief.

"Give Aunt my best wishes," she said.

"I will. And do enjoy yourself this evening."

That was highly unlikely, especially after the miserable day she'd had. But she nodded nonetheless and retreated down the corridor to her bedchamber, finding her lady's maid already there, lining up hairpins on the small table near the looking glass.

"Good evenin', Miss Fernside," she said with a warm smile.

"Evening, Penelope," Lark said, closing the door behind her.

"Not a 'good' evening, then?" Penelope asked.

Lark sighed. "I'm afraid not. My day has been rather disappointing thus far."

"Ah, I am sorry to hear that, miss," Penelope said, straightening a brush next to the hairpins. "But don't give up yet.

Perhaps the evening might surprise you. I've a number of dresses for you to choose from." She gave a little smile. "That always seems to improve your mother's mood."

Lark gave a humored smile. It was well known around Brackenmore Hall that Mother loved dresses and jewelry as greatly as Lark loved birds—just as it was well known that Mother despised birds and nature as greatly as Lark despised dressing in fine clothing.

Not only did it draw an undue amount of attention toward her and her wealth, but she also found fine gowns and cumbersome jewelry impossible to wear while attempting to observe nature.

"If only I could be more like her," Lark mused as she moved to the dresses on the bed.

In reality, she would never want to be like her mother. Lark found far too much joy in simplicity. But she could not deny life would be simpler if she could fit in with Society, as Mother did.

Lark shifted her eyes from the simple pink dress with a higher neckline, to the pea green gown with a bow at the bodice, then finally to the last—an azure blue gown with a sheer overlay and subtly ruched sleeves.

Far too elegant for a dinner with a party of bird observers, but mother had insisted she bring at least a few fine gowns.

"You mustn't dress like the rabble dear, even if you insist on being amidst them."

"Let us do this one," Lark said, smoothing her hand along the modest pink dress.

Penelope didn't respond. Instead she nodded her head and turned away. The young woman had been a constant companion over the ten years she had worked for Lark—when Lark was sixteen and Penelope fourteen. Over those years, their kinship had grown so they could both read each other rather well. As such, Lark knew there was something Penelope was not saying.

"You disapprove?" Lark asked, curious.

Penelope hesitated. "Not disapprove, per se. I was only hopin' to try out a certain hairstyle I saw on a fashion plate last week at Campell's. I believe it will look best with the blue gown, though."

Lark pulled in her lips, eying the blue ribbon around the bodice and lower neckline, though still modest. It was finer than anything she'd worn thus far on the trip, and the sapphire jewelry Mother insisted she bring along *would* pair nicely with it.

"The other women dress fine, as well, so you wouldn't be out o' place."

Penelope had a point. Mrs. Shepherd and Mrs. Chumley were very finely dressed each evening. If anything, wearing the gown would help them to know that Lark was at their level in Society—if not technically above it.

She looked at the dress once again. The color did wonders for her complexion, and the cut and style accentuated her figure perfectly. The green in her hazel eyes was brought out, as well. She always noticed a number of gentlemen's eyes turning when she wore it.

Would Mr. Branok's do the same?

She started at the thought. Heavens above. There was no chance of Lark wearing the gown now. That pathway of seeking a gentleman's approval led only to misery.

"Thank you, Penelope. But the pink dress will suit fine enough."

Penelope accepted the decision at once. "That's fine, miss. I've many other hairstyles to choose from that are just as lovely."

"Thank you," Lark returned. "At any rate, it is better this way. I would not wish to attract any attention, even positive. I've no idea what Mr. Chumley takes as disruption, so I'd rather not risk it."

Penelope opened her mouth, looked at Lark, then paused. "Yes, miss."

Lark had told Penelope of Mr. Chumley's stipulations even before Aunt and Uncle—and Lark had sworn her to secrecy about the hefty price she'd paid as well. Was there something Penelope wished to discuss further in regard to either of these topics?

If there was, she remained silent, helping Lark dress down to her stays and chemise before Lark sat in front of the looking glass as Penelope started her hair.

Throughout it all, Penelope remained uncharacteristically quiet until Lark could bear it no longer. "Have you something on your mind, Penelope?"

Penelope blinked. "I s'pose."

"Would you care to share?"

Penelope didn't look up. "I don't wish to gossip, miss."

Nor did Lark wish to encourage her to do so. And yet, her curiosity always seemed to speak louder than her conscience.

"Is it gossip if it does not leave these four walls?" Lark asked.

Penelope smiled knowingly. "I suppose not, miss. I was only goin' to say, if you are worried about what Mr. Chumley could do to you…I wouldn't be worried about it any longer."

Lark stared. "What do you mean by that?"

"Only, I've heard the chatter downstairs, miss. Talks of allowin' a single female on the excursion. It's unheard of for Mr. Chumley. But apparently, after marryin' Mrs. Chumley two years back, it's she who rules the house now. She heard word of your desire to come and fought for your presence." Penelope paused, looking up at Lark with a mischievous smile. "So if you're worried abou' him sendin' you home, you oughtn't be, for Mrs. Chumley wouldn't allow it even if he tried."

Lark stared, dumbfounded. Mrs. Chumley was the reason Lark was there? Did the woman know of Lark's promise to remain unseen and what she had to pay to join? Lark had the sneaking suspicion that Mrs. Chumley was none the wiser.

"You're certain your source is reliable?" Lark asked. "Forgive me, but Mrs. Chumley hardly seems the forceful type."

"I know, miss. Mrs. Chumley is quite reserved when it comes to new people and large gatherin's. She prefers the company of just a few close friends. I shan't tell you who I heard this from, but I know the person to be a reputable sort. And Mrs. Chumley is quite known at their house for standin' up to her husband."

Interesting. *Very* interesting.

Mrs. Chumley hadn't spoken more than a few sentences to Lark the entire excursion. Lark had assumed the woman was merely distracted with Mrs. Shepherd, but did she truly stay away from new faces out of insecurities? It seemed more than plausible. As did the knowledge that Mrs. Chumley ruled her home above Mr. Chumley.

Truthfully, Lark had wondered—even with her hefty price and promises—how the man had ever been talked into allowing Lark to join. Learning that Mrs. Chumley had been the one to coerce him made perfect sense.

All at once, the cage Lark had locked herself within at the start of the excursion flung open. Courage fortified her wings, and a lightness filled her soul. Did this mean she was free? Could she now act how she wished and speak about birds with her equals without fear of repercussion?

A smile touched her lips, and when she stared at her reflection in the looking glass, she caught sight of the blue gown still laid out on the bed.

Only six days had passed since she'd been in London, dressed up to the nines with Mother night and day. And yet, she couldn't deny that, while such finery was worthless during bird observations, in the proper setting, they gave her great confidence.

When she was younger, she hadn't minded wearing fine gowns and jewelry to balls and dinner parties. But after Mr. Yates's treatment of her eight years before, she'd discovered that dressing simpler—if not dressing down—provided her with far less attention from other fortune hunting gentlemen. The very fact that her being an heiress was on parade when she'd met Mr. Drake was simply further proof that when she dressed wealthier, she was *treated* wealthier. And that wasn't necessarily a good thing.

In truth, this was the real reason she hesitated to wear finery here. Yes, she'd been nervous to provoke Mr. Chumley's wrath, but more than anything, she did not wish to go through what she already had with Mr. Yates and Mr. Drake. Not again.

"Even with that knowledge of Mr. Chumley," Lark said unprompted, as if attempting to convince herself she'd made the right choice, "I still believe the pink gown will be better for this evening."

Once more Penelope hesitated. She tucked in another pin within Lark's blonde curls. "Is your reasonin' the same as before, miss?"

Lark nodded in silence. Penelope had been there through Lark's courtship of Mr. Yates and was no stranger to Lark's fears that had surfaced since. Mr. Yates had told Lark they would be removing her trusted maid from her position as soon as they married—despite Lark's protests. A mere week more of courtship, and Penelope would not be with her today.

"Forgive me, miss," Penelope said softly, "but there isn't anyone to be fearful of here, is there? They all must have their own fortunes to afford a trip like this."

Lark sighed, having had the thought already herself. "I suppose you are correct."

"Most of 'em are married, as well. And happily," Penelope continued. "Those who are single hardly seem a threat. Mr. Dunn is, well, Mr. Dunn"—they shared a smile—"the Kay brothers seem too focused on the birds, and Mr. Branok isn't—"

Her words broke off abruptly, and Lark's eyes snapped to Penelope, who pressed her lips tightly together.

"Mr. Branok isn't what?" Lark asked.

Penelope busied herself with more pins in Lark's curls. "I promised meself I wouldn't say a word, but I s'pose it can't hurt if *you* know."

Lark's intrigue grew, all else forgotten but the man's blue eyes and mischievous whispers.

"On our first night here," Penelope said in a voice just above a whisper, "Mr. Branok's valet drank a bit too much in the evenin' and began to share information with the butler here, who was also drinkin'. They were both speakin' so loudly, I couldn't help but hear it, layin' in me bed. I don't think even the valet's aware of what he was sharin'. At any rate, I heard that Mr. Branok," she lowered to a whisper, "has sworn to never marry."

Lark's spirits fell. There was nothing so disappointing as being promised gossip, only to be delivered news one had already learned. But then, if Penelope knew *this*, perhaps she knew more.

"Did he give a reason for why he would not marry?"

A small smile slipped around Penelope's lips. "Apparently, he had an unfortunate experience with a woman a few years ago. They spent weeks gettin' to know one another. Flirtin' and dancin' and makin' eyes, that sort o' thing. She fully expected a proposal from him, but apparently, he didn't love the woman, so he left on another one of his excursions, hopin' that his absence would end her admiration."

Lark leaned forward in her seat. "Did it?"

"Fortunately for him. When he returned some six months later, the woman had already married another—somehow, with her reputation still intact."

"What a relief that must have been for her." Lark looked away. "Was he upset at all with her marriage?"

"No, the woman never approved of his excursions anyway, so the valet said Mr. Branok was relieved."

"Truly?"

Penelope nodded, removing a pin she held in her mouth before continuing. "Apparently, Mr. Branok's benefactor won't fund his excursions should Mr. Branok ever marry. Though I don't know why."

Lark mulled over the information. So *that* was why he wouldn't marry, because he'd no longer be carted from expedition to expedition.

That made sense, of course, but what didn't was the fact that Mr. Branok would lead a woman to marriage only to drop her days later. Was he truly capable of such unkindness? He'd always been respectful toward her—if a little unruly.

But then, perhaps his flirting was the guise he put up in the beginning to simply receive what he wanted.

A sliver of disappointment settled near the back of her stomach. Was he truly just using her? Were they not friends, then?

"All that is to say," Penelope finished, "you needn't worry about Mr. Branok pursuin' you either. He's clearly unwillin' to give up anythin' for his excursions—even the reputation of a woman. And if his only threat is makin' a woman fall for him, with your decision to never marry, you have nothin' to fear."

Penelope was absolutely correct. Lark *truly* had nothing to fear now. She ignored the disappointment she'd felt before and squared her shoulders. So, the man enjoyed the chase, did he? The chase with no finish line, apparently. If that was what he was doing with Lark—flirting with her, attempting to make her fall in love with him, only for him to jaunt off to another excursion—he had better think again.

Her eyes flicked to the dresses once more. "On second

thought, Penelope, I think I should like to wear the blue gown after all."

CHAPTER 14

Henry gathered with the others in the drawing room, awaiting the entrance of Miss Fernside—the last to arrive before the evening would begin.

"Terribly rude to have her make us wait all this time," Mr. Chumley muttered beside him. "I'm awfully sorry, Mr. Branok."

"Not at all," Henry responded. "It has not been more than but a few minutes since the Kay brothers arrived. And Heaven knows how often I am late to matters."

Mr. Chumley gave an unresponsive, "hmm," clearly unhappy with Henry not engaging in slandering Miss Fernside.

The gentleman's issue with the woman was beginning to wear on Henry's patience. Each one of them had been far later other evenings than Miss Fernside was this evening, and Mr. Chumley hadn't felt the need to issue a complaint about any of *them*.

"It is all rather thoughtless," Mr. Chumley continued before lowering his voice. "Furthermore, my wife has now been appointed to be her chaperone this evening, as the Hasketts have fallen ill. Again."

Henry's eyes darted to Mr. Chumley's. Miss Fernside would

have a different chaperone that evening? He tried not to feel too disappointed, but he could only assume that when someone who was not typically a chaperone became one, she was far more dedicated than a seasoned and more lenient caretaker.

Did that mean Henry would not have the opportunity to speak with Miss Fernside at all? That certainly would put a damper on this evening. He'd been looking forward to speaking with her since departing from the sick-filled carriage hours before.

"I do hope Mr. and Mrs. Haskett feel well soon," Henry said. "The poor couple have certainly been through it all."

"Yes," Mr. Chumley mumbled. "So much so that it makes one wonder if one should not have relented and brought them and their niece along at all." He shook his head. "I simply cannot—"

Mr. Chumley broke off mid-sentence as footsteps sounded near the doorway, and Miss Fernside entered the room.

All eyes fell on her in an instant, but none faster than Henry's. And once he found her, he could not look away. Miss Fernside was always stunning. But tonight? She was regal. Her soft blue gown was the shade of a blue tit's wings and accentuated her blonde curls with an almost angelic effect. Her figure shown so flawlessly—her soft brow and smiling lips so delicately feminine—that a masculine instinct arose with him to protect her, to admire her, and to respect her even more than he already did.

When her eyes met his, lingering a moment longer than anywhere else, he could have sworn he'd seen satisfaction in her smile.

"Miss Fernside," Mrs. Chumley greeted, moving toward her. "What a picture you look this evening."

"You are too kind, Mrs. Chumley," Miss Fernside responded with all the humility in the world, though confidence still shown in her expression. She looked at the others about the room. "You must forgive my tardiness. I stopped first to wish my aunt well before coming down myself."

"I hope she is feeling better," Mrs. Shepherd said, her arched eyebrows pulled together.

"That is very kind of you," Miss Fernside responded. "I'm certain she will be by morning." She turned next to Mrs. Chumley. "I must thank you for agreeing to chaperone."

"It is my absolute pleasure. I was just telling my husband how very glad I am to assist in any way I can. Was I not, Mr. Chumley?"

Mr. Chumley nodded with a tight smile. Miss Fernside met his gaze, but instead of shrinking as she normally did around the man's condemning eyes, she met his stare without reluctance, remaining silent and confident.

Henry couldn't help but stare himself at the woman, startled at the change that had come over her. There was something more certain in the way she held herself, in the way she spoke. Had the gown miraculously given her more confidence? That wouldn't surprise him. She typically wore standard colors with high necklines and simple hems. The blue she wore now was in no way extravagant, but it was elegant in every way—as were the sapphires decorating her pale throat and dangling from her dainty ears.

But then, would a simple change in wardrobe alter the way she behaved around Mr. Chumley, even eliminate her fears of being expelled early from the excursion?

Before he could answer his own question, the party moved to the dining room, and despite his best efforts, Henry was pressed to take a seat beside Mr. Chumley two seats down and across from Miss Fernside, who sat beside Mrs. Chumley near the head of the table.

At least being across from her, he could subtly watch her, but the thought was only a mild balm to his irritated soul as the meal progressed, for not only did Mr. Chumley speak nearly the entirety of the first few courses, but Miss Fernside seemed determined to not meet Henry's gaze for even one moment.

What was this game she was playing at? Or was she simply taken with Mrs. Chumley's conversation? Whatever it was, he found himself growing—embarrassingly enough—*jealous* of the attention Mrs. Chumley was receiving from Miss Fernside. This was a feeling he was not accustomed to experiencing at all, and to be frank, he did not care for it.

He did not care for it at all.

Instead of pining for her attention any longer, however, Henry put forth effort, initiating conversations around the table in the hope that Miss Fernside would take the bait—just as the little brown and white creeper had in the East Indies when he'd laid out food for him.

And yet, with each conversation, she continued speaking with Mrs. Chumley—ignoring all mention of the redstart they'd hoped to see that morning, the birds they wished to see in Cumbria and Cornwall, and the facts they'd discussed that morning in class about the woodcock.

However, when the conversation naturally shifted to lifelong lists—including the birds the party had seen on their own and throughout the excursion—Miss Fernside's eyes were finally drawn to the others around the table.

Of course, Henry had them all beaten with his list of just over a thousand unique birds, though he insisted on not being included in this particular comparison. After that, the others shared theirs—the Kay brothers' one hundred and eleven and one hundred and six, Mr. Gibbon's ninety-three, Mrs. Chumley's twenty-seven, and Mr. Chumley's eighty-nine—before the Shepherds joked about their combined thirteen. Finally, Mr. Dunn mentioned his one hundred and forty-two, which he then proceeded to list off one-by-one.

Henry anxiously awaited a break in his words so Miss Fernside might have the chance to share her number, as his curiosity about that very fact had steadily grown since he'd first met her.

But Mr. Chumley broke through Mr. Dunn's droning words instead. "Now, I must know next how you all..."

His words faded as he met his wife's gaze. Mrs. Chumley raised a subtle finger in the air to signal for him to stop. "Yes, my dear?" he asked.

"Forgive my interruption, Mr. Chumley," she began, "but I'm afraid we did not hear from Miss Fernside what her number is."

Henry could have cheered for the woman.

"Ah, yes," Mr. Chumley began, clearing his voice with another strained smile. "Do share with us, Miss Fernside, what your little number might be."

Henry fully expected the woman to cower beneath his gaze once again, to hide her talent for fear of being met with retribution.

But apparently, the man's belittling words lit a fire within her. Miss Fernside lowered her fork carefully onto her plate, then faced the man directly. No hint of hesitation sounded in her tone, and no inkling of insecurity shone in her eyes.

"As of this morning," she stated calmly, "one hundred and seventy-three."

Mr. Dunn and Mr. Chumley did not react, but the others shared their surprise with open mouths and eyebrows raised in surprise. Henry, on the other hand, was not surprised. He had expected a large number from her from the moment she'd recognized the call of the kingfisher.

Instead, he was impressed. Impressed and even more aware of how he'd been swindled by their competition. Had he any chance of beating her?

"One hundred and seventy-three," Mrs. Shepherd breathed. "That is remarkable."

"And you only remain in Suffolk?" Mr. Gibbon questioned.

"Suffolk and London," she responded.

"Makes me wonder how many more birds we are missing in our own little county," the elder Mr. Kay said as the younger agreed.

"It truly is remarkable," Mr. Shepherd added.

Miss Fernside smiled her gratitude, then glanced at Henry. He gave her an impressed look, and she responded with a simple little shrug—which made him smile all the more.

Until Mr. Dunn spoke.

"Hmm," the gentleman mused. "That number seems a little farfetched to me."

Silence fell around the table, and Miss Fernside's smile stiffened. "Not for one who pays attention to migratory and breeding patterns."

"Yes, but in only the east of England?" Mr. Dunn continued. "I hardly think that's possible."

"I assure you. It is," she stated carefully.

He narrowed his eyes. "Are they unique birds? Or have you counted the same more than once?"

She gave a mirthless smile that showed just how much she was willing to tolerate his words. "They are all unique, sir. Considering there are over three hundred in Suffolk alone, my number is not beyond comprehension."

"Birds that you have seen or heard?" he continued questioning, ignoring her defense.

Miss Fernside's eyes flicked to Henry's as she no doubt recalled the similarity to Henry's own questioning at the beginning of the expedition—questioning he was beginning to slightly regret.

"Not that it matters," she began, "but I have seen each individual bird with my own eyes. I do keep a field journal, if you care to check my work."

She'd obviously meant it as a slight, but the man didn't pick up on it. "I think I might."

She nodded, then the table fell silent as Mr. Dunn continued cutting into the slab of pheasant on his plate.

"Well," Mrs. Chumley said, breaking through the discomfort, "I should like to see your list, merely because I did not know that many birds existed." She laughed at her own self-deprecation, and the others smiled in response. "What a marvelous feat. Is it not so, Mr. Chumley?"

Mr. Chumley nodded. "Indeed. Quite a feat. Especially considering Miss Fernside does not have a husband."

Once more, the table fell silent. Eyes shifted from Miss Fernside to Mr. Chumley. Mrs. Chumley sent a subtle frown to her husband, but he did not see, as his attention was far too innocently focused on his plate.

Miss Fernside, however, merely smiled all the more pleasantly. "It is a shock is it not?" she asked, waiting until Mr. Chumley met her gaze. "Although, perhaps it is because I do not have a husband that I have seen as much as I have."

Henry had to bite his tongue to avoid laughing out loud. He'd been subject to Miss Fernside's serrated words himself too many times to count. To see them directed at Mr. Chumley—whose pride needed a good stripping down—was far more satisfying. Especially when Mrs. Chumley and Mrs. Shepherd both smiled, as well, though they ducked their heads before anyone else could see.

Mr. Chumley stared at Miss Fernside tight-lipped, clearly unable to concoct a response. He was no doubt as confused as the others—as confused as *Henry*—with the change that had come over Miss Fernside. Had she simply found freedom beyond the presence of her aunt and uncle? Or had she discovered something about Mr. Chumley that finally allowed her to be herself regardless of repercussions?

Whatever the reason, he was glad others would now have the chance to enjoy her plucky personality, too.

"Well," Mr. Shepherd said, clearly ready to break up the silence, "whatever it is you are doing, Miss Fernside, it is clear that it is working. If I were you, I wouldn't change a thing."

"Thank you, Mr. Shepherd. I don't intend to."

Mrs. Shepherd paused. "You mean to say, you are *choosing* to remain unmarried?"

Miss Fernside smiled. "Indeed. I have nothing against the institution. But for some, marriage does not suit."

Mrs. Shepherd and Mrs. Chumley appeared intrigued, but the gentlemen—all but Henry and Mr. Watts—watched her with looks of discomfort before focusing on their food instead.

Miss Fernside did the same, though she looked far less discomfited than the others as she ate.

Henry did his best not to stare, but he found it more and more difficult as the meal progressed. She was unlike anyone he'd ever known before, and she was winning his attention more than he'd ever thought possible.

"Did any of you have any luck with your observations after the return journey this morning?" Mr. Chumley asked next, clearly desperate for a semblance of normalcy to return to the table.

A mumble of assent sounded.

"I did," Mr. Shepherd said. "I was finally able to find myself a red-backed shrike, which I've been desperate to see since learning of them."

"I've seen over fifty," Mr. Dunn said.

Mr. Shepherd looked slightly disappointed, and Mrs. Shepherd appeared the same for her husband, but Miss Fernside was quick to respond. "I'm so pleased you've found one, Mr. Shepherd. And a well done to you, for the little creatures are not always easy to spot."

Mr. Shepherd's smile returned, as did his wife's, though Henry hardly noticed, once again captured by Miss Fernside's confidence. To see those around the table—most of them, anyway—begin to embrace her for who she was thrilled his soul.

"Do you know," Mr. Dunn said, apparently unaware of the offense he'd caused, nor the efforts from the others to undo his words, "shrikes impale their food on thorns or wires before eating them? Extraordinary."

No one said a word. Mrs. Shepherd looked slightly unsettled, as did Mr. Gibbon, his small mustache nearly disappearing as he curled his lip up in disgust.

"Thank you, Mr. Dunn," Mr. Chumley finally responded, "I should like to discuss the loggerhead in more detail, however, let us withstand speaking of such barbaric matters until it is just us gentlemen, as I fear females find this sort of detail far too unsettling."

Miss Fernside cleared her throat, and all eyes fell on her again. "Oh, yes," she began, "we women cannot bear to hear of these things. We simply would not know what to do with ourselves seeing such behavior. Barbaric, surely, eating food off a spike."

With great theatrical movements, she stabbed her fork into the piece of beefsteak on her plate, held it upright in the air before her, then plunged the food into her mouth. Finally, she peered around the table with an innocent expression at those who now stared unsettled at their own plates.

Then she paused on Henry. He did not bother hiding his grin this time. This woman had no equal. She was simply perfection.

"Well," Mrs. Chumley said, setting down her own fork with a look of amusement she tried to hide, "I believe that to be the perfect transition to end our meal. Ladies?"

The women departed, Henry's eyes trailing after Miss Fernside until she disappeared around the corner, and the gentlemen resumed their seats.

Mr. Gibbon blew out a breath. "I simply cannot understand Miss Fernside."

"I think she's humorous," Mr. Shepherd said.

"As do I," agreed the elder Mr. Kay.

"Humorous or difficult?" Mr. Chumley muttered. "I am terribly sorry if her presence here has caused any of you grief. I was promised that she would not be a disturbance."

Mr. Dunn snuffed. "She certainly was a disturbance this evening."

Henry leaned back in his seat, thanking the footman for refilling his drink as the men continued. All the while, he fought the urge to sigh with impatience.

"I promise, I shan't allow it to continue," Mr. Chumley said. "It is not fair for one woman to ruin an entire excursion for the rest of us."

"Not right at all," Mr. Dunn agreed. "She so often prevents the rest of us from observing more seriously. I do not care for it."

"My sincerest apologies, Mr. Dunn," Mr. Chumley said. "And to all of you."

The others fell silent. But Henry could not bear it any longer.

He took a drink, swallowed, then straightened. "Forgive me, but I do not believe an apology is necessary. If you ask me, Miss Fernside is not difficult in the slightest. And the way she speaks with humor and honesty is, quite frankly, a breath of fresh air. Furthermore, she certainly does not diminish the quality of this excursion. She adds to it. After all, not one of us can compare to her clear talent when it comes to bird observations. That much is obvious with her list. She has seen far more and has traveled far less."

Her words from their first day in the carriage echoed in his mind, and he couldn't help but smile. If only he'd known then what he knew now about her.

The Kay brothers and Mr. Shepherd nodded in agreement, and Mr. Chumley fell silent, but Mr. Dunn hmphed again.

"If her list can be believed," he muttered, his great, bald head glowing in the candlelight above.

Henry shifted to face him. "You question the woman's honor?" he asked, staring the man down, daring him to press the issue.

Mr. Dunn, for the first time that evening, hesitated. "No, not her honor. But...mistakes can happen."

Henry shook his head in disbelief. The level of petty insecurity from the man—and even Mr. Chumley—was astonishing. But Henry would not stand for it any longer.

"I have seen with my own eyes the level of detail and attention Miss Fernside shows in her journals," he began. "She does not make mistakes."

He ended firmly, with no room to disagree, and finally, Mr. Dunn fell silent.

Mr. Shepherd once again shifted the conversation to more pleasant matters, but Henry had nothing else to say, his mind focused entirely on Miss Fernside.

He needed to speak with her that evening, no matter Mrs. Chumley's chaperoning. He longed to discover what had brought on this sudden confidence in front of others and if it would last. He also wanted to share with her how much he appreciated her humorous comments that evening—and her kindness to Mr. Shepherd.

However, as the gentlemen went through to the drawing room, Henry, bringing up the rear, caught a flash of blue fabric that no one else noticed as it disappeared around the corridor. He paused in the doorway, skimming the party for Miss Fernside before realizing she was not there.

He looked over his shoulder down the corridor, knowing she had left the party early. But, why? Was she unwell? Or was it her aunt?

A sudden urge overcame him to ensure Miss Fernside was well, so he slipped from the room, gave his excuses for a footman to deliver, then strode down the corridor toward Miss Fernside's departing figure.

CHAPTER 15

Lark removed her gloves as she exited another corridor and climbed the stairs toward her bedchamber, stifling a yawn with the back of her hand.

She was thoroughly exhausted. Yes, she'd finally been able to be herself—to defend her skills and be unafraid of Mr. Chumley expelling her from the excursion. But it had taken its toll on her. As had not speaking with Mr. Branok. She had attempted to not even look at him—to make him long for her attention so he might know what it felt like to be flirted with and then ignored.

But the second she'd seen him, his look of admiration, the laughter he'd stifled at her words, and the clear approval of her standing up for herself, she'd realized that the rumors Penelope had heard were just that—rumors. Rumors that were complete and utter nonsense.

Mr. Branok was a gentleman, through and through. He was respectful, encouraging, and kind. And she had made a terrible mistake wearing this dress tonight. It had given her more confidence than she needed. With that and her aunt and uncle's decided lack of presence, she'd unleashed her tongue fully and would now pay for it.

Mrs. Chumley had been an utter delight that evening, so Lark could not regret her actions entirely. But still, she had noticed Mr. Branok's attention, and that more than anything, made her regret her choice. For she'd led him on. Pulled him in. Like a moth to a flame, she'd lured him closer until he had stolen glances with looks of admiration far more than she'd ever seen.

She'd done the very thing to him that he'd been accused of doing to another woman. And she'd done it on *purpose*.

She wouldn't have felt so badly had he been a terrible person, but Mr. Branok was good. He didn't deserve this. That was why she'd left before the men had come through. She knew he would have spoken with her, tried to get to know her better, perhaps be encouraged to even *like* her. But she could not, in good conscience, allow that to happen. Both of them wished to remain single, and she would do nothing to persuade them to wish otherwise.

She wouldn't talk to him alone any longer. She would have a chaperone from this point forward. Otherwise—

"Miss Fernside?"

Lark jumped, whirling around to face the very man occupying her thoughts.

She stood on the step second from the top, staring down at Mr. Branok, who stood just at the side of the stairs.

"Mr. Branok?" she breathed, holding a hand to her throat to quell her racing heart. "I did not hear you coming."

"My apologies," he said, his neck craned to see her easier. "I did not mean to frighten you."

He said nothing more, merely watched her in silence.

"Are you in need of something?" she began, eying the empty space behind him. They were a good deal away from the drawing room, with no chance of being overheard. "Why are you not with the others?"

"I wanted to see…if you were well."

She observed him for a moment—saw the sincerity in his eyes—and her heart attempted to stretch out toward him.

"That is very kind of you," she said. "But I assure you, I am well."

His eyes did not shift from her, so she looked away from *him*. She would not follow through with her previous plan—coaxing him along and dropping him—no matter the softness in his eyes as he peered up at her.

He drew closer, reaching the bottom step and resting his hand on the railing, his voice soft as he spoke. "Are you quite certain?"

She tipped her head to the side as she peered down at him. He looked markedly handsome tonight with his blond hair pomaded into the latest fashion and the light blue of his waistcoat reflecting deeply in his eyes. Instead of the amusement and charm he typically exhibited, his expression was something she couldn't quite put her finger on. Was he hesitant? Unsure, perhaps? But about what, exactly?

"I am certain, yes," she finally replied. "Why do you ask?"

"Due to your early departure. I thought, perhaps, you left due to Mr. Chumley's and Mr. Dunn's shameful behavior this evening."

Once again, the gossip she'd heard from Penelope slipped through her thoughts, and *once again*, she could have laughed at the idea. Looking at Mr. Branok now, his thoughtfulness in seeking her out, his taking her side over the other gentlemen, the truth was clear to her even more.

He was as good a gentleman as she had ever known.

"I did not leave due to being offended," she assured him. "I left due to my exhaustion. I fear I have held my tongue for so long, it was rather strenuous allowing myself to stretch my wings for the first time this evening."

A small smile curved the right side of his lips. "I've been

meaning to ask you about that. Are you no longer concerned about what Mr. Chumley might do to you?"

She smoothed her hand along the banister to her right, her fingers following the grooves of the dark wood shining in the candlelight. "No. I no longer have to worry about him."

They did not raise their voices. Despite the steps between them, their words drifted up and down in an easy manner about the open space.

"May I ask what has changed?"

Lark would not betray the words Penelope had shared with her in confidence, so she simply said, "My knowledge."

The intrigue in his eyes grew, but he did not press her for more information. The silence grew between them, but his scrutiny of her increased.

"What is it?" she asked.

"I merely…" He paused again, taking two steps up the stairs. The candlelight flickered against his jawline, more of his tanned throat visible as he craned his neck to see her. "I am merely attempting to understand you again. Specifically why you are unapologetically yourself around me and not around others."

She thought for a moment. "Have I offended you?"

"Not in the slightest."

She tipped her head in his direction. "That is why. No matter what I have said to you, no matter how I behave around you, you will not be offended."

He smiled. "So you *try* to offend me, then?"

"At times," she teased. "But I believe you already know what sort of person I am, so my causing offense is getting trickier by the moment."

He drew a step higher. "And what sort of person are you?"

"Difficult. That's what most gentlemen say."

He took another step, and the voice inside her told her to excuse herself at that moment, for the light in Mr. Branok's eyes grew increasingly brighter—and increasingly more mischievous.

But her body refused to retreat.

"One man's 'difficult' is another man's 'dream,'" he stated. Then he shrugged. "Or so at least I've been told."

"Who on earth has told you that?"

He delivered a charming smile. "Do not call my bluff now, Miss Fernside."

He paused on the middle step, but she no longer fought to leave. Her desire to be near the man, to speak with him and have his attention on her, was too great to leave now.

"I fear I must call *your* bluff, though," he continued. "I had no knowledge of how many birds you have seen in your life, and I fear I am now concerned over our competition."

He flattered her, that much was clear. He had such an advantage over her, what with more than half a dozen exhibitions under his belt, but he was kind to even suggest she might win.

"Why did you not tell me you'd seen so many?" he asked.

"You have never asked me."

"I…" He paused. "Have I not?"

She smiled. "No, you have. Our first time in the carriage, I believe. I simply refused to answer you."

He narrowed his eyes. "I do recall now."

"You see? You are not offended even when I tell you a falsehood."

He grinned. "Well, despite my inability to take offense at your actions, I do hope you will continue to be yourself around me—and the others. I quite enjoyed seeing Mr. Chumley's and Mr. Dunn's usually sheen feathers fluffing around the table."

"I did, as well," she said with a smile. "Though I fear Mrs. Shepherd might have nightmares about shrikes this evening."

Mr. Branok chuckled, and Lark beamed.

His eyes remained on her, a quick sweeping gaze over her

gown before settling on her features once more, and the humor in his expression softened.

"I do truly hope you were not offended by their words," he said. "Specifically, Mr. Dunn's disbelief and Mr. Chumley's slight about your needing a husband."

Lark thought for a moment. "No, I was not offended by them. In truth, I know they, like most people, do not truly intend to cause offense. Even if they do, I would never wish to allow their actions to cause me such futile anger that my own joy becomes at risk. Life is far better when one forgives, even if —*especially* if—no apology is extended."

It was a truth she'd lived by for years now. Finding forgiveness for Mr. Yates's actions had been difficult and was still something she strived for today. But whenever she put effort forth, her life improved drastically.

She'd had so much practice with forgiveness that she'd managed to do so with Mr. Sebastian Drake after a matter of hours—if not minutes—of his proposal. Though, that did not mean there was not the occasional bitterness that sporadically sprouted from long-forgotten roots of hurt.

"You are truly wise, Miss Fernside," Mr. Branok said, drawing her mind to the present.

The admiration in his eyes was sincere, but she could hardly accept the word. She gave a little scoff. "I do believe that is the first time I have ever been called that."

"Then no one knows who you really are."

How true his words rang. Lark very rarely revealed who she was inside to anyone apart from Aunt and Uncle. At least not in the last ten years. She may have worked hard to forgive, but she had yet to break down the walls she'd fashioned round her heart.

And yet, somehow, Mr. Branok had made his way into that small circle of individuals.

His features were all the clearer from his place midway up

the stairs. Shadows danced across his jawline and the ridges of his cheekbones were made all the sharper due to the candlelight at his side.

He drew a step forward, his voice soft. "If others do not call you wise, what *do* they call you?"

"You already know one. Difficult." She held out her hand and counted on her fingers. "Another is strange. Unbearable. And my personal favorite, *incompetent.*"

Mr. Branok's brow drew deep and low, his voice like unsettled thunder at the edge of a horizon. "Who would dare call you such things? A gentleman?"

"If he could be called as such," she said.

Mr. Yates had given her those qualifiers and more over the short months they'd courted.

"You mustn't walk on your own, Miss Fernside," he would say. *"It isn't safe."*

"Surely nothing can happen to me, Mr. Yates. They are the grounds to my own estate."

"Our estate," he'd always corrected. *"But I must insist that you allow me to help you. Your distraction for birds renders you incompetent."*

Lark hadn't realized until later that everything he had said to her, everything he'd done to her, had been to manipulate her so that he might have full control over her life and property.

Remaining where she stood near the top of the stairs, she released the deep breath she'd been holding onto, letting go once more the frustration that arose whenever she thought of the man.

He was in her past for good now. And in her future was freedom and birds.

"It is no wonder you have such a poor opinion of gentlemen," Mr. Branok said, "if the ones you interact with behave so poorly."

She peered down at him, only a few steps between them

now. "In truth, I haven't a poor opinion about *all* of you. Only some. And those gentlemen are of no importance...any longer."

Mr. Branok's eyes bore into hers, but she looked away, unwilling to share anymore.

"At any rate, I truly am not so very wise," she said, attempting to steer the conversation back to the playful nature from before. "Otherwise, how could I have ever mistaken you for Mr. Dunn?"

It took a moment for his eyes to shift from sobriety to cheerfulness once more, but when they did, her heart took flight.

"You have a point," he said. "I have wondered how on earth you were able to confuse me for a balding gentleman well advanced in years." They shared a quiet laugh. "But that begs the question, were you relieved or disappointed when you discovered who I really am?"

"I was mortified. But you already know that."

"Only mortified? Not relieved? Perhaps, pleased?"

He flashed a smile, and she shook her head. "I'm certain you would love to know precisely what I thought when I first discovered you were not Mr. Dunn. However, I do not believe you need the increase to your pride."

"Are you saying I'm arrogant?" he asked, smiling as he climbed another step. "Is that not you calling the kettle black?"

"I beg your pardon, sir, but I am the furthest thing from arrogant."

He gave her a dubious look, though his eyes still shone with delight. Lark was positively bubbling with merriment. She most certainly should have gone by now. No good could come from blatantly flirting with a gentleman alone after dark. But she couldn't get herself to stop.

"Very well," he said, "perhaps you are not arrogant. But you do have a certain allure about you all the same. An ability to draw others closer to you." He motioned to the step he was on, then to the ones behind him. "The evidence is fairly damning."

She smiled. "You've drawn closer of your own accord, sir. I have no sway over you."

And yet, as his eyes trailed across her features, attraction clear in his gaze, she knew her words weren't entirely true.

This gown *always* did the trick.

A hint of guilt crept up behind her, reminding her of why she'd worn the gown in the first place—and how she'd retreated because of it. And yet, now that Mr. Branok stared at her exactly as she'd hoped he would, she could not find the desire within her to stop him.

Even with *knowing* the rumors about his name.

She hesitated at the thought.

Long ago, when gossip had spread about her around Suffolk —word that she'd scared Mr. Yates off due to her strange obsession with birds or that she was too greedy to share her inheritance with a husband—Lark would have given anything to have the chance to share her side of the story—the *truth*. But no one cared enough to ask.

Had Mr. Branok ever had the opportunity to share the truth? Dare *she* ask?

"Or perhaps," she began, her heart rapping against her chest, "we *both* hold a certain sway over others."

His eyes met hers, curious.

"Or so at least I hear," she ended heavily.

He tipped his head to the side, so the angle of his jaw looked even sharper. Slowly, recognition settled in his expression. "Listening to rumors, are we?"

She shrugged, keeping her shoulder raised in the air. "I suppose I am not so very wise after all."

He eyed her shoulder still raised in the air, then followed the length of her arm before allowing his gaze to linger on her bare hand on the banister.

"What have you heard, then?"

CHAPTER 16

Lark steadied herself on the step as she responded to Mr. Branok's question. She did not relish sharing such things with him. But he had more of a right to know than anyone what was being said.

She would simply have to beg forgiveness in her prayers that evening for breaking her promise to Penelope in allowing the rumors to spread to just one more person.

"There's talk of a woman falling for you," she replied, "incapable of resisting you. But that you could not bear to have your wings clipped, so you allowed her to fall in love with you, only to leave her at the first sign of another expedition."

His eyes found hers. "So nothing new, then."

She paused. He knew? How long had the rumors been spreading? "I must apologize for even mentioning such things," she said.

"Then why did you?" His question wasn't condemning in any way, merely asked with sincerity.

"Because when something is said about a person, that person has the right to know."

He nodded, pensive. "So, your bringing up these matters has

nothing to do with your own curiosity to see if such rumors were true?"

She hesitated until she saw the smile in his eyes. He wasn't upset? How was this possible?

"Very well," she replied. "A small part of me *is* curious. But I did not tell you to force a confession out of you."

He nodded, and to her surprise, belief registered in his expression. "You are as generous as you are wise, Miss Fernside. And I must thank you. Not many would provide such consideration. Although, I should expect such coming from you, knowing the rumors about your own name."

She blanched, swallowing hard as she attempted to speak levelly. "Y-you know of them?"

To her surprise, he grinned. "No. I know of no such rumors. I was merely attempting to catch you out, which I have appeared to do so successfully."

His smile grew as he was so obviously pleased with his subterfuge, and despite herself, Lark smiled in return. "You are a scoundrel, Mr. Branok."

"That will be unsurprising to you, given the rumors about my name," he returned. "But what would you say in regard to the gossip *you've* experienced?"

She thought for a moment. "Like all tattle, what sliver of truth there may be is shrouded by an overabundance of untruths."

He sobered, his blue eyes delving into hers. "Once again, you prove how wise you are. My experience has been the very same, so I will clarify, as much for your peace of mind as my own, that whatever you have heard, I would never intentionally injure a lady."

Instant peace rushed over Lark at the humility, truth, and sorrow within the man's expression. There was no mistaking the hurt hidden behind his eyes, as well, for she had witnessed the very same in her own reflection when she'd borne the brunt of gossip herself.

Nothing was quite so painful as when supposed loved ones spread—and believed—false knowledge for their own entertainment.

"I should like to elaborate, if you care to listen," Mr. Branok continued, his voice soft and deep.

Lark nodded in silence, her heart reaching out to him once again. This time, she did not attempt to hold it back.

"The gossip began nearly four years ago," he said. "A young lady fell in love with me, but I regrettably did not love her in return. I made my intentions clear from the beginning. While I enjoyed her company and conversation to a degree, I had no intention of marrying and held no interest in her as a future wife.

"Unfortunately, she would not accept my words and, as such, spread the false news that she and I were to wed, hoping that would encourage me to do so. I had previously committed to an excursion to South Africa, so when I left—as was always the plan—word spread rapidly that I had abandoned my intended after leading her to believe that I would remain with her."

He paused, his eyes clouding over. "My friends wrote to me of the news, and it truly pained me that nearly all of Society could believe that I would ever treat anyone so poorly. Fortunately, a few of my friends believed me without hesitation. Their loyalty was what kept me going, though I have avoided much of Society since, like one would avoid the plague. Both can be deadly, though one is physical, while the other is social—if not mental."

He drew a deep breath, his shoulders straightening. "At any rate, I was happy for the woman, despite her treatment of me. I will admit, I knew a great deal of relief when I discovered she'd married. I dreaded returning to England for I feared her father would have challenged me to a duel or forced me to marry her to save her reputation, but a marriage between us would have never worked…"

He trailed off, and Lark hesitated. Hearing the truth had not only settled her concerns but had also caused her heart to ache. Nothing was worse than an innocent person being mistreated.

She did not wish to keep dredging up his painful past, but her curiosity about the other woman could not be reconciled. There was something unsettling about the idea of another woman having Mr. Branok's attention.

"Why is that?" she asked. "I mean, why could a marriage not have worked between you two? Simply because of your decision to never marry?"

"That, and there are a few other reasons," he replied. "My benefactor has made it clear that he would cease sending me out on trips if I wed, for my attention would be split."

So *that* had been true. His benefactor could clearly do what he wished with his own money, but Lark couldn't help but feel slightly disappointed for Mr. Branok's sake. If he ever wanted to marry, that is.

"Excursions are quite expensive," Henry continued, "as I'm sure you are aware. He does not wish for his money to be wasted on someone half-interested in discovering birds."

Lark paused, an unsettling feeling creeping up behind her. She knew the cost of an excursion had to be steep—traveling always was. But then, despite Mr. Branok believing otherwise, she did not know the actual cost. If a *viscount* was concerned about not wasting his money, how was she to afford frequent excursions of her own?

"His concerns are not unfounded," Mr. Branok continued, pulling Lark toward the conversation again. "My attention would be scattered. But more than anything, I choose not to marry because I have many places I still wish to see, and…I could never leave a wife at home while I was away. Not only would the action be unreasonable, but it would also be cruel, being parted for months at a time. Wondering if I'm alive or dead. Caring for all the matters at home, children, the estate, tenants—all while I'm living out my dreams. That hardly sounds fair."

Lark's heart softened. This man was truly incomparable. Mr. Dunn and Mr. Gibbon had both made it clear they couldn't wait to be away from their wives. Mr. Chumley always complained about his own. Mr. Yates had often gone to London without allowing Lark to accompany him, always stating he needed time away from her incessant need to be cared for, though she never asked for a thing.

If more men were like Mr. Branok, Lark might have considered changing her mind on matrimony altogether.

But that ship had already set sail, never to return.

"So," Mr. Branok said, still peering up at her from two steps down, "now that you know the truth, what think you? Has your opinion of me been terribly altered?"

"I didn't have a high opinion of you to begin with," she replied.

He laughed. "Just so."

She smiled, delighted that he'd caught her teasing. "In truth, my opinion of you remains the same, if not a little higher. I believe you are an honorable gentleman. You've been nothing but kind to me and my aunt and uncle, when others have not shown the same courtesy. With such actions, how can you be anything but noble?"

Lines of surprise stretched across his tanned brow. "High praise from Miss Fernside."

If only he knew just how highly—and for how long—she *had* praised him and his work. But she would take that knowledge to her grave.

"My good opinion does not come readily any longer," she said.

"Especially toward gentlemen."

Love Is for the Birds

"Yes," she replied honestly.

"I still have yet to discover why."

Why? Because of the pain she'd been caused. Father leaving her in death. Mr. Yates leaving her when she revealed who she wanted to be. Mr. Drake leaving her when he learned he would not receive a penny of her inheritance.

But she was not quite ready to share such things.

"Because," she began, "many gentlemen do not have a high opinion of women. They are too often untruthful with us simply to protect our delicate sensitivities. They believe that because we may dress fine and be told we look lovely in ball gowns, we cannot bear long travels, or early mornings, or talk of birds eating. Femininity is its own form of strength. One can be delicate, one can wish to be cared for, while not being coddled."

"I couldn't agree more," Mr. Branok said softly. "Which is why I complimented your conversation and bravery *before* complimenting the gown."

The air between them instantly changed, sparkling like magic between them. He placed his hand on the banister only a few inches from hers.

"You did not compliment my gown," she breathed, her head beginning to spin.

He moved closer, only one step between them. "Then allow me to now," he whispered, eying the slight slope of her neckline before staring once more into her eyes. "Your gown is beautiful, but no matter what you wear, you are *stunning*, Miss Fernside."

Her breath caught in her throat at the intensity of his words, and she marveled at his ability to share exactly what he was feeling with merely the intonation of his tone and the look in his eyes.

"I can only hope," he continued, "that one day, you might give another gentleman a chance to prove that not all of us are intolerable. To prove that some of us know just how to respect a woman...and to treasure her."

His hand slid up the banister, his finger brushing against hers in the process, and energy surged through her bare hands, spilling heat across her body like a hot cup of tea—invigorating and soothing all at once.

She looked at his hand next to hers, unmoving, then back at him. His eyes had yet to waver from her features. Slowly, deliberately, he moved forward to the step just below hers, their bodies nearly flush, their eyes at the same level due to his height.

"I suppose," she began, forcing her voice to remain steady, "you are just that type of gentleman who knows how to do such things?"

She searched his eyes, attempting to decipher why he was drawing so closely to her—or perhaps to find her own answer as to what she was doing *allowing* him. Both of them had made clear to the other that neither had any interest in marriage. So why did they both allow themselves to pursue the clear attraction between them?

But then, she already knew why *she* did. The very fact that he was attracted to her and she was attracted to him was the chink in her armor. And she was powerless to the look of desire in his eyes as he drew ever closer.

His hand lifted from the banister, moving to rest softly against the back of her fingers, funneling more heat throughout her body. His eyes were soft as they looked between hers, and when they moved to her lips, her heart stamped against her chest.

Mr. Branok, *the* Mr. Branok, wanted to kiss her.

Her. Strange, little, fortune-filled, bird-obsessed Lark Fernside.

She had to be dreaming. There was no possibility this

gentleman, this famed naturalist, writer, bird observer, and world traveler, had any true interest in her.

Or did he?

He leaned closer, his head tipping to the side, his masculine lips parted as Lark did the same. Their breath mingled. Lark's head swirled with desire, disbelief, and longing as her eyes closed of their own accord, as if they knew it would help her live in the moment, relish in his kiss even more.

He hovered just out of reach. If she moved but an inch, their lips would touch. So why didn't she? Why didn't *he*?

Did he not truly wish to kiss her but had been caught up in the moment and was now wondering how to retreat without offending her?

Her heart sank, and she opened her eyes, daring a glance at him.

His own eyes were only half-open, his brow furrowed.

"Mr. Branok?"

"Yes?" He remained where he was, his breath tickling her lips.

"What…what are we doing?"

He did not move, that intense focus remaining on her lips. "I know not."

Just as she'd feared. He did not want to kiss her. "Then perhaps, if we do not know what it is we are doing, we ought not be doing it?"

His frown deepened. "Perhaps." He hesitated. "But I cannot help but wonder if that is the precise reason we *should* do it."

Was there still hope? Dare she believe…

She chewed her lower lip. "You know I shall never marry?"

"Yes," he breathed, finally looking into her eyes. "Just as you know I shall not."

"Then," she began, "your intention is to…"

She didn't finish. She didn't need to. A sudden realization settled in Mr. Branok's eyes, and he pulled back with a snap.

155

He withdrew his hand from hers and then took a step back down the stairs. "Forgive me," he breathed, shaking his head and averting his gaze. "I did not wish…you must think…" He trailed off. "No, I have no excuse. My behavior is unacceptable. Especially after what I shared with you about…Forgive me, Miss Fernside. I shall treat you with better respect from this moment forward."

Understanding settled on Lark. Of course. He feared doing the same thing with her that had been said about him years ago. But that was not what this was. Was it?

"No," she said with a shake of her head. She could not end the evening having him think she judged him or that she was not just as much to blame. "No, you did not act alone. I also…"

But it was no use. He shook his head, backing down another step. "You trusted me, and I would not wish for you to think that what I said before was anything but the truth."

"I do not think that," she tried again.

Once more, he withdrew, turning around and speaking over his shoulder. "Forgive me. I should never have stopped you from retiring from the evening. Goodnight, Miss Fernside. I hope this will not disturb your opinion of me."

With that, he turned around and walked away.

Lark stared after his broad shoulders and long stride, regret overcoming her.

She never should have asked him what he was doing. She'd been foolish. She'd merely wanted a response—words that mentioned how he'd longed to kiss her because he could not help himself, because he found her—the real her—more irresistible than any woman he'd ever known.

But once again, she'd opened her mouth and spoken abrasively instead of holding her tongue.

And how she regretted it.

Wretched dress. She never should have put it on.

CHAPTER 17

Yorkshire – April 16, 1817

Lark's regret for interrupting her moment with Mr. Branok only amplified over the next few days, for the change in the gentleman was palpable. Not only did his stolen glances stop, but so did his sparkling eyes, teasing comments, and encouraging words.

He was not unkind by any means—indeed, he was still tenfold more respectful than Mr. Chumley and Mr. Dunn—but the marked difference was difficult to accept, causing the rest of the week to be more than trying for Lark and her declining mood.

On Wednesday, she gleaned great amounts of information from Mr. Branok about how to make better recordings in her field journal, including how to organize her findings, record weather and location, and write down specifics relating to the environment and habitat in which she observed the bird.

She wanted to share with him how grateful she was for his insight, how impressed she was with his advice and knowledge, but to her disappointment, the man spoke with everyone in the class but her.

On Thursday, he managed to compliment a sketch she'd made of a yellow-throated wood warbler—the exact bird she'd thought she'd seen when Mr. Drake had proposed to her. This memory of Mr. Drake irritated her to a degree, but it was merely a mask to the hurt she felt for Mr. Branok's continued disregard.

By Friday, any hurt or irritation she knew shifted entirely to desperation, so much so that she found herself motioning for Mr. Branok to sit near her for the meal in an effort to let him know that all was well—at least on her side.

However, the man mumbled an unintelligible excuse, then went out of his way to sit beside Mr. Chumley instead. A handful of those nearby saw the dismissive act and cast sympathetic glances toward Lark, which only proved to make her pride smart.

She reminded herself to forgive—just like she'd said she would the night they'd spoken together. After all, she knew he was merely behaving out of guilt and regret for nearly kissing her.

Yet, no matter how many times she reminded herself of those facts, her embarrassment festered until it molded to form a dense lump of anger within her heart.

His treatment of her was entirely unfair. After all, she hadn't asked for his attention. She hadn't asked him to tease her, to speak with her, to whisper with her, to *flirt* with her. Granted, she *had* worn that blue dress on purpose, but then, she'd chosen to leave that evening for a reason. She was—almost entirely—blameless in the situation, and now she was the one suffering because of it. She was the one being humiliated in front of everyone because of *him*.

This knowledge proved to anger her further, so much so that when she retired each evening and was greeted by the sight of his books on her bedside table, she had to fight off any temptation she had to throw them all into the fire so that she might watch the flames devour the man's written words. However, she was intelligent enough to know the wealth of knowledge within them was beyond Mr. Branok's ungentlemanly behavior. So, night after night, they were left untouched on the table.

And night after night, her frustrations grew.

YORKSHIRE – APRIL 19, 1817

When Saturday arrived, the party ventured forth once more toward the sheep farm in a final effort to spot the elusive redstart, which they still had yet to find.

Lark shored up her defenses to ride in the carriage with Mr. Branok, but it was to no avail, for when she joined the others near the coaches, she was approached by Uncle, who told her that he and Aunt Harriet would not be joining them.

"These roads are simply too much for your aunt, I'm afraid," Uncle said regrettably, but Lark was not surprised.

Each day they'd traversed the winding journey to the farm, Aunt had spent the rest of the full day recuperating in bed while Uncle attended to her and Lark aimlessly wandered the grounds alone until dinner where only Uncle joined her.

"If we both do not go this evening," Uncle continued, "I believe your aunt will finally feel up to joining us for dinner."

Lark agreed at once, for Aunt Harriet had taken her meals so often in her room, the others were beginning to worry for her sake.

"Send her my love," Lark said. "I will update you on what I find today."

Uncle expressed his appreciation, then waved goodbye from the top step as Lark entered the coach behind Mrs. Chumley and Mrs. Shepherd—their husbands joining Mr. Branok in the final carriage behind them.

Lark spent the short drive thumbing through the pages of her field journal as Mrs. Shepherd and Mrs. Chumley expressed approval of her sketches and the information she shared about each new bird seen. They marveled at the charming lapwing with its shining green plume atop its head like a feathered cap, and the fluffy, brown common chiffchaff with its twittering song Lark mimicked with a little whistle.

Seeing such birds and speaking with the women was a living dream come true after so many years, and while invigorated by her growing list, there also came the sense of frustration, for each time she added a new bird, she was once again reminded of her competition with Mr. Branok, which in turn frustrated her that she'd agreed to the challenge at all.

But the document they'd signed had been binding. So she would continue adding to her list, if only to prove to him that she was a force to be reckoned with.

Mrs. Chumley and Mrs. Shepherd continued with their admiration of the journal the entire journey to the farm, and while Lark knew they were simply being kind, she appreciated the gesture more than they would ever know.

"You must tell us if you spot this redstart we've heard so much about," Mrs. Chumley said as they rolled down the road. "For if anyone has the ability and skill to spot it, it is surely you."

"Indeed," Mrs. Shepherd agreed. "And you must point it out to our untrained eyes. I'm keen to see it."

"You are both too kind," Lark responded, though their generosity lit a brighter fire beneath her to find the bird—if only to return the gesture of kindness.

While she was looking forward to spending the next week on the east coast observing gulls, curlews, and especially the puffins, she was desperate to add that redstart to her list.

However, any hope she might have had to find the bird

vanished as the morning wore on—and as the others in the party grew impatient. Mr. Gibbon and the Kay brothers wandered toward the nearby forest instead, trying their luck for more birds within the trees, and Mrs. Shepherd and Mrs. Chumley lingered back by the carriage so they might speak more openly without fear of frightening off any creatures.

Mr. Dunn remained near the farm, as did Mr. Shepherd. Both stood a dozen or so feet away from Lark, hunched down and hidden behind the stone wall perpendicular to the nest to keep their presence to a minimum—though Lark believed Mr. Dunn's balding head glinting in the sunshine might have been the very thing preventing the redstarts returning to their home.

That...and Mr. Branok and Mr. Chumley's conversation directly to her right.

She stifled a sigh of long-suffering as their whispers trailed toward her on the wind.

"The excursions are paid for in full by my benefactor," Mr. Branok was saying. "I am very fortunate to have fallen into it."

"Fortunate, indeed," Mr. Chumley said. "Traveling to Europe is one thing, but going to other countries is another ordeal entirely, is it not?"

"Indeed," Mr. Branok agreed. "Most people come away with only a handful of birds unless they have proper guides. I looked into establishing an excursion outside of England a few years ago, but the costs were extortionate. Doing so without a bene- factor isn't worth the money, time, or effort."

Lark's chest tightened as she thought back to the last conversation she'd had with Mr. Branok about the cost of excursions. To give up on her dream now would be the ultimate blow to her spirits, so she flicked the feeling aside.

She didn't care how much of her money she'd have to spend to see the world. She wasn't a miser like these gentlemen. She would not give up for anything.

Mr. Chumley cleared his throat behind her. "Any chance you

might recommend my name to join you on your next excursion, Branok?"

Lark held back a scoff. Had the man no shame? Couldn't join an expedition based off his own merit, so he had to rely on a famed naturalist to bring him aboard?

"Oh, I…" Mr. Branok hesitated, and Lark fought the urge to look over at him. "I suppose I could if you truly wish me to do so, but I must be clear, Lord Blackstone does not allow married individuals to join the expeditions. At least not on his expense."

Lord Blackstone sounded a bit too fastidious in Lark's humble opinion, but she brushed the thought aside in a moment. She didn't care one lick about this Lord Blackstone or Mr. Branok's expeditions or Mr. Chumley's begging.

She only cared about seeing these redstarts.

Seated behind her own section of the wall, she'd discovered a perfect view of the nest through a gap in the stones that allowed her to sit in the grass, instead of kneeling or hunching over like the others.

She would have told the rest of the party about her findings —shared in her wealth, so to speak—but the others had all moved farther east to avoid the patch of nettles to her left. However, the devilish plants were far enough away for her to sit comfortably without any concern about touching the angry, pointed florae, so she remained still, silent, and content.

Until Mr. Chumley's voice projected toward her again. "Why the stipulation?" he asked loud enough for even Mr. Dunn to turn around with a look of disapproval.

Lark couldn't blame Mr. Chumley's stupidity for speaking. He clearly knew very little about bird observation. But Mr. Branok was a skilled bird observer. He knew better than to disrupt silence with conversation.

"I believe it has to do with the lack of focus husbands are prone to have," Mr. Branok responded in a softer whisper. "How they long for the comfort of their wives."

Mr. Chumley huffed out a laugh. "If the man knew my level of desperation to escape my wife for a few months, he would not hesitate to include me as his most focused expedition member."

Lark scowled. The man certainly had a lot of nerve to speak such things about his wife who was just out of earshot.

Her eyes rebelliously wandered toward the gentlemen who were hunched down in the grass, Mr. Chumley's focus on Mr. Branok, and Mr. Branok's eyes on the nest.

That is, until they connected with hers. Instead of pulling her gaze away at once, however, Lark locked onto him, hoping to share her disapproval—with their speaking and their topic of conversation.

Before long, Mr. Branok looked away with a lowered gaze, and she pulled her attention to the nest with satisfaction. She wouldn't waste a single moment longer on the men. Neither of them was worth her time.

She peered through the gap in the wall. The moss and grey feathers the birds had been gathering all week had been fashioned into a proper nest with sturdy walls in a clear bowl shape, though the lingering remains of the bottom of the nest poured out over the stone wall like a petrified waterfall.

How could a bird with only a beak and claws create such a thing? It was quite impressive, really. Almost—

"Lord Blackstone," Mr. Chumley said, interrupting her thoughts once more. "Where have I heard that name?"

Mr. Branok didn't respond. Had Lark's look hushed him for good?

"He wouldn't be the viscount who started the Blackstone's Club in London, would he?" Mr. Chumley asked. "I do not know much about clubs, but I've heard it is one for misfits."

He gave a humored laugh, but silence followed.

Lark did everything she could to keep her eyes from Mr. Branok, but she could no longer help herself after his continued silence. Stealing a quick glance at him, she noticed the look of discomfort rushing across his features.

"Yes, that is the very one," he replied.

Mr. Chumley paused. "You are a member?"

"I am. Though, I've never put much stock into gentlemen's clubs."

Mr. Chumley cleared his throat. "Oh, yes. Certainly. Nor I. Although if it allows me to go on an expedition..." He ended with a light chuckle, and Mr. Branok smiled tightly in response.

Lark narrowed her eyes. Why did he appear to close off when Lord Blackstone was mentioned? Did he take issue with the man?

Before she could presume an answer, Mr. Branok's eyes fell on her again, but this time, she looked away first.

Redstarts. Focus on the redstarts.

And yet, between Mr. Dunn's shining head, Mr. Chumley's continuous, oblivious words, and Mr. Branok's strange reaction to Lord Blackstone, Lark had no chance of focusing.

She tried to tamp down her curiosity, but the questions continued to assail her absent mind. Why did Lord Blackstone only allow misfits to join his club? And more importantly, how on earth did Mr. Branok fit into that category?

Perhaps she could ask Uncle Francis. He, himself, was a part of White's—or was it Beetle's? Boodle's? Well, whatever it was, he prided himself on being a member of a gentlemen's club and would no doubt have heard of Blackstone's.

Then again, why did she care anyway if Mr. Branok was a part of it or not? The short answer was that she did *not* care. Or rather, she was trying hard not to.

Time slowly crept by, a half hour passing in the same manner as the sun stretched higher and higher into the sky before Lark finally acknowledged her inability to ignore the gentlemen and therefore gave up entirely, listening to their conversation unabashedly as it shifted from Blackstone's to India to, inevitably, birds.

"Now, tell me more about this redstart," Mr. Chumley asked. "How many eggs do they lay?"

"A dozen," Mr. Branok responded. "When other birds typically lay half that."

Lark paused, swinging back to look at them. That...that was not accurate.

"Heavens, a dozen," Mr. Chumley mused. "And the color?"

"They are speckled, yellow and brown."

That was *also* inaccurate.

"They're typically in the tops of tall trees," Mr. Branok continued. "Conifers, I believe. So this is strange to see one in the crevice of a wall."

Once again, wrong. But now she understood. He must have confused the redstart with the golden-crested wren. She supposed it was easy enough to confuse the two, what with them both being small and both in Yorkshire for a time...but beyond that, the similarities ended.

"And what of their eating habits?" Mr. Chumley asked next.

"Insects, primarily. I believe..."

His words trailed off as he caught Lark's gaze, and only when he appeared confused did she realize she still stared. She debated whether or not to correct him, then settled on the latter, looking away without a word. Correcting him would only push her to speak with him, and she'd determined to never do that again.

"I believe," Mr. Branok began again carefully, as if expecting Lark to interrupt him with another stare, "they also eat the eggs and larvae of select insects."

"Fascinating."

Lark pressed her lips together. She didn't need to correct him. The gentlemen would be happy enough in their ignorance.

Obviously, Mr. Branok knew the difference and had simply confused the two birds, but that was more than fine.

She stared harder at the nest—the nest that would *not* be housing speckled, yellow and brown eggs—willing her ears to tune out the men, but their conversation continued.

"Redstarts also remain in England year-round," Mr. Branok began. "And…just a moment…that cannot be right."

Lark closed her eyes, fighting the urge to look at him for as long as possible before finally relenting. She glanced over at him, a crease between his brows as he fell deep in thought.

He must have realized he was mixing up the birds. Would he come to the conclusion on his own which ones he'd confused?

"I fear I cannot remember correctly if that is the redstart or…" Mr. Branok paused again.

Do not say anything, Lark. Do not. Do not.

But her tongue had a will of its own. "You've confused the redstart with the golden-crested wren," she whispered.

Mr. Chumley didn't look at her, having obviously learned to tune her out by now. But Mr. Branok stared at her.

"Pardon?" he asked.

Lark finally met his gaze, fully aware of Mr. Chumley watching her now, too. "The Redstart does not remain in England year-round but leaves in the autumn. Furthermore, their eggs are in number, only half a dozen, and they boast a shade of pale blue within their nests which are almost always fashioned in cracks and crevices. It is the golden-crested wren that lays a dozen eggs of a yellow variety in conifer trees."

Mr. Branok, to his credit, at least appeared to contemplate her words, but Mr. Chumley instantly brushed her off with an intolerant scoff. "Thank you, Miss Fernside, but I fear I am more inclined to believe our resident expert on bird observing." He lowered his voice further. "One who has left his own county."

His condescending smile was the last straw—as was Mr.

Branok's continued silence. Praise Heaven for Penelope and the knowledge she'd given Lark, for now she could finally defend herself without repercussions.

She faced the men directly with a smile of her own. "Oh, I understand perfectly, Mr. Chumley, but if you prefer to believe Mr. Branok, I suggest you take your own advice, for my words about the golden-crested wren have come directly from Mr. Branok's own volumes of work. As for my information about the redstart, I'm afraid you'll have to take Thomas Bewick's word for it, as he documents his findings in his book, *A History of British Birds*. Now, correct me if I am wrong, but I do not believe our *resident expert*"—she paused, giving Mr. Branok a fleeting, unimpressed look—"has seen a redstart before. You must forgive a simpleminded girl who has not seen much beyond her own little county, but I am apt to believe Mr. Bewick's firsthand account instead of one who has not seen the bird at all."

She ended with a pleasant smile, noting Mr. Branok's distinct lack of response, then directly faced the nest once again, feeling more than a little satisfied with Mr. Chumley's indignant expression.

As for Mr. Branok, who remained silently watching her, Lark believed she'd finally managed to offend him. And yet, the knowledge did not satisfy her. In fact, it made her regret her harsh words, which annoyed her to no end. The man deserved to be put in his place after he'd ignored her and offended her these last few days.

And what of forgiveness?

She stifled a sigh. When would her conscience give her a moment's respite?

"I must apologize, Mr. Branok," Mr. Chumley whispered. "She does not know..."

But his words faded away as Lark caught Mr. Branok shaking his head. "No, Miss Fernside is right. I confused the birds. I also have not seen a Redstart, so I am more apt to believe her research than my own memory."

A fresh wave of guilt rushed over her, threatening to drown her entirely after correcting him unceremoniously. Mr. Branok was so humble, even though he had every right to be anything but.

She pressed a hand to her brow that pinched with regret, her ears beginning to ring.

Then she paused. That was not ringing.

That was a bird's song.

The others must have heard it too, for silence marked the air for the first time that morning before the jovial twittering continued.

Lark snapped her attention toward the sky, and sure enough, the bird they'd awaited days for swooped into view. Bounding through the air in flight, his orange, flaming tail sprawled out behind him in all its glory. Lark observed it through the gap as the redstart hovered just above his nest, then flapped toward his home with a spare bit of moss in his beak.

Lark could hardly believe it. The redstart had finally appeared—and not a moment too late. She watched in silence, marveling at his movements and his brown, white, and orange feathers, attempting to memorize every detail as she slowly retrieved her journal and began sketching and writing feverishly before he would inevitably depart.

After a few moments, movement occurred behind her, and she managed to tear her gaze away to find Mrs. Chumley and Mrs. Shepherd creep up behind her.

"Is it the redstart?" they mouthed out in sensible silence.

Lark nodded with a grin. They tried to peer over the wall, awkwardly crouching down in the grass, but Lark motioned them toward the crack, standing off to the side so they might have a better view.

They gasped and grinned, which made Lark all the happier.

LOVE IS FOR THE BIRDS

This was what it was all about. Bringing others to find the joy in bird observing.

The women remained there, but Lark was not finished with her own observations. She eyed the space to her right, but the men had drawn closer to see the redstart for themselves. If she joined them, she would have to stand directly beside Mr. Branok, and that was simply not an option.

There was plenty of space to her left, however, so she backed away slowly, keeping her eye on the nest so she did not miss a single moment of observing the bird.

Her skirts snagged onto a bramble, so she raised her hem, but just as she did so, her half-boot caught onto a hidden rock protruding from the grass, and she fell forward with a sharp inhale, catching herself with her hands in the grass just before she might have fallen on her face.

Her first thought was to keep quiet, praying the redstart hadn't been scared off, but when her hands, arms, legs, and cheeks began to sting with unbearable pain, she gasped again, then again.

She scrambled back, still on her hands and knees, desperate to escape whatever insect was biting her over and over again, but in her panic, she finally caught sight of where she was.

Somehow, like a fool, she'd wandered and fallen directly into the patch of stinging nettle.

She could no longer hold it in, the pain far too acute, and a yelp escaped her lips, scaring off the redstart and alerting the others to her agony.

CHAPTER 18

"Miss Fernside!" Mrs. Chumley cried out, but Lark hardly heard a sound.

Pain seared throughout her body, inside and out. She could hardly think. She could hardly breathe. Her only instinct was to flee from the nettle as swiftly as possible.

She tried to stand, but her boots continually stepped on her hem, pulling her back down as the stinging became worse, her palms pressing further into the nettles.

Her whole body was aflame, the plants pressing their needled leaves past her stockings, gown, and long sleeves.

"Help her!" cried out another voice.

Lark winced again, another involuntary whimper escaping her lips as the flames spread down her neck, tears streaming down her burning cheeks.

She once again tried to stand, her breathing coming in shuddered waves, but her breath stopped altogether when strong hands encircled her waist and hoisted her to a standing position.

She stifled a sob, still struggling to comprehend what was going on due to the pain cutting off her logic. She rubbed at her

LOVE IS FOR THE BIRDS

hands and face, trying to stop the stinging before those same arms from before wrapped around the back of her waist and the bend of her knees, scooping her up in a swift motion.

Gasping, Lark grasped onto a gentleman's lapel, her opposite arm encircling broad shoulders, and suddenly, dread overcame her.

Mr. Branok. He'd hoisted her from the nettles and was now carrying her to safety.

Why, why had she wavered from the grass? And why did Mr. Branok rescue her, of all people? At this point, she would have preferred Mr. Chumley.

"We must take her home," Mrs. Shepherd said, speaking from behind as she trailed after Mr. Branok and Lark.

"Yes, straight to the carriage," Mrs. Chumley agreed.

Lark could not even protest if she wished to.

"What in Heaven's name happened?" Mr. Chumley asked, coming up to join his wife, Mr. Shepherd not far behind. Mr. Dunn remained at the wall, face red with anger.

He and Mr. Chumley were no doubt fuming for Lark's disruption, but at least Mr. Shepherd had the decency to be as concerned as the women.

Mrs. Chumley responded to her husband, though her whispers fell so silent, Lark could no longer hear them.

It was just as well. She could hardly comprehend their words anyway. Tears still trailed down her face, though with how hard she now bit her lower lip, her cries of pain had finally ceased.

That, and her pride refused to allow herself to be weak in front of Mr. Branok anymore than she'd already been. She could not bear the fact that he was carrying her so commandingly in his more-than-capable arms.

"I can walk," she squeaked out to him as the others spoke behind her.

She attempted to raise her arm so it might not rest so heavily on his shoulders, but the stinging became more poignant as she moved.

Mr. Branok didn't respond to her weak words. She glanced up at him, his jaw set, lips in a thin line, and brow furrowed.

Was he…angry? At *her?*

"Her face," Mrs. Shepherd whispered, her voice trailing toward Lark. "Did you see the rash?"

"It's all over," Mrs. Chumley responded.

The invisible flames of pain lapped at Lark's skin, and she peered down at her arm, swollen with white bumps and angry red welts. She could only imagine what her cheeks and neck looked like as the women had mentioned.

Humiliation rushed over her, not only at the thought of how she must appear, but also at having made such a mistake and disrupting the others in the process.

"You can put me down," she attempted again with Mr. Branok. "I can walk."

Once more, he did not reply. Was he so utterly inconvenienced by her mistake that he could not manage a single word in response?

"Mr. Branok, how can we help?" asked Mrs. Chumley from behind.

"Yes, what can be done?" Mr. Shepherd asked.

"Dock leaves," came Mr. Branok's gruff reply as he continued carrying her toward the coaches. "They should be near the nettles. Broad, oblong leaves. They will not rid her of the pain entirely, but the sap will soothe the stinging."

The two couples dispersed at once to gather the leaves, and while Lark appreciated their efforts, her pride smarted. So, Mr. Branok deigned to speak with everyone *but* Lark?

Another wave of fresh agony rushed over her, and she couldn't help but squirm in pain.

"You knew the nettle was there," Mr. Branok said brusquely.

Oh, so he *could* speak with her, then.

She frowned, dwelling on her anger instead of her pain. Why in Heaven's name had the coaches parked so far away? This was taking an eternity, even with the gentleman's long stride.

"I was distracted by the redstart," she mumbled weakly in her defense.

"Well, it is gone now."

Her stomach fell. He was blaming her for the bird's departure. In reality, it *was* her fault. "I didn't mean to," she said, a rogue tear slipping down her burning cheek.

"You should have been more watchful."

"We have the leaves," Mr. Shepherd said, returning to them so Lark could not respond to Mr. Branok's insensitive words.

Mrs. Shepherd and Mrs. Chumley rushed forward with more leaves in their hands, though Mr. Chumley remained behind in a weak search for more.

"Mrs. Shepherd and I can apply them in the carriage," Mrs. Chumley said. "Mr. Branok, you must accompany us home so you might carry Miss Fernside to her bedchamber."

Lark would have laughed had she not been on the verge of sobbing. There was no chance she would allow him to ride in the carriage with her while the women saw to her rashes—rashes that had reached more places than any of them had obviously suspected. And even if he took a separate carriage, she would never allow him to pick her up again.

The others behind them spoke in hushed tones about calling for a doctor, and Mr. Chumley finally caught up with them with a single dock leaf he extended to his wife.

Lark shook her head, though she knew no one would listen. "I do not need to be carried," she managed, blinking through her tears. "I am perfectly capable of walking."

"Are you?" Mr. Branok muttered under his breath for only her to hear.

She scowled up at him in shock, his pointed slight cutting through her final defenses.

"Put me down," she commanded at once.

"I cannot."

"Why?" she asked.

"Because I'd hate for you to fall in poison ivy next."

Her mouth hung open as if on a broken hinge. She would have slapped him soundly across his cheek if her limbs would have cooperated.

Of all the pretentious, pompous, presumptuous things to say.

With all that was left of her will, she removed her arm from around his shoulder and firmly pressed both hands against his chest, squirming until he had no choice but to drop her feet to the ground.

She landed with as much decorum as possible, straightening as she ignored the looks of surprise from the others behind Mr. Branok. He glowered at her, hands fisted, chest rising and falling from strain and no doubt frustration.

Facing him with a raised chin, though she knew what a sight she must be, Lark spoke in even tones. "I am well enough to walk. To the coach and to my bedchamber. I do not require the assistance of any gentleman, although I will gladly accept Mrs. Chumley and Mrs. Shepherd's care on the return journey. Thank you."

She shot Mr. Branok a pointed look, refusing to feel an ounce of remorse for her sharp words this time, and turned on her heel to make the rest of the way to the carriage herself.

Mrs. Shepherd and Mrs. Chumley followed behind her in silence, but Lark did not face them. She could not. For if she did, she would have revealed the silent cries now escaping her lips as her pain and humiliation overcame her.

Henry berated himself as the carriage rolled away with the women tucked safely inside.

He should have been more aware. He should have been watching Miss Fernside closer to ensure she did not wander toward the nettle. This was all his fault.

"Women," Mr. Chumley grumbled, shaking his head as he and Mr. Shepherd came to stand beside Henry. "Lord Blackstone has it right. Mark my words, Mr. Branok, I shan't ever allow them on another excursion."

Henry grimaced, remaining silent in response as he pulled his stinging hands behind his back. In retrieving Miss Fernside from the nettles, he'd been caught by a few, but his pain was surely nothing compared to the agony Miss Fernside experienced.

"I'm sorry about all this, gentlemen," Mr. Chumley continued. "That redstart will never return after Miss Fernside's hysterics."

Mr. Shepherd didn't respond, looking away in slight discomfort, but Henry's frown grew. Hysterics? The woman had been in unimaginable amounts of pain. In truth, she'd held it together remarkably well. Far better than Henry had his guilt. Then he'd had the audacity to chastise her, attempting to deflect his clear culpability toward her excited distraction with the bird.

"Are you truly upset, Mr. Branok?" Mr. Chumley asked, misreading Henry's silence.

"Not at all," Henry stated. "And there is no need to apologize."

"I beg to differ. The woman scared off the bird we've been waiting to see for days."

"We all saw it, did we not?" Henry countered.

"We did," Mr. Shepherd said. "And it was remarkable."

"But what of the others?" Mr. Chumley began. "The redstart would have stayed for longer, allowing the Kay brothers and Mr. Gibbon to see it, as well."

Henry remained silent. No one could have guessed how long the redstart would remain. Mr. Chumley was simply being fussy.

"How often she disrupts matters," the man continued. "She promised she would remain unnoticed, but she is failing miserably thus far, I daresay. Mr. and Mrs. Haskett are becoming quite a nuisance, as well, being unable to chaperone their own niece so often."

Henry gave a little shake of his head. He couldn't bear this much longer. He needed to clear his mind. More than anything, he needed space from Mr. Chumley and his incessant speaking.

Ever since Henry had distanced himself from Miss Fernside —attempting to make it easier on his conscience after he'd clearly crossed the line of propriety—Mr. Chumley had seized him at every opportunity, and Henry had allowed it. He'd hoped the man's conversation would be a nice distraction, but it proved to be nothing short of exhausting.

Especially while attempting to observe birds.

"The Hasketts can hardly be blamed for falling ill when they travel," Mr. Shepherd said. "And your wife seems more than happy to help in chaperoning. I know Mrs. Shepherd would be, as well."

"Yes," Mr. Chumley agreed moodily. "But that is also disruptive. Only today, our travel arrangements have been made to shift drastically. But worry not, gentlemen. I'm minded to find a way to convince Miss Fernside to end her time with us before the Lake District. Imagine what a peaceful experience that will be without her."

Disgust gurgled in Henry's chest like boiling mud. Miss Fernside had behaved more like herself in the last week than she ever had—and she'd seemed quite confident that no matter what she did, Mr. Chumley no longer held power over her.

But then, what if he did? What if Mr. Chumley found a way to expel her from the excursion? Henry would never forgive himself.

He never should have allowed the kiss between him and Miss Fernside to nearly occur. But more than anything, he never should have ignored her as he had the last few days. He'd thought perhaps he could convince himself that he'd imagined the connection and attraction between them, but being away from her only proved that whatever he felt for Miss Fernside was growing—whether he liked it or not.

Mr. Chumley might experience peace without her. But if Henry had learned anything in the last week of avoiding her, it was that all excursions from this point forward without Miss Fernside would be decidedly lacking.

And he was still coming to terms with what exactly that meant.

"I think my wife and yours would be terribly sorry if that happened," Mr. Shepherd said carefully.

"I suppose," Mr. Chumley grumbled. "But they are not the only ones whose thoughts and opinions should be taken into account." He shifted toward Henry. "What say you, Mr. Branok?"

Henry rubbed at his burning hands once again. "Frankly?"

Mr. Chumley gestured for him to continue.

"Very well, frankly, Mr. Chumley, I believe your frustrations with the woman ought to be laid to rest. She is not disrupting matters."

Unless he was referring to matters of Henry's heart.

"I beg to differ, sir," Mr. Chumley protested. "What of the way she instructed you today? You cannot tell me you appreciated it."

"I did," Henry replied. "One needs correction when one is wrong."

He gave Mr. Chumley a knowing look, and the man narrowed his eyes a fraction, as if wondering if Henry was speaking of him.

He was.

Henry continued, "I would far prefer her instructing me than the possibility of me relaying false information. I, for one, am glad she spoke up. At any rate, she has just as much right as anyone to be on this trip. She paid the same as the others, did she not?"

Mr. Chumley averted his gaze. "Yes, quite right. Quite right."

He fell silent, then, clearly knowing he was losing the conversation.

Mr. Chumley and Mr. Shepherd soon wandered back to Mr. Dunn, but Henry excused himself. He couldn't take a moment longer of the diatribe against Miss Fernside—especially what would inevitably come from Mr. Dunn. Henry would rather walk home on his own—a solid two-hour-jaunt—then spend a second more in their company.

So that was precisely what he did.

Finding dock leaves along the way to soothe his hands, he allowed his mind to return to Miss Fernside and the pain she must still be in—not only from the nettles but from his treatment of her.

She'd been so generous to encourage him to share his own side of the rumors about his name. But he'd behaved abysmally, telling her he would not injure a woman when, in the next second, he *had* injured her.

Nearly kissing her with no intention of marrying her.

Slighting her when she tried to be his friend. Criticizing her for a simple distracted mistake. What had he been thinking?

He obviously *hadn't* been, and that was the problem.

But he was thinking now. And he knew what he needed to do. He needed to make this right. To apologize for ignoring her and injuring her. And he needed to do it right now.

CHAPTER 19

Lark remained indoors over the next several days, keeping to her room or Aunt Harriet's while using the excuse of recuperating from the rash the stinging nettle had caused. In reality, she was attempting to recover from her humiliation instead.

She took her meals in her bedchamber, accomplished her observations in the early hours of the morning, and ducked down random corridors to avoid any passersby when returning. She skipped Mr. Branok's classes, receiving a review from Uncle Francis about what she missed each time, and had promptly tucked away her list for her competition with Mr. Branok at the bottom of her drawer beneath blank papers and jars of ink.

If he was going to pretend nothing happened between them —not even a friendship—then she would do the very same with their agreement.

Four days after the mishap, her wounds no longer stung, and the unbearable itch had mercifully subsided, as had the angry red welts and spots. As such, Aunt Harriet managed to convince

LOVE IS FOR THE BIRDS

Lark to join the other women for tea and biscuits one afternoon while the gentlemen traversed across the moors.

In the drawing room, Mrs. Chumley was kind enough to reassure Lark that, while the redstart *had* been frightened off, the bird had promptly returned not a quarter of an hour later, and each gentleman had been fortunate enough to observe him for longer.

"Mr. Chumley said it was marvelous," Mrs. Chumley continued. "The female made a showing, too. Although, Mr. Branok disappeared before he had the chance to see them. No one knows why he left, though he ended up walking the great distance back to the house instead of waiting for one of the carriages."

Lark didn't care a lick about what the gentleman did or did not do, but she smiled at Mrs. Chumley nonetheless and merely sipped her tea before returning to her room to avoid any sight of the man.

On Thursday, Lark was back to full health, which caused both Aunt and Uncle to press her to join them at Bempton Cliffs to see the seabirds nesting on the precipices.

"It is a journey I can actually manage with relative ease," Aunt said. "The roads are far less winding."

So, Lark relented.

At any rate, there was only one bird that could convince Lark to join them, however, and that was the puffin. So, with great reluctance, she joined the others, swallowing her pride with every greeting and every look of curiosity—or in Mr. Chumley's and Mr. Dunn's case, every look of intolerance—before loading into the carriage with Aunt, Uncle, and Mr. Branok.

To her eternal frustration, Mr. Branok had the audacity to act as if nothing out of the ordinary had happened between them, behaving as he had before their moment on the stairs.

"I'm so pleased to have my carriage companions again," he said with a smile that swept about the coach.

Lark smiled politely but kept her eyes focused on the horizon, refusing to give him an inch of generosity.

"And you, Miss Fernside," Mr. Branok pressed, as if he hadn't been unthinkably cold with her over the last week. "It is lovely to see you out and about this morning. We've all been wondering when you would feel well enough again to make your return. To be back in time to see the puffins is providential."

Insufferable man.

"Yes, I am quite pleased," she responded.

"I see your rash has subsided," he continued. "I trust your discomfort has, as well?"

Apart from experiencing this conversation? "It has, thank you."

"And I am certain you are anxious to find more birds for your...*list*."

He ended the word heavily, and Lark turned to see his knowing expression. His blue eyes were hope-filled, as if he were trying to mend the gap between them. Lark almost gave in until she reminded herself of all that had occurred between them.

"You know," she began, "I quite forgot about the list while I was convalescing. I was more focused on how to better recognize stinging nettle and poison ivy so I might prove I'm capable of walking sensibly again."

She smiled sweetly at him, and he shifted his gaze away with a discomfited clearing of his throat.

She'd hoped perhaps she had heard the last from him, but he spoke once again.

"Your knowledge was greatly missed in my classes," he attempted. "I would be happy to share with you all that you have missed."

LOVE IS FOR THE BIRDS

He really was trying now. But it was too late. Their fate had been sealed, no matter how her conscience begged her to reconsider.

"Thank you, but my uncle has kindly already done so."

Aunt and Uncle watched her carefully from across the coach, no doubt wondering why she was behaving so unkindly, so she added a smile in Mr. Branok's direction, then shifted her body closer to the window.

To her relief, Mr. Branok finally took her not-so-subtle hinting and redirected his attention to Uncle Francis and Aunt Harriet instead until the carriage finally rolled to a stop.

As they joined the others at the cliffs, Lark finally allowed herself to anticipate being out of doors again—and especially seeing the puffins.

"I'm so happy you joined us," Aunt said, looping her arm through Lark's as they stood at the cliff's edge, watching the puffins on the next cliff over.

"I am, too," she replied.

And she was. Observing these birds was another experience entirely. The sunshine had disappeared, replaced with overcast skies, and the wind held a chill as it blew in from the North Sea, but in that muted lighting, the puffins themselves were striking in every sense of the word.

Having never seen one in real life, with only the drawing in Bewick's book to rely upon, Lark was unprepared for how much delight she experienced in seeing the little creatures.

Their colorful beaks and orange, duck-like feet stood out from the mossy white crevices in which they built their nests. But what struck Lark more than anything was the smoothness of their black and white feathers—and how approachable and kind their eyes were, as if they held a deep innocence about them.

But as she overheard Mr. Branok speaking—though she did

her best to ignore him—she was surprised to discover they, perhaps, were not as gentle as they appeared.

"Puffins are carnivores," he taught, standing near enough to the group to be heard by them all. "They eat mainly fish and can carry as many as ten at a time. Their beaks are also strong enough to crush mollusks and other crustaceans, while their tongues have spines to hold the fish in place while they eat."

Lark had read as much in his novels, but she was happy to see he'd gotten his facts right this time.

She sighed at her own condemnations. She was beginning to sound rather petty, and it wasn't a nice feeling at all.

"And those who are romantics at heart will be happy to hear this," Mr. Branok continued. "It has been observed that puffins mate for life."

"Oh, I do like that," Mrs. Shepherd said, encircling her arms about her husband's, who responded with a smile of his own.

Lark nearly blushed at the look the couple gave each other, so she turned swiftly away and wandered down the cliffside, anxious to escape their words—and Mr. Branok's.

Leaning against the stone barrier with a perfect view of the puffins, she watched the sea roar below. The puffins called out their low, guttural, croaking cries as they rested in their nesting grounds.

So they mated for life, did they? What nonsense. They were no doubt attached to the location rather than the bird. At least, that's what Lark's experience had been. Men were always more interested in her home and the location of it—and by extension her wealth—more than who she was as a person.

"I take it you did not find the notion as romantic as Mrs. Shepherd?"

Lark started, whirling her attention to Mr. Branok, whom she had not heard approaching from her side.

He'd come alone, the others a good distance away so they would not be overheard—as if he'd done so on purpose.

LOVE IS FOR THE BIRDS

"What notion?" she asked, playing innocent.

He leaned against the barrier, motioning to the birds. "That puffins mate for life."

"Oh. I suppose it is romantic enough."

"Why does that not surprise me?"

She eyed him, still perturbed that he thought he could treat her as his friend even after ignoring her, rejecting her, and chastising her.

"Why does *what* not surprise you?" she asked with narrowed eyes.

"That you are not a romantic."

She frowned. "Why does it not surprise me that *you* are?"

"On the contrary. I am not."

"Except for the fact that you just said it was romantic," she countered.

"I said it for the benefit of the others."

He motioned to the Shepherds, Mrs. Shepherd clinging to her husband so tightly Lark wondered if Mr. Shepherd was beginning to lose feeling in his left arm. He hardly seemed to mind her grasp on him, though, his smile ever wider.

"In truth," Mr. Branok continued, "I think it a ruse."

Lark bit her tongue to prevent herself from conversing further, but her curiosity won out again. "A ruse for what?"

"For others to believe in romance and marriage. In reality, love better suits birds than it does us humans."

He'd said the words lightly, and though they were bitter, they didn't sound as such.

He looked over at her, catching her staring, so she put another inch of distance between them. "I suppose we can agree on that, then. Love is for the birds."

"Certainly." He studied her still. "I know why I believe so, but may I ask why *you* feel such a way?"

She didn't consider his words for a moment. "No."

He pulled back, obviously surprised. "Why not?"

"Because only true friends ought to speak about such matters."

"And are we not true friends?"

She looked at him with a focused gaze. "Why do you not rehearse how you treated me before and after I fell into the nettle, then tell me if we are true friends."

To her relief, he finally shed his confident expression, and a regretful wince crossed his features.

That was enough for her—to simply know that *he* knew.

"Excuse me," she muttered, backing away, not wishing to hear what excuses he had to share. "I must return to my aunt."

He held up a disarming hand, his humble look of pleading stopping her at once. "You will not allow me to explain?" he asked softly.

Her defenses began to slip down from around her heart, but fear gripped her soul. She could not give in to this. She could not welcome him back into her life. She'd grown too used to his friendship before, so much so that no longer having him in her daily life had hurt too greatly.

She was far better off keeping her distance from him indefinitely.

"No, Mr. Branok," she said softly. "We needn't pretend any longer to be friends. You clearly wished to keep your distance before, and I was hurt because of it. But I assure you now, I understand and agree that we ought to maintain distance from one another. We shall remain professional acquaintances and nothing more. Good day."

"No, Miss Fernside—"

But she shook her head in silence, walked around his outstretched hand, and left him alone.

CHAPTER 20

Lark was eager to see the last of Yorkshire.

The day after observing the puffins, her final day on the coast had been an utter failure. She had become obsessively preoccupied with avoiding Mr. Branok, so much so that she'd wandered away from the group and drew closer to an unsuspecting wave that had managed to catch her up to her knees.

She'd yelped in surprise with the cold water and subsequently frightened away the gulls that the party had been observing nearby. Shortly after, a gust of wind sailed toward the beach, blasting sand toward her and causing her eyes and nose to be filled with grit.

Not only could she not see properly, but a fit of sneezing had overcome her to the point that every bird they attempted to approach afterward was promptly scared off.

Aunt Harriet had insisted they return home for Lark to change so she would not catch a cold, and Lark did not protest. While she may not have cared any longer about upsetting Mr. Chumley, she truly did not wish to disturb the observations of the others, and at that rate, she most assuredly had been.

Fortunately, as they were traveling to the Lake District come morning, Lark had made the excuse of remaining in her room to prepare for the journey, even though, once again, she was merely avoiding others.

The morning of their departure ultimately arrived, and Lark joined the group on the gravel drive outside the house. She cast one final glance at the grandiose structure that had once held so much promise for the excursion—but had ultimately turned into a contemptuous representation of the failure that was this journey.

She could only pray the Lake District held more for her.

And yet, as they ventured forth, her fortunes did not change, for Mr. Branok still attempted to speak with her, and her aunt and uncle cast more and more concerned glances in her direction.

Lark ultimately feigned sleep to avoid such stares and conversation, though she remained wide awake, her mind abuzz as she listened to them chatter about birds, travels, and the countryside.

The one positive throughout the journey was Aunt and Uncle's improved health. When the doctor had come to prescribe Lark a salve for her nettle, he'd overheard Uncle speaking of Aunt's carriage illness. The day after, the physician returned with a tonic to soothe any future head pains or nausea.

Lark hadn't the faintest idea what was in the draught, but it had put both Aunt and Uncle in decidedly jovial moods, which at least proved to soothe Lark's concern for them.

She was also happy that their wellness allowed them to capture Mr. Branok's attention entirely, for she had been serious in her words with him before. They were to be acquaintances. Nothing more, nothing less. No more private chatting. No more flirtatious smiles or glances. And certainly no more whispering.

While she was still coming to terms with the decision and all that it entailed—including losing out on a friendship with the first gentleman who seemed to understand her and accept her for who she was—she was determined to keep her distance from him.

So, when their day-long journey from Yorkshire to Cumbria drew to a close, and the house came into view, Lark blew out a silent breath of relief. That is, until she took in the sight before her.

Greygrove Manor, with its moody exterior and gloomy turrets, was the perfect reflection of her mood—and no doubt a prediction for what was to come over the next fortnight.

She thought perhaps the grey, gothic home was half-hidden by the thick shrouds of dark trees surrounding the property, but as they drew nearer, she realized the manor was truly *that* much smaller than Dreyton Park.

Which meant she would have *that* much more difficulty avoiding Mr. Branok.

Still, the view of Lake Windermere from the entrance of the house was unmatched. As she stretched her limbs from their tightness, she admired the calm, bluish-grey water in the placid aura of the early evening. She hoped to be able to see the water from her bedchamber, but as she was led to where she would reside for the coming fortnight, she soon discovered her only view was of the dense trees at the back of the house—trees that were far too thick to even see a foot within.

She plopped down onto her bed, her shoulders slumped forward as she rubbed the sleep from her eyes. She may have pretended to rest the entire journey, but she hadn't managed a wink in between all the talking of the others.

Perhaps she could take advantage of that now and sleep until morning. It would be a fine excuse not to join the others for dinner tonight. Or maybe she could get by with feigning sleep for the next fortnight so that she might flee to London without another sight of Mr. Branok.

Then again, their convalescence in Town hardly sounded restful with the balls and dinner parties Mother no doubt had lined up for Lark each night. The two-week rest they had from the excursion would absolutely be another strain on her will to survive before they picked back up again and finished the expedition in Cornwall.

A sigh escaped her lips, and tears pricked her eyes at the feeling of confinement now pressing down on her. She just needed to rest. That was all. Tomorrow would not seem so bleak if she simply slept.

But then, what if nothing improved? What if the entire expedition was as disappointing and unbearable as her last week in Yorkshire had been?

A tapping on her door pulled her from her thoughts, and she looked over her shoulder at the closed entryway.

"Come in," she called, ready to tell Penelope she would need help to dress down instead of up that evening.

But when Aunt and Uncle appeared instead, she stood to face them with a look of surprise. "Oh, I did not expect you both this evening."

They closed the door behind them, then faced Lark in unison with pleasant smiles, albeit worried brows.

"Is everything all right? You're both feeling well?" she asked.

Aunt and Uncle exchanged glances of concern, then nodded in unison.

"We are both well, dear Lark," Aunt Harriet replied. "But... are you?"

"Why, of course I am," Lark lied.

Another look between her aunt and uncle was shared, then Aunt reached for Lark's hand and led her to sit on the bed beside her, Uncle remaining standing before them.

"I am glad you say you are well," Aunt began gingerly, "but your Uncle and I cannot help but notice that you do not *seem* so very well. Nor have you the last few days—particularly during the journey here."

Lark didn't know what to say. She knew she hadn't been hiding her moodiness very well, but she hadn't wished for her aunt and uncle to confront her about it.

"I've been a little out of sorts, it is true," she began. "I admit, my pride has been rattled to a degree after falling into the nettles. And then there was the matter of scaring off a number of birds in the days after that."

"Any person would be a little unsettled after those experiences," Uncle reassured her. "But if I may be so bold…?"

He hesitated, pausing until Lark motioned for him to continue.

"You have dealt with far more painful experiences," he began, "and prevailed each and every time. You must allow yourself the opportunity to do so again."

His words spoke a comfort to Lark she wasn't aware she needed. Comfort and encouragement.

She felt the weight shifting around her shoulders, though it did not remove entirely.

"Talk to us, my dear," Aunt gently coaxed, resting a hand on Lark's in her lap. "We are here for you. Always."

Lark drew a settling breath. Aunt Harriet was right. They *were* there for Lark. Not only emotionally, but physically in the Lake District. They had literally come on the excursion *for her.* The least she could do was talk to them, help them understand what she'd been experiencing of late.

"I cannot thank you both enough for being so aware of me and my needs," she began. "And I must admit, I have not been feeling myself lately. This excursion, the entire experience…It has been more difficult than I anticipated."

"In what way?" Aunt asked.

Lark wasn't about to admit the fact that she may or may not have found herself in a compromising situation with a gentleman which led to a desire to kiss him. They would no doubt worry over her as they had with Mr. Yates.

Granted, with Mr. Yates, they had the right to be concerned. But Mr. Branok was no threat. Not anymore.

"I suppose I'm finding it difficult to...to find my place," she stated instead. "I am either too distracting, too knowledgeable, too honest, or too loud. I cannot seem to fit in with anyone— even with like-minded bird observers. I'm too strange wherever I go. I must accept that again."

Aunt squeezed her hand tighter. "My dear, you put far too much pressure on yourself to fit in when you were never meant to."

"But everyone else seems to," Lark continued. "They all have friends and significant others who share their love of observing birds. They all seem to make friends so swiftly, whereas I..." She trailed off with a shrug. "I only wish I could find someone like me with whom to be friends."

Aunt was silent for a moment. "Were you not satisfied with the friendship Mr. Branok offered?"

There it was. The question Lark had been dreading. "No, of course I was grateful for that. But you know full well, a single female cannot be simply friends with a single male, no matter that both of us have decided against matrimony. At any rate, he is far too close with Mr. Chumley, and any gentleman who could befriend such a man could never be a friend of my own."

Uncle seemed to accept her excuse, nodding in agreement. He'd always been protective of Lark due to the gentlemen who mistreated her. He'd taken an instant dislike to Mr. Yates for that reason.

But Aunt hardly seemed convinced with the answer, her eyes studying Lark in silence.

Lark was finished with the conversation, though, so she straightened on her bed and pulled on a smile. "I suppose, if I desire friends, I have to leave my room to find those friends. Mrs. Shepherd and Mrs. Chumley have been generous and kind. Perhaps I can speak with them more at dinner this evening."

"That's my girl," Uncle said with a wink. "Darling?" He offered his hand to Aunt, which she accepted.

"We shall see you downstairs?" Uncle asked.

"Certainly," Lark said, smoothing her dress. "I shall call for Penelope presently."

Uncle nodded, then shuffled down the corridor. Aunt, however, lingered behind. "I'll be just a moment, Francis," she called out, then she turned back to Lark.

"What is it?" Lark asked, feigning curiosity, though dread filled her.

Aunt hesitated again, her eyes narrowed as she lowered her voice. "Forgive me for asking, but…is there anything going on between you and Mr. Branok?"

Lark's cheeks warmed. "Between me and Mr. Branok? Heavens, no. Why do you ask?"

"I used to see certain looks pass between you two during dinner and throughout his classes," she began. "But now, you hardly speak with him. I could not help but wonder if something occurred between the two of you to cause the change in your relationship."

Lark drew steadying breaths. "I assure you, there is no relationship between us, nor shall there ever be one. We are similar in some regards, which can lead to disagreements, but we are acquaintances and always will be."

She spoke so assuredly that Aunt seemed to accept her words. "Very well," she said. "I must have imagined matters. I am wont to do such things, Francis tells me. Well, I shall see you for dinner, yes?"

"Of course."

"Will you not wear the blue gown once again? I did not get

to enjoy seeing you in it the other evening, and Mrs. Chumley went on and on about how beautiful you were."

Lark smiled to hide her grimace. She would never wear that gown again. "I think I would prefer a different color this evening."

"Very well," Aunt shrugged off. "You look lovely in any color."

She bade Lark farewell, then disappeared down the corridor as Lark shut the door behind her.

She shouldn't have agreed to go to dinner. She should have hidden her true feelings, blamed her lack of enthusiasm on being excessively tired.

Because now, she *was* excessively tired, if only due to the very notion of having to play the part of the amiable, approachable Miss Fernside when all she wanted to be was sulky, jaded Lark.

Unfortunately, the only person who accepted her as both was the only person she'd sworn to never be around again.

CHAPTER 21

Dinner passed by slowly, despite Lark being actively engaged in conversation with Mrs. Chumley for the majority of it. Fortunately, Mr. Branok was seated at the opposite end of the table again, though his eyes continuously flitted away from Lark's each time she caught him watching her.

After dinner, Lark was sorely tempted to leave before the gentlemen joined them in the drawing room, but Aunt Harriet must have known she would have attempted to do such, for she kept Lark the center of attention until the men came through.

To her relief, Uncle Francis occupied the standing space to her left—and Aunt sat beside her on her right—so once again, Mr. Branok had no chance to speak with her.

Lark sat near the fire, feeling cold and tired despite her proximity to the flames. The drawing room was comfortable enough with its maroon walls, the wooden flooring covered with large, red and gold tapestries, but she still longed for her warm bed and the privacy of her bedchamber.

The crackling fire in the small, dark hearth punctuated the air between the soft murmur of voices around her, and she felt her attention waver as her eyes grew heavy and dry until she slipped in and out of consciousness.

She hadn't realized she'd dozed off fully until a shuffling on the couch beside her jarred her from her sleep. Her eyes opened, and she straightened from her slightly slumped position to stare at the fire.

"Feeling tired from the journey here?"

Lark stiffened. Mr. Branok's voice spoke beside her instead of Uncle's. That must have been the shuffling she'd heard. How often was this man going to pounce on her when she was unaware?

"I am a little weary," she responded truthfully, though it was not due to the journey.

She glanced around the room. Aunt Harriet spoke on the opposite couch with Mrs. Shepherd, and the rest of the gentlemen stood away from the fire on the other side of the dark, wood-paneled room—Uncle included.

Lark pulled in her lips. Mr. Branok must have been watching her until she'd been left alone, then seized his opportunity to...to what, exactly? Why did he insist on speaking with her, even after she'd been more than clear that they needed to stop?

"I trust you had a pleasant meal," he said next.

She placed her hands in her lap, leaning slightly away from him. "I did, thank you."

She wouldn't ask him how his meal was in return, no matter what politeness demanded.

She faced Aunt and Mrs. Chumley, striving to hear their words so she might join their own conversation to dissuade Mr. Branok from continuing, but the women spoke so quietly, Lark had no hope of hearing them.

"You must be looking forward to your morning walk tomorrow," Mr. Branok said. "Especially in a new location."

Lark pushed aside her conscience. He was trying so hard and

seemed earnest in his endeavors. But she would not give in. Doing so would only open her up to more disappointment.

"I am looking forward to it," she replied. "But I suppose I should retire now so I might awaken early enough. If you'll excuse me."

She made to stand, but his whispered words, soft enough for no one else to hear, reached her ear.

"Miss Fernside, please."

She was going to pretend she hadn't heard him, protect her heart and her peace of mind. But when she made to stand, the subtle movement of his leg made his knee press up against hers, and she paused.

Heat seared through her thin gown, and the desire to feel that warmth for longer grew so strongly within her, she could not pull back. Instead, she peered up at him, the firelight dancing in his eyes and highlighting the look of pleading within them so brightly, she found herself nodding before sense could convince her to do otherwise.

Mr. Branok glanced around the room, no doubt to ensure their conversation remained unheard, but he kept his knee against hers as his voice dropped lower. "I shall be succinct, but if you still wish for our friendship to end, I will, of course, respect your decision." He waited for another nod of understanding from her before continuing. "Firstly, allow me to apologize for my behavior on the"—he cleared his throat—"stairs."

Lark blushed at the mention. More than a week and a half had passed since that night when they'd nearly kissed, but still, the memory was forever branded in her mind. The look of desire in his eyes, the heat blazing through her limbs at his touch, the stirring in her heart to feel him closer. It was as if it had happened yesterday.

"I thought it best to keep away from you after that," he explained, "hoping that would prove my respect for you, but all it did was make me more and more irritable—resulting in my frustration with you falling into the nettles. But I must clarify that I was in no way upset with you and solely upset with myself, for if I had merely behaved as your friend, you would have come to stand beside me when observing the redstart instead of getting caught in the nettles. For that also I must beg your forgiveness, as well as for not keeping you safe to begin with."

Lark listened to his reasoning, each word another salve to place upon her wounds. Her confusion over the last week, her frustration and anger over the man's behavior, slowly seeped away until she was left with nothing but a stirring in the base of her stomach at the knowledge that he had wanted to protect her —that he had wanted her to respect him.

Of course, his actions weren't the best way to go about that, but truthfully, she could see his logic and could not deny that she wouldn't do something similar.

"So," he finished, "shall I leave you alone or...or can you find it in your heart to forgive a fool such as I?"

Lark sighed. "As foolish as you are," she whispered, "you are too charming not to forgive."

His shoulders visibly lowered, and the lines in his brow grew faint.

"But," she continued, "the question remains...are you foolish enough to forgive my own intolerance and curt words?"

"Surely you must know I already have."

They shared a smile, and the tension between them faded. The fire popped beside her, and Lark turned her attention to the flames, watching them lap at the logs within the hearth, though her thoughts were centered instead on her burning skin that was nearly numb now due to Mr. Branok's leg still pressed up against hers.

She sent a quick glance to Aunt, though Mrs. Chumley still spoke with her animatedly, which meant Lark's proximity to Mr. Branok remained unnoticed in the dim light of the room.

Love Is for the Birds

That was more than a relief, for Lark would hate for Aunt to notice—just as greatly as Lark would hate to pull away.

Was Mr. Branok feeling the very same? Was that why he remained with his body shifted toward hers? Or was her spirit longing to be near an ever-unattainable soul?

After another moment, he shifted beside her, moving his leg away from her in the process, and she struggled to keep her spirits up.

"I know we cannot ask after specific numbers," he began in a whisper, "but I have been dying to know, how fairs your list?"

Lark chewed on her lower lip. "You wish me to be honest?"

"Of course."

"I nearly threw it out a hundred times last week."

His lips parted in surprise. "My dear Miss Fernside, how dare you? My being ungentlemanly is in no way an excuse for us to sever the binding agreement we have made for this challenge. We signed the papers, after all."

She attempted to hide her smile at his overt teasing. "Yes, well, I was perfectly ready to accept the consequences of my forfeit."

He paused, holding his chin with his forefinger and thumb in a thoughtful gesture. "You know, I think we quite forgot to establish what those consequences would be."

"You're right. Somehow, I overlooked it. I thought I had been so thorough."

"Not thorough enough, I suppose."

He winked, and she shook her head, though within her, the fire of competition had been relit—as well as another flame within her heart. But this one was sparked by the gentleman beside her and was already glowing so brightly, she wasn't sure she would ever be able to douse it again.

CHAPTER 22

The Lake District – April 27, 1817

Lark's mood the next day improved, but her insecurity around the others remained, for she dreaded making further mistakes and frightening off more birds.

Still, knowing Mr. Branok was on her side once again encouraged her to try a little harder and to be a little braver around the rest of the observers.

As such, when the rain let up that afternoon after church and the party meandered around a section of Lake Windermere, observing the birds flying over and drifting upon the water, she made a calculated effort to not disturb the others and to be the type of observer they would wish to be around. She was polite, kind, and kept her distance. And most importantly, she didn't sneeze, yelp, or fall into nettle.

However, after an hour or two, she grew weary once again of holding her tongue and attempting to be the perfect companion. Did she truly have to be mute to be accepted by others? And if that was the case, did she truly wish to be *around* the others.

Mr. Branok kept her spirits up, which she was more than grateful for. Even if they didn't speak as much as she would have preferred, he kept her on her toes by sneaking glances and sending hidden smiles in her direction as he taught the moving class more about the birds they spied—great crested grebes, cormorants, and terns—and the hungry ducks that circled around them, including goldeneyes, tufted ducks, and red-breasted mergansers.

After a quarter of an hour, the group discovered a few mute swans across the lake, and they shared spyglasses to observe them from their viewpoint at the top of a raised bluff overlooking the water.

Lark joined them in silence, but the edge of the steep-sided bank was narrow, allowing only a few of them at a time to observe the swans. Giving up her position to Mr. Dunn—who grumbled a begrudging "Thank you"—Lark awaited her turn again by peering down the bluff at the opposite side.

Mud filled the bank below, webbed footprints scattered here and there, and Lark narrowed her eyes at the sight of large droppings near the thick bushes that overhung much of the bank.

As improper as it was, she recognized the deposits as those of mute swans, due to their size, shape, and color, as she had observed them from time to time in Suffolk.

With a quick glance at the others who remained preoccupied with the swans in the distance, Lark made her way off the bluff, then down and around to the bank below. Sidestepping mud and droppings, she cast her eyes about the space.

Just as she'd suspected, though still to her delight, through the thick leaves of the bushes at her left, two swans with glorious white feathers floated in the calm water at the edge of the bank, completely hidden from the upper bluff.

Lark smiled at the sight, then softly gasped as one of the swans shifted round to reveal three fuzzy cygnets tucked safely within their mother's wings atop her back. Grey-haired and black-beaked, the baby swans peeped and chirped contentedly at their parents as they enjoyed their moseying on the water.

Lark marveled at the view for a moment, sketching the serene scene and taking avid notes before glancing at the bluff. No one else had peered down to where she was, so no one else knew of the swans and cygnets. She would not wish to disturb the small family by bringing the entire party to see them, but one or two others would not hurt.

Especially if Mr. Branok was one of them.

Anxious to share with the gentleman her discovery, Lark walked back up the muddy pathway, but as she neared the top, she heard Mr. and Mrs. Shepherd instead.

"I'm certain we will have the opportunity to see them again another time, my dear," Mr. Shepherd said softly.

"Yes, I know," his wife returned. "I am merely disappointed, that is all. They were so very far away, I could hardly make them out at all. And…" She dropped her voice further. "And Mr. Dunn is so very large, I feared he might push me over the edge accidentally with his swinging elbows."

Lark stifled a smile as she met them on the pathway.

"Oh, Miss Fernside," Mrs. Shepherd said with a genuine smile. "I wondered where you had got to."

Lark did not hesitate a moment. "Were you hoping to see the swans?"

"We were," Mr. Shepherd said. "My wife has always had a particular affinity for them, but I'm afraid there was not much room for us."

Lark could only smile. "Follow me."

The Shepherds exchanged looks of intrigue as they followed Lark down the muddy pathway to see her findings, and the expression of joy on each of their faces—Mrs. Shepherd as she admired the swans and Mr. Shepherd as he watched his wife—was worth everything to Lark.

Before long, the three of them made their way back up the

pathway, discovering the others had already carried on with their walk along the lake.

"It is unfortunate they were too impatient to wait," Mr. Shepherd said.

"Too impatient and not as skilled as Miss Fernside here," Mrs. Shepherd agreed. "I'm certain you could find any bird you set your mind to."

Lark smiled with humility, and the discomfort she'd felt before shifted off her shoulders.

"Were you able to hear much of Mr. Branok's teachings about the swans earlier?" Lark asked, braving to be herself even more.

"Only a little, I'm afraid," Mrs. Shepherd said. "Do share with us your own knowledge."

Lark was happy to oblige, sharing information about the mute swans mating for life—"Quite like the puffins"—how they ate aquatic vegetation, and how predatorial they become during breeding season.

By the time they caught up with the others, the Shepherds were marveling at Lark's knowledge and about the birds themselves, thanking Lark profusely for sharing the spot with them.

"It was my pleasure," Lark assured them. "Bird observing is far better when shared with others."

She, more than anyone, knew the truth in those words.

They joined the rest of the party, and Aunt and Uncle asked after Lark's location until Mr. Branok spoke about the mallards nearby.

"I've a few of these in my collection," Mr. Gibbon said, motioning to the ducks as they stood together in a half-circle, facing the water licking the shoreline.

"Collection?" the younger Mr. Kay asked.

"Indeed. I've a room dedicated to the several birds I've had stuffed. Unique ones, too. Parrots. Buzzards. Even flamingos."

Lark hid her look of disgust. Taxidermy. She could never

understand such a thing—especially done by those who claimed to love birds.

"You know," Uncle Francis interrupted, "I went to an exotic animal shop once. Cutler's Emporium of Curious Creatures. I went there to speak with...Well, never mind whom. I did, indeed, see the most curious of creatures, though, while there. All living, too. Iguanas, snakes, even a marmoset."

"Mr. Branok," Mr. Chumley said thoughtfully, ignoring Uncle's words, "the owner of your club has a particular affinity for mounting, does he not?"

Mr. Branok's jaw visibly stiffened. "He does."

Lark watched him carefully. Just like before when his club had been mentioned, Mr. Branok grew silent, as if closing off to avoid any mention of it. She still had yet to decipher why, though—and more importantly, what sort of misfit he was to have joined such a club.

"Does he have a large collection?" Mr. Gibbon asked, intrigued.

"Yes. Quite a number of rare animals."

"Marvelous," Mr. Gibbon breathed. "I'd love to see."

"You'll have to get past Lord Blackstone first," Mr. Chumley said with a chuckle.

"Blackstone?" Uncle Francis's blurted question ended the conversation between the others. "As in...*Blackstone's*?"

Lark stared, wondering at his sudden exclamation.

"Yes," Mr. Chumley replied stiffly. "I believe that is what I said."

The lines in Uncle's forehead increased tenfold as he faced Mr. Branok. "You belong to said club?"

Mr. Branok shifted his footing. "I do."

"For how many years?"

"Five, sir."

Uncle didn't respond. Lark stared between him and Mr.

Branok, anxious to decipher what was occurring, but neither man would look at her—and now avoided each other.

The conversation shifted to the ducks once again as Mr. Gibbon asked a clarifying question about which was male and female, but Lark didn't hear Mr. Branok's response, for Uncle pulled Lark behind the group, shifting away to speak in a whisper.

"Did you know Mr. Branok belonged to Blackstone's?" he asked.

Lark shrugged. "He has mentioned it a time or two to the other gentlemen, but I quite forgot until now. I believe Lord Blackstone funds his excursions."

Uncle didn't respond, merely looked away, deep in thought.

Lark had been tempted to ask him about the club long ago, but ever since she'd fallen into the nettle, she'd been determined to forget any thought or care about anything related to Mr. Branok.

Now that things had changed, however, perhaps she could ask him.

"You seem distressed, Uncle. What is the significance of Blackstone's? Is this the club you belong to?"

Uncle straightened. "Certainly not. White's cannot be compared to...Blackstone's is known for ..." He shook his head with a sigh and cast a sidelong glance at Mr. Branok. "Never you mind. Come. Let us rejoin the others."

Lark hesitated, an unsettled feeling burgeoning in the pit of her stomach as concerning thoughts swirled round her mind. Why did Uncle appear so uneasy with Mr. Branok being a part of Blackstone's? Was it simply due to the stigma of those who belonged being misfits? Or was there something else that frightened Uncle? Something that should frighten Lark?

Though she longed for answers to her questions, she did as she was told and rejoined the half-circled party.

"Do tell us, Mr. Branok," Mr. Dunn was saying, "why are females always the uglier of the birds?"

Lark pulled a face. This was one surefire way to ensure she focused on the present—listening to Mr. Dunn's thoughtless words. Only an ignorant, unobservant simpleton would call female birds *ugly*.

Mr. Branok caught her eye. Before, he'd averted his gaze with discomfort due to the conversation. Now, he watched Lark unabashedly, amusement alight in his features, no doubt at the disdain clearly written across her own—especially as Mr. Dunn continued.

"One would think the females would put in a little more effort to be more eye-catching," he said.

Mr. Branok sent Lark a subtle nod of encouragement as if to say, *"Go on, Miss Fernside. Tell him what you truly think."*

She did not have to be told twice.

"One *would* think so," she said, stepping forward to face the entire party. "However, I find that female birds, while unattractive to the untrained eye, are some of the most striking creatures on earth. Yet, even if the females *were* dull and ordinary, the male birds would still do whatever they could to attract—nay, *beg* for attention." She paused, looking to the women around her who were already smiling at her response. "At any rate, no matter the creature, human or bird, the men always do whatever they can to attract attention. All we women must do is simply breathe and they come flocking, do they not?"

Mrs. Chumley, Mrs. Shepherd, and Aunt Harriet laughed in unison. Uncle Francis, though clearly distracted, still smiled, and Mr. Shepherd cried out a, "Hear, hear," with another loving look at his wife.

Mr. Dunn was the furthest thing from being impressed, and Mr. Chumley looked as angry and red as a robin's breast.

Mr. Branok's reaction was what she was most interested in,

however, so when admiration shone in his blue eyes that matched the sparkling water nearby, her heart spread its wings and took flight.

"Right you are, Miss Fernside," he said. "Right you are."

CHAPTER 23

he Lake District – April 30, 1817

A few days after their arrival, the weather took a turn for the worse, and Aunt insisted on keeping Lark inside for fear of her catching a cold.

"It is only ten days until we return to London," Aunt Harriet said. "I cannot in good conscience allow you to return to your mother with a chest cold."

Lark had reluctantly agreed, especially when she discovered the men would be remaining indoors, as well.

However, instead of being treated to time with Mr. Branok, when the group gathered together for tea and conversation, she discovered his absence immediately.

She remained for as long as possible with the present company but soon found herself longing for solitude—if only so she might not have to feign interest in the conversations around her.

Excusing herself, Lark returned to her bedchamber, gathered her collection of Mr. Branok's and Thomas Beswick's books, then made her way to the library where she swiveled around an oversized, single-seat chair to face the window.

There, she nestled into the cushion and pulled out the first volume of Mr. Branok's works, rotating between his words and the view she had out of the window as rain poured down onto the green grass and thick trees beyond.

The room was warm and comforting, the dark wood shelves and green furnishings made only slightly brighter by the dim light seeping in through the many windows that made up nearly all of the west wall.

Lark breathed a sigh of peace, finally feeling at one with herself.

The last few days she'd had with Mr. Branok had been a dream—occasionally flirting, regularly whispering, and frequently sharing in the joys of observing new birds like ospreys, ring ouzels, and jackdaws. Mr. Branok had often sought her out and asked for her knowledge on the birds they discovered, as well as any other information she might be willing to divulge, causing Lark to feel seen, heard, and appreciated.

Yes, she was quite content with their relationship the way it was—their *friendship* the way it was.

And yet, her emotions continually and errantly strayed. Each time he helped her down from the carriage, warmth rushed through her limbs to remain in her heart like an inextinguishable flame. And each time they spoke in hushed tones by the fire at night, her soul yearned to be nearer to him, so much so that when she was away from him, she could hardly focus on anything *but* him.

This was her problem now. For even though she attempted to read more about the schomburger from the West Indies and its reddish-brown color and long bill, all she could think about was Mr. Branok, if he had discovered the bird during his own time in the West Indies…and how he might have looked in the heat of the day while there.

Tanned features. Sweat beading across his brow. Dark blond

hair dipping over his bright blue eyes that matched the skies above. Cravat and waistcoat gone—it was too hot to wear such things out there, after all.

He would be hunched over low, hidden in long grass. A thin shirt stretched across his broad shoulders. Perhaps he'd unbuttoned the top, allowing the contours of his chest and collar bone to be just visible. His lips would be slightly parted as he released soft breaths to avoid scaring off the bird. Lips that were formed, wet from just licking them to keep them moist, and then—

Footsteps sounded behind her, and Lark started, hefting herself out of her very unladylike daydream. With a racing heart, she peered around the corner of her chair to see who had disturbed her from such enjoyable thoughts.

Her stomach dipped at the sight of Mr. Branok himself entering the room. He didn't see her, moving instead to the bookshelf where he faced the six shelves stuffed with brown, red, and blue leather-bound books.

In silence, she shifted her own books on her lap so Beswick's was on top. Once secure in her knowledge that Mr. Branok would not discover her reading his books out of her own personal collection, she took a moment to unabashedly observe him as he perused the shelves.

He wore no jacket—and his waistcoat was buttoned to his cravat—but it contoured his broad shoulders closely as he held his hands behind his back.

She should probably be more ashamed of spying on him, but the time between them had been so comfortable, so casual, that she could not help but treat this situation as *he* would. It was much more fun this way anyway.

After a moment, he turned away from the shelves and faced the windows instead, walking forward to better view the grounds. Was he watching for birds? As Uncle would say, *"The weather is not even fit for ducks."*

He appeared pensive, a small smile on his lips, and Lark

longed to know of what he thought until he turned to leave. Before he managed two steps, however, he caught her gaze and stopped, pulling back with a smile.

"Miss Fernside? My apologies. I did not see you there."

"I know," she answered with a smile of her own.

He narrowed his eyes. "How long have you been watching me?"

"Since you entered the room."

"And you did not think to alert me of your presence?"

"I thought it would be more enjoyable this way."

"You are beginning to sound like me, Miss Fernside."

They shared a smile.

"Did you not wish to visit with the others this morning?" she asked.

"I did, but my time was spent this morning writing letters of business to my steward." He paused. "Did you not wish to visit with them either?"

"I was for a moment, but I prefer reading."

Mr. Branok glanced toward the doorway, as if wondering whether or not he should leave since the two of them were alone, but he seemed to think better of it, taking a few steps toward her instead.

His gaze dropped to the books in her lap, and she breathed silently in relief that she'd thought to hide his books. They'd grown closer as friends, but not nearly close enough for her to reveal just how obsessed she had been—and still was—with his writing.

"Reading, I take it?" he asked, motioning to the books.

"I was, yes."

"Which books?" He tipped his head to the side to read the spines, but she discreetly shifted her hand to hide them.

"Thomas Beswick," she said.

"Ah, of course. I trust you are not using the birds within those pages to add to your list."

He gave her a look of warning, and she attempted to tamp down how greatly she enjoyed the attention.

"I would never dream of breaking the rules, Mr. Branok. You know that."

"Mmm. Yes, I do." He tipped his head to the side again. "What other books have you there?"

"Oh, just more of his."

"I wasn't aware he'd written so many."

She scrambled to think of a response, and in so doing, Mr. Branok had a moment to witness her hesitation. Once again, he narrowed his eyes. "Is there a reason you are keeping the other books from me? To hoard the knowledge to yourself, perhaps? Become the better bird observer, after all?"

"No, that would be ridiculous," she replied.

"Then why do you not tell me what other books you have?"

"I never said I would not."

"Very well, then tell me."

She drew a deep breath. Perhaps she could play it off coolly, as if she hardly cared. She raised Beswick's to reveal Mr. Branok's own books. "Oh, they are yours, I suppose."

"You suppose?" He was barely restraining his smile now as he took a step closer.

"Yes. I...I just saw them and thought I might peruse them." That was more or less the truth. She needn't mention they were her *personal* copies, nor that she'd "just" seen them on her bedside table.

He moved forward, leaning toward her. "Which volumes?"

"Let us see," she began, reading them as if she didn't already know. "Volumes one, three, and...five."

"Ah, of course."

He peered closer, his head just over her shoulder. Her mind swirled at his closeness as the scent of his earthy cologne wafted around her. Still, she forced herself to remain still, if only to pretend she was unaffected by his proximity.

LOVE IS FOR THE BIRDS

"Those volumes hold some of my favorite birds I've ever recorded," he said. He wandered away from her, taking a seat diagonally from her, though he faced away from the window and toward Lark. "Have you read them before?"

This was the question she'd been dreading—no doubt the question he'd been dying to ask her for weeks.

The innocent smile on his lips and the mischievous look in his eyes told her that he already knew the answer to that question. After all, she'd essentially admitted to reading his work when she'd critiqued him for mixing up the redstart and the golden-crested wren. But her pride hindered the truth from coming forth more fully, so she remained silent.

"It is a simple enough question, Miss Fernside," he began. "Yet I detect a struggle within you to reply. Why is that?"

His smile grew ever wider.

"Truthfully?" she asked. He nodded. "I do not wish to inflate your head to an even greater size than it already is."

He laughed. "Always the flatterer."

"I do try."

"Come now, my friend," he coaxed. "Surely you can tell me if you have read my work before now."

Lark pulled in her lips. Very well. If he wished for her to bear her soul, he would need to bear his own first.

"I will tell you that and more," she began, "if you tell me why you become upset whenever Blackstone's is mentioned."

Instantly, his features fell, but he picked them up swiftly with an easy smile. "You do drive a hard bargain. Though I am minded to accept your suggestion. But first answer me this…Do you care that I am part of such a club?"

"Not in the slightest," she answered truthfully. "I know nothing of gentlemen's clubs. I am merely curious after seeing your reaction when speaking of them."

And Uncle Francis's reaction, but she would keep that to herself.

Mr. Branok seemed to relax more, resting his elbows on both sides of his chair, causing his shoulders to lift as he laced his fingers together before him. "I am more than happy to explain then. You see, many years ago, my father belonged to White's. He spoke so highly of the club, I had a mind to join after his death. However, when a friend of mine was denied membership due to his reduced circumstances, I realized how shallow most of the members were and promptly severed any desire to join. Lord Blackstone discovered what had occurred and invited me to join his club, instead. It is as simple as that."

But Lark was not quite satisfied. "I have heard Lord Blackstone's club is filled with…"

"Misfits?" Mr. Branok finished. "Those who do not fit into Society's standards? That is precisely what we are."

She paused. "Forgive me, but I struggle to see how you fit into that category. Indeed, *I* would fit within such a club better than you."

He chuckled. "It takes more than being an outsider, I'm afraid." He glanced at the doorway, then back at her. "Lord Blackstone only permits men to join who have been blackballed from other clubs."

Her brows pulled together. "Blackballed?"

"When someone is denied membership in a club," he explained, "for one reason or another."

Her mind raced. "So you were blackballed yourself?"

"I was."

He gave nothing more, so she did not press him. It really was none of her concern. At any rate, if his friend has been denied due to social status, then whatever Mr. Branok *had* done could not be so very bad either.

"This is why I tend to keep my membership of the club quiet," he said. "Many men look down on Blackstone's due to its beginnings, and while I try not to trouble myself over other's

LOVE IS FOR THE BIRDS

opinions, I find most of Society is far more agreeable when they are in the dark about certain matters."

Lark raised a shoulder. "Or they become more dangerous."

His eyes met hers. She knew he wished to ask her to clarify, but all he responded with was, "Just so."

She looked away, fearing he might read her very thoughts, and it seemed to break the spell between them.

"What was it about Blackstone's that made you wish to join that club, as opposed to all the others?" she asked next.

"In truth, I didn't wish to in the beginning," he replied. "But Lord Blackstone approached me and convinced me to join with the promise of funding my expeditions."

"It certainly isn't a terrible trade."

"No, indeed. I owe him a great deal." His eyes took on a far-off look. "There are times when I wish I wasn't a part of the club. But were it not for Lord Blackstone and his funding, I would not be where I am today."

Dread crept up behind Lark like a dark cloud. He'd mentioned this before—how expensive excursions were—and she had done her best to tamp down her fears. But now, she had to ask. She had to know if her dreams of exploring the world were even a possibility.

"Is that true?" she began. "Surely you could have accomplished the traveling and publishing on your own."

Such an idea wasn't too far-fetched. The man was wealthy enough—he'd mentioned having his own estate before and certainly looked the part.

But Mr. Branok shook his head resolutely. "No, I would not have published a single volume of work without his endorsement. Field journals do not generate much of a return, and even though they sell now more than ever, it is due to Lord Blackstone's agreement with the publishers and printers. He gives generous donations, and they continue printing my volumes of work."

Lark's heart thudded painfully against her chest. "And the excursions?"

He leaned back in his seat with a sigh. "They would be even more impossible to continue without Lord Blackstone. I attempted to embark on a voyage on my own once. I'm sure you can guess where."

She pressed down her swirling stomach to answer. "India?"

He smiled. "India. My parents longed to see the country—its culture, wildlife, mountain ranges, and deserts—so when they passed, I adopted the dream myself. To be able to see what they longed to see…I could only imagine how wonderful it would be. However. I was woefully unprepared to accomplish all that is required. For officially sanctioned excursions—which is what is necessary to see more than a handful of birds—not only is the cost incredible to begin with, but it increases exponentially with each new day spent away from England. One must also take into account the proper permissions to travel from the Crown itself, as well as the countries one is visiting. A ship must be procured and an able-bodied crew.

"There is also the matter of supplies, different money for each country, food to eat, and accommodations for all involved. One must also acquire a knowledgeable and dependable guide so time is not wasted exploring areas with no birds. There is also the risk of contracting potential diseases, so one must know how to handle sequestering." He ran his fingers through his hair. "The list goes on and on. Fortunately, Lord Blackstone has endless wealth *and* unbelievable connections in seemingly every part of the world. Without them. I wouldn't have a hope of seeing what I have. Nor would I have any chance of one day exploring India."

He finally stopped, peering over at Lark. "So there you have it. All the reasons for why I keep quiet about my membership to Blackstone's—and why I must remain a part of it. Despite my disapproval of Lord Blackstone's *collection*."

Love Is for the Birds

He grimaced, and Lark forced a smile, though she felt her world caving in around her. Were her dreams truly for naught? She had wealth enough for an excursion or two, she was absolutely certain. She didn't need to go on hundreds of them. But if Mr. Branok, famed and well-known as he was, had to rely on this benefactor, how would Lark ever be able to accomplish on her own all that he'd laid out? And how would she *ever* find someone to help her and be willing to invest his time in a single female who had only been on one excursion in her life?

"Have I upset you?" Mr. Branok asked. "Do you disapprove of me remaining in such an odious club?"

"No," she said truthfully.

She could not blame him for missing the real reason she was upset—she'd always told him she was happy with simply exploring England. She also couldn't blame him for swallowing his pride to fulfill his dreams. Not when her *own* dreams were being ignited by a flame of disappointments. She would do anything to see them realized. But then, what if there was *nothing* to be done?

"Are you certain?" Mr. Branok pressed, his brow pursed with concern after her silence.

Lark forced her mind to remain in the present. She didn't know what the future held. But she did know, in this moment, she was on an excursion *now*—with Mr. Branok, no less—and for the time being, that would be enough.

"Yes," she replied, her smile more sincere this time. "I care not what club a man belongs to, nor what he did to become rejected by others. One's actions speak louder than another's words anyway."

His eyes softened as he watched her. "Once again, wise words from Miss Fernside." His smile faltered. "But unfortunately, many men, even *good* men, cannot look beyond this sort of thing."

His eyes delved into hers, and Lark knew he spoke of Uncle

Francis. His reaction to Blackstone's three days prior had been obvious. But she wasn't concerned. She would simply tell Uncle he needn't worry over Mr. Branok belonging to such a club. After all, how terrible could Blackstone's be if they welcomed individuals who did not belong elsewhere?

"My Uncle is of a sound mind and heart," she said softly. "He is protective of me, as any guardian ought to be. But he knows a good man when he sees one, I assure you."

Mr. Branok's eyes still searched hers warily, but he nodded all the same before clearing his throat and blinking away the last of their serious conversation.

"Well," he said, patting his hands against his thighs, "I believe it is your turn to speak now."

Lark's stomach flopped over itself with nerves. He was right. It was her turn.

"Yes," she finally responded. "I have read your books before."

His smile filled her soul with as much warmth as the sun.

"How many of them?" he asked.

She closed her eyes. "All of them. Except your latest, of course. And…" She paused, pressing her hands against the books on her laps. "And these are my own personal copies."

"I assumed as much. They look a little worn." His voice held a smile to it. "Just how many times have you read each of them?"

Her cheeks warmed. "I cannot be sure."

"How about you give me an estimation, then."

She opened one eye, peeking at him through the crack between her lashes. He was positively beaming. "More than…six or seven times each. If not more."

His brow raised. "Truly?"

She opened both eyes and faced him more directly. "Do you believe I would ever admit to such if it were not true?"

He didn't respond, staring at the pile of books in her lap as if attempting to calculate her response.

"Back on our first day in the carriage," he began, "you

mentioned books that took you on figurative trips around the world. That they provided you with being able to see more than you ever would have dreamed." He caught her eye again. "You were referring to my own books?"

She swallowed the last of her pride that remained and nodded. "Yes, I was specifically referring to yours. I know nothing of the world beyond your books."

He didn't say anything, his eyes searching hers in silence.

"What is it?" she asked. "Attempting to decide how best to tease me?"

CHAPTER 24

No, Henry was not attempting to decide how to best tease Miss Fernside. He was attempting to decide how to respond at all.

He'd had a handful of individuals express their love for his volumes of work, but he was no fool. They were field journals, not literary masterpieces.

So, now, to have this intelligent, observant, talented woman admitting to reading his books multiple times to help her see the world when she was incapable of doing so...he was overcome.

"I put in a great deal of work with each book," Henry began, "and I always hope that my findings will inspire others. To hear that...To see that you..." He trailed off with a shake of his head. "You have touched my heart this morning, Miss Fernside. Touched my heart and humbled me."

Her embarrassment melted away, her hazel eyes watching him with such focus, he nearly became unnerved, but he maintained her stares so she might know he spoke the truth.

"You must have thought me so callous, so detached from reality when we first met," he continued. "To think I attempted to prevent individuals from calling themselves observers simply because they were incapable of leaving their homes." He grimaced. "I truly did not wish to cause offense. And I am sorry that I so clearly did."

Her features softened as much as her voice. "All is well, Mr. Branok."

And just like that, she'd forgiven him again. He could not look away from her this time. She glowed in the grey light of the morning's rain. Flawless skin, warm eyes, soft curls. Lips coaxing and tempting as they smiled at him. Lips he'd had the chance to taste before—but would never have again.

He and Miss Fernside had made such progress to become better friends. But then, the look in her eyes—and what he assumed was in his own—was anything but friendship.

Which was precisely why he needed to look away. Doing so would help him prevent another mistake of nearly kissing her. He respected her too greatly—just as he respected their mutual desire to remain single—to allow himself to falter again.

Unless...unless Miss Fernside just so happened to change her mind in a few years.

He cleared his throat, setting aside the ridiculous notion to return to the more platonic—and safer—conversation from before.

"So you truly have read my work over and over again?" he asked.

She sighed, clearly giving up her denial. "I have."

"Then how on earth did you confuse me with Mr. Dunn if you were so intimately aware of my work."

Her high cheekbones painted pink. "I had never seen you before. Though that was not due to any lack of effort. You are the reason I chose to—"

She stopped abruptly, her eyes wide and lips parted.

"I'm the reason you chose to what exactly?" he pressed.

She held her lower lip between her teeth, tantalizing, though he knew she was not meaning to be. "Never mind."

As if there was any possible way he could let his curiosity go. "Come now, Miss Fernside. Surely we are past feeling embarrassment around each other."

"Surely we are not."

He scooted forward to the edge of his seat, shifting to face her more fully and casting her his most charming smile. "I promise you are safe to tell me."

"No, it is far too telling."

"What if I promise not to tease you?"

She shook her head.

"If I promise not to respond at all?"

"No."

"It really is that telling?" he asked.

"It really is that *humiliating*."

He thought for a moment. "What if I agree to remove ten birds from my list?"

"That would be against the rules."

"Very well. May I beg?"

"Certainly. But it won't work. There is no amount of begging in this world that would convince me to—"

Her words stopped, and she gasped as Henry left his chair behind to take a knee before her, wrapping his hands around one of hers as he held it just above her lap.

With wide eyes, she stared across at him. "Mr. Branok, what on earth are you doing?" She glanced over her shoulder at the empty doorway. "Suppose someone sees you. Imagine what they would say."

He ignored her words, catching her eyes and refusing to let go as he stroked his hands across her bare fingers. "I am begging you, Miss Fernside, on bended knee."

She blushed, shaking her head as amusement returned to her eyes. "You have clearly taken leave of your senses, sir."

She tried to pull her hand away, but he held fast. Perhaps he *had* taken leave of his senses. Did he not just tell himself that drawing closer to her would be a mistake?

Ah, well. What did he know anyway?

"Miss Fernside," he began with an airy tone, "would you please do me the honor of telling me the truth about what you had been about to say? For I must confess, I shall die a slow and agonizingly painful death should I live out the rest of my days without the knowledge. I beg you, my lady—nay, I plead with you—to release me from my prison."

"Very well," she said in a sharp whisper, "I shall tell you, but only if you release me from this compromising position."

He grinned. "Your wish is my command, my lady." He bowed over her hand, then finally released her as he sat back in his seat.

"Heavens above," she muttered, holding her hands in her lap as she shook her head, though her eyes shone with delight.

"So," he began, not missing a beat from where they had been before he'd knelt, "you were saying."

She hesitated again, and he made to move toward her, but she held her hands up to stop him. "Very well, I shall tell you. I was merely going to say, that..." She paused. "That I came on this tour with the very purpose of meeting you and being instructed by you."

Henry stared. She had to be teasing. "Miss Fernside, you promised to tell me the truth."

"That *is* the truth," she insisted.

He narrowed his eyes, still unconvinced. Although, hadn't she let it slip weeks ago that she'd come for him? "I thought you came for the birds."

"That was only my second purpose. More than anything, I wished..." She blew out a sigh, pressing a hand to her brow. "I cannot believe I am admitting to this." She muttered another unintelligible sentence before continuing. "I have longed to meet you for years now, ever since I first stumbled upon your books. So when I saw your name on the list, I knew I would join the excursion with the main purpose of seeing you and telling you how long I've admired you and your works." She buried her face in her hands. "There. Are you satisfied?"

Henry thought he had been surprised before. Now? He was astonished. She'd come...for him?

"Have you nothing to say to the woman you've just discovered to be a shameless, prowling huntress?" she asked, peeking just above her fingertips.

"I...I find myself speechless," he uttered.

"If I would have known that was all it took to silence you, I might've told you all of this weeks ago."

He laughed. "I am equally flattered and surprised. And a touch frightened."

"Due to my clear obsession, no doubt."

"No. I am frightened that I've been an utter disappointment."

She lowered her hands with a sigh, her petite shoulders slumped slightly forward. "Well, you oughtn't be concerned on that account. At the risk of further puffing up your pride, I will tell you that being with you has far exceeded my expectations."

Her sincerity touched him again. He longed to tell her his own feelings about the expedition—how she'd made it the most wonderful and engaging of his life. How she'd brightened his world and soothed his soul.

But she spoke again before he could say a word in response.

"Will I see you at dinner tonight?" she asked softly, staring at her fingers splayed across her books—*his* books.

She was ending the conversation, which was probably for the best. He needed to leave before he said something he couldn't take back. "Yes, I will be there. I trust you will, as well?"

She nodded in silence.

Regretfully, he stood. "I will take my leave of you, then. So long as you promise we shall speak more this evening?"

She peered up at him, her eyes soft. "Of course."

He gave a short bow, then turned to leave, but she stopped him. "Mr. Branok?"

"Yes?"

She hesitated. "Thank you."

"For what, Miss Fernside?"

"For accepting me as I am." To his surprise, tears glistened in her eyes.

Henry could not keep from her any longer. Slowly, he reached down, taking her hand in his and bending low to place a kiss on the back of her soft skin.

He closed his eyes as he did so, lingering a moment, memorizing the feel of her hand in his, the warmth of her skin upon his lips, the scent of her swirling in his mind, until finally, he pulled back with a lingering look in her direction.

"It is my pleasure to know you as you are, Miss Fernside," he whispered, then he gently released her hand, delivered another bow, and walked from the room.

CHAPTER 25

The Lake District – May 5, 1817

Over the next several days, the rain fell in droves. Though the women remained indoors, the men ventured forth each morning, returning in good spirits despite being thoroughly drenched.

Henry could only imagine how Miss Fernside felt, being trapped within the confines of Greygrove Manor, but they'd both agreed to continue their challenge, despite her being locked away.

"I do not think it fair for me to add birds to my list when you cannot," Henry had told her.

But Miss Fernside had insisted. *"If you don't know I am still looking for birds out of the window every moment of the day, you are a greater simpleton than I thought."* Then her hazel eyes had sparkled.

So, Henry did his best to continue finding birds around him as he walked with the other gentlemen each morning, if only because he'd promised to do so.

But despite his best attempts, the birds were fewer and farther between, which pecked at the other men's patience.

Henry tried to keep them all satisfied, but doing so was difficult when something else was also niggling at his repose.

That of Mr. Haskett's new and decided intolerance for Henry.

Henry had hoped he'd imagined the change that had come over the gentleman, but ever since Lord Blackstone's name had been mentioned a few days prior, Miss Fernside's uncle had essentially ended all friendly interaction with Henry.

Mr. Haskett was still respectful, but gone were their conversations during carriage rides, replaced with stiff silence and lowered brows. And gone was Mr. Haskett's interest in Henry's travels, for the man could barely stomach a glance in his direction, even when Henry instructed the party or taught more about the birds in the Lake District.

Henry had attempted to speak with Miss Fernside on the matter, but their conversations when her uncle was near had become painfully stinted, for Mr. Haskett's hawk-like eyes watched them devotedly.

One morning, nine days after their arrival in the Lake District, Henry plucked up his resolve to confront the gentleman. He hardly cared if Mr. Haskett approved of his choice in club, but knowing that he was Miss Fernside's uncle, Henry needed to put forth more effort, if only to keep his friendship with Miss Fernside intact.

With the rain still pouring forth from the dark skies above, Henry joined the gentlemen on their daily walk near the lake. He attempted time and again to walk beside Mr. Haskett, but the man was adept at avoidance.

Still, after his fourth attempt, Henry was successful, catching Mr. Haskett when the man became distracted with a nearby eider duck.

"Strange to see one so far beyond the coastline," Henry began, "is it not?"

Mr. Haskett visibly stiffened. "Indeed, sir."

His cravat stood tall and crisp, skimming the bottom of his ears as he maintained his view directly ahead.

They stood for a moment in silence. Henry struggled internally between his lack of concern over the man's opinion and his desire to maintain a positive relationship.

Think of Miss Fernside.

"How are your niece and wife fairing remaining indoors so frequently?" Henry asked next.

"I believe they are quite content."

Henry could have laughed. Did the man know his niece at all? Miss Fernside was no doubt beside herself.

"You must miss walking with them," Henry tried next.

"I do." His jaw flinched, then he turned to face Henry directly. "So you are a member of Blackstone's."

Henry nearly balked at the sudden change in conversation—and what it shifted to. This was the last thing he wished to discuss with the prejudiced gentleman.

"Yes, I am, sir."

"And you find that Lord Blackstone treats you well?"

"Indeed. He is a kind man, if not a little eccentric. But then, most of us are in our own ways."

He needn't share how greatly he disapproved of the viscount's gallery or the way he prattled on and on. Mr. Haskett hardly seemed impressed as it was.

"And are you acquainted with many of the men in your club?" the man asked next.

Henry hesitated. Mr. Haskett was clearly fishing, but for what fish, Henry couldn't be sure. "I am with a certain number."

His lips thinned. "What of Mr. Sebastian Drake?"

Mr. Drake? What on earth had he to do with anything? "I know him, yes."

"Are the two of you merely acquaintances or have you struck up a friendship with him?"

Henry fought his every instinct to maintain his footing. Mr.

LOVE IS FOR THE BIRDS

Haskett's questioning was so forceful, so strange, Henry wasn't quite sure what to make of it. What was with this sudden obsession with Mr. Drake, of all people?

Furthermore, what right did Mr. Haskett have to interrogate Henry in such a way? He had a mind to fight back.

Miss Fernside. Think of Miss Fernside.

"We are merely acquaintances, sir," Henry replied, his jaw tight. "But what I know of him, I believe to be honorable."

Mr. Haskett sniffed, raising his chin with an air of superiority Henry couldn't understand. "If you'll excuse me. I promised Mr. Dunn I would share my latest find with him."

With that, he bowed, then turned on his boot and stalked away.

Henry stared after him, dumbfounded and crestfallen. That simply could not have gone worse.

"Morning, Mr. Branok."

Henry turned to find Mr. Shepherd by his side, a friendly smile on his face.

"Mr. Shepherd," he greeted. "Good morning."

Mr. Shepherd's smile faded. "Are you well, sir?"

Henry stared after Mr. Haskett's departing figure, the man walking right past Mr. Dunn to forge ahead of the group.

"Yes, I'm well," Henry replied. "Though I fear Mr. Haskett is not."

To Henry's surprise, Mr. Shepherd chuckled.

"Why do you laugh?" he asked.

"Well, because it is obvious," Mr. Shepherd said knowingly. "Mr. Haskett's changed behavior. His sudden interrogations. It all adds up rather nicely."

Henry faced him more directly. "Adds up to what, exactly? Him disapproving of my being a part of Blackstone's?"

Mr. Shepherd pulled back with a frown. "Blackstone's? Heavens no. He differs now in his behavior toward you because of…" He hesitated. "Because of your marked interest in his niece."

The blood drained from Henry's face. "What?"

Mr. Shepherd's mouth opened as he struggled to speak. "I… forgive me. I thought, well, it is rather obvious that you and Miss Fernside have taken a liking to one another. I could only assume that Mr. Haskett is attempting to decipher if you might be a good enough match for his niece."

The air rushed from Henry's lungs as if he'd been struck, the words swimming through his mind.

Rather obvious.

Taken a liking to one another.

Might be a good enough match.

Good heavens. What had he done?

"I'm terribly sorry, Mr. Branok," Mr. Shepherd said, looking truly repentant. "I did not mean to assume…"

Henry shook his head. This was his own fault. This was all his own doing. Flirting with Miss Fernside, singling her out, *seeking* her out. He'd hoped, being on this excursion—being so used to living out of Society's notice on his *own* excursions— that his time with Miss Fernside would be ignored, chalked off as innocent fun. After all, the entire party had been made aware of his and Miss Fernside's distinct desire to remain single.

But of course others would assume that their fun was a mask for something more between them. And of course Mr. Haskett would think the same.

Would the man press them to marry simply to save Miss Fernside's name from ruin? Or worse…had Henry done anything *to* ruin her name? He would never forgive himself if he injured the woman—or forced her to marry when she so clearly did not wish to.

But perhaps he'd caught the rumors in time. Perhaps he could put an end to them now, at this very moment. Save them both from going through the same thing he'd experienced years before.

"There is no need to apologize," he reassured Mr. Shepherd, who looked more and more regretful of his words. "I am grateful you have made me aware of what is being said about Miss Fernside and myself, but I must say, I am quite shocked. For she and I have both shared many times with nearly all of you that we have no interest in marriage—whether between ourselves or others."

Images flashed in his mind as he spoke the words. He and Miss Fernside standing before a vicar, exchanging vows of eternal companionship. The two of them venturing forth to distant lands, discovering new birds. Smiles shared, love shared...

But he set them aside. That was in neither of their futures. They'd both made it abundantly clear from the start—and so had Lord Blackstone.

"Mr. Shepherd," he continued, "if you would be so kind to tell me, how far have these rumors spread?"

"I am uncertain," Mr. Shepherd said at once. "Most of the men here do not care about such matters. The women might speak more, but my wife..." He hesitated. "My wife speaks with me often. She notices things many do not. Miss Fernside's eyes on you. The way she brightens when you are near. Perhaps she was mistaken, though."

Was that true? Did Miss Fernside watch him from afar? Did she find happiness when they were together?

He pressed a hand to his brow to force these new images aside. He should not care at all what Miss Fernside did in regard to watching him or her feelings for him—other than that of friendship.

Anything else would force both of them to alter lifelong plans, and neither of them were willing to do so.

"Might I ask a favor of you?" Henry asked next.

"Of course. Anything, Mr. Branok."

"I know rumors have minds of their own," he began, "but if you were to hear any other words about Miss Fernside and myself, would you be so kind as to correct them directly? I do not wish for Miss Fernside to be damaged by any of this."

Mr. Shepherd nodded at once. "Of course, sir. I will see it as my duty. Mrs. Shepherd will be more than happy to oblige, as well."

Relief filled Henry's heart, though he was not naïve enough to believe the rumors had not already spread. If one person noticed, many more would in time.

"I can't thank you enough, Mr. Shepherd," Henry said, delivering another nod of gratitude before excusing himself.

He strode away in the opposite direction of the others. He needed time to think. Time to decide how to best proceed.

And more than anything, he needed time to figure out how exactly he would tell Miss Fernside that their friendship was being sabotaged by the opinions of others, all while keeping to himself that his own wayward and confusing thoughts of spending the rest of his life with her were also to blame.

CHAPTER 26

Lark feared she might truly go mad. Multiple days indoors would do that to anyone, but to her? She couldn't take it any longer.

Sitting in the drawing room with the other women, she stared at her journal in her lap. Over the last few days, she'd spotted only three birds from the window, and each time, they'd been so far away, she hadn't been able to decipher what they were.

After such disappointment, she'd resigned herself to looking at the birds in her books. But not even that had managed to capture her attention today, so she'd turned her focus to updating her lists—her lifelong list, the birds she'd written down for the challenge with Mr. Branok, and the ones she'd cataloged for Mr. Chumley's future use.

That had only taken half the morning, however, so now, she sat near the window, staring mindlessly at her journal as the other women sat near the fire with their stitching.

"I've a cousin who lives near here," Mrs. Shepherd was saying. "in Coniston, I believe. Amy Paxton. Although, I suppose it is Amy Eastwood now. She married Mr. William Eastwood not too long ago."

She continued speaking of how her cousin came to move to the Lake District, and Lark did her best to listen, but soon, her mind wandered as she stared at the raindrops sliding down the window.

She enjoyed walking in the rain. The cold was always invigorating, and the sound tranquil. She wasn't allowed to walk in it very often, though. Aunt and Uncle truly cared for her well-being, and she understood their concern, but she'd always had trouble remaining indoors during rainstorms ever since Mr. Yates.

He hadn't ever allowed her out in the rain. His was not for care, but for control. If she did venture forth, he had taken to berating her for days, criticizing her, and threatening to withhold his supposed love from her. Ever since then, remaining indoors and not having the freedom to explore on her own, always brought back those unpleasant memories.

Lark pressed her eyes together, squeezing the thoughts out as she laid her head against the back of her chair.

"Poor Miss Fernside," Mrs. Chumley said from across the room. Lark looked over to see compassion in the woman's eyes. "You must be so terribly bored, my dear."

Lark forced a smile. "I am well enough. Though, I do wish for the rain to cease."

"As do we all," Mrs. Shepherd agreed.

"Indeed," Aunt Harriet said.

"I become restless when I cannot walk outside," Mrs. Chumley continued. "When Mr. Chumley leaves for weeks at a time, I grow ever so weary. That is why I forced myself upon this expedition with him," she said with a conspiratorial smile. "And why I coerced him into bringing women along this time, too."

LOVE IS FOR THE BIRDS

Lark smiled. The woman must be a force to be reckoned with in her marriage. She seemed so softspoken and passive.

Mrs. Shepherd looked at Lark. "You must simply find something to do to occupy your attention, Miss Fernside. Do you have any stitching? If my hands are busy, so are my thoughts."

Lark agreed. But not even drawing helped this morning. "Thank you. But I'm content enough to sit here for the time being."

"Poor dear," Mrs. Chumley repeated with a sigh. "This is why husbands come in such use. If you ever change your mind about matrimony, Miss Fernside, you must find a husband who does not mind the rain and loves birds as much as you do, my dear. Then you shall be able to do all sorts of things."

Lark tensed. She so despised this conversation. No woman could ever understand her desire to remain unmarried. Then again, no woman understood the heartache she went through with Mr. Yates.

No woman aside from Aunt Harriet. She glanced at Lark with a wary smile, but Lark gave her a settling nod. When she was younger, she'd found it difficult to stand up for herself. Now, however, she was more than capable of doing so.

"Thank you for the suggestion," Lark said genuinely, then she stood from her chair and closed her book. "I do believe I shall take Mrs. Shepherd's advice and find my stitching. If you will excuse me, ladies. I shall return in a moment."

They nodded, and Lark gave Aunt another reassuring smile before leaving the room. In the corridor, she finally allowed her shoulders to fall and her smile to fade away.

She would not be returning to the drawing room. Not that morning, anyway. She'd been indoors for long enough—she'd been subjected to memories of Mr. Yates for long enough—that she was finished.

Donning her half-boots, pelisse, bonnet, and thick gloves, she sent a note to Aunt to let her know she should not expect

235

Lark to return for an hour, then slipped down the stairs in silence.

She did not breathe easily until she left the confines of Greygrove behind and stepped onto the wet, green grass at the back of the manor.

There, she paused, allowing the tapping of the rain on her bonnet to fill her senses and the cool air around her to fill her lungs. This was precisely what she'd needed. She was feeling better already.

While fully aware that the drawing room was on the other side of the house and the gentlemen were still on their walk, Lark still wished for privacy. So, with a smile—a true smile—on her lips, she crossed the grounds in peace toward the thick grove of trees at the back of the property.

The wind slipped around the nape of her neck, invigorating her steps and pushing her forward until she was in the shelter of the trees. There, she removed her bonnet and raised her face to the branches above, allowing the few droplets of moisture that slipped past the leaves to caress her face.

Finally, she'd escaped. Finally, she felt free. It was as if she'd stood up to Mr. Yates all over again, and the notion was intoxicating.

She drew deep breaths, relishing in the moisture on her eyelashes and lips, her smile growing ever wider.

But when a rustling sounded to the side of her, followed by a swift clacking, she paused, whirling around to face the direction from which the sound had come.

Nothing was there. Her heart raced, her breathing stinted as she strained to hear the noise again.

A minute passed by. Then two. She was beginning to believe she'd imagined the noise. But after another moment, the clacking came again, as if someone hit two pieces of wood against each other.

Love Is for the Birds

Lark tiptoed forward, straining to see through the thick bushes and grass.

More rustling. More clacking. Whatever it was, it sounded large. But then, what on earth could it be? A deer? A badger?

A warning voice from within told her to keep her distance, but her curiosity got the better of her, and she crept closer and closer to the unpredictable noises until finally, she caught sight of something large and grey in a small clearing of trees, rain pouring down upon the mound.

As she finally recognized what she saw, her breath was snatched away. There, in the center of the clearing, caught in a bird snare, was a large, tawny owl. Her brown and white feathers resembled the trunks of the trees around them, and her black eyes—perfect, still orbs—continuously looked around her.

Lark was absolutely certain the owl had already seen her. But still, she remained silent, hoping the creature knew she was safe with Lark.

And yet, the owl continued to click its beak—a sign of its feeling threatened. Lark remained where she was, dropping her bonnet to the ground and lowering herself between the branches, straining to see where the owl was caught or if she was injured.

One of her white legs was stuck in between the wires, her black talons large and on full display as she attempted to rid herself of the snare, but her effort was to no avail.

Anger surged through Lark. The snare had no doubt been laid to capture a pheasant or other game, but this was precisely the danger of setting them. To capture and possibly injure a creature as beautiful as this owl? It was unthinkable. Was the bird a young mother? Had she been hunting at night and been stuck since then? Were her babies starving and frightened?

Lark shook her head. She had to do something. She *needed* to do something.

Her mind raced, but with each solution, another problem

arose. She could not safely release the owl on her own, that much was clear. None of the women back at the house were strong enough to help, and the men were long gone. A servant, perhaps? Maybe the very one who set the trap?

Leaving her bonnet behind, she backed away slowly, then sprinted toward the servant's entrance the moment she reached the open grass.

However, as she neared the home, a gentleman rounded the side of the house, striding toward the back entrance, and she gasped.

He would help her.

"Mr. Branok?" she cried out. "Mr. Branok!"

CHAPTER 27

Finally, Mr. Branok turned, facing Lark with a look of confusion, which swiftly shifted to concern.

"Miss Fernside?" He moved toward her directly, removing his hat. Rain poured down around his features. "What is it? Are you hurt?"

She shook her head, breathlessly speaking. "No, there's—there's an owl—she's caught—a snare—in the woods."

"Take me to her."

She nodded, running back the way she came with Mr. Branok in tow.

Together, they made their way through the trees, slowing down as they approached the owl and attempting to level their breathing.

"She's just there," she whispered, pointing through the clearing.

Mr. Branok hunched down beside her, their shoulders grazing as he looked through the bushes.

"Do you know how long she's been there?" he whispered through the owl's clacking beak.

Lark shook her head. "I can only imagine through the night."

He nodded, dropping his hat on the ground next to her long-forgotten bonnet and removing his greatcoat from around his shoulders. "We must try to release her from the snare."

We? He wanted her help?

He handed Lark the coat, and she took it without question, the fabric heavy as she folded it over her arms.

"Put that on," he commanded. "It will protect you from the rain."

Lark hesitated, then did as she was told, the scent of his cologne muddling her senses. "What about you?"

He removed his jacket, revealing his dark blue waistcoat and white shirtsleeves speckled with rain. "I'll be fine. I'm going to cover the owl with this"—he held up his jacket—"and when I have hold of her securely, I'll give you a signal. Then you must help me untie the snare. Do you think you can manage?"

He'd asked the question not out of doubt, but out of care. Lark could see it in his eyes.

"Yes," she stated firmly. "I can do that."

He nodded, loosening his cravat then moving from their hiding place.

Lark watched him slowly creep out of the woods into the clearing and toward the owl. The creature remained still, her obsidian eyes unflinching. The only sign she was agitated at all was the clacking of her beak and thinning of her body as she stretched taller.

Mr. Branok didn't speak, merely approached the owl in silence, the only sound being that of his footsteps in the soft, wet grass beneath his boots.

He paused a few feet away, holding the jacket up slowly, then in one swift movement, he tossed the cover toward the owl.

She responded with a sudden screech, and Lark gasped as the owl flared its wings, attempting to escape, but the snare caught harder around her leg.

Mr. Branok retrieved the discarded jacket, stepped a few feet away, then did the process again, and again. On his fourth attempt, the jacket landed squarely over the owl, and he launched forward, wrapping his arms around the bird to secure his hold of her.

He maneuvered around the grass until he settled in a seated position, the owl holding still and silent now she could not see the danger around her.

Lark waited with bated breath. Finally, Mr. Branok met her eye and nodded. Swiftly, she left her shelter in the trees and joined him in the clearing, kneeling at his side with his greatcoat heavy around her shoulders.

"Careful of her talons," he instructed in a soothing voice, holding the owl more securely.

Lark nodded in silence, examining the knots in the snare before reaching forward, acutely aware of the black claws and foot of the owl stretching out nearly five inches. They would shred her gloves in a heartbeat.

"Are you frightened?" Mr. Branok asked.

She was going to lie to save her pride, then decided against it. "Yes."

She glanced up at him, his eyes steady. "I promise you, I will do my part to keep you safe. You do yours to keep *her* safe." He motioned to the bird, giving Lark an encouraging nod. "You can do this, Miss Fernside."

She drew a steadying breath. If Mr. Branok had faith in her, she would have faith in herself, too.

Upon her first touch, the owl reacted with another screech, attempting to spread its wings again and thrashing about its talons. It caught the end of her dress, but Lark dodged out of the way before any damage could be done to her flesh.

Mr. Branok held fast, his features strained with effort. "Are you hurt?" he asked, frowning.

"No. No, I am well."

Then she moved toward the snare once again. She wrestled

with the wire for nearly a quarter of an hour as Mr. Branok held the bird until finally, the snare was freed from the owl's legs, and Mr. Branok motioned for Lark to return to the trees.

She did so at once, holding his greatcoat securely round her, ever grateful for the shelter it had provided. She turned back around to face him as soon as she was in the midst of the trees, then watched him roll his body to the side, release the bird and jacket, and back away slowly toward Lark.

The owl didn't move for a moment, merely clacking her beak in warning as Mr. Branok joined Lark behind the bushes.

"Is she injured?" Lark whispered.

"No," Mr. Branok responded. "Look."

They watched in silence as the owl remained still. Then all at once, the bird splayed out her greyish brown feathers, knocked the jacket to the ground, and beat her wings against the air until she took flight in silence, as if nothing out of the ordinary had just occurred.

They watched her fly away, a sense of accomplishment swelling within Lark's heart as the owl flew above the trees until she disappeared out of sight.

Lark and Mr. Branok remained in their hiding spot, though they straightened in silence before looking at one another.

"That was…" she began, shaking her head.

"Incredible," he finished.

Lark had to agree.

She stared at the snare the owl had left behind, Mr. Branok's jacket crumpled to the side of it. "How did you know how to do that—hold her, I mean?"

"Our guide did the very same to a pelican while we were in Hudson's Bay. I had no idea if it would work with an owl." He smiled. "Thank heavens it did."

She breathed out a laugh of relief. "Thank heavens, indeed. I don't believe she would have been alive for much longer had we not helped her."

LOVE IS FOR THE BIRDS

"No." Mr. Branok's brow creased. "Although, it never should have happened in the first place. More care needs to be given to snares and where they are placed. You were fortunate to have found her out here." Then he paused. "Why *are* you out here? And on your own?"

"I needed an escape."

"From being indoors?"

She hesitated. "From being with my own thoughts."

He watched her, clearly waiting for more of an explanation, but she wasn't certain she was ready for that. "Why did you return so early? And in the back entrance?"

He hesitated then, too. Rain had soaked through his shirt-sleeves while holding the owl, and now, the see-through fabric clung to the contours of his arms.

"I needed an escape, too." He averted his eyes. "And I needed to speak with you."

Her stomach tightened. He hardly sounded pleased.

"About what?" she asked, attempting indifference.

He stared at the grass between them, water droplets clinging to the ends of his dark blond strands. "A delicate matter. And slightly awkward. But I must be honest, for I have learned from my mistakes before and will not avoid you again."

She waited for him to continue as he drew a deep breath, his blue eyes soft, though weary. "It would appear there are some in our party who have misinterpreted our friendship and suspect there is something more between us than there is. Unfortunately, I believe your uncle is one of them. Not only does he seem upset with the very idea, but he also appears quite troubled due to my involvement with Blackstone's..." He trailed off, shaking his head before continuing. "However, I would hate for his assumption to encourage him to act recklessly—specifically, to force the two of us to wed."

Lark reeled at his words—not over the information, but over

the very fact that Mr. Branok was speaking about such matters with her. Did his honesty know no bounds?

"Furthermore," he continued, "I recognize the coincidental timing of all of this. Directly after I assure you the rumors about me being a scoundrel were untrue and that I would never intentionally involve you in anything that might sully your good name, *this* just so happens to occur. I cannot tell you how greatly upset I would become should anything adverse happen to you, or should you be persuaded to believe I was speaking anything other than the truth. I only pray this does not create mistrust between us, for I should like our friendship to continue. However, I will respect your decision whatever the outcome."

He stopped, facing Lark directly with a tight jaw.

Lark replied at once, anxious to soothe his concerns. "Sir, I thank you for your transparency, but you must allow me to settle your troubles immediately. I assure you, I trust you now more than ever. And I appreciate your honesty more than you'll ever know."

Relief shone in his eyes as she continued.

"As for my uncle, I meant what I said before, about him not being cause for concern. He is merely protective due to…to my past."

He watched her, his gaze heavy. She tried to hold her tongue, but his honesty before about his past produced the desire within her to share about her own.

"I do not wish to intrude," he said softly.

"I know. But I am ready now." She drew a deep breath. "You once asked me why my opinion of gentlemen is so poor. It is due to one man in particular. A man I'd once planned to marry."

His jaw, still wet with rain, twitched. "I see."

"When I was eighteen," she continued, "I thought I had fallen in love. Mr. Yates was charming, handsome, and came from a well-respected family. At first, he doted on me, but little by little, he revealed his true self. In every way, he controlled my actions. I was no longer allowed to observe birds, walk around my own estate, or even speak with my aunt and uncle. Matters became worse when he defended the fact that he was…fraternizing with other women all while expressing his love for me."

Mr. Branok's brow hung dangerously low over his eyes, a subtle shaking of his head revealing how exactly he felt about Mr. Yates's actions. "I'm sorry," he muttered. "I'm sorry you ever experienced such a betrayal."

"Thank you," she said. "But I assure you, I have healed greatly over the years. In truth, I could almost see why Mr. Yates did what he did."

"There is no excuse," Mr. Branok said firmly.

Lark could have thrown her arms around his neck at the words. Such honor, such loyalty, she'd never experienced beyond her own family. "I agree. There is no excuse. But Mr. Yates was obviously desperate—if not a little deluded. You see, as the youngest of eight sons, he was anxious to make a name for himself, so he thought he could do so by marrying me…a young, moldable, impressionable heiress."

Lark watched Mr. Branok carefully, studying his surprised expression. "You are an heiress?"

Warmth swarmed her heart and filled every inch of her. Of course he would not know. Of course he had not given a single thought to her fortune.

"I am," she replied. "My home is Brackenmore Hall in Suffolk. For obvious reasons, I tend to keep that side of my life as silent as possible."

"I can understand," Mr. Branok stated. "Though, you should not have to hide who you are to avoid despicable men from misusing you."

"No, I should not," she said wryly. "And yet, I must. Even just recently, I was proposed to by a gentleman after merely a week of knowing one another, for he was in search of a fortune himself."

She gave a small, mirthless laugh at the memory. She'd become frankly unhinged at Mr. Drake's sudden and unexpected proposal. She'd been minding her own business, seeking out a bird, when he'd confronted her with the question.

And worst of all? Lark had laughed.

She'd *laughed*. In her defense, it *had* been a laughable moment, for they had not spoken above a handful of times before he was expressing his desire to wed her.

Still, she held no ill will toward the man. Mr. Drake had never been unkind. Not like Mr. Yates.

"While I still intend to keep the knowledge of my wealth to myself," she continued, "I am no longer afraid. I have help now. My uncle was the one who discovered Mr. Yates's infidelity so I was able to cast the man out before I could seal my fate with his. Ever since, he and Aunt Harriet have taken me under their wings, protecting me, watching over me, and ensuring I lead the life I wish to."

Mr. Branok's features softened. "I am glad you had them at your side through all of it."

"As am I."

The strain she'd felt before at having to reveal Mr. Yates's cruelty was now growing fainter as it lifted from her heart and reminded her of the light that had come into her life since.

The light that had come into her life in the form of Aunt Harriet, Uncle Francis, even on occasion her mother.

And now, a light beamed brighter than all the others in the form of Mr. Branok.

She peered up at him, feeling the warmth and glow of that very light now as his eyes perused her features.

"So you see?" she began. "There is nothing to worry about

concerning Uncle Francis—what he may believe or what others may say. He knows I do not wish to marry and would therefore never force me to. If I *were* to have a husband, that would only occur because of my wholehearted desire to marry you."

Their eyes met, and suddenly, Lark was struck with what she'd said. "If-if I had such a desire to marry *anyone*," she corrected, but the words had already been spoken.

The intimacy of the situation settled around her. They were alone again. Secluded. No chance of being spotted or inter-rupted. And they had spoken of marrying one another.

No, they had spoken of *not* marrying one another. That their plans to remain single forever had remained unchanged.

And yet, the words jumbled in her mind, confusing her desires and muddling her logic.

"What a relief," Mr. Branok said, staring down at her, his voice as deep and soothing as when he'd spoken near the fright-ened owl.

She needed to say something, to let him know she did not truly wish to marry him. Or at least, she did not *think* she wished to marry him.

Her eyes dropped to his shoulders, the ridges visible through his wet shirt. "I believe it is foolish for anyone to assume some-thing is between us," she said distractedly. "Other than friend-ship, I mean."

"Quite foolish," he agreed. "But I would hate for your name to be tainted with rumors, nonetheless. Especially rumors I could have prevented."

The raindrops tapped lightly against the leaves around them, muting the air and creating an ambience of peace. Of privacy. Where words could be shared without being overheard, and actions could go unnoticed by all but themselves.

Her eyes rose to his lips, moisture clinging to the tops of them.

"Rumors are as untamable as a free bird in flight," she replied, taking a step toward him. "I would never blame you for that."

"What *would* you blame me for?" he asked in a whisper.

He remained where he stood, his brow furrowed, though his eyes dropped to her mouth for half a second.

That was all the encouragement she needed. "I would blame you for increasing my desire to be near you."

"And why do you wish to be near me?" he asked, his gaze stalwart, no hint of teasing in his eye.

Whispers of waterdrops slipped past the trees, falling down around them. The air was still, no breeze to be felt, and any chill Lark might have experienced was warded off due to Mr. Branok's greatcoat still draped round her shoulders.

"Mr. Yates did not allow me to walk in the rain because of how it made me appear—ragged and weary."

Mr. Branok frowned, his jaw twitching in disapproval, but she continued.

"My aunt and uncle do not allow me to come out into the rain for fear of me catching a cold." She drew a step closer. "But you? You believed in my ability to help with the owl. You did not push me back indoors. You are the only gentleman who has not told me to hide from the rain. Instead, you *protected* me from it…and sacrificed your own comfort to do so. *That* is why I wish to be near you."

Her hand moved as if of its own accord, sliding down the shape of his shoulder to the lines in his upper arm.

Mr. Branok swallowed hard. "You deserve to make your own choices in life, Miss Fernside," he began, his voice husky.

"All of them?" she asked, peering up at him through her own wet lashes.

She had taken leave of her senses. What other excuse had she to draw so close to him, to make her desires so known—directly after she'd told him she still had every intention of remaining single?

What was her intent to be near him, then? To ask for his kiss, but to remain unattached?

The truth of the words slipped into her conscience like the rain to the earth below. That was precisely her intent. She'd longed for it ever since that night on the stairs. Just one kiss. That would surely satisfy any desire she had.

Perhaps that truth made her a scoundrel herself. A broad. A...a loose woman. But as she stared up at Mr. Branok, the man whose work she'd admired for years, the man who'd seen her for who she was and allowed her to be—*encouraged* her to be— her true self...She did not care what she was labeled, so long as the label was *Mr. Branok's desire.*

But she would not push him further.

The line between his brow deepened, desire clear as day within those blue eyes she'd grown to love, and her heart dipped with anticipation.

Just like before, the space between them sparkled with energy as if anticipating a lightning strike. But unlike before, Lark would not say a word. Instead, she kept her eyes on him, her lips slightly parted, open and ready to accept his affection.

An errant raindrop splashed against his cheekbone, sliding along the side of his features. It lingered at the edge of his jaw, and Lark hesitated a moment before reaching forward, gently wiping the moisture away.

Mr. Branok's broad chest rose with a deep breath, and he closed his eyes with a furrowed brow. When they flashed open again, his gaze was more intent, and the determination within them caused her stomach to turn pleasantly.

His jaw flinched, again and again, as if he fought an internal battle to keep away from her. She longed to tell him he was fine, that she did not think less of him for having the desire to kiss her—that she thought *more* of him.

She longed to let him know that all would be well after the kiss, that they would both be able to maintain their plans to remain single.

But she knew, one word would break the spell.

She could do nothing but wait.

Now, it was up to him.

CHAPTER 28

Henry knew Miss Fernside wanted this. He knew it as perfectly as he knew he wanted it himself.

And though he'd fought a good fight for as long as possible, her touch and the look in her eyes broke down any remaining barriers until he was finally ready to admit that his will had lost—and his heart had won.

He knew the consequences to their actions. She had to, as well. But clearly, they were past the point of caring. Clearly, it was now time to act.

He stared down at her, her eyes wide and receptive, her lips pink and parted. How he'd kept himself from her for so long was beyond him.

With her hair wet from the rain, her cheeks rosy from the cold, he'd never seen anyone so alluring—so stunning. His greatcoat draped over her shoulders caused her to appear even more petite, and his desire to protect her, to defend her, amplified.

Learning what she'd endured as an impressionable young woman had been almost unbearable to listen to. And now,

Henry simply wanted to hold her. To cradle her. To show her how a true man treats a woman for whom he has feelings.

But he could not continue. Not unless he knew she was absolutely certain this was what she wanted, as well.

"Miss Fernside…"

"Yes?" she breathed, her eyes fluttering as she looked at his lips.

Desire for her swirled in his stomach. "I cannot proceed unless I know…this is what you truly wish for."

The stalwart look in her eyes ended any remaining concerns.

"It is," she stated.

His heart tripped. That was all he needed.

He stepped toward her, using every ounce of strength within him to move slowly, to prolong the moment he'd dreamt of for weeks.

He reached up, sliding his right hand across her lower jaw, ending when the tips of his fingers reached the nape of her neck. She raised her chin to maintain contact with his eyes, and he bent low to do the same, so drastic was the difference in their height.

He leaned closer. She wet her lips, and he was gone. Their eyes closed, and he pressed his lips to hers. He was finished fighting his desire, fighting his thoughts, fighting his longing for Miss Fernside. Instead, he breathed her in.

She was soft, though warm. Gentle, yet sure. He leaned his head to the side, pressing his lips more firmly upon her own, and she responded with a sigh that caused his legs to tremble.

This woman was everything. And he was nothing without her.

LOVE IS FOR THE BIRDS

LARK HAD NEVER KNOWN SUCH EUPHORIA AS BEING KISSED BY Henry Branok.

Henry Branok, of all people. Never in her wildest dreams, never in her greatest desires, would she have ever guessed this would occur. Not only that she would get to kiss him, but that he would *want* to kiss *her*.

For he did. She could feel it in her very soul. His right hand cupped her jawline and neck, his left slipping beneath his great-coat still about her shoulders. As his fingers slid along her waistline, the warmth from his hand seared through her pelisse and dress to heat her skin.

She'd kept her hands to herself, not wishing to pressure him further, but as he drew her closer, his fingers pulling gently at her side to move her nearer, her heart raced, and she leaned against him, resting a hand upon his chest where the rain made his shirtsleeves so thin, she wondered if it was still there.

Their mouths remained still, moving occasionally as one, though they remained present, deeply aware of one another. His breath tickled her cheek—warm, comforting, living—just like the heat radiating from his rapidly beating heart against her fingers.

She opened her eyes for but a moment, slowly moving her fingers up his chest and noting his brow flinching with emotion as she did so.

This was what she'd wanted for so long. Not only his kiss, not only the affection, but the attention—and the sure knowl-edge that Mr. Branok felt something for her. Something beyond friendship.

And it was the same for her. Unfortunately, that knowledge frightened her as much as it excited her.

What were they to do now?

Mr. Branok must have felt the change come over her, her question coming through her kiss, for after another lingering moment, he pulled back, slowly, yet intentionally.

He moved his hand away from her neck first, then his fingers from her waist, and the cold enveloped her.

Lark didn't know what to say. Neither of them spoke, neither of them looked at one another. Only the sound of the rain surrounded them.

Finally, she dared a glance up at him, his brow no longer furrowed, though raised in a somber manner. She did not have to ask why, for deep inside, she felt the very same.

Their time together had ended.

"You must be cold," she said, motioning to his wet shirt.

He merely shook his head.

Even still, she knew he had to be. Slowly, she removed his greatcoat and handed it to him. Their fingers brushed in the process, the connection from before sparkling between them, but he looked to the ground instead, retrieving his hat and her bonnet.

As he extended it to her, he was careful not to touch her this time.

Was he upset with their exchange? Or upset that it wouldn't happen again?

Lark accepted the bonnet, keeping it in her hands as the awkwardness between them grew, neither of them daring to ask what the other thought.

"I...I'd better return indoors. Aunt will be wondering where I am."

Mr. Branok nodded. "If you go in first, I shall remain out here for a moment to avoid the suspicion from others."

She nodded with gratitude, backing away. "Thank you for your help with the owl."

"Of course." He paused. "That moment was...unforgettable."

"I'm certain the owl will remember it, too."

His eyes bored into hers. "I was not speaking of saving the owl."

Her breath caught in her throat at his meaning.

Silence once more punctuated the air between them. Lark couldn't put off leaving any longer. She curtsied in departure and turned away.

That kiss had done the exact opposite of what she'd expected—allowing her some form of satisfaction. For now, she knew she would never be satisfied until she was able to kiss Mr. Branok for the rest of her days.

ONCE SAFELY IN HER BEDCHAMBER, LARK CHANGED INTO DRY clothes, did what she could to fix her hair, then retrieved her stitching, intent on returning to the women in the drawing room. But just as she was headed out, a maid delivered a note to Lark with the invitation from Uncle to meet him in the library.

Fear tightened her throat. Did Uncle know what had just occurred? Had he somehow seen or been told what she and Mr. Branok had just done? Or was she merely spotted in the rain and would now be instructed to rest for the remaining days of the week?

Instead of allowing her thoughts to run rampant, Lark made straight for the library, finding Uncle with his hands behind his back as he stared at the rows of books before him.

"Uncle," she began, "you sent for me?"

He turned to face her with a kind smile, though it did not reach his eyes. "Thank you for coming so swiftly."

He eyed her wet hair with suspicion, so she rushed forward to distract him.

"Did you enjoy your walk this morning?" she asked.

"No, the weather was abysmal. Come. Sit with me."

Together, they sat beside one another on the sofa. Lark did

her best not to wring her hands in her lap, instead wriggling her toes—just as she'd done right before first meeting Mr. Branok.

Never in a million years would she have guessed that they would have ended up as friends...if not more than friends.

She bit her lip to hide her smile.

"How have you been?" Uncle asked. "Remaining indoors, I mean?"

"I've been faring well enough," she replied, then her guilt nudged her further. "Though I will admit to walking out in the rain a time or two to maintain my sanity."

"I assumed you would do as much," he said with a motion to her wet hair.

She felt better already being honest with him, but when his features fell again, she hesitated. "Is something wrong, Uncle?"

He released a heavy breath. "Yes. I called you in here to tell you that I must return to London this morning."

Lark pulled back. "London? Is something wrong? Mother?"

He shook his head, quelling her worries. "No, nothing like that. I only have...business to attend to. Answers I must seek."

He fell silent, deep in thought.

"Answers to what questions?" she asked.

He blinked, drawing out of his reverie and facing her squarely. "You are aware that Mr. Branok is a member of Blackstone's Club in London."

Lark nodded, a pressure falling on her chest. "Yes, you and I have spoken of it, if you recall."

"I do. However, I must ask if you are aware of the reputations that come with being a member of said club."

Her uneasiness grew. "Only that those who are members have been blackballed from other clubs due to simply not belonging in Society."

"That is only part of it, I'm afraid. More than anything, Blackstone's houses those who have been excluded from other clubs for very *specific* reasons. You see, a gentleman is only blackballed—at least in my experience—due to despicable or otherwise appalling behavior that cannot be tolerated by the *ton*."

Lark's ears began to ring. Despicable? Appalling? Mr. Branok was neither of those things. But then, he'd merely said they were a group of misfits. He hadn't told her exactly *how* he'd been blackballed, had he?

"I have known only a handful of men who are members of Blackstone's," Uncle continued. "But the most concerning member...is that of Mr. Sebastian Drake."

The breath rushed from her lungs. Mr. Drake? The fortune-hunting, propose-after-a-week Mr. Drake?

She swallowed hard. "Does Mr. Branok know him?" she asked, attempting nonchalance.

"Yes," Uncle stated gravely. "Not only are they acquainted, but Mr. Branok *defended* the man's character."

Lark stiffened at the worlds colliding around her. The men knew one another? Did that mean Mr. Branok was aware that his acquaintance was the very man Lark had mentioned that morning?

"Does he..." she began, "does he know of my history with Mr. Drake?"

"I do not know," Uncle said with a wince. "I could not ask without betraying what happened to you. Though his knowing what had occurred would not surprise me."

Her head began to spin. If Mr. Branok *did* know, he would have already suspected Lark to be an heiress, but he was sincere in his surprise earlier. It was far more likely that he knew of no connection between her and Sebastian Drake.

Still, how could Mr. Branok defend a fortune-hunter's character? Unless, of course, he was unaware of the man's actions altogether.

"Lark? Are you well?"

Lark nodded, though her worry threatened to boil over. If

only she had mentioned Mr. Drake by name that morning. All of this would have been resolved.

Or…or matters would have gotten worse, preventing their kiss.

Uncle took her hand in his, directing her attention to him. "Lark, I know this is difficult, but we must be vigilant. We must discover why Mr. Branok was blackballed. Sebastian Drake was prohibited from joining due to his being a fortune hunter but—"

Lark paused. "How do you know that?"

Uncle raised his chin. "Because I was the one who did it."

A sliver of guilt struck Lark's heart. All Mr. Drake had really done was propose to her. True, his fortune-hunting was contemptible, but was he truly deserving of being blackballed?

Was Mr. Branok?

"As for Mr. Branok," Uncle continued, as if reading her mind, "we must know what his offenses are if we are to continue any sort of acquaintanceship with him. Otherwise, we risk injuring our own reputations and place in Society."

Lark looked away, unable to agree. She stood by her words from before—it was none of her business why Mr. Branok had been blackballed. But if Uncle thought he'd done something heinous, Lark would settle his concerns by asking the source directly.

"I will speak with Mr. Branok myself," she offered.

"Heavens, no," Uncle said at once. "That is the last thing you should do."

Lark pulled back. "Why?"

"Who is to say he will speak the truth?"

"He is a gentleman," she defended.

Uncle sighed. "So claimed to be Mr. Yates. *And* Mr. Drake."

Lark held her tongue. Uncle had warned her of Mr. Yates from the beginning, but Lark, in her naivety of youth, had ignored the signs Mr. Yates had given early on. Mr. Drake gave no such sign as to being despicable, only misguided. And Mr.

Branok? Mr. Branok had only ever revealed himself to be honorable and respectful.

But she knew Uncle, and he would not be convinced of Mr. Branok's goodness until he'd received word of it from others— others *aside* from Lark.

"Very well," she relented, "then what is to be done?"

"I sent an urgent letter to a colleague of mine in White's," Uncle said. "But he has told me no one can seem to recall why exactly Mr. Branok was blackballed, as it was nearly half a decade ago. That is why I must return to London early. And... and why I want you to come with me."

CHAPTER 29

ark's mouth opened wide. "What? Uncle, I cannot…"

But he held up a hand to stop her. "Please, Lark. Only hear my reasoning. I cannot in good conscience leave you here when I do not know of what Mr. Branok is capable. I would be remiss in my duty to protect you."

Lark could understand Uncle's plight. But she had paid far too much money and had waited far too many years to join an expedition, only to leave it five days early.

"Uncle, you know how greatly I appreciate all you've done for me, how you've protected me, but surely you must know…" She softened her voice. "I will not leave early."

Uncle looked as if he wanted to protest further, but he sighed, his shoulders dipping. "Yes. Yes, I assumed you would say as much. But I had to try."

She released a breath, grateful he did not push her. "Aunt is remaining, is she not?"

He nodded. "We have spoken already. She told me you would deny my request to leave and has already promised to remain at your side."

LOVE IS FOR THE BIRDS

"You may rest assured that I am in capable hands with her, then," Lark said, though she tried not to feel dread at the notion.

She loved Aunt Harriet. But Lark had grown used to tasting a small amount of freedom on this trip. She could not say goodbye to that already.

"There, you see?" Lark said. "I will be more than watched over. And truthfully, whatever Mr. Branok has done, he cannot have done anything so terrible that I would feel unsafe around him."

Especially after this morning. Saving the owl. Speaking with her honestly. Asking Lark before he kissed her.

Still, Uncle gave her a skeptical look. "Perhaps, but I must request that you do not seek out the gentleman while I am gone. Avoid being with him at all costs. I cannot bear the thought of something happening to you again."

Lark had expected this. She knew his restriction came from a place of love—but also of fear. She longed to shout out, *"Nothing will happen to me if Mr. Branok is by my side!"* but she held her tongue, for Uncle was just as stubborn as she was.

"Lark?" he pressed. "Please. Promise me you will do this."

She looked away, knowing already this was a losing battle. "Mr. Branok has never revealed himself to be anything other than trustworthy, Uncle," she tried once more.

"That may be so. But we cannot be sure until we know why he was blackballed." He waited until she met his gaze. "I beg of you to keep away from him until we know. Just until we see one another again in London. Surely you can manage five days for the sake of your reputation and future."

Lark felt hollow inside. Five days. Five days of not speaking with Mr. Branok—of not sneaking off to enjoy his company or his...his kisses. Kisses she wanted to taste again and again.

She released a sigh. Perhaps this was for the best. Perhaps time away was all she needed to realize she *could* live without

Mr. Branok's attention and affections because right now, she could think of little else.

Slowly, she nodded. "Very well, Uncle. I shall do as you wish."

He released a sigh of relief, then stood to leave, giving her an affectionate kiss atop her head. "I'm sorry about all of this, Lark. I know how greatly you admired Mr. Branok. To have matters sour so swiftly…" He trailed off with a disappointed shake of his head. "I will let you know the moment I become aware of his transgressions."

Transgressions?

Lark pulled back at the word, only vaguely aware of Uncle taking his leave as she remained seated on the sofa, her mind a torrent of tumultuous thoughts.

According to Uncle, heinous acts had to be made to become blackballed. Lark was certain Uncle would not be convinced that Mr. Branok was honorable—just as Lark would not be convinced of the contrary.

Mr. Branok being friends with Sebastian Drake was not a strong enough reason for her to keep away from Mr. Branok permanently.

But one question did prove to unsettle her.

Why had Mr. Branok not told her why he'd been blackballed?

Henry didn't have the opportunity to speak with Miss Fernside after their kiss. She'd been more than willing to share that kiss with him, and yet, that night and each subsequent day after that for the duration of their time in the Lake District, any chance they had to speak, she shifted uncomfortably away and deliberately tried to involve anyone else aside from him in the conversation.

Matters were made even trickier with Mrs. Haskett ever-present at her side, which Henry could not help but feel was intentional, as well.

Henry figured Miss Fernside's behavior was due to one of two reasons. Either she regretted kissing him and was attempting to create distance between them, or her uncle—who had mysteriously departed to London on some undivulged business—had requested she no longer speak with Henry due to his association with Blackstone's.

Either way, he was torn. He longed to speak with her again, to tell her that their kiss could be the first of many or the last of one—for he would be willing to consider both. But those solutions would either lead them toward a deeper relationship or no relationship at all, and each pathway was more frightening than the other.

There was another side of him that begged to carry more pride. If Miss Fernside did not approve of him any longer because her uncle did not, Henry should not wish to be friends with her either.

In truth, he was slightly hurt by her calculated dismissal of him, especially after the progress they'd made to be honest with one another. But of course he couldn't blame her, for he had done the very same to her in Yorkshire. Even still, it was not a pleasant situation to be involved in.

As their time in the Lake District came to a close, he determined to speak with Miss Fernside on the journey home, as it was his final chance before she'd no doubt be smothered by Mr. Haskett, as well.

London would not provide any opportunity for the party to come together until they met again to travel to Cornwall, so he planned to speak with Miss Fernside while Mrs. Haskett slept off her inevitable illness.

However, with Mr. Haskett's absence, the Chumleys thought it best for the women to join in one carriage while the others transported the men. Henry could hardly protest, though inside, he dreaded the notion of listening to three days of Mr. Chumley complaining against women and Mr. Dunn droning on and on about his special lake and the birds he captured while there.

As they loaded into the carriages that would soon be London bound, Henry stole a glance at Miss Fernside, who waited behind Mrs. Shepherd and Mrs. Chumley as Mrs. Haskett disappeared within the coach first.

Now was his chance—his one and only opportunity to speak with her before they would not see one another again for a fortnight.

Swiftly, he headed in her direction, standing at her side as the women settled within the carriage. "Miss Fernside, may I have a word?"

Her light brows rose in surprise, and she shifted a wary gaze toward the coach. "I-I do not wish to keep them waiting."

"Please. It will only take a moment."

She hesitated again, then nodded, stepping off to the side with him.

Henry knew he did not have long. Mrs. Haskett would no doubt be in search of her within the minute.

"I merely wish to ask if I might call on you while in London," he began. "I've much on my mind of late and wish to discuss it with you."

Her lips parted—those lips she'd once allowed him to taste. "Sir, I am sorry to say that my time in London will not be my own."

His heart dropped. "So you do not wish to speak with me?"

"I do. But current circumstances demand…discretion."

"Your uncle?"

She glanced over her shoulder at the carriage, the doorway

LOVE IS FOR THE BIRDS

still empty. Mrs. Haskett must be distracted with the other women to have not come in search of her niece yet.

"I cannot say," she whispered. "Only that...I had hoped in five days...But no, I think it best if we do not see one another until Cornwall. Excuse me, I must go."

He reached out, wrapping his hand around her wrist to stay her. His act was brazen but done so out of desperation rather than control. She focused on his fingers around her arm, and he softened his hold.

"Tell me," he whispered back. "Is this your own choice? Or is someone else making the decision for you?"

Their eyes met, hers wide with—With what exactly? Fear? Realization? "It is my own choice," she answered weakly.

"Is it?" he pressed.

"Lark? Lark, are you coming?"

Mrs. Haskett's voice reached them from within the carriage, and Henry gritted his teeth.

"I must go," Miss Fernside whispered again.

Henry released his hold of her completely. "So this is how you wish to proceed? After..." He dropped his voice. "After everything that has occurred between us?"

"Lark?" Mrs. Haskett called again.

Miss Fernside backed away. "I am sorry. None of this is how I wish it to be. But I do not have time to explain right now. Please, wait for Cornwall."

Cornwall? Two weeks from now? She could promise no such thing, for who was to say if Mrs. Haskett would not demand her presence further—or worse, if Mr. Haskett demanded she never speak with Henry again?

Henry shook his head. He was finished begging. He was finished pining after her. "Do not trouble yourself. You have made your wishes clear enough. Goodbye, Miss Fernside."

"Lark, my dear?" Rustling sounded in the carriage, as if Mrs. Haskett made to stand.

"Mr. Branok?" Miss Fernside called after him, but he ignored her, stalking away to his own carriage and climbing within the confines of his cage.

Unfortunately, the three-day journey proved to be *precisely* a cage. However, Henry had finally had enough time away from Miss Fernside to determine that her avoidance of him was for the best—as would be the next fortnight in London.

Each moment he'd spent in the woman's company had pulled him closer to her siren's call, causing him to forget the very reason he'd chosen to remain single in the first place.

However, after bidding farewell to the others—everyone aside from Miss Fernside and her aunt—Henry returned to his room on the upper floor of Blackstone's. There, he opened a letter from the viscount himself—written on pink stationary, of course—that reminded him once again why he would forever remain unmarried.

Mr. Branok,

Welcome back. I look forward to hearing about your travels, however I admit I have news myself.

Do come at your earliest convenience this afternoon to the card room. I have something to share with you that I believe will be met with great interest.

Lord Blackstone

With excitement he tried to convince himself was stronger

LOVE IS FOR THE BIRDS

than ever before, Henry made his way to the card room on the ground floor, finding Lord Blackstone seated at the foremost table with a group of gentlemen.

"Mr. Branok!" Lord Blackstone called out, waving him toward the table.

Henry made his way across the green-blue carpet, passing gentlemen with their fine clothing, top hats, and canes before reaching the viscount and taking the final seat around the green fabric of the table.

He greeted the others, sharing information about his trip around England as they asked for details before he faced Lord Blackstone.

"I believe you have news for me, my lord."

Lord Blackstone did his best to hide his smile, though his eyes shone with delight. "Yes, indeed. I have brought you here to ask if you'd like to take part in another excursion. This time..." He paused for dramatic effect, "to India."

Henry felt...To be honest, he did not know *what* he felt. He knew he should have been excited. Ecstatic. He'd been longing to go to India for years—for himself and for his parents. But something was preventing him from feeling the joy he'd expected.

Something...or *someone*.

"He's clearly in shock," Lord Blackstone joked with the other men. "That is why he does not speak."

"Or he is merely tired from his travels," one gentleman guessed.

Henry attempted to clear his thoughts. "I am equally both."

"Not excited, then?" Lord Blackstone asked.

Pull yourself together, Henry.

He cleared his throat, smiling. Honestly, this *was* excellent news. Leaving England, focusing on finding other birds—it would be just the thing he needed to forget about Miss Fernside altogether.

267

"On the contrary. I am thrilled," he responded. "I cannot wait to leave. When is the departure date?"

"There he is," Lord Blackstone said with a chuckle to the others. He faced Henry again. "The ship will set sail the first week of June. I had to pull quite a few strings to make this happen, but we must jump on this opportunity. It took…"

Henry's heart fell, and Lord Blackstone's words faded away. The first week of June. That was a week before Cornwall wrapped up. That meant he would miss seven days of the excursion. And seven days of Miss Fernside's presence.

Such knowledge should have excited him further. After all, why should he care about leaving her? They had been friends, nothing more, and he'd been leaving behind *good* friends for years.

And yet, the twisting pain within, the emptiness that filled his heart at the knowledge of no longer seeing Miss Fernside, was nearly unbearable.

"Of course," Lord Blackstone continued, "this means you will have to cut short your trip now, but that won't be a problem, will it?"

Henry stared. Yes, it would be a problem, but not because of what the viscount thought.

This was what Henry had been trying to prevent all along. This was why he'd never wanted to marry. Because he wanted to travel without regret, without leaving anyone behind. He wanted to join these excursions because there was no reason *not* to.

The noise around the cardroom pressed down on him, the heat from too many bodies and shining candles causing beads of sweat to slide down his back.

Leaving on excursions was far easier knowing his parents were gone and he had no other immediate family members living. Leaving behind Miss Fernside would make him long for home—long for her presence, effectively causing the excursion to be one filled with pain, regret, and loneliness, even more than he already experienced.

But he should not be feeling any of this. Miss Fernside had, in an essence, rejected him. Chosen her uncle over himself. So how had she captured him so fully that he was already regretting the time he *wouldn't* get to spend with her? How had he allowed himself to be so wrapped up in the mere memory of her affection that he'd even considered beginning a deeper relationship with her?

He wouldn't stand for it.

"I see no problem at all," Henry stated calmly, ignoring the way his voice echoed mutely in his own thoughts. "I will simply tell the host I've no other option but to leave early."

Mr. Chumley would have no problem with that. Henry would be finished with his teaching by that point, anyway, and the others would be allowed to venture forth on their own to put into practice all they had learned.

And Miss Fernside would…Well, she would do whatever she wished to do, and whatever that was, it wasn't Henry's concern.

"Excellent," Lord Blackstone said, beaming.

He carried on about plans for the expedition, and Henry did his best to listen and show his excitement, despite the trepidation unsettling his happiness.

Leaving Miss Fernside would be painful. He was man enough to admit it. So departing from Cornwall early was for the best—for both of them.

This way, she could remain single and free to live her own life. Henry could do the same. And both of them would be happy in their decisions.

At least on his part, he hoped that would be the case. For as of right now, all he could think of was how departing from Miss Fernside was not the answer to his happiness.

The last few weeks had made that clear enough.

CHAPTER 30

ondon – May 15, 1817
Since her arrival in London two days prior, Lark had been to more social events than she wanted to for the rest of her days. Granted, there had been a single dinner party, two promenades through Hyde Park, and only one ball, which she was attending currently, but still, she was utterly spent.

Apparently, she had grown far too accustomed to being around like-minded individuals whose first love was a bird. The people she was forced to associate with now were as drab as dry dirt, going on and on about "this hairstyle" and "that cravat" and always the latest gossip.

Even so, Lark would do her duty and play the part of the amiable female in search of a husband to fulfill her agreement with Mother—even if it was all for pretend.

"Stunning, is it not?" Mother commented as they entered the ballroom.

The grand space was as bright as day with countless candles flickering above the room and about the walls.

"Quite breathtaking," Lark said, though her eyes were on the hordes of people already filling the dance floor.

She dreaded the number of times she would be asked to dance tonight—and all by acquaintances of Mother who'd heard tell of her stunning, wealthy daughter.

Mother had been thrilled to welcome back Lark after her travels. To her credit, she'd listened to Lark's full account of the expedition thus far—omitting a few happenings, of course. But after that, Mother had not wasted a single moment making up for lost time, pulling Lark from person to person at each event they attended.

"My friend puts on quite a show," Mother continued, commanding the space she walked.

She looked as regal as ever in her white gown that draped flatteringly over her figure.

"He does, indeed," Lark agreed.

The ball tonight was put on by the Duke of Rockwood, yet another of Mother's many friends. Her connections truly knew no bounds—which was unfortunate for Lark and her desire to remain unnoticed by all.

Well, not all. But the one person she wished to be noticed by was the one person she *hadn't* seen for two days.

It was just as well. She couldn't speak with Mr. Branok anyway. Nor would he wish to speak with her. She'd burned that bridge to cinders, and her charred heart was proof enough of the fact.

Soon enough, Mother and Lark found Aunt and Uncle, the former joining them as they walked about the room, and the latter retreating to the card rooms almost instantly.

Lark wouldn't mind hiding away with no responsibilities for an evening. Oh, to be a gentleman.

Instead, she remained at the forefront of attention with Mother introducing her to more faces and individuals than she could ever hope to remember.

After a quarter of an hour, Mother was whisked away by a group of women who strikingly resembled a gaggle of Roman geese as they walked about the room in unison, their heads held high, ready to cast judgments on all who dared approach them.

For the moment, Lark was left to her own devices. She joined Aunt at the edge of the room, observing the dancers on the floor, and Lark stifled a yawn.

"Tired already?" Aunt asked.

"I've been tired since we left the Lake District."

Aunt Harriet smiled encouragingly. "You'll need to rally your energy this evening. This may be the last dance you have without a partner."

Lark's shoulders dipped. Aunt was right. It was only a matter of time before Mother returned to her side with a row of gentlemen behind her for Lark—goslings behind the mother goose.

"Would I could be a wallflower," Lark muttered, longingly eying the young girls sitting demurely at the sides of the room, anxiously staring at each gentleman who passed them by without notice.

Her heart reached out to the ladies. They were pretty, but nowhere near fine enough to be noticed by the pompous *ton*.

Lark would know. Mother had dressed her in her finest gown this evening—the deep red gown with pearls sewn down the center and around her waist and neckline was even more grand than the blue dress she'd worn on the expedition.

The blue dress that had caused so much trouble between her and…

Her heart twisted, but she ignored it as best she could—just as she'd done from the moment she'd sworn to Uncle she would not speak with Mr. Branok.

The days since had been the most difficult of her life. She'd hoped, upon her return to London, that Uncle would have good news concerning Mr. Branok, but his words had been bleak.

"I still have yet to discover a single person who is aware of what he did to be blackballed," Uncle had told her upon her return. *"This can mean only one thing. Mr. Branok must have hidden his actions due to their egregious nature. I can only imagine what heinous behavior he must have exuded. I can hardly bear the thought of meeting up with him again in Cornwall in two weeks' time."*

Once again, Lark had soothed her uncle's anxiousness, for she still felt the same about abandoning the expedition too early —there was no chance she would.

Just as there was no chance she would believe that Mr. Branok was capable of doing anything *egregious* at all. But she'd decided, for now, to allow Uncle Francis time to calm down before she voiced her continued desire to ask Mr. Branok herself what he'd done.

She'd longed to do so during their final days in the Lake District, but true to her promise to Uncle, she'd maintained her distance. And Aunt, true to *her* word, had not left Lark's side for a single moment.

Of course, when he'd approached her at the carriage, everything had fallen to pieces.

Lark winced at the memory. How she'd longed to share with him then and there that Uncle had made her promise not to speak with Mr. Branok, that those five days apart had been the longest of her life. She'd realized that she'd have to wait even longer to speak with him if she had any hope of doing so away from the ever-watchful eyes of Uncle, Aunt, and Mother. That was why she'd hoped he would have agreed to speak in Cornwall, but she knew why he did not.

She had injured him. And he would not forgive her.

"You see? Your mother is wasting no time collecting your partners for the evening," Aunt said, motioning across the room.

Sure enough, Mother had surrounded herself with four young men, pointing over at Lark and speaking behind a fluttering fan.

Lark looked away, pretending not to have noticed the men veritably salivating, no doubt at the knowledge of Lark's wealth.

"Do you know any of them?" Aunt Harriet asked.

Lark focused on the dark-haired gentleman at the front. "Only Mr. Taylor. Mother thinks we would get on splendidly because he enjoys hunting." She cast Aunt a sidelong glance. "Shared interest in birds, you see."

"Oh, yes. That is *just* what you would want in a husband."

"Indeed. I know Mother means well, but she is so often misguided by her own desire to see me wed. I cannot blame her, though. The poor woman will never get to plan her own daughter's wedding."

Aunt eyed her. "Will you be happy if you do not get to plan your own wedding?"

Lark hesitated, focusing on the image in her mind's eye of her standing in front of a church, a man with blue eyes like the sea at her side...

She blinked the image from her mind. "More than happy. If anything, this expedition has only proven to reinstate my desire to remain single so I will be able to enjoy trips like this forevermore."

She merely had to simply readjust her dreams. She might not be able to procure passage to other countries now, lacking the expertise and connections of Lord Blackstone, but she could still manage a trip around England every now and again. Perhaps even Europe. It was all dependent on her hope and efforts. Was it not?

"And yet," Aunt Harriet continued, "would you not enjoy these experiences better with a husband at your side? I know I do with your uncle. Mrs. Shepherd does with her husband, as well." She hesitated. "I know Francis does not approve, but Mr. Branok..."

Lark shook her head, praying Aunt wouldn't finish the sentence. It was too painful to entertain such thoughts, especially knowing Aunt still enjoyed Mr. Branok's company, even if Uncle did not.

"He appears to be your equal in every way," Aunt continued, despite Lark's prayers. "Have you ever considered..."

Once again, Lark shook her head.

Yes, she and Mr. Branok shared similarities. But one of those similarities—their attachment to remaining single—was to their detriment. Should he give up his bachelorhood, he would also be relinquishing his frequent expeditions, publications, and essentially, his freedom. He would never wish to marry her, as he would be gaining nothing from such a relationship—so a marriage between them was out of the question.

She, on the other hand, would be gaining far more. Freedom, protection...love.

She shook her head. The idea was absurd. Mr. Branok did not love her. She wasn't even certain if he wished to remain friends after last week.

"No," she replied softly. "He is determined to remain single. And I am quite content with my choice. But thank you for always being so aware of my happiness, Aunt."

Aunt gave her a saddened smile, then turned to face the dancers. However, her features shifted to surprise when she focused directly ahead of them. "Is that Mr. and Mrs. Chumley just there?"

Lark followed Aunt Harriet's line of sight, and to her surprise, a flutter of excitement occurred in her chest at the sight of the couple half-hidden by a gentleman in front of them.

She'd missed Mrs. Chumley, and she'd almost been away from Mr. Chumley long enough to consider tolerating his presence again.

"I believe it is them, yes," Lark replied.

If the Chumleys were here, did that mean other members of their bird observing party were in attendance, as well?

Do not dwell on false hope, Lark.

"Oh, they've seen us," Aunt said.

Mrs. Chumley made eye contact with Lark across the floor, her eyes brightening as she smiled and waved in greeting. She pointed Lark out to her husband, who appeared less than thrilled at the sighting.

But Mr. Chumley's actions were lost on Lark when, in the next moment, the gentleman who'd been in front of them turned and revealed himself to be the very man Lark had convinced herself it was not.

Mr. Branok.

"Lark..." Aunt spoke a voice of warning next to her, for she must have seen the man, too.

But Lark could not utter a single word. The blood rushed in her ears, and her heart thumped painfully against her chest when his eyes connected with Lark's, surprise in his expression.

What was he doing here? Had the Chumleys invited him? From the look on his features, he hadn't expected to see Lark, either.

Mr. and Mrs. Chumley led the way forward, and Mr. Branok very clearly hesitated before following behind them.

"Do you wish for an escape?" Aunt asked under her breath.

Lark was tempted to accept the help, especially as Mr. Branok averted his eyes from Lark, but she knew she could not avoid him forever.

She could only thank the Heavens that Uncle had disappeared within the card room. One could only imagine the disgruntled comments that would occur should the two see one another again.

"No," she whispered. "No, I am well."

Aunt nodded just as the group reached them.

"Mrs. Haskett, Miss Fernside," Mrs. Chumley greeted first as bows and curtseys were exchanged. "We had no idea we'd be having the pleasure of seeing you this evening. What a delight!"

"Such a pleasure to see you all, as well," Aunt Harriet responded.

"I cannot tell you how pleased I am to see familiar faces," Mrs. Chumley continued. "I do find these sorts of gatherings difficult, but knowing I have friends here certainly makes it more bearable." She sighed happily, looking around at the small party. "Who knew we would have a little reunion between us? I feel as if we ought to retreat to the gardens to see if we can spot a few birds."

The group laughed. Even Mr. Chumley cracked a smile in silence. Lark dared a glance at Mr. Branok, but he pulled his eyes away from her in an instant.

Her heart rapped against her chest, as if attempting to break free so that it might join Mr. Branok across the circle. She did not blame it. He looked flawless tonight. Green waistcoat, pomaded hair, jaw firm. But more than handsome features, there was who he was as a person—a person Lark desperately missed. His conversation, his encouragement, his kindness.

"Miss Fernside," Mrs. Chumley said, interrupting her thoughts, "your gown is gorgeous. Whoever is your modiste?"

Once more, Mr. Branok hurriedly looked away when Lark caught him watching her.

"Oh, my apologies," she began. "I cannot recall, for my mother had it made for me."

"Your mother?" Mrs. Chumley asked with excitement, leaning forward. "Is she here this evening?"

"She is," Lark said, tension rising within her.

This was the last thing she wanted—for Mother to meet the group.

Or worse, Mr. Branok.

Her eyes traveled across the room to where Mother stood, her eyes already fixed on Lark as she took note of the party around her daughter. True to form, within a matter of seconds,

Mother excused herself from the gentlemen of her own circle and forged her way toward them.

"As a matter of fact," Lark began, sending a passing glance at Mr. Branok, "this is her now."

Mother entered the circle right on time, her sweeping movements graceful. "My dear," she greeted, "I see you have made friends. Do introduce me."

Lark nodded, attempting to swallow her anxiousness. She had intentionally omitted any mention to Mother of Mr. Branok being young, single, and handsome. Mother was politeness herself, but she was shameless in her efforts to marry off Lark. What in Heaven's name would happen when she discovered Mr. Branok's amiability?

"Mother," Lark began, "these are our friends from the expedition."

She went around the group, introducing them as Mother smiled at each around the circle, though her curious gaze lingered on Mr. Branok.

"*You* are Mr. Branok?" Mother asked after the introductions, surprise in her tone.

"I am, ma'am."

She looked as if she wished to say more, but Mrs. Chumley spoke next. "It truly is such a pleasure to meet you, Mrs. Fernside. Your daughter has been an utter delight on our journey. Has she not, Mr. Chumley?"

Mr. Chumley cleared his throat with a nod that looked very much like it pained him, and Lark couldn't help but smile at the sight.

Penelope had been right. Mrs. Chumley certainly ruled the roost, or Lark would have been vanquished from the expedition long ago.

"I am so pleased to hear that," Mother said. "More of the world needs to discover how charming my daughter is."

She glanced again at Mr. Branok.

"And her knowledge is unmatched," Mrs. Chumley continued. "She is even giving our resident expert a run for his money."

Mother homed in on Mr. Branok. "And I take it you are the expert?"

Mr. Branok gave a rigid smile. "I am no expert, ma'am."

Mother leaned toward Lark, speaking in a voice loud enough for all to hear. "Is he being humble, daughter?"

Lark met Mr. Branok's gaze. "Very much so."

"I thought as much." Mother smiled. "I have heard great details about your expeditions over the years, Mr. Branok. My daughter seems to speak of nothing else. She takes a keen interest in your books."

Lark blushed, stealing a glance at the gentleman.

Before, Mr. Branok would have teased her with knowing glances and sparkling eyes. Now, he merely ducked his head with modesty as Mother continued.

"Do tell me what is so engaging about your volumes of work that makes my Lark so obsessed with them."

"That I could not tell you," he replied. "She may be the only other person who has read them."

The group laughed.

"Nonsense," Mrs. Chumley said. "My husband has read them, have you not?" Mr. Chumley nodded. "And I, myself have managed a page or two. Though, I admit, I am not your target audience."

"My daughter certainly is," Mother continued. "Mr. Branok was the sole reason she signed up for your tour, Mr. Chumley."

Mr. Chumley snapped a condemning look at Lark. She'd never told him that Mr. Branok was the reason she'd attended, fearing he would never say yes if he knew the truth. However, there was no purpose in hiding it now.

She raised her chin, then glanced at Mr. Branok, who watched her carefully with an unreadable expression.

Was he upset? Sorrowful? Did he regret ever speaking with someone who was so clearly obsessed with him?

"Now tell us, Mr. Branok," Mother said next, "does your... your wife go with you on your many excursions round the world?"

Heavens above.

"No, I am not married. My expeditions do not allow me the luxury."

Mother's look of disappointment was clear, but she brushed it aside and smiled anyway. "I find when one wants something badly enough, one can make anything possible."

Her eyes lingered on him, and Lark gave a subtle nudge to Mother with her elbow, praying for the man to find some relief.

However, distraction came in another form as Mr. Taylor from before stood beside Lark with a toothy smile. "Miss Fernside, may I have this next dance?"

Lark stared, only aware in that moment that the music from the previous dance had ended and another was about to begin.

"Oh..." Lark hesitated.

She glanced at Mr. Branok, but he would not meet her gaze.

Crestfallen, Lark returned her attention to Mr. Taylor. "Yes, of course. I would be happy to."

She excused herself from the others, feeling Mr. Branok's eyes on her as she walked past and away from the circle, though she did not turn around.

Doing so would only lead to greater disappointment, for he was the only man she wished to dance with that evening—and she knew he was the only man who would not ask her.

CHAPTER 31

Henry was grateful when the small circle disbanded so he no longer had to speak.

His mind was too muddled, too confused. Seeing Miss Fernside in all her scarlet glory was even more unsettling.

He stood on the outskirts of the ballroom, doing his best not to watch as she twirled, spun, and clapped during the dance with her partner. The only knowledge that comforted him in that moment was knowing that the gentleman appeared far happier than Miss Fernside did.

Although, that didn't surprise him. From what she had said before, he could only imagine how miserable she had to be within the confines of the ballroom instead of freely exploring the world—and birds—around her.

If only he could help her.

He closed his eyes, drawing a deep breath before looking away from her. Such thoughts would not lead to anything productive. He was already confused enough. Wanting to ease her burdens, help her be happier, would only draw them closer together, and that was not what he wanted.

Or was it?

He blew out an aggravated sigh, rubbing his fingers against his temple to dispel the growing ache in his head.

He'd tried to forget about her. He'd tried to convince himself that she was not worth a second of his time. He'd tried to wrap his mind up with India so much he could care about nothing else. He was finally fulfilling his dream, his *parents'* dream.

But none of it worked. She was the first thing he thought of when he woke up, the last thing he thought of when he fell asleep. Even then, he did not feel relief, for his dreams were filled with images of her smile and warm eyes.

Thinking of her wasn't even the worst of it. It was the longing he had not expected. It was as if his very soul yearned to be with hers. To be strengthened by her, comforted by her, even challenged by her.

Even now, he had to fight to keep himself from striding directly toward her, interrupting the set, capturing her hand in his, and begging her to dance with him for all the rest of his days.

He turned away, but it did not help. Nothing ever did.

His eyes trailed to her once again. Her blonde curls were piled high and elegant atop her head as she danced. Rubies dangled from her ears, swinging jovially back and forth as she smiled at the couple dancing down the set.

Her gloved hands tapped in time with the music, and with each clap, Henry's heart beat against his chest.

His time away from her was supposed to have subdued any attraction he held for her. But all it did was dissipate his hurt and anger. All it did was make him uneasy about the coming days when he would be without her. He could hardly manage two days. How was he to manage one hundred and fifty?

The same panic that had been growing for days sparked again inside his chest, igniting a greater desire to speak with her. If he still had to leave for India, if he still had to be parted from her, could he at the very least speak with her now? Would she allow him that much?

She'd wanted to before, had told him they could speak in Cornwall, but he'd promptly set her aside. Perhaps...perhaps he could ask her to dance now and tell her he would wait. Her mother would allow him the opportunity to dance with her, surely. She seemed eager enough for her daughter to draw closer to him. And with Mr. Haskett nowhere in sight, Henry had more of a chance than ever.

He unabashedly observed Lark as she neared the end of the dance, his heart racing at the thought of speaking with her again, telling her he was bound for India, but that he wanted her —needed her—to still be his friend when he returned.

That knowledge would surely be enough to sustain him through their many months apart, would it not?

The music neared its completion. Henry tapped his fingers anxiously against his thighs, waiting for the song to end. However, when he glanced at his left and spotted Mr. Sebastian Drake standing nearby, Mr. Haskett's words from before flooded his mind.

"Are the two of you merely acquaintances or have you struck a friendship with him?"

Henry had noticed Mr. Haskett becoming visibly agitated when Henry had called Mr. Drake honorable, and Henry had been wanting to decipher the meaning of that conversation since. Perhaps now would be the perfect time to do just that —*before* he spoke with Miss Fernside.

He glanced at her, her figure still dancing around her ever-smiling partner, then he made for Mr. Drake.

"Branok," the gentleman greeted. "I hear you are headed to India."

"News travels fast."

"When it comes to Lord Blackstone, it certainly does. When do you depart?"

Henry glanced anxiously toward Miss Fernside, the music finally ending as the dancers clapped.

"First week of June." He hesitated, then, at the risk of being seen as impolite, pushed forward. "Mr. Drake, may I ask you something?"

Mr. Drake faced him more directly. "Of course."

Henry drew a deep breath. It was time to get to the bottom of this.

Exhausted already, Lark allowed Mr. Taylor to lead her from the floor, but before she could even be returned to Mother's side, another gentleman, Mr. Jensen, swooped in with a small smile.

"May I have the pleasure, Miss Fernside?"

Lark graciously nodded, though her insides screamed in protest. She couldn't take another dance with another polite gentleman. Not unless that gentleman was Mr. Branok.

But he had already no doubt left the ball, having had no desire to occupy the same room as Lark, let alone the same set.

"I have so looked forward to this moment, Miss Fernside," Mr. Jensen continued. "I truly—"

"Lark, I must speak with you."

Lark stood back at Uncle's sudden presence, his eyes wide and figure cutting off Mr. Jensen entirely.

"Can it wait, Uncle?" she whispered, motioning to the gentleman who looked positively affronted. "I was just about to dance with Mr. Jensen here."

Uncle dropped his voice. "Is Mr. Branok here this evening?"

"I believe he was," she replied as passively as possible.

"Then no, it cannot wait. Mr. Jensen, do excuse us."

LOVE IS FOR THE BIRDS

Lark gave the man an apologetic look, though she could not feel any regret herself, as she had just been rescued from at least one dance this evening.

She followed Uncle through the crowds. He moved to the outskirts before facing her with a look of urgency.

"I am sorry for the interruption, Lark, but this could not wait." He drew a deep breath, his eyes focused. "I have discovered the truth about Mr. Branok just now in the card room. No one talks like a man filled with brandy."

Lark grimaced, her stomach unsettled, as if she were being tossed about by a rowboat. She hadn't received enough sleep or rest in the last few days to be able to manage this right now. "Uncle, I'm not sure..."

But he stopped her with a shake of his head. "I know this is difficult, but it must be known, Lark."

Lark looked away, knowing Uncle would tell her even if she begged him not to. She knew he was simply trying to protect her, but listening to this felt like a betrayal.

"As I was playing," Uncle began, "I overheard an older gentleman from Blackstone's sharing that Mr. Branok has just recently agreed to a new excursion. This time to India. He will leave a week before our own expedition ends."

Lark's heart instantly lifted. India. He was finally going to India. She couldn't imagine the joy he must be feeling. And yet, her own spirits slowly lowered as she realized what that meant for her—losing out on an entire week with Mr. Branok.

It shouldn't have upset her as much as it did, seeing as how Uncle was attempting even now to sever her relationship with Mr. Branok. But still, she'd thought she'd have longer to prepare before her time with him completely ended.

"I heard this news and instantly sought the man out," Uncle continued, oblivious to the torrent within Lark. "From him, I discovered that Mr. Branok was blackballed because..." He glanced around them, ensuring they were unheard as he whis-

285

pered. "Because he published a series of articles criticizing every club owner within London, spreading false rumors, and tearing them apart—all anonymously."

Lark hesitated, the information settling over her as slowly as a sparrow-hawk coming in for a leisurely landing. The information certainly wasn't as heinous as Uncle had first led her to believe.

"What sort of things were written?" she asked.

"The older gentleman said they were so horrible, he dared not repeat the phrases. But the club owners were deeply injured. Years later, they are still dealing with the aftermath of the rumors."

Lark frowned. To think of Mr. Branok spreading rumors and injuring other people simply didn't suit.

"If they were done anonymously," she questioned next, "how could they know it was him?"

"I asked the very same question," Uncle said. "Apparently, Mr. Branok slipped in small hints within each article for the men to know exactly who was writing such things. Furthermore, Mr. Branok did not deny his part in writing them when asked."

Was no denial the same as a confession now? Or had Uncle's source simply been exaggerating? "Uncle, I am unsure of all of this. Mr. Branok hardly seems the type to do such a thing."

"Did we not both think the very same about Mr. Yates and Mr. Drake?" Uncle asked with a wince, his words softening further as he continued. "Who's to say we are not doing the very same with Mr. Branok?"

Lark turned away. She had known from the start that Mr. Yates was hiding something. And she was still convinced that Mr. Drake was truly a good man inside.

As for Mr. Branok...

"In what way has Mr. Branok revealed himself to be untrustworthy?" she asked.

Uncle leaned forward. "The very fact that he is friends with Mr. Drake," he whispered. "When a man keeps company with a fortune hunter, there is no telling what his limits are."

"How do you even know they are friends?"

Uncle pressed his lips together. "My source has told me so. He has also alerted me to the fact that Mr. Branok is fully aware of Mr. Drake's intent to marry wealthy and has even aided him in his endeavors, finding young women who are inexperienced in the ways of the world to fall for the scoundrel." Uncle shook his head, leaning back. "I am sorry, my dear niece, but Mr. Branok is a deceptive scoundrel who has lied from the start." He dropped his voice further. "Apparently, both men come to these balls to scope out potential females for Mr. Drake. I would not be surprised if Mr. Branok was the one who pointed Mr. Drake toward you all those weeks ago."

Lark couldn't believe it. She wouldn't believe it. The timing simply didn't align, nor did Mr. Branok's actions over the last few weeks. "How could Mr. Branok behave so innocently if he was not innocent?" she mused aloud.

Uncle's voice softened. "Tell me, did you speak with him about Mr. Drake's proposal?"

Lark hesitated. "I mentioned it without the use of Mr. Drake's name."

"And what was Mr. Branok's response?"

The memory flooded her mind, filling her heart with confusion and despair. "He...he said nothing about him."

Uncle gave her a sorrowful but knowing expression. "Can't you see, my dear? Yet another despicable gentleman has managed to convince us of his feigned goodness."

The weight of the world pressed down upon her shoulders as she stared out across the teeming ballroom. The heat from the candles produced beads of sweat upon her brow, and the noise from the hundreds of attendees grew louder and louder in her ears. She couldn't breathe fully. She couldn't think clearly.

Mr. Branok wasn't capable of such deception. It was ludicrous. Preposterous. Unbelievable.

But when her eyes focused across the room, the crowd parted at just the right moment to reveal Mr. Branok himself speaking with none other than Sebastian Drake.

Lark's stomach curdled. It couldn't be true. They were not friends. Mr. Branok was not Mr. Drake's assistant.

Or was he? Were they there together tonight, finding more women to capture in their web of deceit?

"The blackguards," Uncle spoke from beside her, having spotted the gentlemen, as well. "I'll confront them myself now."

But Lark put a settling hand on his arm. "No. Uncle, I will take care of this."

He pulled back. "You most certainly will not. I—"

"I will," she stated firmly.

Without waiting for a response, Lark moved toward the gentlemen, feeling as if the world was speeding up around her, though her footsteps moved slowly, as if through sticking, wet mud.

Finally, she reached them. They both turned to face her in unison, eyes wide with surprise.

Neither of them said a word.

"So, it is true, then," she stated. "You two are friends. You *have* been helping him."

Mr. Branok frowned, while Mr. Drake looked as if he wished to crawl into a very large, very deep hole.

What a fool she'd been. How blind she'd been—just like before.

"This clears up matters perfectly," she said, though nothing was clear at all.

"What matters?" Mr. Branok questioned, his brow furrowed.

Lark hardly heard him, her mind connecting the dots from here and there as she tried to make sense of Uncle's accusations and Mr. Branok's behavior that just didn't match up.

"Why didn't you tell me that you knew him?" she asked in a haze. "And why didn't you tell me why you were blackballed?"

His look of confusion grew. "Miss Fernside, please…"

But she shook her head. "No, it doesn't matter any longer."

And it didn't. She was past the point of caring. Her anger, her stress, her will to fight slipped through her fingers.

What did it matter if the men were friends? What did it matter how he was blackballed? And what did it matter if she ended her relationship with Mr. Branok? It never would have lasted anyway.

She raised her chin. "I hear you are off to India."

He hesitated, clearly confused with the shift in her persona. "Who did you…I was hoping to tell you myself."

Mr. Drake looked between them, appearing more uncomfortable by the second.

"You needn't tell me anything now." She took a step away from him. "I truly hope your time there is a success. As for our challenge, we may render it void so you will be under no obligation to finish it."

His features fell, but she refused to apologize.

She looked between the men. "I hope you both find what you are looking for, though I pray it is not at the expense of *another* woman. Farewell, to you both."

Mr. Drake remained silent as Mr. Branok called after her, but Lark marched ahead. She was finished. Finished being whipped from one emotion to the next, and one gentleman to the next.

From now on, she would simply be *Miss* Lark Fernside.

Forever and always…alone.

CHAPTER 32

Henry stared after Miss Fernside, utterly speechless. What on earth had just happened? He and Mr. Drake had been having a civil enough conversation. Henry had asked if he knew Mr. Haskett, Mr. Drake had hemmed and hawed, then without warning, Miss Fernside had appeared.

She was clearly upset, believing he and Mr. Drake were close friends, then she'd written Henry off, as if she never meant to speak with him again. How had she jumped to such an act?

"Deuces," Mr. Drake muttered under his breath.

Henry looked at the man, an awkward expression across his features.

"Branok, I owe you an apology for dragging you into this."

"Dragging me into what, exactly?" Henry asked. He had utterly no idea as to what had just occurred.

Mr. Drake glanced over his shoulder toward the door, then back at Henry. "I must make this brief. I...I have somewhere I need to be. But first, you must promise to repeat this to no one."

Henry hesitated. He knew Mr. Drake to be honorable enough. But to be sworn to secrecy? And yet, if this allowed him

LOVE IS FOR THE BIRDS

to understand what had just occurred with Miss Fernside, he would do anything.

"Of course, sir."

Mr. Drake leaned toward him, his words swift and soft. "I cannot explain in detail why, but I have no other choice but to marry money."

Henry groaned inwardly. He had a feeling as to where this was headed.

"As such, I made the mistake of asking for Miss Fernside's hand after only a week of knowing her."

"That was *you?*" Henry asked, his jaw slack as he recalled Miss Fernside's words from before.

Mr. Drake grimaced. "You've heard, then. Well, she readily— and laughingly—declined. However, her uncle, Mr. Haskett, discovered my actions and sought to punish me by blackballing me." He shook his head, rubbing a hand at the back of his neck. "I regret my actions heartily if I injured her. But I *must* do this."

He finished, and Henry blew out a heavy breath. He had never seen the man speak so forcefully. Henry could only guess what Mr. Drake's motivations were, but the circumstances must be dire, indeed, to push him to wed for money alone.

Now *Mr. Haskett's* anger with Henry made sense. It must have sounded as if Henry were defending Mr. Drake's actions by calling him honorable.

But as for Miss Fernside's anger…"What was she saying, that I was helping you?"

Mr. Drake shook his head. "As to that matter, I've no idea. Unless perhaps Mr. Haskett has heard other rumors to hold against me."

Henry mulled over the information as the men departed from each other. He needed to find Miss Fernside straightaway to hopefully explain things from his view.

But before long, he discovered from the Chumleys that Miss Fernside, along with her aunt, uncle, and mother had left the ball early due to a "sudden and swift ache in Miss Fernside's head."

Henry knew exactly what that meant. Miss Fernside didn't wish to speak with him. But he would not give up. He'd come too far to give her up now.

CORNWALL – JUNE 2, 1817

Lark had never been more relieved to see the last of London. While she would miss Mother and her constant doting, Lark had been pushed and prodded to enough social outings to last her a lifetime, and she was more than ready to spend the next fortnight out of doors with the birds.

She truly had been unknowingly spoiled on the expedition. She couldn't wait to get back to the world the excursion had created for her, even with all of its many flaws.

With feelings of relief and hope, she stared out of the coach window, taking in the view of Gwynnrudh House, their new place of residence in Cornwall.

"It is pronounced 'gwin ruth', I believe," Mr. Chumley had said at the start of their journey. *"But you know these Cornish names are always so difficult to say. Marazion. Fowey. Golowduyn."*

Despite the difficulty in its name, Gwynnrudh was a charming home, three stories tall with a grey, slated roof and nearly pink walls surrounding the entire edifice. Awnings decorated each framed window, and the drive wrapped around a quaint circle of grass in the center of the space in front of the home.

The building quite reminded Lark of a dollhouse she'd had as a child, and for a moment, she was lost in her memories of the past—when she'd acted out a husband and wife always doting on one another, their house full of children who played and laughed all day long.

Lark had always imagined her future would turn out the same. But nothing in life ever did.

A loud snore tore through the small carriage, and Lark jumped in surprise, turning to face Mr. Dunn, who was seated beside her.

Aunt shook her head with a look of long-suffering, but Uncle merely smiled encouragingly at them both. He would never admit to being tired of their new carriage mate, even if he *had* grown weary of him, for Uncle was the one who had chosen him.

"He will be far better than Mr. Branok," he'd said at the beginning of their journey.

"I hope you managed the switch with discretion, Francis," Aunt had said with a frown. *"I should hate to offend Mr. Branok, no matter what you believe he did."*

"Of course I was discreet," Uncle had defended. *"I merely told Mr. Chumley that others ought to have the opportunity to ride with Mr. Branok, and he readily agreed."*

They'd loaded into their carriage after that and had subsequently spent three solid days of travel with Mr. Dunn mumbling on about his property, bragging about his list of birds, and snoring so loudly, Lark feared the carriage walls would crumble to pieces due to the noise. The only fortune they had was that Aunt and Uncle were able to fend off much of their carriage illness this time due to another draught prescribed by a fine physician in London.

Even still, the sight of Gwynnrudh House was *more* than welcome to Lark.

"We should awaken him," Uncle said, motioning to Mr. Dunn who sprawled out across more than half the seat.

"Must we?" Lark asked. "We can still have half a minute to revel in without his conversation."

She and Aunt shared a covert smile, though Uncle woke the man, nonetheless.

"Mr. Dunn, we have almost arrived."

Mr. Dunn grunted, grumbled, then looked outside. "Ah, yes. Is this the house? It is a bit too pink for my liking."

Lark ignored him. It wasn't too pink. It was charming.

The carriage rolled to a stop, and Lark was finally released from her boxed torture, stretching out her limbs in delight before she caught sight of Mr. Branok.

His eyes were already on her, but she swiftly looked away. There was no purpose in encouraging him with a lingering look of her own—no matter how badly she wanted to. Her friendship with the man had effectively been terminated.

At the thought, her mind filled with the conversation she'd had with Mother just before she'd left.

"Why will you not pursue him, Larky?"

"We wouldn't suit, Mother."

"Stuff and nonsense. Anyone in love would suit."

"But I do not love him."

And yet, ever since she'd said the words aloud, she'd wondered at their truthfulness.

While she'd managed to overcome Mr. Drake's actions quickly, Mr. Branok was another matter entirely. He'd attempted to call after the ball, but fortunately, Lark and Mother had been out. Still, to avoid another surprise visit, Lark had written him a note, telling him she was far too busy to entertain any callers for the foreseeable future and that he should keep his distance.

He had respected her wishes, but now that they were on the excursion together, she had a feeling he would not stop until he did speak with her.

In truth, Lark should have already given him the opportunity to do so, especially after she'd pounced on him and his friend at the ball. She had been in a state of panic that night, overly exhausted, overwhelmed with the socializing she'd done, stressed with the evening ahead of her, and completely disrupted by the reminder of her growing feelings for Mr. Branok. All of these contributed to Uncle persuading her to see something that frankly was not true.

Yes, Mr. Branok might be friends with Mr. Drake, but she couldn't truly believe that Mr. Branok would deceive a woman to marry a fortune hunter. Nor could she believe that he'd spread vitriol about other men to injure them.

It was more likely that Uncle had been misinformed, for Lark *knew* Mr. Branok to be a good man. He'd never in all their weeks together given her any reason to believe otherwise.

She had been hurt, afraid, and persuaded by Uncle. But now it was too late because Mr. Branok was leaving for India, and matters would be far easier to let their friendship—or what was left of it, anyway—slip quietly into the abyss.

Although, such a thing was easier said than done, especially when she'd seen Mr. Branok in the Chumleys' parlor three days prior.

All of her memories with him had been brought back. The way they'd met, his challenge issued, his rescuing her from the nettles. Their kiss. The fact that he was the very reason she'd joined the excursion. All of it.

And now, as she stood on the drive before the pink house with Mr. Branok's eyes still on her, she winced at the pang of longing in her chest to be near him, to listen to him, and to give him the opportunity to defend himself.

But in that moment, Aunt and Uncle came up to stand at both sides of her, preventing her view of him any longer, and she was reminded once again that her time to be with Mr. Branok was over.

As much as her heart tried to convince her otherwise, she wasn't there for him any longer. She was there for the birds.

Throughout the rest of the day, she had to remind herself of that very fact as Mr. Branok taught a brief class, led the party through the pristine grounds of Gwynnrudh, and finally, in the evening, when he shared with them news of a rare bird, a nightjar, being spotted in the woods right next to the house just the night before.

"They are nocturnal and extremely difficult to spot," he shared, "but those of us who wish to brave the darkness and cold Cornish air can venture forth this evening."

Lark had known no small amount of excitement, but she tampered it when Mr. Branok met her gaze.

He would be gone soon. Not only from Cornwall but from England altogether. It would be better not to share in any joy with him, for that would make his absence all the harder.

When darkness fell, most of the party gathered in the front entryway, though Mrs. Chumley and Aunt Harriet had opted out that evening on account of the cold.

As they stepped out into the brisk air, Lark could not blame the women, for it was, indeed, a frigid wind that blew. But she merely focused on the warmth her pelisse afforded her and forged ahead with the others.

Mr. Branok led them through the darkness, holding a lantern aloft to guide them deeper into the woods.

"Stay close to me, Lark," Uncle said, offering his arm to her.

Lark accepted his help, doing her best to stifle her independence, for Uncle's constant companionship was worse than Aunt's. Where Aunt allowed her a certain amount of freedom and space, Uncle had become like a growth on her side.

Throughout the next hour, his close eye on her continued until, to no surprise of her own, the party disbanded.

"We may try again tomorrow night," Mr. Branok assured the group, most of whom were ready to be warm once again.

He gave Lark an encouraging nod, but she looked away without a response, smiling to herself. She didn't need any encouraging or coddling.

LOVE IS FOR THE BIRDS

Not when she had a strategy of her own.

"I am sorry, dear niece," Uncle said, patting her hand in a reassuring manner as they returned indoors. "I know how you were looking forward to finding that bird."

She shrugged. "All is well, Uncle. There is always tomorrow."

She gave him a smile, and he looked at her with surprised delight—no doubt shocked at her uncharacteristic adapting—before he walked her to her door and left her for the evening.

She half-expected him to sleep just outside of her bedchamber, what with how protective he'd become, but she was relieved he did not, for otherwise, there was no way she would be able to enact her plan.

She waited an hour after Penelope had helped her undress, then finally, at midnight, she redressed herself in silence, donning extra layers to ward off the cold that would no doubt be more cutting than before.

Peering outside, she could no longer see candlelight pouring forth from the windows below or to the side of her, and she breathed a settling breath.

It was time.

Tiptoeing her way through the dark house, she made her way to the front door, relieved to find it wasn't locked. If it was unlocked before she left, it would be unlocked when she returned.

Silently, she opened and closed the door behind her, then raised her cloak over her head as she crossed the drive, her boots mutely crunching the dirt and rocks beneath her soles until she reached the soundless grass.

There, in the shadows of the trees, fully hidden from any wandering eye spying her from Gwynnrudh, Lark removed the hood of her cloak and sighed.

She was free. Finally free.

Grinning, she moved forward, the anxiety she'd felt before aiding her warmth as, sure enough, the temperature had dipped again. Still, she took comfort in that fact, for she knew no one in their right mind would be out there that night but her. If she wasn't going to be able to go on excursions of her own in the future as often as she'd once hoped, she was going to take advantage of *this* one.

Now, onto the nightjar.

She walked in silence, pausing every few steps as she relied on each of her senses more fully to find the bird in the darkness —listening for any unfamiliar sounds and sniffing for any unfamiliar scents.

In the research books she'd read, the great eared nightjar resembled a miniature dragon, one Lark had seen in medieval paintings of old. But the more common nightjar that migrated to England—the one she might see tonight—boasted smoother features, its feathers said to perfectly match the grey bark of a tree, almost as if the bird was armored.

To see one during the day was unheard of. At night? Impossible. But the sound…She was certain if she could just hear the sound—described as that of a cricket though more elongated— she might follow it to discover where the nightjar was perched.

She moved through the thick trees, ensuring she did not stray too far from the house, the silhouette of the home lit by the nearly full moon that shone that night.

Crickets chirped all around her, the distant rushing of the ocean's waves the sound of heaven's breath on the wind. Even if she did not find the nightjar, coming out here on her own had already been worth it.

She felt as if she could breathe for the first time since the Lake District. And nothing could disturb her peace. Nothing could—

"Have you taken leave of your senses, Miss Fernside?"

CHAPTER 33

Lark jumped in the air, a quiet yelp erupting from her throat as she swiveled to see who had snuck up behind her.

Fear caused her brain to delay recognition, but as the outline of broad shoulders greeted her, and the deep, soft voice finally settled in her mind, she knew at once who it was.

"Mr. Branok," she breathed.

Her limbs felt like gelatine as relief rushed through her to know it was not a burglar in the night.

Then all at once, indignation ignited. "How dare you startle me in such a way?" she said in a harsh whisper, reaching forward to give him a whack on his arm.

He chuckled in the darkness. "How dare *you* become angry with *me* when I am merely out here to look after your well-being?"

"Fine job you're doing at it. You nearly scared me to death."

She could just see the flash of his smile. "My apologies. But truth be told, you really should have expected me."

"How do you figure that?"

"After those cryptic smiles you were attempting to keep to

yourself earlier, anyone with half a brain could see you were concocting a plan to sneak back out here."

Lark stared. "Very well, perhaps I was not as discreet as I ought to have been. But I thought I did a fine enough job at keeping it from the others. I daresay my uncle was not aware of my desires."

"That would not be the first time, would it?"

He'd spoken the words without guile, but he'd made his point.

For just a moment, matters between them had felt like before, when she could speak comfortably with him, playfully. But too soon, Lark was reminded of all that had happened between them—and it was too much to pretend like it hadn't.

"Well," she began, smoothing out her pelisse, "I thank you for your efforts to look after my well-being, but I assure you, I am quite well. You needn't concern yourself over me any longer, Mr. Branok. Goodnight."

She turned on her heel and made her way through the darkness, but he caught up with her, running around to stop her with both hands raised in a disarming motion. "Miss Fernside, please. Forgive me. I did not mean to cause offense. I simply have kept silent for so long, I only want…"

She stopped, folding her arms. "What, Mr. Branok? What is it you want?"

He hesitated. "A single moment of your time."

The pleading in his tone, the softness of his words, tugged at her defenses, just like they had by the fireside when he'd first begged her forgiveness.

But she could not tear them down this time—not when her heart still needed protecting.

"I do not know if that would be wise," she answered truthfully.

"Because you do not care to hear what I have to say?"

"No, I do care."

"Then, why?" he pressed.

"Because my *uncle* thinks it unwise."

He didn't respond for a moment, and she could only guess what words he was withholding. "And what do *you* think?"

"It matters not what I think."

"It does to me," he answered promptly.

Lark could no longer meet his gaze. She wanted to believe him, but whispers of doubt echoed in the deepest recesses of her heart—doubt that had been planted there by Mr. Yates long ago.

Mr. Yates had partially hidden his sharp teeth and cruel claws until she'd finally dared to speak her mind.

"I cannot marry you, Mr. Yates. I will not," she'd said.

He'd let loose in a rage, criticizing every inch of her personality and soul, then moved on to her family. She'd been crushed in the moment, but over the years, she'd discovered that the words—while unpardonable—were spoken out of his own insecurities and had nothing to do with herself.

And yet, the unsettling feelings borne from Mr. Yates's cruelty returned to plague her. Was she truly unlovable? Was she really so strange that no one could bear to listen to her?

She hadn't realized she'd shaken her head until Mr. Branok dipped his chin to meet her gaze.

"Do you not believe me?" he asked.

When put so plainly, she couldn't deny it. She *did* believe that he cared what she thought. Ever since they'd first met, he'd listened to her and welcomed her conversation. He was the first man, aside from Father and Uncle, who genuinely seemed interested in what she had to say.

But she still couldn't comprehend *why*.

"I believe you," she responded. "But I cannot understand it."

"You cannot understand what?"

"Why my opinion matters to you."

He tipped his head to the side. "Because *you* matter to me,

Miss Fernside." He drew a step closer, his softened features just visible in the light of the moon slipping through the trees. "I cannot tell you how I have missed your company and your friendship. I have spent the last fortnight crushed, knowing how poorly you must think of me, and I cannot bear to live another moment without at least attempting to modify those thoughts."

His words filled every bit of her. Her defenses dispelled, making room for a poignant twinge of regret at not allowing herself to listen to him before now.

She'd promised Uncle she wouldn't, but what good had that done? Uncle was still filled with fear concerning Mr. Branok, Mr. Branok had clearly been hurt by her actions, and Lark? Lark was more miserable than ever because she was being told what to do and what to think *again*.

From the moment she'd met Mr. Branok, she'd been unapologetically herself—snapping at him, correcting him, and speaking her mind—and he had responded in stride, unafraid to speak the truth back but always willing to apologize when he had been in the wrong.

And, despite it all, he still accepted her. He still wished to be near her. He had been nothing but honorable and gentlemanly from the start.

And Lark was tired of being told to believe otherwise.

"I will leave you if you still wish it," Mr. Branok said, taking her silence as a dismissal.

But she shook her head. "No, I should like to listen to what you have to say. In truth, I have wanted to do so for weeks."

He hesitated. "Forgive me, but if that is true, why did you not allow me to do so before now?"

Ashamed, she hung her head. "I was confused. And fearful. Uncle said many things."

"About my alleged friendship with Mr. Drake? Or about why I was blackballed?"

LOVE IS FOR THE BIRDS

"Both," she admitted. "I was afraid that everything Uncle said was true."

Mr. Branok was silent for a moment. "*Was* afraid?"

"Yes." She raised her chin. "No matter what the truth is, no matter what Uncle says, no matter how you vex me...I cannot think poorly of you, Mr. Branok."

His lips formed into a small smile. "I can't tell you how happy I am to hear that, Miss Fernside. However, I should like to address your concerns if you are so inclined."

She nodded in silence. She was more than inclined—she was ready.

Mr. Branok drew a deep breath. "Firstly, concerning Mr. Drake—I have not spoken with the gentleman above a handful of times. After you left us at the ball, he admitted to his proposal, and while I do not know his reasons behind his actions, he appeared truly regretful for causing you any discomfort."

A soothing warmth wrapped round Lark's heart at the words. She had already forgiven Mr. Drake's actions. But now... she was *healing* from Mr. Drake's actions.

"Until that evening," Mr. Branok continued, "I was entirely unaware of his desire to marry money—and entirely unaware of his connection to you."

Further peace seeped through Lark's limbs. She'd known the truth all along, but hearing the words from his mouth was more than validating—it was comforting.

"As for why I was blackballed," Mr. Branok continued, "I should have told you from the start. But I was frightened of admitting to my behavior, afraid that I might disappoint you. I can only assume now that you have heard of the articles."

Lark held her breath unconsciously, nodding. So he *had* done something—something that might disappoint her. But could his actions be as bad as Uncle had said, spreading false rumors and injuring others?

At once, she pushed the worrisome thoughts away. She was finished listening to words born from fear and mistrust. Instead, she would listen to her heart, to the words that brought peace to her mind—for that was how truth was distinguishable from lies.

And being around Mr. Branok always brought peace to her life.

"I did write the articles," he began softly. "There is no excuse for my penning them, but I will say that I was young, my parents had only just died, and I was in a very dark place. You recall me telling you how my friend was denied membership to White's, resulting in me losing all desire to join myself?"

She nodded, and Mr. Branok ducked his head, rubbing his hand at the back of his neck. "Well, I did not simply *lose* a desire to join. I *found* a desire for retribution. In an act of solidarity—and I admit a hearty helping of pride—I took it upon myself to write a series of articles about the clubs in London, likening them and their members to a murmuration of starlings. Territorial. Ravaging all in their wake. Mimicking other birds and having no individual thoughts of their own. Screeching loudly so no other sounds can be heard. That sort of thing. I admit, it was childish, but it did the trick. I was blackballed from every club. Not soon after that, Lord Blackstone sought me out."

He looked down at Lark again, his eyes glinting in the moonlight. "Had I known it would ever lead you to think less of me, I assure you, I would have stopped myself from publishing the articles. But I cannot regret doing so. Not when it led me to the life I've been able to lead thus far."

He finished, and Lark stared up at him. Was that it? Was that all he had done?

"Are you so very appalled?" he asked with a sort of wince.

To her own surprise, Lark laughed. "Appalled? Certainly not. I'm intrigued. And, frankly, I should like to see a copy of these articles myself."

Surprise registered across his features, then a grin spread upon his lips. "I may or may not have kept a few for posterity's sake."

She laughed, relief overcoming her. "That is truly all you did? No vicious rumors spread, no cruel untruths said about any individual?"

Mr. Branok pulled back. "Of course not. The articles were entirely in metaphor. I shared no lies and mentioned no names, only clubs in general. The worst thing I said was that starlings were known to suck the eggs of other birds, likening the clubs to sucking the lives from gentlemen before they could even begin to participate in the club." He gave an awkward sort of smile. "I took the metaphor a bit too far in that regard, I suppose."

But Lark's smile only grew. She knew it. She *knew* it. She knew the rumors had been untrue, that Mr. Branok could never do anything so unkind.

A lightness continued to fill every inch of her, an airiness lifting her heart to soaring.

"So," Mr. Branok said, peering into her eyes through the darkness, "you are still willing to associate with me despite all of this?"

She beamed. "More than willing, sir."

"Even if your uncle does not approve?"

"*Especially* if." Uncle Francis would simply have to take her word for it from this point forward. Mr. Branok was in her life to stay.

"Excellent," Mr. Branok said. Then he sobered. "However, there is still one matter we must resolve."

"What matter is that?"

"That of our challenge ending early."

Her stomach dipped. "Oh, I see."

All at once, her joy and elation dissipated like smoke in the air.

India. She'd forgotten about India.

He would be gone in four days' time, and she would be left alone again.

How could she have been so stupid? Here she was, thrilled to be talking with Mr. Branok once more, to be back in her fantasy world the excursion had provided for her...only for the gentleman to be stripped from her presence again in less than a week.

How had she allowed herself to become so wrapped up in this relationship that she couldn't even think straight? That she couldn't protect her heart enough to shield what would inevitably damage her more than anything—being physically and emotionally separated from Mr. Branok?

She knew the reason. Her *heart* knew the reason. But she couldn't admit to loving the man aloud. That would only make saying goodbye more painful.

This was why she never should have allowed herself to fall for him. This was why she'd wanted to remain single. All of this heartache, this regret, could have been avoided had her heart simply behaved.

"Do you still wish to cancel the challenge?" he asked.

Lark turned away, grateful for the darkness that provided her emotions time to settle. Yes, she loved the man. Yes, she longed for a perfect world in which she could marry him, and he could marry her—where both of their dreams could be fulfilled and carried out without issue.

But such a world did not exist.

A world in which their friendship continued, however, *did* exist.

With a deep breath, she faced him again. "We can continue the challenge and see who is victor on the day you leave...on one condition."

"Name it."

"You must let me know the moment you publish your book

Love Is for the Birds

about all your bird findings in India so I can be the first in line to purchase it."

She'd expected a smile from him in return. Perhaps a chuckle. But when his features softened, and he fixed his attention on her, a fissure of delight stirred in her stomach.

"Miss Fernside," he said, "have you any notion how fortunate I am to simply know you?"

A sudden emotion washed over her, a perfect mixture of love and sorrow. Tears pricked the corners of her eyes, but she blinked them swiftly away. She shouldn't be feeling any more attraction to Mr. Branok. She shouldn't be falling in love with him any more than she already was. But how could she not when he spoke such lovely things to her?

He took a step toward her, his intent clear as he closed the distance between them. He reached his hand to her cheek, her skin tingling with anticipation.

Snap!

A twig broke behind them, followed swiftly by voices, and Lark's heart jumped to her throat.

They were not alone out there. If she and Mr. Branok were to be discovered...

She shot a look toward him, but he was already in motion. He seized her hand and pulled her deep into the woods.

CHAPTER 34

Mr. Branok led her through the forest, weaving their way around trunks and bushes until he pulled her behind a wide tree. He leaned his back against the trunk, pulling her body face forward against him to shield her from any sighting. She clung to the sides of his jacket, her chest rising and falling with rapid breaths, though she tried to stifle it, for each breath pulled her closer to Mr. Branok. He held her in place, his strong hands searing her upper forearms with heat, as if his protective hands would be branded into her skin forever.

At least then she would have a part of him with her when he left.

The voices grew louder, a distinct male and female tone marking the air.

"Who are they?" Lark dared to whisper.

Mr. Branok didn't respond for a moment, then he bent down, whispering in her ear, "Shepherds."

His breath tickled the side of her neck, and pleasant chills ran up and down her skin. She closed her eyes to balance herself, his proximity making her head spin as he straightened, though he kept hold of her behind the tree.

LOVE IS FOR THE BIRDS

She strained to listen to the couple approaching, finally hearing their words.

"This is utterly ridiculous, Mr. Shepherd," Mrs. Shepherd said in a voice that Lark guessed was supposed to be a whisper.

"Ridiculous?" Mr. Shepherd returned. "My dear Mrs. Shepherd, this is *romantic*."

Mrs. Shepherd giggled, and a small degree of Lark's nerves settled, at least in regard to being discovered. Of all those in their party, the Shepherds would cause the least amount of damage.

Though Lark had always said she cared not what Society thought of her, she did not have the energy to go through whatever rumors would abound should she and Mr. Branok be caught in such a compromising situation. As such, she sealed her lips as the couple drew closer.

"Come along, my darling," Mr. Shepherd was saying, "where is your sense of adventure?"

"I never had one, if you recall. You would no doubt be better off on your own out here."

"Nonsense," Mr. Shepherd said at once. "I am far happier with you than without. After all, what would be the purpose in partaking in an activity like this if I cannot share it with the one I love?"

Lark felt the hair at her brow shift back and forth with the breeze, only to discover it was Mr. Branok's breath instead, warm and steady against her skin, his fingers still encircling her in a protective yet gentle manner she'd never before experienced.

"It is freezing out," Mrs. Shepherd continued, her voice jerking as if she shivered. "Why can we not find the bird in the daytime?"

"You heard Mr. Branok. The bird is most active at night. Come now, I shall keep you warm."

Silence followed. The couple must have stopped just a few

feet away from the tree Lark and Mr. Branok had hidden behind, for Mrs. Shepherd's giggling sounded louder. "I thought you brought me out here to find that night...ling? Night...tern?"

"Night*jar*," Mr. Shepherd said.

"I still cannot imagine why you are so determined."

"Imagine the look on Mr. Branok's and Miss Fernside's faces when we tell them we discovered it first," Mr. Shepherd said.

They laughed together, and Lark pulled back to meet Mr. Branok's gaze. They shared a look of amusement in the darkness, but as her eyes dropped to the smile tipping his own lips upward, her heart thudded dully in her ears.

They were so close to one another. Her fingers loosened round his jacket, no longer clutching at the fabric but resting at his sides.

"You are mad if you think that possible, my dear," Mrs. Shepherd responded. "Those two could find a flock of birds with their eyes closed at the bottom of the sea, I'm sure of it." She broke off with a sigh. "They are quite a formidable pair. When will they finally see reason and wed?"

Lark stiffened. She dropped her gaze, though she felt Mr. Branok's watchful eye on her as the conversation continued.

"I don't know," Mr. Shepherd said. "We both know they have no plans to do so."

"Yes, that is what they've said, but it is another matter entirely what they *feel*. Surely you've seen the way Miss Fernside brightens whenever his attention is upon her."

Lark could no longer feel the chill on the air, heat rushing through her body. Mr. Branok still stared down at her, but she could not lift her gaze. Her humiliation was already acute.

"They're always sneaking off together, too," Mrs. Shepherd continued, her voice dropping to a whisper, though it carried on a draught. "And the way *he* watches her? There are veritable stars in his eyes. Surely you have noticed that."

Lark fought everything within her not to look at Mr.

LOVE IS FOR THE BIRDS

Branok. She had seen those stars far too often in his expression. They would be ingrained in her memory for eternity.

"I couldn't say I *have* noticed that," Mr. Shepherd responded. "We gentlemen aren't the most observant when it comes to such matters."

"Hmm," Mrs. Shepherd hummed disappointedly. "Then there is nothing recent you've seen or heard from Mr. Branok that would point to his feelings for Miss Fernside?"

"I'm afraid not."

"Pity. I was certain just one small piece of information would make me so happy, I'd be in a *very* accommodating mood…"

She trailed off knowingly. Silence followed, then Mrs. Shepherd giggled again.

"In that case," Mr. Shepherd said, "I do have a bit of knowledge that might satisfy you. Have I told you about Mr. Branok standing up for Miss Fernside?"

Mrs. Shepherd gasped. "Do tell."

Lark was certain Mr. Branok could feel her heartbeat thudding against his own as Mr. Shepherd spoke.

"It happened after dinner one evening," he said. "Mr. Chumley was carrying on as usual, complaining for one reason or another about Miss Fernside."

"Insufferable man," Mrs. Shepherd muttered.

"Indeed," Mr. Shepherd said grimly. "At any rate, most of the men allowed the words to progress. But not Mr. Branok. Not only did he compliment her humor and honesty, but he also confessed that her talent for bird observing was unmatched, even with himself. He ended with defending her honor, as well, when Mr. Dunn dared question the accuracy of her list. Needless to say, the men do not speak so unjustly about Miss Fernside any longer—especially when Mr. Branok is around."

Mrs. Shepherd responded with an airy sigh, but Lark heard nothing else. She frantically blinked to rid her eyes of the tears threatening to spill down her cheeks. The knowledge of Mr.

Branok's defense of her was not a surprise, nor were the words he'd spoken that he'd never meant for her to hear. Instead, they aligned with exactly who she knew him to be—the only man who would ever hold her heart.

Unable to help herself any longer, she raised her gaze to his, the movement causing a tear to slip from her eye. It trailed down the side of her features, leaving a cold path behind it.

Mr. Branok studied her, his brows turned up with emotion as he focused on her eyes, lips, then teardrop.

The air hummed around them with the crickets chirping and the distant sea's waves rumbling, though the energy between her and Mr. Branok was the loudest of all.

"Did my information make you happy?" Mr. Shepherd said, his voice a distant echo in Lark's mind.

"It most certainly did," Mrs. Shepherd whispered. "But I fear I am far too frozen to do anything about it."

"Then let us return indoors, my darling."

"What about the bird?"

"What bird?"

She giggled, and the two of them wandered toward the house, their voices and laughter carrying on until the sounds disappeared on the air.

All the while, Lark did not step back from Mr. Branok, and Mr. Branok did not remove his hands from Lark's arms.

Instead, they stood there, silent, staring, hearts beating wildly as their longing for each other became so palpable, Lark felt as if she could almost grasp it, never to let it go again.

That was what she wanted, for Mr. Branok to be hers. She wanted to be his wife, for him to be her husband. She wanted to spend the rest of her days in his arms, observing birds, creating challenges together, believing in each other.

And as Mr. Branok stared down at her, she could only hope that he wanted to be with her the very same. He leaned closer, his hands finally moving, sliding up her arms, cradling her neck, tipping her chin for him to better place a kiss upon her lips.

She leaned back, eyes closed, lips parted, and waited.

But a sound pierced the air, a chittering loud and long, and Lark's eyes flew open.

She met Mr. Branok's gaze, excitement alight within them that matched her own.

"Is that..." he began.

Her heart skipped. "The nightjar!"

CHAPTER 35

There could be only one thing that would stop Henry from kissing Lark Fernside, and it wasn't a bird.

It was Miss Fernside *hearing* a bird.

Had it been up to him, he would have ignored the sound of the nightjar altogether, kissed the woman until they were both senseless, then maybe, if there was time, gone to see if the bird was still there.

But he knew how excited she would be at the sighting, so he'd stopped before they'd even begun.

Sure enough, her eyes brightened, and her grin grew as she stared in the direction of the sound.

He dropped his hands as she did the same, and together, they slowly followed the chittering through the trees. The noise grew as they drew nearer and nearer until finally, it was so close, Henry knew they could spot it, so long as they positioned themselves in the right location.

As Miss Fernside searched the trees, however, Henry had a difficult time focusing on anything aside from the memory of her body pressed against his. The way she'd cried when she'd heard of him defending her. The way she'd listened to his side of the rumors again—believed his words *again*.

Her goodness knew no bounds.

"I can't find it," Miss Fernside whispered in the darkness.

Henry once more pulled back to the present. He needed to focus. He needed to find this bird. Not for himself, but for her.

He leaned down, shifting back and forth to see the silhouette of the trees against the moon above. He'd learned how to find night herons this way in the West Indies, and he could only pray it would work the same for the nightjar.

A few minutes later, he spotted it. The bark-like feathers were impossible to see in the darkness, only a black silhouette visible with the lack of light, but he was certain it was the bird they sought.

With a stuttering heart, he tugged at Miss Fernside's arm until she leaned closer to him.

"There," he whispered in her ear.

She peered down, looking back and forth with a shake of her head. "I can't see…"

Knowing he was simply allowing himself to drown faster, Henry wrapped his right arm around her shoulder and pulled her closer to him until their faces touched. There, he pointed with his left hand where the silhouette of the bird stood out against the dim light, perched at the very edge of a leafless branch.

He knew she'd seen it when she breathed out a sigh. She'd done the same when she'd found the redstart and the kingfisher. Would her eyes be sparkling as they'd done with every other bird?

He forced his attention to remain on the nightjar still chittering away, the bird's chest puffing out with each call. But before long, Henry was once more drawn to the woman beside him.

Removing his arm from around her shoulders and straightening his stance, he took a moment to observe her. Sure enough, her eyes sparkled, and he couldn't look away.

For years, he'd told himself that there would never be a female he loved more than his love for observing birds. But now he'd been proven wrong. Absolutely wrong. He was left with two choices. He needed to either give up his love for Miss Fernside and continue with his expeditions, or he needed to marry her and give up all he'd built for the last half-decade.

Such a decision should have been painful. Impossible, even.

But as he caressed her features with his eyes, watched as another tear trailed down her skin, Mr. Shepherd's words echoed in his mind.

"What would be the purpose in partaking in an activity like this if I cannot share it with the one I love?"

Henry had always loved bird observing. But never more than this last excursion. Instead of the standard joy he felt when finding a new bird, Miss Fernside's joy doubled his own. The same went for his excitement over each bird pursuit, each conversation, each rescue, and each new sighting. He felt all the same emotions, but they were multiplied to the point where he could hardly bear it.

Mr. Shepherd had been absolutely correct.

Why in Heaven's name would Henry ever choose to give up a life with Lark Fernside when it would be exponentially better than anything he'd ever experienced alone?

He *wouldn't* give it up. It was as simple as that.

But would Miss Fernside wish to do the same?

She must have felt his gaze on her, for in the next moment, she met his eyes. The very air between them pulled them closer, and Henry faced her more directly. When she did the same and her eyes dropped to his lips, a pleasant, nervous energy surged within him.

He took a step toward her, wanting to feel her kiss on his lips again, wanting to feel her in his arms forevermore, and more than anything, wanting to know what it felt like to kiss the woman he now knew he loved.

Before, he'd taken their kiss in steps, needing her approval, needing to test the waters of her affection. But now, the desire in her eyes was clear. Now, hesitance for what the kiss might do vanished.

For he was ready to give up anything and everything to be with Lark Fernside. He wouldn't stay back a moment longer.

Lark saw the switch in Mr. Branok's expression. Something warm had held his features before—a kindling of desire, but now fire flashed in his eyes.

In an instant, he closed the distance between them. His right hand slid round her waist, settling at the small of her back as he pulled her toward him. His left fingers slipped through her hair, cradling her head in his palm. Then his lips were on hers.

Lark only took a second to respond. Her arms wrapped around him, his firm back beneath her fingertips as she tipped her head to the side, kissing him with as much fervor as he kissed her.

Their mouths pressed against each other, working in unison, both of them expressing their desire to continue the affection for as long as possible. Lark's heart had never beaten so powerfully, so wildly. But then, that was because she had never felt such love before—for Mr. Branok and *from* Mr. Branok.

Seeing the nightjar had been a dream come true. But sharing this moment with him was heavenly.

At the thought of him truly loving her, an overwhelming sensation of joy and peace rushed over her. How was she so fortunate as to have won his affection? She'd never known such a love could exist. It furnished her desire to be closer to him, to remove any remaining distance between their souls, just so she might connect even deeper than before.

She moved her hands from around his waist to slide up his chest before wrapping around his neck, bringing her as close as possible to him. He sighed in response, securing both arms around her, splaying his fingers across her as he felt every inch of her side and back, though he never strayed from propriety— for that was just the sort of gentleman he was.

For a moment, he broke off from their kiss, allowing her to catch her breath as he trailed his lips around her cheek and brow before capturing her mouth once more.

Lark couldn't help but compare this kiss to the one before. Where once he'd been reserved, now he commanded attention. Lark was more than happy to surrender, if only because she trusted this man with her whole heart. She *loved* him with her whole heart.

Tonight had been perfect. Her time with him had been flawless. Old wounds had been laid to rest. Bridges had been mended. Hearts had been sealed together. And now, she and Mr. Branok would be able to…

To what? Have a future together?

The question slipped past her euphoria, shooting thorns of doubt onto the flowers of their affections, and her mood plummeted.

They *had* no future together.

Mr. Branok pulled back slowly, clearly sensing her shift just like before. He stared down at her, his eyes alight as he took her hands in his.

She couldn't allow this to continue.

"Mr. Branok…" she began.

"We are far beyond that now," he said, his voice husky. "Henry."

The ache in her heart caused her to wince. "I...I don't think—"

"Marry me."

Lark stared, stunned. "What?" she breathed.

"Marry me," he stated more firmly, his eyes caressing every inch of her features. "I know what you said before, that you don't wish to wed, that you don't want your life dictated by another. But I swear right now if you'll be my wife, you will want for nothing, and that includes freedom. Freedom to explore whatever part of the world you wish to. Freedom to remain home should you wish it. Freedom to command *me* to remain at home. Anything you desire, it shall be yours. Even, and especially, my love for you."

Tears sprung to her eyes. This was everything she'd ever wanted. A gentleman to love her, to provide for her, to be her everything. For she was willing to be the same for him. She would have gladly given up her decision to remain single. She would have gladly remained at home to wait for his return from his exhibitions.

But then, that was just it. If he married her, there would *be* no more exhibitions. There would be no more published books. There would be no more fulfillment of his dreams to travel to India. She could use her fortune to get him there, but then what? They had no connections, no permissions, and no knowledge of how it all worked.

He'd said it himself weeks before. If he married, he would be forced to give up everything.

Lark knew what it was like to give up a part of herself for someone. That was why she could not have Mr. Branok do the same.

At the realization of what she was about to do, fresh tears sprang to her eyes. "I'm sorry," she forced out with a broken whisper. "But I cannot marry you."

She tried to pull her hands from his, but he held steadfast, his eyes steady. "Because of your promise to remain unwed?"

"No. Because of another promise I made long ago. That I would never ask anyone to give up who they are for me."

"Traveling for excursions is not all of who I am," he said at once.

"But it makes up such a large part of who you are. I could never take that away from you."

"You wouldn't have to," he said firmly. "I would be giving it up on my own."

But she shook her head. "You can't. I would never forgive myself. I would always feel as if some part of you regretted leaving the opportunities you have now, and we...we could never be happy because of it."

The words were like daggers to her own heart. She could only pray they wouldn't be to *his*. And yet, she needed to be truthful. She needed reality to settle between them to make things easier when he left for India to fulfill more of his dreams and she never saw him again.

The silence between them stifled the air, and only then did she realize the absence of the nightjar's chittering.

"Forgive me, Mr. Branok," she said with finality, pulling her hands from his as she stepped away from him. "I can't go through with it."

"Do you love me, Lark?"

Her name on his lips, the question on his voice, made her pause. He stared at her with patience, but she couldn't answer, for if she spoke at all, she would speak the truth.

Instead, she turned around and fled through the trees, ignoring his calling out for her, ignoring the pain he must have felt, and praying Heaven guided her steps through the darkness —as well as through the rest of her life as she now tried to figure out how exactly she was going to live without Henry Branok by her side.

CHAPTER 36

ornwall – June 3, 1817

Henry awoke the next morning, not ready to face the day. Of course his lack of sleep and the discouraging thoughts that plagued his mind hadn't helped matters, but more than anything, he was crushed due to the simple fact that Miss Fernside loved him, but she still would not be *with* him.

He didn't blame her for her refusal. The proposal had been too sudden. There had been no notice, no romantic words, no promises or plans for their future—even though he had them all. Instead, he'd been caught up in the moment, unwilling to wait a single second longer to begin their life together. But how he regretted his hastiness.

He'd prayed a good night's rest would have helped to change Miss Fernside's mind, but when she didn't appear for breakfast nor at one of his final morning classes, he knew she was avoiding him again.

"Can we expect your niece to be down soon?" he asked Mrs. Haskett as the group gathered in the gardens, a large tent and chairs having been set up for their comfort. "I am happy to wait for her."

"She is feeling excessively tired this morning, I fear," Mrs. Haskett responded quietly with a fleeting glance at her husband, who stood across the grass speaking with Mr. Dunn. "I do wonder if she's merely resting now to be ready to find that nightjar this evening."

Henry forced an innocent smile.

"At any rate," Mrs. Haskett continued with another glance at her husband, "she sent me a note this morning, giving her excuses, so you needn't wait for her."

Henry nodded, though the disappointment stung.

His lesson—timely focused on how to find birds in the dark of the night—was painful to teach with the constant reminder of the previous evening, so once he finished, Henry escaped from the others and retreated to his bedchamber. He'd hoped to see Lark along the way, but she was nowhere in sight.

The rest of the day progressed in the same insipid manner— Henry moving from space to space, praying to catch Lark, becoming disappointed when he didn't, and always fighting his desire to appear outside her door and beg her forgiveness— until dinner finally arrived.

But once again, Lark made no appearance, and the Hasketts gave their excuses for her a second time, all while Mr. Haskett looked condemningly at Henry.

Had Lark told her uncle what Henry had done? Or was he simply blaming Henry for something else? It certainly wouldn't be the first time.

The meal was served earlier than normal to allow the party more time out of doors to spy the nightjar later that evening. For obvious reasons, Henry couldn't get himself to join in the buzz of excitement around the table, nor could he focus on the conversations around him.

He was defeated. Exhausted. And more than anything, depleted of all hope.

As such, he slipped out of the drawing room after dinner

LOVE IS FOR THE BIRDS

without notice by the others, asking a passing footman to call for a horse. After scribbling out a quick letter in his bedchamber, Henry tucked the correspondence inside his waistcoat pocket, then left Gwynnrudh House without a sound.

He pulled on his gloves and made ready to leave as the groom delivered a black horse. Henry thanked him and grasped the reins. Just as he was about to mount, the door opened behind him.

"So, you're leaving, then?"

Henry turned to face Mr. Haskett, the man's features tight and rigid as he stared at Henry.

"Off to London without even a goodbye to anyone?" Mr. Haskett continued.

Henry was about to respond, then thought better of it. Whatever he said in defense of himself, Mr. Haskett was not going to believe him.

True to form, the gentleman sniffed with derision at Henry's sustained silence. "It is just as well. At least this way, you will stop injuring my niece even more than you already have."

His niece.

Henry looked away with a shake of his head. "You are aware that Miss Fernside does not belong to you, are you not?"

Mr. Haskett narrowed his eyes. "Are you aware she does not belong to *you*?"

"Keenly."

This placed a look of satisfaction on Mr. Haskett's face. "It would appear that she has finally taken my advice, then, and dropped her acquaintance with you."

Acquaintance. If only Mr. Haskett knew how *acquainted* Henry and Lark actually were.

"Well, this can only be for the best," the man continued. "You have been nothing but trouble for her from the start."

Those words, coming from the gentleman who'd bled Henry

dry for information about his travels and gushed over his knowledge about birds? Henry couldn't help but scoff.

He should have walked away right then. But his pride securely rooted his boots to the gravel drive. "I'm sorry you think that, Mr. Haskett. Because I have been nothing but kind and respectful to you, your wife, and Miss Fernside from the beginning of this excursion."

Mr. Haskett opened his mouth to protest, but Henry drew to his full height, commanding silence as he continued. "My membership in Blackstone's may have sullied your opinion of me forever, as well as the rumors surrounding my name. But I would have assumed, knowing what you do about Miss Fernside's own suffering, that it is far better to judge a person off his or her own actions than what others say. Otherwise, it speaks much more about a person willing to believe in tittle tattle than it does about the man or woman whose name has been tarnished by brazen deception."

Mr. Haskett's stiff look faltered only a degree, but it was enough for Henry.

"As for Miss Fernside," Henry finished, "you ought to trust her more than you do. Perhaps then you would be able to learn more about honor and respectability."

He tipped his head in departure, then mounted the black horse.

"You will not tell Lark you are leaving?" Mr. Haskett snapped back at him. "Where is the honor in *that?*"

Henry merely cast the gentleman a look of long-suffering then trotted away on his horse without a word or a single glance back.

LOVE IS FOR THE BIRDS

LARK JERKED AWAKE AT THE SOUND OF SOFT TAPPING AGAINST HER door. She sat up straight in the chair before her desk, slightly disoriented.

Light still shone through her window, though it appeared more golden than before. Had dinner passed already? She'd been staring mutely at her field journal before she had fallen asleep upright at the desk. Her lack of sleep last night must have finally caught up with her.

Rising from the desk, she rubbed the sleep from her eyes, smoothed out the fabric of her light blue dress, and answered the door.

She wasn't surprised to find her aunt and uncle standing before her, though she *was* taken aback by the concerned look in Aunt Harriet's eyes and the anger in Uncle Francis's.

"What's the matter?" she asked at once, opening the door wider to allow them within.

They moved through the doorway, neither of them speaking as she closed the door behind them.

"What is it?" Lark asked again, looking between them both, her stomach churning with nerves.

Had they heard that she'd snuck out last night? That...that she'd denied a proposal from the only man she'd ever loved?

Aunt Harriet spoke first, her brows pointed up. "Mr. Branok is gone."

Lark blinked, a cold wave of shock rushing over her. "Gone?" she breathed. "What do you mean, gone?"

"Your uncle saw him leave just after dinner."

Still, Lark couldn't understand their words. "Well, where is he going?"

"London," Uncle stated gruffly.

"No," Lark said at once, her mouth parted in stunned disbelief. "You must be mistaken."

"I am not. I asked, and he did not deny it."

Lark still shook her head. "He does not leave for another three days."

Another three days would allow her time to process his request. To rally her defenses. To beg his forgiveness. And to... to reconsider.

After all, that was what she'd been doing all day in her bedchamber on her own. Seeking out an answer to their problem. Praying for a solution to ease her concerns, to provide a resolution where they could both receive what they wished. Where Henry could still travel the world, could still publish his findings, and she could be with the man she loved.

But if he was leaving for London—leaving for India—she had already lost her chance to beg him to propose again.

"What have I done?" she asked aloud, shaking her head in dismay.

"What do you mean?" Aunt asked, her brow now furrowed. "You've done nothing to warrant..."

She trailed off when Lark shook her head again. "He proposed last night."

Aunt gasped, and Uncle frowned all the deeper.

"The scoundrel," Uncle growled out, but Lark hardly noticed, continuing as if she were the only one in the room.

"But I said no," she said, a hopelessness filling her soul to near drowning. "I said no."

"That is a fine thing, Lark," Uncle's voice said, echoing in the recesses of her empty heart. "You will heal from the wounds he has caused, and you will be far better without him."

The words were just another shovel of dirt into the grave that was her hope.

"You're certain he left?" she asked him again.

"Quite," he stated firmly. "Really, Lark, this is for the best. You—"

His words were cut short when Aunt placed a soft hand on

LOVE IS FOR THE BIRDS

his arm. He looked at her questioningly, but Aunt gave a subtle shake of her head.

"Do you..." she began gently. "Lark, darling, do you regret your refusal?"

Lark looked between her aunt and uncle, fearful of their response, but when she hooked onto Aunt's gentle gaze, she could no longer deny the words aloud.

"Yes. Very much," she breathed.

Aunt's eyes glistened. "You mean to say you wish to accept him?"

Lark's heart overflowed at the very notion. "Yes, very much," she repeated. "I have to tell him. I have to let him know."

Aunt's smile spread across her lips as she turned to Uncle. "You said he only left an hour ago?"

"Well, yes, but I—"

"Call for a carriage, Francis."

"Now see here, she cannot—"

Aunt turned to face him with a tight-lipped expression Lark had never before seen. "No, *you* see here, my dear," she stated firmly. "Lark is old enough and of a sound mind. If she says she wishes to accept an amiable gentleman's proposal, there is no reason for us not to lend our undying support."

Uncle's face grew red. "If he were amiable, that would be fine, but he is not. He is a member of—"

"Oh," Aunt Harriet broke off, casting an impatient look to the ceiling. "If I hear one more word about 'Blackstone's this' and 'White's that,' I shall go mad."

"It matters!" Uncle exclaimed. "He is not a good man, he—"

"Uncle?"

This time, Lark interrupted, her voice soft through their argument. They faced her, both falling silent at her words.

"I know you wish to protect me, and you always have," she began, "But I am older now than I was with Mr. Yates. Older and wiser. I have learned much. And I can say assuredly that

Henry Branok is a good man. He is the *best* of men. And I will accept his proposal and marry him, if he will still have me."

Uncle grew more and more flustered, huffing unintelligible words as fear shone in his eyes.

Lark's heart reached out to him, and she placed a soothing hand on his arm. "I cannot thank you enough for always being there for me, Uncle Francis. Though, I assure you, I know what I am doing. You will see in time. But right now, I must find him." Then she looked to Aunt. "Will you help me?"

Aunt beamed. "What are we waiting for?"

Together, the two of them ran from the room, Uncle following closely behind them, still red in the face, though silent as they reached the entryway and Mrs. Chumley and Mrs. Shepherd walked in at that same moment.

"Heavens, what is all this about?" Mrs. Chumley asked, looking from person to person.

"Where are you off to in such a hurry?" Mrs. Shepherd asked next.

Lark met her eyes. Mrs. Shepherd would never know what Lark had overheard the other night, but Lark felt a kinship with her she'd never experienced with anyone other than Aunt.

As such, she smiled at her knowingly. "I'm going after Mr. Branok."

Mrs. Shepherd's eyes lit with joy.

"He left?" Mrs. Chumley asked, glancing between the others again.

Lark caught them up to speed while Uncle steamed silently in the background, and moments later, Mrs. Chumley herself called for a carriage.

"We're coming with you," she stated. "This is far more appealing than making ready to find some bird in the cold tonight."

Mrs. Shepherd nodded, and Aunt happily agreed. "Any amount of carriage sickness is worth this."

LOVE IS FOR THE BIRDS

Lark could only smile.

"And what am I to do?" Uncle stated from the background as the women spilled out of the front door as soon as the carriage rolled up.

"Join the men back in the drawing room," Lark said, "and tell Mr. Chumley thank you."

She ran down the stairs, the women already piling into the carriage.

"Tell him thank you for what?" Uncle called after her.

She climbed into the carriage, then popped her head out of the door. "For his attempts to keep me from joining the excursion! Were it not for his efforts, I never would have had the pride to keep fighting to join!"

And with a grin, she backed into the carriage and leaned into her seat, her heart and mind racing in time as she contemplated what she'd say to Mr. Branok and if she truly had another chance at happiness.

CHAPTER 37

Henry slowed his horse to an easy walk as he faced the sun sinking lower in the sky.

Petite sea pinks dotted the golden-green grass across the cliffside, disappearing over the edge as if they made up a flowering waterfall pouring into the glistening sea below. Beyond, the sun slowly lowered in between a hazy yellow sky and the blue-grey waves drifting toward the Cornish shores. Herring gulls cried overhead with their signature calls, and black-headed gulls swooped closer to the water below, hoping to snatch a quick treat before tucking in for the night.

Henry couldn't deny the appeal of the serene setting. Any other night, he would have stopped to breathe it all in, to relish in his blessed life and good fortune.

But right now, he had somewhere he needed to be. Posting that letter had been his first task. Next would…be…

His thoughts trailed off as rumbling wheels and a rattling carriage sounded ahead of him. Directing his horse off the small road—that was more an impression in the grass than anything —he waited for the coach to pass, eyeing the charging, black horses.

LOVE IS FOR THE BIRDS

Horses that looked quite like the one he now rode.

He narrowed his eyes. That was the coach they used during the excursion, was it not? And certainly they were Mr. Chumley's horses.

Who was within the coach, though? And why did they travel with such haste?

The wheels slowed only a degree as the carriage passed him by, but Henry felt as if time stood still as he peered into the window and fixed on a pair of almond-shaped, hazel eyes.

"Lark," he breathed.

Where was she going? Was she fleeing to London to be rid of him earlier? Or had something happened—an illness or injury, perhaps?

She noticed him in the last second, her eyes widening and mouth dropping open. But in a flash, the carriage charged past him.

His horse stamped his hooves in protest, snorting as Henry reined him in for half a second before allowing the gelding to charge after the carriage. To his relief, however, the coach was already pulling to a stop.

He pulled in the black steed just as the door swung open and Lark leapt forth in a single motion, the footman having no chance to open the door for her first.

"Lark," he said, dismounting at once and facing her with concern, "are you well? Is something wrong?"

She shook her head, breathless, the footman moving to the door to prop it open for her. "No. No, all is well. I am well."

"You are certain?" He perused her up and down, ensuring no injury had befallen her as he stood a few feet away from her, clutching the reins in his left hand.

"Yes."

Relief overcame him, and he took a moment to take in her appearance. She wore no bonnet, her soft dress was wrinkled across the front, and her piled hair drifted slightly to the side, the strands about her features no longer curled but hanging limply near her cheekbones. Her eyes were slightly reddened and weary, as if she hadn't slept the night before, and her cheeks were pink, no doubt from the heat of the carriage.

Henry had never seen her so beautiful.

"Where are you—" he began.

"What are you—" she said at the same time.

Both stopped their words, and Henry motioned for her to continue, but she fell silent.

"Go on," a whisper sounded from within the carriage, a hand slinking forth to push Lark forward.

She took two steps, allowing just enough space for the footman to move behind her and lean toward the door, clearly beckoned by whoever was inside.

He nodded, closed the door, then moved to Henry's horse. "Sir," he said, bowing as he took the reins, tied them to the carriage, and tapped for the coach to move ahead.

All the while, Lark didn't drop her gaze from Henry's, not even when the carriage rode forward, leaving the two of them alone.

Obviously, whoever was within the coach—Mrs. Haskett, perhaps?—had requested the coach to be pulled ahead, but then…why?

Lark spoke before he could concoct an answer. "Where are you going?"

Henry paused. She didn't know already? "Why, back to Gwynnrudh."

Her brow pursed. "You are not going to London?"

"London? No, I was not to leave until Friday."

"But my uncle said…"

Realization dawned. Henry should have known Mr. Haskett would have muddled this. "We spoke after dinner," he explained. "He assumed I was headed to London, and I, in my pettiness, chose not to correct him." He dropped his gaze. "You must

LOVE IS FOR THE BIRDS

forgive me for arguing with him. He did see me leave, but I was merely on my way to post a letter."

"A letter," she repeated.

So she wasn't concerned with the argument, then. He couldn't deny his relief.

The carriage's departing wheels quieted, and he looked beyond Lark to see the coach stopped at the bend in the road, allowing them privacy.

A shadow moved across the back window of the carriage, then another, and he narrowed his eyes. "Who has accompanied you?"

Please, let it not be Mr. Haskett.

"My aunt, Mrs. Chumley, and Mrs. Shepherd."

Henry pulled back in surprise, having not expected the trio. They were better than anyone else in the party, however. Had Mr. Haskett come, he would already have challenged Henry to a duel.

But then, why *were* they there?

Henry had a hope, but he needed to be absolutely certain before he could proceed.

"Where exactly were the four of you headed? And in such a rush, no less."

Lark chewed on her lower lip. "Well." She broke off with a sigh and averted her gaze. "To be honest, we were...coming after you."

His heart thumped against his chest. "And why would you do that?"

She gave a sigh of long-suffering, obviously wishing to end her discomfort. "I'm sure you can decipher that for yourself, Mr. Branok."

"I'm sure I could. But even still, I should like to hear the words come from your own mouth. Plus, I do enjoy seeing you blush."

She pulled in her lips to hide a smile, and sure enough, her cheeks pinked.

The breeze from the sea below blew strands of hair across her smooth brow, and the light of the setting sun caused a halo to glow around her golden hair.

"Very well," she finally said, her voice smooth as she gave in. She drew a deep breath, then continued. "I feared you would leave for London—for India—before I could...before I could tell you that you must still go on the excursion and all future excursions for Lord Blackstone."

Henry waited with bated breath. This was not what he'd been expecting. He only had his prayers to rely upon now.

"But," she continued, "this time, you shall have someone waiting for you."

His chest rose and fell, his lungs tight. "What are you saying, Lark?"

She swallowed. "I am saying that *I* will wait for you, Henry. For years, if I must. No matter how long it takes for your dreams of traveling and writing to be realized, I will be here for you, supporting and encouraging you from afar until you are ready to come home."

The words soared through Henry like a peregrine falcon in flight, diving straight to his heart and striking him with such power, such emotion, he nearly had to take a step back. "You would do that for me?"

"Yes. I made a mistake last night. But if it is too late..."

Her words trailed off, her chin quivering, but Henry could no longer keep himself from her. He closed the distance between them, removing his gloves, and cupping her face in his hands.

"My darling Lark," he said softly, "with you and I, it is *never* too late."

And that was the truth. For he had spent his entire life seeking lasting joy in places he could never find it. But with

Lark, he knew he'd finally found home. And he would never let it go again.

She drew in a calming breath, closing her eyes and leaning into his hand.

"But I will not be going to India," he finished.

Lark's eyes flew open, and she straightened, pulling away. "What?"

He took her fingers with his own, bringing up her hands to hold against his chest. "The letter I sent," he began, "it was to Lord Blackstone. I told him quite clearly that I would no longer be agreeing to any further excursions unless he allows me to set my own schedule—and bring along my wife and future family."

LARK STARED. SHE HADN'T HEARD HIM CLEARLY. HAD SHE?

"You...you really wrote that?" she asked.

"I did."

"The...the part about...your wife?"

He grinned.

"And your future family?"

"Yes."

"But how did you know I would change my mind?"

"I didn't know. I merely had to hope."

Lark was certain she would melt into a puddle at his feet. How could she ever thank Heaven enough for blessing her with such a man?

"You would truly wish to take me with you?" she asked, still finding the knowledge hard to believe.

"More than anything," he returned, pulling her closer. "Now that I have you, why would I ever wish to be parted from you?"

She couldn't help her growing smile. She must be dreaming. Such magic did not happen in reality—at least not hers.

"But what if Lord Blackstone doesn't agree?" she asked, trying to diminish any gap in their otherwise perfect ending.

"I expect I'll be blackballed from his club, too," he joked. "But worry not. I've another article planned. This time…pigeons."

She laughed, shaking her head. "Truthfully, Henry. You cannot give up your excursions, your writing and publishing, your traveling. It's who you are. I said before, I cannot have you lose that…not for me. I will wait years if I must. I will fund the excursions myself. They might be fewer and farther between, and you might not see as many birds or have the best guides or travel to the best places, but I will be your benefactor. I…"

She trailed off at the sight of tears shimmering in his blue eyes.

"What have I said?" she asked, concerned she'd upset him.

"You're willing to do all of that for me?"

Her heart swarmed with love. "That and more. Whatever you need."

"But don't you see, Lark?" Henry asked, leaving her hands pressed against his chest as he held her waist. "I don't need your fortune. All I need is *you*." He brushed the curls blowing over her brow. "Traveling and writing and exploring—that is not who I am. That was what simply fell into my lap after my parents died. I had lost who I was before that. But being with you…I have *found* myself again."

Lark drew in a shuddering breath, staring up at him to see his own eyes shining with tears in the glowing gold of the fading sun as it hedged closer to the horizon.

"With you," he continued, "I have known no greater joy. Any other excursion I could go on would pale in comparison—and that is purely because of your presence on this one." He paused, staring deep into her eyes and speaking with such fervor, she could hardly breathe. "I know you have dreams of your own to travel, and I will do everything within my power to help them come to fruition. I will work day and night just to have you by my side. From this moment forward, I cannot be parted from you, my darling Lark. Please tell me we may live the rest of our lives fulfilling *both* of our dreams. Together. Please tell me..." He broke off, his voice overcome with emotion. "Please tell me you will accept my hand in marriage."

Lark stared up into his eyes, feeling his heart racing beneath her hands and overwhelmed with her own love for this man bearing his soul to her.

"Yes, Henry. With all of my heart, I will marry you."

He let out a breath as he smiled, as if he'd been holding onto both until she answered.

"As if there ever could have been any doubt," she said with a laugh, though her tears were now steadily streaming.

"You cannot say that after last night," he joked right back.

He wiped away her tears, both hands cupping her face now. He smoothed his thumbs across her cheeks before leaning down to settle a soft, lingering kiss upon her lips.

She accepted it, returning his affection with such overwhelming love, it could hardly be contained.

After only a moment, Henry pulled back, staring into her eyes. "I would love to give you more, were it not for our audience."

His eyes flicked over her shoulder, and she turned back to the carriage where faces pressed against the glass like children ogling through the window of a pastry shop.

She couldn't help but laugh. "I suppose we ought to go share the good news with them."

He offered her his arm, and she wrapped her hands around it, leaning into him closely as they meandered toward the carriage, the sun dipped halfway into the Cornish sea.

"I take it your aunt does not disapprove of me too heartily?" Henry asked.

"On the contrary, she's the one who pushed me out of the carriage to begin with."

Henry chuckled. "Perhaps she can help her husband approve of me again."

"Yes, but that will take some work," Lark admitted.

"I fear I did not seek his permission to marry you." He dropped his tone. "Not that he would've given it."

She waved a passive hand. "I give my own permission. At any rate, Mother heartily approves already."

He peered down at her. "Does she?"

"Oh, yes. She will be quite happy when I tell her that her plan to have me wed by the end of the Season has been accomplished."

He stopped, facing her directly with mild curiosity. "Plan?"

She raised an uncaring shoulder. "Oh, did I not tell you? My mother and I made an arrangement. I could only go on the excursion if I agreed to do my best to find myself a husband before, during, and after."

"Oh, you did, did you?" he asked, narrowing his shining eyes. "So this has been your plan all along, has it? To enchant me and entrap me to be your husband?"

"Heavens no. It only became my plan *after* I discovered you were not Mr. Dunn."

He threw back his head and laughed, then wrapped his arms around her waist and lifted her in the air before spinning her round and round.

Lark laughed with delight until he set her feet back down on the ground and kissed her once more. Afterward, he pulled back, took her hand in his, then continued on their way.

"Now," he said, "speaking of arrangements...Are we still in agreement to carry on with our own?"

"You mean to see who shall win the title of 'Best Bird Observer in All of England'?" She gave him a knowing look.

LOVE IS FOR THE BIRDS

"Sir, we have signed a binding agreement. Of course we shall carry on. The full two weeks now, as first discussed."

"Excellent," he said. "And we needn't make any changes due to our impending marital status?"

"No, I think all is in order still." She gave him a sidelong stare. "Unless you intend to distract me, in which case, we shall have to add another rule."

"However could I distract you?" he asked innocently, though the glimmer in his eyes told her he knew exactly how he could —and would.

"We *really* should return to the others now," she said.

His wink sent her heart into a frenzy, but she welcomed it.

For as she faced the carriage—Aunt Harriet and the others rushing forth from the door to join Lark and Henry with open arms and happy tears—Lark knew that perfect joy she now experienced was only a small taste of what was to come.

And she couldn't wait to experience the rest.

EPILOGUE

Cornwall – June 15, 1817

"Are you certain you're ready?" Henry asked.

Lark held her book behind her back, her finger holding the right location in the pages. "Yes," she breathed. "I'm ready."

She faced her betrothed—*her betrothed*—who held his own book behind his back as they stood upon Tregalwen Beach. They'd already lagged behind the others, the rest of the party following common sandpipers and charming dunlins seeking mollusks in the sand.

Days before, the party had congratulated them as a whole upon their return to Gwynnrudh, though some were more enthusiastic than others. Mr. Dunn had given a grunt of approval, and Mr. Chumley, well, his wife very clearly pressed him to speak at all.

"What shall we gift them for their engagement?" Mrs. Chumley had said at once. *"Oh, it must be something related to birds."*

"Perhaps Mr. Chumley would consider returning the cost of my extra entry to the excursion," Lark had whispered into Henry's ear.

He'd responded with a questioning look.

LOVE IS FOR THE BIRDS

"I shall tell you later," she'd said, smiling to herself.

Uncle had remained in the background, excusing himself without saying a word. Lark had spoken to him in private often since then, and Henry, too. While Uncle was still unsure, fearful, and rather stiff, Lark had every confidence that he would most certainly come around one day.

Even now, he wasn't watching them like a kestrel as he'd been apt to do the last few weeks. Instead, he focused harder on the gulls circling above.

A storm was blowing in, dark clouds looming ever closer to the tanned lighthouse in the distance, Golowduyn already shining its beacon out at sea. But none of them could resist being outside one last time in search of birds. Today was their final night in Cornwall, and tomorrow, they would be headed back to London, their excursion finally completed.

That meant one thing. She and Henry needed to see who had won their challenge.

"On the count of three, we reveal our number," he said.

She nodded with approval.

"And whoever wins receives the title," he continued. "Agreed?"

"Agreed," Lark said.

Henry narrowed his eyes, facing her as if they were about to duel. "Right. Three, two, one."

At the same time, they revealed their books, opened to the correct page, and showed each other their number. Lark stared in stunned silence.

"Congratulations, Miss Fernside," Henry said, a smile on his voice. "Or should I say, Congratulations, Best Bird Observer in All of England?"

There had to be some mistake. Lark could not have won. But as she read the numbers again, there was no denying it.

Henry: 175
Lark: 211

Her eyes snapped to Henry's. "Did you follow Rule Six?"

"Which one was that?"

"Agreeing to do our best."

Henry dipped his chin. "Do you truly think I would do you the dishonor of *not* trying? One hundred and seventy-five is a formidable number for anyone. You were better than I, as simple as that."

Lark stared at the numbers once again, allowing the truth to sink in. She had done it. She'd beaten Henry Branok at his own game.

Of course, she'd had far more time to explore, for she hadn't been teaching, speaking with others, and answering as many questions as he had. But then, he'd also been out of doors on average more days than she had, hadn't he?

They reviewed each other's lists of the birds they'd seen, and Lark glowed as Henry marveled over the ones she'd observed that he hadn't.

"Reed bunting, sedge warbler, golden plover," he recited. "Nuthatch—how did I not manage that one? Oh, a marsh harrier, very nice. Tree pipit. Well, there is one bird on mine you do not have."

She looked between the lists. "Which one?"

"A lark."

Lark stared at the birds' names. "I don't see that on yours."

"I'm looking at her right now. You can add that to your list, if you'd like."

She met his gaze, his eyes on her, and she laughed with a shake of her head. "Very clever, Mr. Branok."

He delivered a proud smile. "Be prepared to hear such comments for the rest of your life, my darling." He wrapped her in his arms. "You are my favorite bird, after all."

LOVE IS FOR THE BIRDS

He pressed a quick peck to the tip of her nose. "Now, what shall you do to celebrate your victory?"

Lark had imagined months ago what this would feel like and what she might do. And yet, now, looking back at the months she'd spent falling in love with Henry, she found she truly wasn't bothered by her victory in the slightest.

She had already won the best reward of all.

She closed the book and peered up at her husband-to-be, staring into the stunning pools of blue and sighing. "I think I'm more interested in what we agreed to do if we did *not* win."

His eyes narrowed. "Surely we had spoken those in jest."

Swiftly, Lark flipped to the front of her book where the signed agreement rested, and she pointed to the final rule they'd added only last week.

"'Rule Seven,'" she read aloud with a growing smile. "'The individual who is *not* the victor shall either, one,'"—she raised her finger—"'eat a full pheasant for dinner, two, ask Mr. Dunn for a recitation of his lifelong list thus far, or three, mimic the ritualistic mating dance of a sandhill crane.'" She pointed to his name next to the list. "And I will remind you that these were *your* ideas that were absolutely not suggested lightly."

He sighed, pulling his lips to the side. "Hmm. Not a *great* selection to choose from."

"You only have yourself to blame for that," she said. "You didn't like the suggestion I offered."

"I can't imagine why. Falling into a patch of nettles seems appealing now."

She grinned. "Stop putting this off. Which do you choose?"

He rubbed at his jaw, peering out at the sea. "I can't stomach eating a full pheasant. I'd be as sick as your aunt on a carriage ride. And listening to Mr. Dunn is even more unappealing than that." He sighed. "Very well, I have made my choice." He faced Lark. "Prepare to be *wooed*, my love."

Lark stared, trying to hold in her laughter. "What? No,

you're not supposed to do the mating dance for *me*, just in general."

"No, no," he said, removing his jacket and laying it on the sand, dropping his journal on it next. "This is for your pleasure. I've seen this very dance performed by the cranes while I was in the Americas, and it was remarkable. You shall certainly fall more in love with me than ever before after this."

Lark was already laughing as Henry secured his footing, then splayed out his arms to the side of him.

"Stop laughing," he said, pulling on a look of extreme concentration. "This is serious."

But Lark couldn't help it.

He continued, dipping his head up and down before jumping in the air and spinning in a complete circle.

Another laugh blasted forth from Lark. "Oh, heavens," she said, covering her face with a hand. "Stop, you're embarrassing yourself."

"Rules are rules, my love."

He made the motion again, kicking up an errant leg every so often which made her laugh even harder.

"Now this is the best part," he said, a look of excitement on his boyish face. "The sound they make."

He made a noise akin to a monkey's chatter at the back of his throat, and it echoed around them.

Lark laughed, glancing at the others, though Aunt Harriet was the only one who'd turned at the noise. She smiled in amusement, then continued her walk with the rest of the party.

Lark watched Henry again as he kicked up his leg again, sand flying into the air with his movements.

"Stop!" she cried out, her side beginning to ache due to her laughter. "You look utterly ridiculous!"

"Utterly ridiculous? I can assure you, I am putting every sandhill crane to shame right now due to my fluid movements."

He ducked his head back and forth again, smiling as he used

her embarrassment to his advantage. "Now, the dance mustn't end until the other crane joins in."

He looked at her with a waggle of his eyebrows, but she shook her head. "There is no chance. *I* didn't lose the challenge."

He walked toward her, stalking her like she was his prey.

"No, Henry," she said, holding up her hands between laughs.

But he seized her, securing her hands in his and pulling her arms up in the same flapping motion he'd done before.

"There you go," he said, laughing now in return. "I tell you, I'd take this sort of dance over the ones at the balls in London any day."

"Perhaps you can start a movement next time we're there. Mother will be thrilled."

He laughed, still flapping his arms madly. "Now the spin!"

He released her, spinning around again, but this time, his boot caught in the sand, and he fell on his backside with a grunt.

Lark could no longer stand up straight. She doubled over, gasping for breath in between her laughs.

"Are you all right?" she asked, rushing over to him and kneeling at his side.

Henry laid back in the sand with another laugh, shaking his head as grit stuck against his tanned skin and dark blond hair. "Better than ever," he said, though clearly winded.

She brushed aside the sand from across his features, peering down at him with a grin.

"How was that?" he asked, still lying down. "Are you officially wooed?"

She shook her head. "I am officially *something* right now."

He looked up at her from the sand, then slid his hand round the nape of her neck and pulled her toward him. She leaned over him, returning his kiss in between their labored breaths.

After a moment, he abruptly pulled back and laid deeper into the sand, splaying out his hands at the side of him. "I'm ready to sleep now, I think. That dance was exhausting."

She smiled. "It certainly looked it."

"Are you glad you won now," he asked, sitting up to better face her, "so you could witness that?"

"It was an utter treat for my eyes, I assure you. Although, in hindsight, I think I prefer the ending."

"When I fell?"

Once again, she laughed. "No, our kiss."

His eyes dropped to her lips. "Perhaps that's what we do for our next challenge, then."

"And what challenge will that be?" she asked.

He stood, helping her up, as well, before pulling on his jacket. "Perhaps you can try to best me with your lifelong list."

"Oh, you've far succeeded in that regard. I don't think there's any catching up to you."

He held his book in one hand, then grasped her fingers with his other. "All in good time, my love," he said, then he placed a lingering kiss atop her brow and led her down the beach.

The wind whipped Lark's skirts against her legs and pulled Henry's hair across his brow in an unwieldy manner that made her want to kiss him senseless right there.

"I cannot wait until we are on our own excursions," Henry mused. "I can only imagine the birds you'll be able to spot."

"The birds we'll be able to spot *together*," she corrected.

He smiled down at her, lifting her hand to kiss the back of it. "Just so."

India – April 9, 1818

Ten Months Later

Sweat dripped down the center of Lark's back, tickling her skin where the moisture pooled at the small of it. She dared not

LOVE IS FOR THE BIRDS

rub it away, though, for any movement might frighten away the Indian paradise flycatcher whistling just a few feet above them.

They'd been tracking the bird for days—Henry, herself, and their enthusiastic local guide—and now they were enjoying the fruits of their labors as the black-headed bird fluffed up its wings and preened as he sang.

The blue ring around his eyes and his cinnamon-colored wings glinted in the hot, Indian sun, but what stole attention more than anything was the foot-long feathers of the bird, producing a streamer-like tail dangling down from its short body.

"The long feathers are used to attract mates," their guide whispered.

"Glad I didn't need some of those to capture your attention," Henry whispered into Lark's ear. "Only a certain dance."

She nudged him softly, if only to stop herself from laughing. Her husband was insufferable, charming, and the love of her life all at once.

Their trip to India together had been a perfect dream come true—as had the months leading up to it. But then, what else could be expected when she'd finally married the man who made her feel worth more than gold?

They continued to watch the bird in silence, writing down their observations and scribbling a few sketches before the bird eventually flapped away, his feathers streaming out behind him in a fluttering that seemed to wave goodbye.

Then, the three of them wandered through the hot, thick forest, in search of the next bird—whatever that would be. Lark had quickly come to realize that the most thrilling part of excursions was the unexpected occurring. They never knew what they were going to discover, and each new step, each new location, each new breath, brought another adventure—which was exactly how she preferred it.

"We must write to your mother tonight," Henry said as they

traipsed through the thick trees. "Tell her we've spotted another unique bird."

"Oh, yes. But perhaps you can do most of the writing. I think she treasures your letters more than mine now." She shared a knowing smile with him, having spoken the words out of delight rather than envy.

Mother—who still watched over Brackenmore Hall—had taken the foremost seat at their wedding, sobbing tears of joy. She'd also invited half of London to the ceremony, but Lark hadn't minded. She was happy to share her joy with any and all who wished. And the way Mother loved Henry had filled any gap in Lark's relationship with her.

"You are just exactly who my daughter needed," she continually told Henry. *"I am thrilled to see the two of you so happily settled. Now...I do not mean to pry...but when shall I have a grandchild?"*

Lark smiled. *"As soon as the stars align, Mother,"* she'd always replied.

In truth, she and Henry couldn't wait to have children of their own, but first, they needed to get back to England. Lark had little desire to travel across the sea again when she was already nauseated doing so.

"We must respond to Mrs. Chumley, as well," Lark continued. "And the Shepherds."

They'd kept in contact with both couples since the excursion. Mr. Chumley, who had slowly come around to Lark due to her keeping silent about his charging her extra for his expedition, had even come to thank her for her collection of birds she'd written down for him.

"This will come in great use," he'd said with strain, then told her she would be more than welcome on any of his future excursions.

Lark had certainly taken that for a victory, even if he'd invited her simply because she and Henry were now married.

"Yes," Henry responded. "And Lord Blackstone, as well."

"Oh, he will no doubt be wondering if you are working on your next volume out here or if you have been too thoroughly distracted by your wife."

Henry wrapped his arm around Lark's shoulder. "Little does he know I have not even started it yet."

Lark laughed. Last year, when they had returned from Cornwall, Lord Blackstone had met with them both. Upon learning that *Lady* Blackstone was friends with Lark's mother, Lord Blackstone had been coerced into granting Henry's alternate agreement, that of Henry being in control of when to go—and with whom.

The viscount was reluctant to agree, but after some charm on Lark's part—particularly the compliments she paid to Lord Blackstone and his *"animal collection"* she'd heard of, though she would happily never see—the man had seemed to come around to the idea of Lark joining the excursions with Henry.

Matters had been fully settled, however, when Henry had vouched for her keen ability to find birds.

"If she's better than you, perhaps I'll simply pay for her to go instead of you, Branok," Lord Blackstone had joked.

Fortunately, however, they'd both been allowed to come together.

She and Henry ducked below a low-hanging branch. "You will be in for a world of hurt if you are late turning in the book," Lark advised.

"Well, if you would stop kissing me so often," Henry whispered down to her to avoid being heard by their guide, "I might have time to *do* other things. You are like those alluring mallards you complimented last year. You simply must breathe, and I cannot help but flock to you."

She laughed. "I've not heard such a complaint until now. But you may rest assured that I will stop—"

"Now do not be hasty, Mrs. Branok," Henry said, whirling around in the middle of her path and wrapping her in his arms.

"I was not complaining about your kisses. If anything, I would complain that they are not frequent enough."

"Is that so?" she asked, wrapping her own arms around him.

They were a hot, sticky mess together, sweat beading on each of their tanned brows, but Lark hardly cared. She stood on the tips of her toes and placed a lingering kiss to his lips.

Pulling back, she smiled. "How was that for a kiss?"

He licked his lips. "It was a bit salty."

She laughed, playfully swatting him on his chest. "Fine. We shall wait until I have bathed, then."

"If you insist," he said with a wink.

She gave him another shake of her head, then they walked through the trees, still hand-in-hand, and though their eyes were focused on the trees up above, their hearts remained ever with each other.

Lark supposed she'd been wrong all those months ago.

Love wasn't *just* for the birds.

THE END

Bachelors of Blackstone's

A Bachelor's Lessons in Love by Sally Britton
A Trial of His Affections by Mindy Burbidge Strunk
A Gentleman's Reckoning by Jennie Goutet
To Hunt an Heiress by Martha Keyes
Love Is for the Birds by Deborah M. Hathaway
Forever Engaged by Ashtyn Newbold
A Match of Misfortune by Jess Heileman

Author's Note

INTRODUCTION

This is one of my favorite parts about writing books—when I get to defend all of my choices as a writer and disguise it as Author's Notes! So, here comes an info dump you never knew you needed.

BIRDING BEGINNINGS

My husband and I often brainstorm about books during drives around the countryside or to the local bird reserve. We talk about the books I'm currently writing, as well as ideas for future novels. Since we are both big into birdwatching right now—hence the many trips to the bird reserve—we talked about how fun it would be for me to write a birding book set in the Regency Era.

The pastime wasn't really popular until the Victorian Period, so writing this book has been tricky in finding the balance between entertainment and accuracy. How do I share the correct information about birds even though in the 1800s, their

AUTHOR'S NOTE

knowledge was limited? And how do I balance all that information with romance, which is primarily what the book is about?

The answer? Well, I never found one. I just did my best to balance it all and be as accurate as possible—and that's all a person can do, really. As for everything else, that's what this Author's Note is for!

BIRDWATCHING IN THE REGENCY ERA—NOT REALLY A HUGE DEAL

First off, let's dig into the words I chose. "Birding" was used in Shakespeare's *The Merry Wives of Windsor,* so the word was definitely around since the 1500s. However, it was used in the context of *hunting* birds...more specifically, finding a wife, so I wasn't super confident in using it.

"Birdwatching," as far as I could discover in my research, came much later, in the mid-1800s, so I couldn't use that word either. As such, I settled with "bird observing," since that sounded the most "Regency-like" to me. How's that for accuracy? (Being a Regency romance author for more than a decade and writing nearly twenty books gives me enough street cred, right?)

As I mentioned earlier, birdwatching wasn't really popular until much later, however, observations of the natural world were beginning to pick up steam, so I have every confidence in assuming that there were like-minded bird observers in England during this time.

As for "Life Lists"—individual records of the birds one sees over his or her lifetime—these also weren't common until the 1900s, so I made another assumption and chose to believe that some passionate individuals would have kept "Lifelong Lists" to keep track of the birds they'd witnessed.

BIRDING BOOKS: RIVETING READS

AUTHOR'S NOTE

I ended up purchasing a few modern-day birding books to add to my library, and while they were helpful with photos and colors and descriptions and information...they just didn't give me the historical vibe I was seeking. So I picked up some contemporary sources from the Regency Era—books that Lark and Henry absolutely would have read.

The first was Thomas Bewick's, *History of British Birds*, with one volume accounting for the land birds, and the other accounting for the water birds. Another book was *The Natural History of Selborne* by Gilbert White, and finally, *A Natural History of Uncommon Birds* by George Edwards.

It was fascinating reading these books. Not only could I read firsthand accounts of bird sightings and descriptions that pulled me into a historical mindset, but it also allowed me to immerse myself in Lark's world of reading books and Henry's world of writing them. They were just what I needed to feel as if I was a historical bird observer myself.

The thing I found the most interesting? The descriptions! They went on and on and on and were so detailed down to the color and size of every inch of the bird. It makes sense, seeing as how the only reference these readers had were the drawings and sketches of each bird—no high-res color photos for Regency folks!

BIRD FACTS...ISH

I strived to make every single fact accurate that I gave for each bird, even if the knowledge might not have been known at the time.

For example, Bewick's books suggest that those in the Regency Era *did* know about puffins mating for life. However, there are recent studies that claim that puffins might possibly become attached to the location more than the bird. I would

AUTHOR'S NOTE

rather be like Mrs. Shepherd and think romantically, however Lark and Henry would obviously see the logic in both.

On one other instance, I leaned into the historical name of a bird. The golden-crested wren is now called the goldcrest bird or the golden-crowned kinglet, so I went with the original name solely because most of the others' names have remained the same over the years.

As for the known species in England during that time, I went with the logical conclusion of four hundred, though present-day England has over six-hundred.

LOCATIONS AND LOGIC

I found it really difficult to narrow down my selection of English counties to only three. At first, I had the excursion hitting up five different areas, then four, then finally, I settled on three, because I didn't want a 7,000-page book. (Maybe next time.)

I wanted to go with places I had actually been myself, some of my favorite spots in the UK, as well as locations that would provide the company the most variety of birds.

Yorkshire was a given. It has gorgeous moorlands and cold coastlines, so I found it really easy to choose that county. What was really fun was that my husband actually got to go back to England (he was born and raised there) in April, and while there, he spent some quality time birding across Yorkshire. I was able to live vicariously through him, and it was a dream! I could just imagine Lark and Henry ducking behind the stone wall to catch that redstart.

The Lake District, or Cumbria, was another easy choice. I've loved the time I've spent there, but it is my husband who has a deep and abiding passion for that area. I was more than happy to include it as the mid-stop for the excursion.

Finally, do I need to even mention why I chose Cornwall? I

AUTHOR'S NOTE

mean, it's Cornwall. (If you haven't read my Cornish Romance series yet...what are you doing??? Go read them right now! The audiobooks are free on YouTube, and the eBooks and paperbacks are all over Amazon! You won't regret reading them. Okay, pitch done.) If you haven't gathered yet, I love Cornwall, so I had to include it as the ultimate engagement location!

Also, did you catch the names of Golowduyn and Tregalwen at the end?? Read the Cornish Romance series to be able to find out why *those* are significant locations.

WHAT'S IN A NAME?

I love placing Easter eggs in my books, and one way I do this is by choosing special names for my characters, locations, and houses.

First off, Lark. Pretty obvious why I chose that name. Plus, it's the name of the sister of a woman I have always admired, so that was a lovely nod to think of each time I typed out the name.

Next, Henry Branok. I desperately wanted to name him Peregrine, but I thought that was a bit too "on the nose," so I chose to go with something more subtle. Branok is Cornish for "crow" or "raven," so not only did I get to use an awesome name with an awesome meaning, but I also got to go with something Cornish! So, when Lark calls him as cunning as a crow, she wasn't wrong. ;)

Most of the locations I used in the novel were real places, but the house names were each made up and were symbolic for how Lark is feeling at that point in the story.

For example, Deryn Park is the picture of uniformity and order with its bold red bricks and stately presence, and this is exactly how Lark feels at the beginning of her journey. Everything is going according to her plan, things are hopeful, and she's ready to seize the day. Furthermore, "Deryn" is a Welsh

AUTHOR'S NOTE

name that means "bird" or "blackbird," and since I'm writing a book set in Wales soon, I thought this was a great addition.

Next, Greygrove Manor is aptly named and described as grey and moody, which is how Lark feels when she gets to the Lake District. Everything is very dark and moody, but when she sees the grove of trees with the owl within, things start to shift.

Finally, we have Brackenmore Hall in Cornwall. My husband loves bracken, which is a type of fern, so I wanted to add it in as a nod to him. And of course, "more" is all about our desire to see more bracken in our lives! This house is pink and reminds Lark of an old dollhouse she had as a child, so in Cornwall, she learns to be hopeful again like she was when she was younger.

So there you have it. Who knew authors put this much thought into stuff, eh??

STINGING NETTLE & DOCK LEAVES

I added the dock leaves to help Lark, even though the internet told me that there's no evidence that they actually work against nettles. It might not take the pain entirely away, but it can certainly help ease the stinging, if only due to the coldness.

I've been stung by stinging nettle only once, and it was a tiny amount on my hand, so it was difficult trying to imagine what a full-body stinging would feel like. Luckily, there were YouTube videos on that. Go ahead and have a look if you want some uncomfortable entertainment.

ACCURATE BIRD COUNT? IMPOSSIBLE!

Attempting to create an accurate account of all the birds Henry might have seen on his excursions, all the birds Lark might have seen in Suffolk, and all the birds the party might have seen in three different counties during the Regency Era is veritably

Author's Note

impossible. It was by and large the hardest thing I had to figure out while writing this book.

Not only did I have to take into account the fact that there were no cars, phones, internet, apps, tracking devices, birding lists, or even good maps, I also had to factor in the number of birds that had been discovered in each county and country in that specific year, even though that number was unknown and vastly different from what the number of birds is now.

For example, in South Africa, there are around 850 recorded birds year-round, though only 725 of them reside there, then some migrate to other countries, while others don't come back year after year. Trying to figure out how many birds Henry might have seen in the country in the year 1817 during a specific month with no electronics and no duplications, then going into Lark's circumstances, and then everyone else's...let's just say, I was going crazy trying to figure it all out.

Now, where I live, local birders took part in a "Big Day" to see how many unique birds they could find in twenty-four hours just in my county alone. They came away with 145 bird species under their belt. Isn't that incredible?

If Lark and Henry had cars, GPS, phones, fast food, coolers, and 24 hours in a day to do whatever they pleased, I imagine they would have been just as successful. However, seeing how restricted they were in time, resources, and everything else *but* money, I think my assumptions were about as logical as one could get.

Here's a bit more insight into what I had to do to figure out how many birds they would have seen in one county alone:

In Yorkshire, 470 are recorded today. In the nineties, a birdwatching group found around 150 in a day. In the Regency Era, not a great deal of recording was done in reference to bird species, so I had to logically guess a safe number, this being 189, in the two weeks they were there. Then I had to factor in the birds that would be unique that Lark hadn't already seen in

AUTHOR'S NOTE

Suffolk, comparing both lists. So I had to write a list out of birds Lark had already seen—around 150 of them—then I had to see what birds were unique to Yorkshire that she wouldn't have already seen. After all this, I figured she would have probably added around 20-30 unique birds during this time.

Needless to say, this was all very time-consuming and frustrating, because no matter what, there was no way to be one hundred percent accurate. I just had to give my best guess. So if you think the numbers are farfetched, whether too low or too high...tell me when you write your own bird book. :)

MY OWN BIRDING EXPERIENCES

My mom instilled a love of birds in me ever since I was a little girl. She'd name each one she saw, whether robins, canaries, chickadees, or quails, and could recognize them by their songs. This love stayed with me for a long time, though it remained relatively quiet until my husband started taking photos of birds years ago during our long drives to get our kids to sleep.

It's amazing now to see how our eyes have opened to the world around us. Now, it's no longer, "Oh, that's another robin. Oh, just another seagull." Instead, it is, "Wow, that's a Say's Phoebe! Look at its head all puffed up!" And "Can you believe the subtle difference between the Western Grebe and the Clark's Grebe? Amazing!" We really have come into this "old-person" hobby full force, and I wouldn't change a thing!

I will say, though, my husband is a far more formidable birder than I. His photos are incredible (check them out on his Instagram @thebritishbirder, you won't regret it), and his knack for spotting the winged creatures at great distances and recognizing them from their song alone is amazing. He's the true inspiration behind this book, and I wouldn't have written it without him!

AUTHOR'S NOTE

Now, go find some birds and tell me if you don't become hooked on this hobby like we are!

THANK YOU

I'm so grateful to each and every one of you who has taken a chance on my story and read it from cover to cover. *You* are the reason I write. Thank you.

If you want to learn more about me and my writing, please join me on Instagram and Facebook, then sign up for my newsletter to never miss a new release. I'd love to have you join me!

Also, if you enjoyed this book, please consider leaving a review. Reviews help indie authors like me because that is how others hear about my books. I will always appreciate you spreading the word!

Thank you for reading!

Deborah

Acknowledgments

I am so grateful to all those who helped me get this book out from start to finish. After every book I write, I'm astounded that I was actually able to finish it, but I couldn't have done it without these individuals.

First, I have to thank Rachel Law for inviting me to her Sweet Romance Spectacular. From my two-hour drive there and two-hour drive back, I was able to voice-to-text most of my outline and brainstorming. I have never been able to get that part of my story out so quickly, and I have her and her event to thank for it!

Next, I want to thank my critique partners for reading the beginnings of this book and keeping me motivated. Each time a new week started, I got my backside in gear so I could have your extremely helpful eyes on the book, so thank you, Martha Keyes, Kasey Stockton, and Jess Heileman.

A special shoutout has to go to my beta readers—Kasey Stockton, Brooke Losee, Emily Flynn, Marlene Willis, and Rebekah Isert. Thank you all so much for your invaluable feedback and getting your responses back to me so swiftly. I couldn't have done this without you!

I want to thank my little kids for being so supportive. It's been incredible watching you all grow into lovely human beings who encourage me, help each other, and genuinely want to be good people. You are the *best* people, and I love you all.

I always love the chance I get to thank my husband for his support because he is genuinely the reason I am able to write.

He talks me off my imagined cliffs, pushes me up my imagined mountains, and pulls me out of my imagined pits. You inspire me, and I love you. Now go get the kids in the car. We're going to the bird refuge.

My final expression of gratitude must go to my Heavenly father and my Savior and Friend. These last few months, I have been buoyed and strengthened by Their love. Each time I pray, I have felt my mind opened. Through all the stress and outside forces fighting against me, They have sustained me, helping me focus on what matters most, but also helping me fulfill my own dreams. I am so grateful for Their love. I know They love you, too.

BOOKS BY DEBORAH M. HATHAWAY

A Cornish Romance Series

On the Shores of Tregalwen, a Prequel Novella

Behind the Light of Golowduyn, Book One

For the Lady of Lowena, Book Two

Near the Ruins of Penharrow, Book Three

In the Waves of Tristwick, Book Four

From the Fields of Porthlenn, Book Five

Belles of Christmas Multi-Author Series

Nine Ladies Dancing, Book Four

On the Second Day of Christmas, Book Four

Seasons of Change Multi-Author Series

The Cottage by Coniston, Book Five

Sons of Somerset Multi-Author Series

Carving for Miss Coventry, Book One

Christmas Escape Multi-Author Series (RomCom)

Christmas Baggage

Castles & Courtship Multi-Author Series

To Know Miss May, Book Two

Men of the Isles Series (RomCom)

Winning Winnie's Hand, Book One

Driving Maisie Crazy, Book Two

Ruling out Robyn, Book Three

Bachelors of Blackstone's Multi-Author Series

Love Is for the Birds, Book Five

About the Author

Deborah M. Hathaway graduated from Utah State University with a BA in Creative Writing. As a young girl, she devoured Jane Austen's novels while watching and re-watching every adaptation of Pride & Prejudice she could, entirely captured by all things Regency and romance.

Throughout her early life, she wrote many short stories, poems, and essays, but it was not until after her marriage that she was finally able to complete her first romance novel, attributing the completion to her courtship with, and love of, her charming, English husband. Deborah finds her inspiration for her novels in her everyday experiences with her husband and children and during her travels to the United Kingdom, where she draws on the beauty of the country in such places as England, Ireland, Scotland, Wales, and of course, her beloved Cornwall.

Printed in Dunstable, United Kingdom